CU

BOOK 3 OF THE HAUNTED SERIES

TONY MARTURANO

a Different Angle

Published in the United Kingdom and the rest of the world by a
Different Angle 2021

Cambridge, England

A catalogue record for this book is available from the
British Library

ISBN
978-0-9540137-8-3

For Anna, my ray of sunshine.
Thank you for being you. x

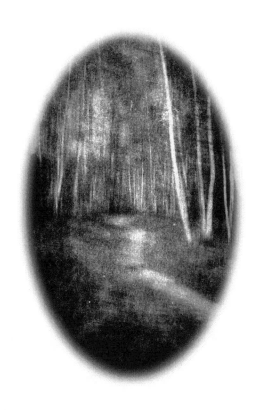

PROLOGUE

The house is tomblike still. The world beyond the window hushed like audience sibilance at the start of a play.

I address the woman sitting on the sofa across from me in a low soft tone, "Lucy, how are you feeling? Are you sitting comfortably?"

"Yes."

"Okay. I want you to completely relax into the softness of the couch. Completely relax your neck, arms, legs, and let yourself be absorbed into the plumpness of the cushion. Can you feel it? Soft and fluffy. Soft and fluffy. And as you do so, feel your eyelids getting heavier. So heavy. Very heavy. So heavy that you can no longer open them. So let them close. Let them close until there's nothing but darkness. Nothing but blackness, Lucy. Nothing, but the sound of my voice. Listen to my voice as it will be your guide. Can you hear me, Lucy?"

"Yes."

"Great. Now picture in front of you a set of doors. Can you see those doors? Theatre doors to a giant auditorium. Can you see the doors, Lucy?"

"Yes."

"Good. So now, follow my voice. Follow my voice through the doors into the giant auditorium. Can you picture it? A giant dimly lit empty auditorium where you can now see rows and rows of plush red empty seats. Rows and rows of empty seats, and you are sitting on one of them. You are seated in the middle row, looking forward towards the stage where the giant safety curtain is all you can see right now. Can you see that? Can you see the giant safety curtain covering the stage, Lucy?"

"Yes."

"Good. I want you to focus on the curtain. Focus on it. Focus until it becomes brighter and whiter. Brighter and whiter. Brighter and whiter until it becomes a giant projector screen. Bright and white. Bright and white until it's nothing but a pure white blank sheet. Can you see that?"

"Yes."

"Okay. Good. Now, feel your seat getting lighter. Lighter and lighter. Lighter and lighter until it starts to lift from the floor, just like a balloon. Can you feel that, Lucy? Gently lifting your feet off the floor and rising above the other seats. Slowly drifting upward and then forward. Drifting upward and forward until all you can see is the whiteness of the giant screen in front of you. Can you see the clean white canvas in front of you?"

"Yes."

"Okay, Lucy. That's good. That's very good. This canvas is for you. It's all for you. I want you to use it. I want you to use it now to project your thoughts. Your memories. Project your thoughts, your memory, just like a movie, onto the big white screen. Can you do that? Can you do that for me, Lucy?"

"Yes."

"Okay. So, I want you to go back to that night. I want you to go back to a few seconds before you get ready for bed. Go back, then use the screen to project what happened. Use the screen to see everything in crystal clear detail. Crystal clear. Then I want you to describe it to me. Can you see that night replaying on the screen now? Can you see it, Lucy?"

"Yes."

"Describe it to me."

"It's cold inside the house. Really cold." She embraces herself, her lips trembling. "The, the weather. It's very bad. That night. It was the night of the storm, and the whole house seemed to come alive."

"Okay. What do you mean by that? What do you mean by come alive?" I ask quickly.

"The doors, they keep rattling and screaming. The windows keep crackling and drumming with the rain. There's a lot of rain. I can see it. Dripping in from the ceiling."

"There are leaks in your bedroom?"

"Yes, but I'm used to them, so I place the pot underneath, and it starts to drip... drip... ting... drip... drip... ting. Drip... drip... ting."

"How are you feeling? Can you tell me how you're feeling? What's your state of mind?" I watch the young woman's face for a reaction, but there isn't one. It seems peaceful. "I'm fine," she says. "I'm relaxed. It's cold in here, but I'm alright."

"The storm isn't worrying you?"

"No. I've seen worse. Much worse."

"What are you doing right now?"

"I'm getting ready for bed. I can't wait to get under the blankets. It's freezing in here." I watch her lips tremble and her shoulders hunch. "It's so cold that I pull on socks and then throw a blanket over the bed."

"Why? Is there no heating?"

"There is, but it doesn't seem to be working. I don't know what's wrong with it."

"What about the room? Can you describe your room to me?"

"It's simple. Normal room. A single bed. Side table. Old wardrobe. There's a small lamp on the bedside table.

"Okay. So, what are you doing now?"

"I'm getting into bed now. Under the blanket... oh!" She jumps back into the sofa.

"What is it? What happened?"

"The thunder. It's so loud. It's like it came through the ceiling. It made me jump!"

I expel the breath I'm holding. "Okay. But you're still feeling okay. Yes? Everything alright?"

"Yes."

"Tell me what else you can hear."

"The saucepan... the tune has changed now. Ting... ting... ting... drop... ding... ding... ding... drop. It's making me feel sleepy. Ting... drop... drop... drop."

She pauses here for several seconds, breathing deeply and heavily. In and out. In and out. And I find myself leaning in to listen.

"Lucy? Are you still with me?"

No response.

"Lucy?"

"Oh no!" She breathes suddenly, and it startles me, although I try not to show it. I take a deep breath. "What? What just happened, Lucy? Tell me what just happened."

"An explosion. Outside. It woke me from my sleep."

"An explosion?"

"Yeah. Really loud. It woke me up. I think it's thunder. Yes. Thunder. I don't like thunder."

"It's okay, Lucy. You're safe in your bed. Safe. I'm right with you. You're perfectly safe. Can you tell me what else is happening in your room right now? Can you describe it to me?"

She swallows loudly like her throat is dry. "I, um, the lamp is still on. I thought I turned it off, but it's flickering again like there's something wrong with it. Like it's going to explode! Oh…I… I can't move."

"What do you mean you can't move?"

"I'm trying to move to switch it off, but I can't. Something… something is sitting…on my ch… che… est, push… push… pushing me down… press… pressing me into the bed."

I watch her struggling to breathe—breaths are coming fast and shallow. "Lucy. Lucy. Listen to my voice. Listen to my voice. You're okay. You're safe. You're safe; just breathe deeply. Breathe normally."

"I can't… I can't! It's on me… it's holding me down!"

"What is, Lucy? What's holding you down? Tell me. Describe it to me, Lucy. Who is holding you down?"

"I… I… I can't. I c… c… can't describe it… the… there's nothing here. But I can smell it! Oh, it's… foul! It's foul…b…but there's nothing there…nothing there."

"It's invisible? Is that what you're saying? Something invisible is holding you down on the bed?"

"Y… yes. It's strong. So strong." She starts wailing, "Aahhhhh… get it off… get it off me!"

"Okay. Alright. Lucy… remember to listen to me… listen to my voice. Just listen to my voice," I soothe. "There's nothing holding you down. Nothing is holding you down. This is a movie, remember. It's just a film about what happened. It isn't real," I chant.

She gasps, then jolts sideways suddenly. "Oh no... oh God... oh no.... There... there's something outside my room. Outside my bedroom door."

"Outside your door? Someone else. Someone else outside your door, Lucy?"

"It's... they... it's coming for me."

"Lucy. It's okay. It's Alright. You're alright, remember? This is just a film. It's just a movie. You are safe. I am here. Tell me, how do you know someone is outside the door?"

"I can hear *it* out there. I can hear it moving around... I can hear its nails tapping on the floor! Oh, Noooo! Noooooo!" She starts wailing, "Noooooooooo!"

"Lucy. What's happening? Talk to me... tell me what's happening."

"Not again... no... no... no," she hyperventilates, then adds in a whisper, eyes bulging out of their sockets, "It's moving the handle. It wants to come inside! Noooo!"

"What does, Lucy? What wants to come inside? Describe it to me. Describe it."

"Nooooo," she cries, "noooooo! I c... c... can... h... h...ear... it in my head! I c... ca... can't breathe... h... h... help me.... HELP ME! HELP ME!"

"Lucy... listen to me... listen to my voice... there is *nothing* in your room... it's just paralysis. Just sleep paralysis. There's nothing in your room. Just breathe, normally. Breathe normally."

"Oh, God! It's opened the door! It's coming for me! It's coming for me!" she cries, head lolling from side to side before she starts moaning. The sound is low and guttural at first but soon metamorphoses into loud wailing once more. The sound is so agonised. So pitiful that it rakes shivers down my spine.

"Okay. Lucy. Listen... listen to me... listen to my voice. There's nothing in your room. It's just a video —like a home movie. You are safe now. You are safe with me," I say, but my words don't seem to have any effect on the woman in front of me who is holding up clawed hands in the air as if trying to fight an invisible assailant.

She starts screaming. The sound is loud, raw, and hysterical.

"Okay... Lucy... I want you to stop looking at the screen now. Stop looking at the screen. It's time for you to wake up. Time for you to come back. I'm going to count to three. Okay? Lucy... listen to me... listen to my voice... okay? One..."

...screaming. Eyeballs swivelling behind closed lids.

"Two."

Back thrust into the couch. Belly thrust into the air.

"And...."

Everything stops. My heart thumps. Ears ring as I watch her sit up in her seat, eyes shut tightly, facing me.

I lean forward. She's breathing loudly, heavily, chest expanding and contracting.

"Lucy?" I attempt.

Silence.

"Lucy? Can you hear me?"

I'm about to lean in closer but stop when her eyelids suddenly spring open, revealing nothing but black ocular cavities that bore into my very soul before she finally speaks, but in a voice that shoves a dagger of ice into my stomach, *"Daddy? Is that you? Come find me. Daddy... come find me."*

SUMMER

JULY

1

THIS IS WHERE IT BEGINS

I'm boring.

Yes, try not to fall off your chair. I know that's a wild statement coming from someone as fascinating as me, but, well, as much as it pains me to say it, I am thoroughly, unashamedly, unrepentantly, unabashedly, deliriously... Yeah, enough of that.

It has been a year and almost seven months to the day since the event at Porthcove—yes, that's the life marker by which all days are now measured—and life has been pretty much uneventful since. And that's fine by me.

Don't get me wrong. Uneventful doesn't mean we haven't been busy. We've both been very busy; Sarah, studying for and passing her exams to become a vet. Me, trying to get enough practical supervised experience to complete my degree as a psychologist and open my own practice.

It's been tough. All work and no play. And, if I'm perfectly honest, it suited me just fine.

Ethan calls it *avoidance*. My way of coping with what happened. His theory is that if I don't stop long enough to think or talk about it, it didn't happen.

Um, no, if I don't think or talk about it, I don't feel like shit.

Endlessly going over all the things that I could or should have done differently that may or may not have resulted in a different outcome in which I might now be living a different life. One that might even include my son still being alive.

What if?

That sentence has been haunting me ever since I conjured it all those months ago and now remains the precarious bridge between real life as I know it and the imaginary one I wish it to be.

Not that I don't appreciate or regret in any way my life with Sarah. What I do regret is coming back to the city.

Don't get me wrong. After what happened, getting away from that place by the ocean felt good. At the time, it almost felt like coming home. I say almost because it's become clear to me that the hustle and bustle of the city will never feel the same again without the family that I was once a part of there.

And I had made my peace with that because I'd set my mind to think that maybe, just maybe, I could hit the reset button with Sarah. You know, forge a new life. New memories. But all I seem to do is replay what was or could have been. It's like the bloody hard disk of my mind is stuck on *overwrite protect,* and I'm incapable of creating things that are new and meaningful.

Sarah, on the other hand. Well, she appears to be smitten with the big smoke as most people tend to be when they first arrive there. London is vibrant, alive, and so far removed from the quaintness of Porthcove that it's easy to be seduced by all its exciting promise.

At least that's the impression I have. We don't really talk about it that much, and when we do, she seems perfectly content with life in the city, affording herself only the occasional trip back to *Tellytubbyland,* where she was born and raised.

But then, if Sarah were unhappy, I wouldn't really expect her to show it. She's nothing like my wife. Which, by the way, is the other uncanny thing that I've been wrestling with this past year. Technically, I'm still married to Ellie. And if I allow myself to think about it long enough, albeit metaphorically, it feels like the equivalent of being shackled to one of those dead twins. I know that's a grotesque analogy, but then so is the thought of still being married to a woman who cheated and then tried to hatch a poorly orchestrated plan to have me committed.

And yes, I can hear that too. Hypocritical much. I'm referring to the cheating, of course. But the rest of it. Well, shit, how would *you* feel about that?

So yeah, Sarah's nothing like Ellie. She doesn't sweat the small things. She's pragmatic that way. And I both love and envy her for it. She's one of those people who could spend hours baking and decorating a cake only to drop it at the last minute and think, *Oh well, I can bake another, and that one will be better.* That, or she'd suggest we go out and buy one and make a trip of it.

Not that she's done much of that lately because of the whole *being busy* thing. But you get my point. I love that about her as well as her boundless enthusiasm for most things and her ability to look for the good in everything. I have never heard her speak a bad word about anyone. She's fearless, generous, and has a special knack for starting a conversation with anyone about anything. Which, as you can imagine, has been something I've been trying to warn her about. *London isn't Porthcove,* I tell her. And she'll say that people are people wherever they live. *Yeah, but some like to drug you, bundle you into the boot of their car, and drive you out to the middle of the woods at night.*

She hasn't been dissuaded, though. At first, I thought it was her naivete. She is, after all, a few years younger than me. Oh, alright, because I know you're probably counting, she's a little more than a decade younger than me and, shit, I feel that every time I think of it that way. And I'm often reminded in other ways, insignificant ways like popular culture stuff, songs, films, sayings.

Although, to be fair, and as twee as this is going to sound, she's much older than her years. And I mean that. Her outlook on life, which probably will come as no surprise to you, is often more balanced and measured than my own.

For Sarah, the theory is simple; *life's too short.*

It took the event at Porthcove to teach me something that she had already been subscribed to for years. We only have one life. *We* choose how we're going to live it.

Kind of.

That's what Sarah wants me to believe. That's what I would like to believe. I really do. Every day, I wish I could look at how we all survived that place, appreciate it for the miracle it was, and move on with the rest of my life. I wish it were that easy. I wish I could tie what happened into one neat little bundle along with everything else that happened and use it as a viewing platform to a whole new perspective on life.

And while I'm at it, I wish I could miraculously be cured of all my psychological scars, my idiosyncrasies, to put them mildly, and the legion of demons that stalk my days and my sleep. Be that Ellie holding me under the water with a maniacal grin on her face or being shoved off a precipice to plummet straight into the fiery pits of hell.

As hideous as these images might be, they pale into insignificance when compared to the emptiness that smothers me each time I'm reminded of the loss of my son. Although it feels a little easier now, thanks to Buddy and my controversial belief of how and why he was brought into my life.

These are the mental scars that no amount of time or therapy will heal, for they are now part of me, as is the ever-present danger of a relapse.

What if?

Yeah. I know. Try not to roll your eyes, but I should warn you now that you're most likely going to get frustrated with me as most do when presented with a relative or friend who is in some kind of crisis and appears incapable of shaking it. Month after month, banging on about the same stuff, pining over the same things.

I'm still the same fucked up weirdo I was before all of this. A somewhat diluted version, maybe. Fewer teeth, but I am still me.

Broken.

Most don't notice this because I've managed to make an art of hiding it. Smiling when uncomfortable—Porthcove taught me that—ignoring the knife to the gut every time I pass a landmark now a milestone of a former life. And all the things I see, hear or smell that relentlessly and sadistically remind me of the family I'll never see again.

The most innocuous thing can set me off and have me thinking that I'm spiralling back into the abyss. Worse, as if that isn't bad enough, I now appear to have developed a mild sense of paranoia. If someone does something in a certain way or says something to me, I find myself analysing and questioning why they said that. What did they actually mean? What's in the subtext?

Bored yet?

I am. It's bloody exhausting being me. This is why I think I've thrown myself wholly into my new, fully signed up for, and acknowledged profession because if I'm busy dealing with other people's problems, then I'm not thinking about and working on repressing my own.

Sorry.

I know you may have come back here thinking all is well in the land, but it isn't. And, for your information, it rarely is for many people around the world who struggle with their everyday existence like me. Be that depression or other forms of mental illness. Many are seldom cured. They just become better at dealing with or masking it, as have I.

Of course, that doesn't stop me from telling myself to *man up*! I mean, bloody hell; I've been given countless opportunities to right wrongs and start anew. Not many people can say that. Similarly, I may have had a new life thrust upon me, one that I would never have chosen for myself, but at least I still have a life. This is more than I can say about the other three people claimed by the ocean that night.

That's got to count for something. Right?

And so, this is the character. This is the role I play daily. And you see the irony in that, don't you? People keep telling me that I look like that Irish actor from that sex film about the billionaire, and now... well, now I've become one. I'm happy-chappy-big-hand-clappy for most of the time. Grateful to be here. Grateful to be alive.

Literally.

That said, there has also been another exciting development in my life. But before I tell you about it, a question... do you believe in fate?

I used to. In that, I believed everything happened for a reason.

Until that day.

After that, everything changed. There was no reason, no life lesson important enough for my son to be taken from me like that. None.

And then....

Remember when we first met a couple of years back? Back then, I was one of those blokes who was always broke, barely two pennies to rub together, and practically living off credit cards.

Well, I hope you're sitting down, but all that has changed.

As you already know, a few months after what happened at Porthcove, I was contacted by our insurance company, informing me that they were going to pay out on Ellie's life insurance.

At the time, I spent hours thinking about all the things I could do with that money. Buy property. Start a new business. All kinds of wild stuff like you do when you come into some cash. And before you shake your head, saying, *I wouldn't know,* I'm not necessarily just talking about inheriting something. The same can also be applied to finding cash you didn't think you had in a coat pocket, stuffed down the sofa, or even on the street. Those scenarios are familiar to me because I remember how euphoric I'd be as I went about deciding what I was going to do with the cash. Often, it would be a little something for Toby or Ellie. Mostly Toby because my wife was rarely impressed with anything that didn't have at least a couple of zeros on it.

Anyway, I received this cheque, and I was excited. I had never seen that amount of cash in my name before. And yet, try as I did, I couldn't decide how to spend it. I mean, we were living out of a bloody B&B at the time, so the logical thing would have been to rent, maybe even buy a small place to call home.

And yet....

Every time I thought about spending that cash, my brain, like a box of fireworks, would explode and crackle with all these ideas, but then they'd all just fizzle out to none.

Days turned into weeks and then months.

Nothing.

The very thought of spending money I received as a direct result of my wife's death—no matter what she tried to do to me—repulsed me. It didn't matter what anybody else did or said. I just couldn't spend it.

Then, one day, I received a letter from my father's solicitor. Remember him? He's the same pompous man who informed me that I had inherited Dolce Vita. He asked me to visit his office. Of course, me being me, I made a joke; I asked, *You're not going to tell me that I've inherited more property that's going to sink into the ocean and kill a bunch of people, are you?*

I stopped laughing after about five seconds when I realised he wasn't laughing with me.

Anyway, I met with the man, and, well, you won't believe it. I didn't. If it wasn't for the fact that I was sitting in front of that podgy saggy face that looks like a smacked old arse, I would have been more inclined to believe that I was having another relapse or maybe even a non-shitty but altogether different wet dream for a change.

I wasn't.

It turns out that along with being the executor of my father's financial affairs, the lawyer was personally responsible for taking out insurance on the property formally known as Dolce Vita. I imagine that's when his balding head was thicker with more colour, and one would hope he possessed some kind of youthful personality.

Somehow, and we don't know how, but unlike most policies of its kind, this one did not contain any clauses that precluded it from paying out in respect of so-called *Acts of God,* which good ole saggy-chops was quick to point out was most irregular before sliding a sheet of paper across the desk to me. It detailed the amount of money that would be wired to my account as soon as I shared my bank information, minus his fee, of course.

I was struck dumb for at least several seconds. I could not believe what I was seeing to the point where I no longer trusted myself to accurately read the numbers on that sheet of paper. I had to refer to the part in brackets in which the total value of the wire was spelt out in words.

It was what people call *life-changing.*

My father, who was rarely there for me in life, was right there for us in death in a way he'll sadly never know.

I did the math. The pay-out was just over eighty-five per cent of what I would have received had Dolce Vita sold. It was more than the total of Ellie's cheque and more than enough for us to start anew comfortably.

I used some of the money to buy us a place not far from Camden. Nothing exciting, just a bank reclaim, auctioned off low for fast disposal because it was listed as *needing major repair*.

Well, I already knew a crew that could help with that. They did such a fantastic job of Dolce Vita before the ocean gobbled it up. I couldn't see any reason why this place would be any different.

Irvin was reluctant at first. He estimated that it would take two or three weeks to make that place good, and he didn't fancy leaving the countryside for that long. So, I deployed countermeasures in the form of a good dollop of the old Battista charm.

He went for it.

So, I booked out a small B&B nearby, and while we were out learning, they were busy transforming what was effectively a dumpsite into a palace. In fact, they did such a great job that I couldn't see any value in moving in. It's not as if we had furniture in storage or anything. Now that I think about it, Sarah and I don't really own much together. At least nothing in terms of possessions. We literally just have each other and a big soppy golden retriever who, may I add, needed a room to himself.

So, we stayed at the B&B and put the house on the market. It sold within a month, almost doubling what I invested back.

And that got me thinking. The plan had always been to start a business. The potential here was obvious. I mean, you always hear stories of people making a living from *flipping houses*.

Why not me?

It made perfect sense.

So, I talked to Irvin, who understandably wasn't that keen. He'd already spent almost a month in the city with just the occasional visit home. And I know how I felt when I first left the city for Porthcove. That, and he didn't like the idea of putting all his eggs in one basket. He told me that he'd owned his own business since he was a teenager and that this felt like he was giving up his independence to work for someone else.

Yeah. He took some persuading, but I assured him that Irvin & Sons would merely be a permanent subcontractor of Battista Properties with all the benefits that entailed. Eventually, he gave in.

We've since *turned over* three more properties. Two sold straight away. The third, an old ten-bedroom hotel in Finchley, Barnet—which is just on the outskirts of London—was double the size of the other two and proved a tad more ambitious. Unsurprisingly, it took almost double the time to make good, but it also almost doubled what I paid for it when it sold not long ago.

And so. Yeah. It would appear that I, Marco Battista, you know, the bloke who gets excited when he finds a fiver in his pocket, the delinquent with no money and no prospects—according to Ellie's parents, oh and my stepmother—has managed to turn himself into one of those people—yeah still can't bring myself round to saying that word—in the space of a year, all without buying a lottery ticket. Oh, and let's not forget, I am now also a bonafide fully certified therapist well on his way to becoming a clinical psychologist.

Can you believe that? I can't. Still.

And the best bit. Once the first sale went through and the money was deposited into my account, it suddenly became clear that I could never have used Ellie's insurance money. It would never have felt right because I never earned that money.

So, instead, I decided to revisit good old saggy-chops. And you should have seen the look on that lawyer's face when I handed him that cheque. Almost made all the shit I went through worthwhile.

I told him that I wanted to set up a charity. One that would offer financial support to bereaved parents during their most hideous time. *The Little Man Foundation*, named after Toby's nickname, will offer just that because it's awful enough mourning the loss of your child without having to worry about the bills too.

No parent should have to go through what Ellie did.

And so, it's been busy. Not least because while Battista Properties and the Little Man Foundation were taking shape, Sarah also landed herself a placement as a junior veterinarian.

We've both been working sixty-something hour weeks. I say we've well and truly earned some downtime that doesn't involve me listening to other people's problems or Sarah spending it with her arm shoved up a cow's backside. Yeah. Her recount of the experience was as funny as it was disgusting.

So, I've hired a car for the weekend. The sun had barely opened its eyes when we were loading the vehicle with overnight bags, an overenthusiastic golden retriever, and driving out of the city and southwest.

When Sarah asks where we're going, I tell her that it's a surprise, and she's okay with that on the understanding that our destination is nowhere near an ocean.

Yeah. That's been our thing since Porthcove. We try to avoid the sight and the sound of the sea even when it's on T.V.

No. Where we're going is somewhere completely different. A place where there's a lot of peace, tranquillity, and who knows, maybe the start of something new.

2

HOLT

The New Forest National Park is in the county of Hampshire and is about an hour and a half drive southwest of London, England.

William I, otherwise known as William, the Conqueror, was the first Norman King of England. He established *Nova Foresta* in 1079. It is 566 square kilometres of vast tracts of unspoilt woodland, heathland, and river valleys. Deer, horses, ponies, cattle, and an array of other animals and birds roam freely in this spectacular car-free haven.

William took his hunting seriously and created the *Nova Foresta* sanctuary to preserve the *beasts of the chase* and their habitat by declaring it *royal hunting ground* and enshrining this in Forest Law.

There have been various changes to the law since, but it was only in 2005 that the New Forest was officially designated a national park. An area of outstanding natural beauty featuring a series of picturesque towns and villages throughout, as well as the renowned Buckler's Hard situated on the banks of Beaulieu River that slices for twelve miles through the southern edge of the park. It was here that Admiral Nelson's—known for seeing off the combined naval forces of Spain and France at the Battle of Trafalgar—ships were built.

At least that's what the leaflet says. We picked it up at a petrol station when we stopped off to get fuel and supplies. And part of me wishes we hadn't since the mere mention of Lord Nelson turns my stomach because I'm instantly reminded of Toby.

My son took after his grandfather and had a thing about ships. He knew all about Nelson and, as you already know, is the reason why we ended up buying a drone shaped like a Galleon and the reason why I've been a grieving parent ever since.

To hear me now, you'd think that I'm stuck in the same place I was a year or so back. I'm not. Don't get me wrong, I still ache for my boy, but it is a little easier now. And I have Buddy to thank for that. He brings comfort where there was once nothing but grief for reasons I've already explained. I know you might think that's weird. Shit, I do. But after what happened at Dolce Vita, I find that my mind has been well and truly opened.

Anyway, as you can imagine, there's much to do in one of England's most stunning national parks. We opt for archery which I didn't realise pulls on arm tendons I didn't even know existed. Segway is next, and it feels like I'm riding a bloody pneumatic drill for most of the time. And then, horse riding that stretches my thighs so wide apart, I'm now walking around like John Wayne.

But we laugh. Oh God, we laugh.

And it feels so bloody good!

It's actually quite tricky to put the feeling into words, but I suppose I will try.

After Dolce Vita, all the survivors managed to resume some semblance of a life, but for Sarah and me, well, it feels like it's only now that we've stopped filling our minds with study and work that we've both realised that it's okay to appreciate being alive without feeling crushed by remorse. It's only now that we've quite literally stopped to smell the sweet scent of flowers while picnicking under a magnificent age-old tree that we've started to learn how to live again. To make the transition from guilt-stricken survivors to human beings once more.

Then, as the mellow rays of a brave sun make their last stand against an armada of sullen black clouds, and exhaustion from the day's activities presses on us, we're about ready for some food and rest.

The Stag & Owl is a cute little pub with a thatched roof and a cloak of ivy. It was a chance find, appearing to us out of a sudden and heavy downpour. We dine on hearty pub grub and even allow ourselves a couple of the local brew.

I've been laying off the proverbial sauce for some time now, especially since I was told in no uncertain terms by Ethan that alcohol interferes with my meds, and I've been teetotal ever since.

This, of course, means that I've become a bit of a lightweight now, so it doesn't take much to make me merry, which apparently, is something that Sarah loves about me. And is why a couple of hours later, ensconced in one of the tiny rickety little rooms above the pub with creaky floorboards and an oversized bed, we manage to find enough reserve energy to kiss and fumble clumsily with each other's clothing all while giggling like teenagers at a sleepover as we try to make love in the squeaky old bed as quietly as possible.

It's only after, to the sound of the rain rapping against the window, that I allow sleep to finally claim me. And it was delicious, deep, and through the whole night. Nightmare-free!

I emerged from my blissful rest to the sound of bird chorus and the smell of fried bacon, feeling invigorated albeit still a little sore from yesterday's shenanigans, but in a good way.

Over breakfast, we plan our day. Surprisingly, Sarah's the first to say that she doesn't fancy doing anything too energetic and that she'd rather just *take it easy* until it's time to return to the city. This, of course, is music to my ears. Only because we did enough of that yesterday, you'll understand. I wouldn't want you to get the wrong idea. There's still a lot of life in this forty-four-year-old stallion, you know. It's just that these days, I like to pace myself a little.

I've really enjoyed my time out here. And, I dare say that Sarah has too. She even said she was going to miss this place. I don't know if I'm reading into that, but it very much seems that, like me, she's in no hurry to return to that place of smog and noise.

So, I ask her if everything's okay. She tells me she's fine, just a little worn out. I accept her reply but can't help but wonder if there's more to this. However, I don't press her. Mostly because I don't know how much of my assessment is accurate and how much might be wishful thinking.

I guess we're going to find out soon enough.

And so, I swagger over *a la John Wayne* to the driver's side of the car and slide behind the wheel, groaning like an old man as I go.

Sarah giggles then suggests that we take the long route home as the leisurely drive will allow us to enjoy more of the area and maybe, time permitting, stop off for a spot of lunch before joining the concrete highway back to reality once more.

I agree, especially since the sun has made a most welcome return by bringing a sparkle to the rain-drenched world and dialling up the saturation on passing trees, meadows, and quaint hamlets.

We're about half an hour into our leisurely journey—shades on, music playing—when I find what I'm looking for and pull over.

Sarah looks at me. "What's up?"

"Sorry. Just need to check something on my phone." I make a show of tapping the screen. "I saw this layby and thought it would be safer to pull over."

She nods and turns to look out of the passenger window. "Oh," she says, "this isn't a layby. It's a driveway."

"Is it?" I ask, following her line of vision out of the passenger window to a sabre arch of trees fading into the gloom of the woods.

There's a brick column to one side wearing a gold plaque that reads:

HOLT

Underneath, in smaller print are the words: *no thru road.*

"Oh, you're right," I say, pushing the car into gear and then piloting it onto the gravel drive.

"What are you doing?" Sarah asks.

"Taking a closer look."

"Marc, this is private property," she protests.

"It's okay. If anybody stops us, we'll just tell them we took the wrong turn," I say, eyes fixed on the drive ahead.

We journey for a least a minute through a woodland of dappled sunshine, shadows, and verdant haze that begins to feel otherworldly by the time we emerge onto a meadow of grass and flowers sloping up to a large, seemingly black house.

We both turn to look at each other with wide eyes as I bring the car to a smooth stop under the shade of a tree and kill the engine.

Instantly, we're engulfed by the sound of… nothing.

It's surreal. As we move in our seats, the only loud noise is the click of seatbelts and the swish of clothing. It's like we've driven onto a sound stage. I don't think I've ever experienced anything like it.

I crack all the windows. "And you, trouble," I say, turning to the dog in the backseat. "You need to wait here. We'll be right back."

We pull on our door handles with peculiar synchronicity and step out into a cool breeze—heady with the earthy scent of moss, the pine-like aroma of wood bark, and the musky smell of leaves naturally blended and diffused into the inimitable tangy freshness of the outdoors.

I take a long deep breath. Sarah looks at me, grins, and mimics the action.

Birds serenade us with a chorus of song punctuated by the caw of crows, wood pigeons, and a medley of peaceful woodland sounds.

Other than that.

Quiet.

Seclusion.

Tranquillity.

It's as palpable as the fresh air. All the tension, the anticipation I'd built up minutes before, scattered like leaves on the wind.

After what happened at Dolce Vita, it would be easy to think that I'd be done with the countryside and that I'd be all about crowds, noise, and anything that avoided my feeling alone, with myself.

And it's odd because that's exactly how I felt. For a while, at least. But I soon learnt that leaving Porthcove didn't mean leaving the dark thoughts that live inside my head.

I feel Sarah take my hand.

There are trees as far as the eye can see. The leaflet I picked up yesterday informed me that Oak, Ash, Elm, and Beech trees are indigenous to the New Forest and support a whole echo system of life here.

I take another deep breath. The air tastes so good that it teases a smile from my face. And if you remember my reaction to the oak tree at Dolce Vita, you'll have some idea of what I'm talking about. It's enchanting.

"Come on," I say with a smile. "Let's explore!"

"Marc," is Sarah's semi protest, but I know she's just as captivated as I am.

As we draw closer, I realise that the house isn't painted black but is covered in some kind of abrasive cladding that's an almost identical match to the bark-adorned trunks of nearby trees.

We're standing on the stone-slabbed driveway now. It slopes upward towards a blue Golf parked in front of a large double garage.

"Oh, I am sorry," says a short, thin man with a perfectly groomed mop of black hair and matching beard as he appears around the garage corner carrying a small box.

"This is a no-thru road," he adds with a faint accent to match his olive skin and middle eastern looks. "There should be a sign at the entrance, but I bet it's fallen over again," he says with a smile before wrestling with the tailgate of his car and the box in his hands.

I laugh. "That's really good, Kal."

The man with the tailored blue suit and shiny brown shoes asks in a posh accent, "Was I convincing?"

"Oscar-worthy," I say.

"I'm Khalil," he adds, proffering a hand to Sarah. "Khalil Khan, but everybody calls me Kal. And you must be the lovely Sarah."

Sarah gives me an equivocal look.

"He's also a resident comedian," I say, shaking the man's hand. "Kal's an agent. He helps me find suitable properties for the business. He's also the one who found this place along with what may well be my next major project."

Kal bows his head. "So, are you guys ready to take a look around this beauty?"

"That's why we're here," I say with a shrug.

Sarah looks at me again, and it's my cue. "Sarah, I have a confession to make."

She cocks her head expectantly.

"A while back, Kal sent me details on a property near here. He also told me about this place. Now, I know we haven't managed to discuss anything yet, but with your placement not far from here, I thought—"

"Stop," she says suddenly, "you had me at *that's why we're here*," she says with a grin.

"Really?"

"Well, there's no harm in looking, is there?" she says, linking my arm once more as if she's about to board a theme park ride. And I love that wonder in her.

Kal stands back to face the building with us and deliver the patter he's undoubtedly been longing to all day.

"Beautiful, isn't she?" he says dreamily, then immediately turns to Sarah. "I mean *it*, *it's* a beautiful building," he says, holding out apologising hands. "It's a new build. About three years. Previously a prototype slash show-home. Still absolutely immaculate throughout. Immaculate and unlike anything you've ever seen before. Designed by Klarkson exclusively for the owner. The plans underwent several modifications before it was granted approval status as a *Paragraph 55 development project*." Kal turns to us and adds somewhat seriously, "This is a rare form of planning permission, you understand, for such a location. Granted only when the building is deemed to be of *outstanding innovative design with significant architectural merit*."

"I'm not sure I know exactly what that means, Kal, but it sounds impressive," I say with a chuckle.

"It means that they would not have had a chance in hell of building in this location of outstanding natural beauty if they hadn't designed something truly unique," the agent says, dreamily taking in the building as if he's seeing it for the first time.

"Holt is made up of two rectangular volumes of glass and steel stacked on top of and overlapping each other. Set on a flood-resistant concrete foundation. The total living space of its geometric shape is 4,352-square-feet or approximately 404-square-metres. Its exterior walls are covered in a specially designed, fully sustainable polycarbonate cladding that allows the house to blend and almost disappear into the woodland surrounding it. Most of the glass walls open onto terraces on both floors in a semi reverse living configuration designed to maximise the occupant's experience of living amongst the trees." He pauses here and sighs before adding quickly, "You wait until you see it from the inside. It's going to blow your mind."

Then, when he notices us staring at him, he offers. "I wanted to be an architect. My parents. They had other plans for me." When neither of us contributes to that, he quickly adds sheepishly, "My full name, or at least the name by which my mother insists on introducing me to everybody she knows is *Doctor* Khalil Kahn. Long story. Let's just say that hospitals and suffering kind of gets you down after a while. And so, executive property management is the closest I could get to being an architect. Ideally, I'd like to retrain, but with a couple of little ones and another on the way, you know, one needs to be practical." He laughs. "Anyway, I'm so sorry. You're not here for my life story, are you? You're here to see this beauty's true potential from the inside, aren't you? Aren't you?" he prompts like an overzealous compere warming up his audience.

"Yay!" Sarah says, taking her cue and clapping her hands together.

Kal leads us around the double garage, where we're presented with a pair of tall windows and an oversized double front door.

Hammered onto the wall to the right are mirrored letters that spell the word *HOLT.* It means *wood or wooded hill.* In North America, it's also a dialect for getting *holt* of something.

Yes, I googled it.

"So, how many bedrooms does it have?" Even though I already know the answer.

"Holt has three bedrooms, all on-suite and with stunning views."

Where did you hear that before? Exactly. I'm reminded of my overenthusiastic American estate agent and the day she told me that Dolce Vita wasn't worth anything. I shiver away the memory.

"So, now I'd like you to take a second to consider what normally happens when you reach your front door. One puts a key in the lock, and the door opens, correct?"

Sarah and I look at each other and nod.

The estate agent waves an electronic tag like a car fob at the door. That's right, waves it, seemingly more for show than necessity, and part of the wall clicks open.

Shit! I know it sounds somewhat juvenile, blokey maybe, but

that excites me! And I'm reassured that Sarah thinks it bloody cool too because she turns to me and grins.

Kal continues, "While everything at Holt is about sustainability and the importance of existing only to complement its habitat, it is also state of the art, boasting its own solar array built into the roof, smart home service in every room, and, of course, a Rottweiler security system, featuring perimeter sensors with movement detection, lighting, video surveillance, and alarm with 24 hours security service."

Noticing our blank expressions, he adds, "One of the best alarm systems that money can buy with video cameras all over the house viewable from anywhere in the world via an app on your mobile device."

The agent then pushes on the door slash wall with a flourish, and we watch how a whole part of it swivels on a pivot like a revolving door.

Front door open. Alarm deactivated. Welcome, Kal and guests, a softly spoken male voice says seemingly from inside the walls.

"That's Holt. He's the AI quite literally built into the house."

"Built-in?" I echo.

"Yes. As mentioned, this house was the actual prototype for what is now being included as standard in Carson luxury homes throughout the world. Don't worry. It's nothing like *Demon Seed*," he adds with a chuckle. I laugh along with him, but Sarah frowns, and I'm reminded of the age gap between us. "Old film," I say.

"Based on the book," Kal adds.

"That's right," I nod; then, somewhat stupefied, I ask, "Kal, what the hell is this place?"

"I had a feeling you were going to ask," the estate agent says with a grin. "As mentioned, Holt is the brainchild of Nathaniel Carson. Heard of him?" He pauses to read the blankness on our faces and then continues. "He's often in the news. Business reports mostly. Major entrepreneur with a whole portfolio of blue-chip companies. From new tech to construction. He initially started building Holt as a sanctuary for himself and his wife. Somewhere for them to escape to. But then, in true entrepreneurial fashion, he realised that with its unparalleled green technological credentials that it would fit perfectly into his portfolio of properties."

"So why is he not living here himself?" Sarah asks with usual directness.

Our tour guide shakes his head thoughtfully. "I'm not sure of the details, and you'll appreciate there's only so much I can say, but it's believed that the lady of the house upped and left for reasons unknown and, consequently, Mr. Carson no longer wants anything to do with the property."

"Well, doesn't sound like he'd miss the money. Why doesn't he just give it to us to maintain as a show home? We don't mind people dropping in from time to time," I say.

Kal acknowledges my comment with a lift of the eyebrows and a smile. "I think it's already served that purpose. Carson Holmes is already building houses like this around the world. I say similar because there are elements of Holt that are unique, and it will forever remain that way in accordance with Mr. Carson's wishes. So, are you ready to have your world completely rocked?"

Sarah and I nod like eager children.

"And so, this is the entrance hall," he says, which is more like a large area with tall windows on either side. "Through here," he says, pointing to a room opposite, "is the dining area. As you can see, there's plenty of space for a large family. Do you have any little ones?"

Sarah looks at me, and I take the cue. "Just an overgrown dog," I say quickly.

"Well, there'll be plenty of room for him to run around at Holt. The property comes with four acres of land. Most of that, of course, is woodland."

The estate agent then skilfully steps aside, allowing us to see through the wide archway into the dining area, where a hunk of dark wood shaped into an oblong banquet table with room for at least eight people takes pride at the centre. It's flanked by wooden benches topped with plush cushions. Hovering above the table, as if suspended in mid-air, are what looks like old glass milk bottles. There must be at least a hundred of them clumped together at intervals like grapes.

"All reclaimed," Kal narrates, "Mr. Carson is an ardent

environmentalist. He heads one of the world's largest charities dedicated to the conservation of natural resources. Most of his companies are pledged to carbon neutrality targets. As you can see, this area doesn't have any doors. It was designed this way with subtle lighting specifically so that diners can enjoy the view of the outdoors with their meal both during the day and at night. This is a wonderful space both for dining and, of course, for business meetings. I know you conduct much of your business from home, Marc... Shall we?" He adds, gesturing into the dining room.

It's bright in here thanks to the giant picture window overlooking the front lawn, garden, and out to the driveway.

"The kitchen can be reached through here, but there is also a hallway entrance further down the corridor," Kal says, pointing to a set of restaurant-style swing doors.

Sarah is the first to push them open, and when she does, it's to a shimmering rectangular marble island. The room is flooded with daylight to the point that it appears as if we've stepped outside again. I look up to see the silhouette of tree branches peering down at us through a large steeple atrium.

An expletive forms at the back of my throat but comes out as a, "Wow."

"Impressive. Isn't it? Trees provide a natural shade, but Mr. Carson was adamant that living amongst the trees should not mean living in the shadow of them."

"What about sunlight?" Sarah asks, "I mean, the light's flooding in here, and it should feel as hot as a greenhouse, but it isn't."

"All of the glass at Holt is specially treated so that it lets in light but not the heat. Instead, that heat is siphoned off to the solar energy batteries located in the loft, which is stored and consumed when required. Naturally, there's also climate control throughout the building. Underfloor heating and discreet vents located in every room to ensure that Holt maintains the perfect temperature at all times."

I nod. Impressed. I've barely seen this place, and I already know I want us to live here.

"Needless to say, the kitchen is top of the range. Mr. Carson is an avid cook. It helps him relax. What about you?"

Sarah and I both stutter and talk over each other as if it would be some kind of sacrilege in this temple of culinary practice to confess that I'm pretty much limited to a decent Italian three-course meal while Sarah... Well, let's just say cooking isn't her favourite pastime. But neither of us is nor has any aspiration to become any kind of food alchemist. And yet, when I look at the 12-ring stove and ovens built into the wall, the sunken dual sink, the pans suspended from the ceiling, the breakfast bar at the island with room for four people, and the general sense that this is undoubtedly the place where serious non and professional chefs may enter, I nod and say, "Oh yes, we're always in the kitchen. Every spare moment we can get."

Sarah glances at me and suppresses a snicker.

"Well, you're going to feel right at home here. The kitchen is fully kitted out with top-of-the-range equipment modern appliances, most of which are monitored and controlled by Holt. Again. All of this is included in the price."

"Come again?" I say.

"All of the furnishings are included in the price."

"No. The bit about Holt."

"Oh. Well, it's a smart home. Holt controls all of that, so you don't have to. A bit like some of those smart appliances that you can get now. Only he's much better. For example, he'll monitor the fridge for things you might be running low on and automatically add them to the shopping list for your approval later. You can also tell him about essential items such as milk, bread, butter, and he'll make sure you never run out. Or, and this is something I know my wife would love, if you need to use the oven, you can tell Holt to warm it before you use it.

This is one of my favourite spaces in the house. It's spacious yet cosy, if you know what I mean."

And strangely enough, I do. It's quite a large space, especially by kitchen standards, and yet, the rustic light wood fitted cabinets, the floating shelves with glasses and dishes on display, and that fantastic giant picture window with that enviable view over the front garden and woodland sets this place off beautifully.

When he spots me looking at the floor, our tour guide—because at this stage it very much feels like the man is showing us around a home of historic importance—adds skilfully, "Reclaimed dark wood. And, as mentioned, underfloor heating, which can be controlled via any of the smart displays. You'll find one in every room controlling a variety of things. Lights, blinds, shutters, etcetera. Or via the app or, of course, by voice command. In fact, it's a bit chilly in here, don't you think?" the estate agent asks, dramatically rubbing his arms. The man then looks up to nowhere in particular and says, "Holt?"

"Yes, Kal," responds that smooth disembodied male voice of earlier.

"Set the thermostat in the kitchen to 20 degrees."

"Of course."

With a grin, the estate agent points to the smart display on the nearby wall. Sure enough, the temperature counts upward to 20 degrees then stops.

"Holt is fully customisable. Responses. Zone themes. Routines. You just teach him your biometric profile, voice, fingerprint, face, eyes, and he'll personalise all your interactions accordingly. He's intuitive and user-friendly. In fact, if you know how to use one of those things from Amazon or Google, Holt works a bit like one of those. Only better. Much better. For example, he can tell when you're looking up and talking to him or about him." There's a smirk on our estate agent's face as if he personally designed the AI. "Now, tell me you're both technophobes," he says with a grin that instantly slips before he asks, seriously, "You're not, are you?"

Sarah and I look at each other because, well, I can't say I'd thought about it until now. "We love technology, don't we, Sarah? Where we come from, we'd be glad to have power most of the time," I say with a smile.

"Really? You mean London?" he asks, perplexed.

"By way of Porthcove," I say with a groan.

"Oh, I've heard of that place. It's beautiful, so beautiful down there. My wife and I went there for our holidays last year, beautiful, so beautiful. We didn't actually get a chance to visit Porthcove because, well, Alexandra, that's our youngest, she got car sick and threw up everywhere. But then, we heard what happened on the news. My wife was like, *Oh Kal, look, that's the place we were going to go to.* Such a shame. Such a terrible shame what happened. Wait… you didn't know any of those people?"

I look at the agent's eager face and realise for the first time that I've been working with the man for the best part of a year, and he doesn't really know anything about me. So, I shake my head. "No. Nobody we knew," I say, forcing a smile.

Kal breathes a visible sigh of relief. "Great. So, how about I show you the rest of this beauty before we lose all the light, eh?" he says, pointing to a nearby door. "The utility room is just through here, but I'm sure you've seen plenty of those. It has everything you could possibly need, including a mini shower area to rinse off those muddy paws."

"Yeah. Sarah can get herself into a right mess sometimes," I say.

"He's talking about the dog," Sarah says, playfully punching me in the arm.

"Oh right," I say with a grin, "right."

When we walk back into the dining room, the bottles hovering above the table spring to life along with the wall lights situated at the four corners of the room.

"Ah," the estate agent says with a smile. I'd hope you'd see that. It's cool, eh? All the lights in Holt are controlled by thermal, motion, and light sensors. That's why there are no light switches on any of the walls. Everything is fully automated, but, of course, should you need to control the lighting for whatever reason, you can always ask Holt." The agent speaks at the walls again, "Holt, turn the dining table lights up."

Done, the voice responds as the lights automatically burn brighter.

"That is so cool," Sarah says, "can I try?"

"Of course."

"Holt, dim the lights in the dining room."

Thank you, guest. Dimming the lights now.

"Holt can be programmed to respond only to the voiceprint of house occupants or has an option to accept limited instructions from house guests too. Shall we?" the estate agent gestures towards the hallway, where I pause for several seconds until the lights go off. And for some reason I can't explain, it brings a grin to my face.

There's a junction at the end of the hallway with corridors leading left and right, but my eyes are drawn to the gloss white floating switchback staircase directly in front of me. It is awash with daylight, thanks to a giant cathedral-like window. Beyond it–

"OH MY GOD!" Sarah's voice drifts out from a room off to my right. "I've never seen anything like it," she's saying as I walk over to the doorway and freeze.

"Oh, Marco. I was wondering where you'd got to. Did you stop to see if the lights went out?" Kal asks with a wry smile.

I smile at him and want to answer, but the words fail to form in my mouth, for my eyes are drawn to the wall of light on the opposite side of the room.

"So, of course, this is the lounge," Kal narrates in the background, "as you can see, the stunning ten feet floor-to-ceiling glass wall offers an immersive view of the lake and woodland on either side. "The elevation was specifically designed this way to give a feeling of floating, of being suspended in mid-air."

And it works. The view, framed by two giant sycamore trees, is of what looks like a giant meadow sloping down to a jetty that reaches out into the surreal mirror of water, reflecting the parallel world of the sky above and that of nature basking in the afternoon sun below."

"It's like a living painting," Sarah breathes as if she's reading my thoughts.

It's stunning. I imagine Carson and his family here. Family. Barbeques. Laughter.

I feel something cold and wet touch my hand. It startles me. I look down; Buddy is nuzzling my hand. "Hey, you. How did you get out of the car?" I say, glancing up at Sarah, who shrugs. The dog's only response is to wag his tail while observing me with those big doe eyes of his.

I think of Toby and Ellie, and I find myself fantasising, replacing the faceless Carson family with us. I dream of another life with them. Here. The image is beautiful as it is crushingly sad. And my stomach lurches when I hear Toby's excited voice in my head.

Come on, Dad! Let's explore!

I focus on the dog's face again. He's still watching me with those beautiful brown eyes. *You wouldn't know which part of the undergrowth to sniff out first, would you, mate?* I think the dog appears to have inherited my boy's boundless vitality for life.

Suddenly, I'm feeling nauseous. Overwhelmed.

"These plush chesterfield sofas are, of course, included, as is this solid mango wood side units and table. The lamps. Pretty much everything you see here can be included in the offering. Oh, hello," Kal adds, spotting the dog.

Sarah is looking at me. There's a smile on her face, but I watch it disappear as she performs a double-take. "Are you okay?"

I take a few seconds to tune in, to recognise those eyes gleaming green in the brightness of the room.

"Yeah. I'm good. I'm fine."

"Are you sure?"

"Yes. I'm sure."

"Would you like some water? A snack, perhaps?" Kal chimes in.

I shake my head. "I'm fine, really," I say.

Get a grip, Battista. What's wrong with you?

"Marc?" Sarah is still looking at me.

I force a smile. "Wow. This view, eh?" I say, looking out, "it takes your breath away."

"Happens to me every time," Kal says, "are you okay to continue?"

"Yes. Of course," I say, "lead the way." Then, turning to the dog, I add, "And you, be good."

The agent leads us out of the lounge and back into the hallway, probably one of the darkest rooms I've seen so far. And we all know how I feel about dark hallways after Dolce Vita. The good thing here, though, is that there are large arched windows at both ends of this one, looking out onto woodland.

"So, down there, you'll find the other entrance to the kitchen that I mentioned earlier and the water closet, toilet if you prefer. Bathroom if you're American. But I'm sorry to say while it's certainly large enough, it does not include a bath. You're most welcome to take a look."

"It's okay. We've seen toilets before. What's down here?" Sarah asks, pointing down the opposite end of the hallway.

"That's exactly where I was going to take you next. The study. But please, feel free to take a wander," Kal says, gesturing ahead.

Sarah grins at me, and then, with that boundless childlike enthusiasm that I love so much about her, she links my arm and pretty much skips us down the hallway to a closed door on our right. It's brighter down here, which I imagine is partly because the study door is made mostly of opaque glass.

I can sense Kal behind me. Presumably holding back so as not to spoil the wow factor of the room by installing himself in it first, and Sarah is obviously of the same mind because she relinquishes my arm and places it on the small of my back, ushering me inside.

And....

To the left is a wall-to-wall shelf laden with books of all sizes and colours. Against the right wall is a desk. At least, I think it is because it's fashioned and gleams like a polished desk but bears the circles and patterns of a tree trunk. Behind it is a brown leather swivel chair.

But the thing that has my jaw hitting the floor is the view in front and to the side of me. I can only shake my head in wonder as I walk into the space. There's no barrier in front of me but for a sheet of glass from floor to ceiling that looks through tree branches, across the lawn, and out to the lake.

The left façade of the room is also made of glass, only this view is out and through the forest. Two completely different perspectives. One absolutely stunning room.

I can feel Sarah's warm hand on mine. "It's as if this place was designed with you in mind," she says gently.

I can't rip my eyes away from the dual vision that has us quite literally immersed in nature. And, like some big girl's blouse, I'm feeling emotional. Quite literally overwhelmed by the beauty of this place.

Can you believe that? Marco hard-nut-Battista? You know, I still blame Ethan for this new mushy lump of goo I've become.

"It's okay," Kal says, "I had exactly the same reaction when I first entered this room." I'd forgotten the agent was here. "Like everything else, the furnishings are all included in the price."

He's referring to the twin couches facing each other in the

middle of the room along with a black wingback swivel chair strategically placed opposite them so that it can spin from socialising with guests or to either of the views this incredible room has to offer.

"I don't want to go back to London," Sarah says suddenly.

I turn to her. "Really?" She nods enthusiastically. "I wasn't sure if you wanted to leave the city?"

"Are you mad? I've wanted out of that place for months. And with the placement out here, I don't really have a choice."

"Oh, Sarah. That makes me so happy!"

"Really?"

"Well, yeah. I thought I would have to make a list of reasons why we should move out here. You know, prepare a whole presentation."

She laughs. "A presentation? Marc, have you seen this place? And it's going to be close to my job. But what about you? What will you do all the way out here? I doubt you're going to find many clients."

"I don't worry about me. All being well, my work will be just over there," I say, pointing out of the glass and across the lake to the building perched atop its own grassy hill. A picture-perfect fairy-tale mansion as beautiful as the landscape it inhabits. "See that place?"

"Yeah, I noticed it earlier. I was going to ask."

"That is Frost Lake Manor. And that, subject to Uncle Irvin's seal of approval, is going to be Battista Properties' latest, and, dare I say it, most ambitious projects."

Sarah gasps. "You've bought that place?"

I exchange looks with Kal. "Not quite yet, but I'm considering it."

"Really? It must cost a fortune!"

I can feel my heart thudding. "Yeah. Something like that."

"And this place too?"

"No. Holt is separate," Kal contributes, "they used to be part of the same estate, but Holt now stands on what used to be the servants' quarters."

"Servants' quarters?" Sarah echoes.

"We call it staff accommodation these days," I say.

"Why are they so far apart?" she asks, "you would have thought they'd be closer together."

I shrug. "Indeed, you would, my dear lady," I say, putting on a posh accent like I know what I'm talking about, but really, well, we've all watched Downton Abbey. "One assumes that the former lord of the manor didn't enjoy mixing with *the help,*" I say, lifting an eyebrow.

"It was sold off a while back," Kal contributes, "the so-called *Lord* needed a cash injection and sold this part of the estate along with the adjacent woodland and even half of the lake to Carson Enterprises." There's a pause as we all gaze out at the view. Birds sing. Then, "So, would you like to see the rest of the house?" The agent offers.

"There's no need," I say decisively. "Just tell me how much and how I can afford it."

AUTUMN

OCTOBER

3

REMORSE

FRIDAY

I am spinning like a ragdoll in a washing machine of saltwater. The freeze, wrapped around my chest like a vice, is squeezing, pushing, and forcing every bubble of life support from my body until there's nothing left but paralysis. Limbs no longer thrashing. Lungs are no longer working. It's time for me to accept. I'm well-versed at that now. I know what to do.

Daddy!

Toby. My flesh. My blood. My pride. My joy. I can hear you, buddy, through the water. I can feel you all over me. And it's no longer cold. No longer freezing. That smile of yours is as warm and as bright as the sun itself.

This is where you end.

This is where I end.

No. Daddy. Look closely.

Toby. Is that you?

Daddy. Look closely. I'm alone.

Toby, is that you. Buddy. I can hear you, but I can't see you.

It's so dark down here. So dark.

I am alone.

Toby!

Alone.

"Toby? Am I dreaming again? I'm not, am I? This isn't the usual dream. Feels different this time. Vivid. Darker. Colder. And no matter what I do, I just can't seem to swim upward.

I'm sinking!

This is where you end.

No! This isn't where I end. No! It isn't! I survived! This is where I survived! I SURVIVED!

"I'M ALIVE!"

I wake with a start, gasping, spluttering, and hyperventilating as if I've just emerged from a thousand leagues beneath the surface.

I clutch at the burn in my chest like I'm about to snuff it at any second, but I'm not. I know I'm not. It was a nightmare. Just another shitty nightmare.

Calm down. Calm down. Breathe deeply. Slowly. That's it. Breathe deeply and slowly, deeply and slowly.

"Oh shit," I sigh, "Oh shit." These bastard things are back.

This is what it used to be like. Every night I would drown in that ocean again and again. And each time with the same terrifying intensity. But then, as the months went on, as I worked the sessions with Ethan, they became more manageable until they faded, but now, suddenly, they're back. And you don't have to be a psychoanalyst to know why.

Anxiety.

"Oh, God." I run hands through my hair that could use a trim. On the bright side, at least it's still relatively thick for a man of my age.

Ugh. Did you just hear that? *Man of my bloody age!* There's nothing wrong with me. I'm still young, virile, and, um, a... fucking wreck.

I punch the air with both hands. "Yay!"

I could use a bit of the verve I had that day back in July when we drove out here, and I made that executive decision to finally lay the past to rest and start anew.

It has felt like I have lived most of my life waiting for the other shoe to drop. Being loved by my mother, accepted by my father, forgiven by my wife, hounded by the debt monster, plagued by grief, and haunted quite literally by ghosts.

But that day, I decided that to take my destiny into my own hands, that I was no longer going to be afraid because there really isn't any point in surviving Dolce Vita if I'm not going to *live* my life.

Or some such shit.

I had wanted to make some grand gesture to Sarah that day. You know, drop to my knees, and ask her if she would move in with me again. Only out here. But then we got so caught up in the moment that the move simply made sense.

Although it wasn't all plain sailing. After we got back to the car – which by the way, had one of the backdoors wide open. I can only assume the golden wonder somehow managed to open it – Sarah told me she was worried that my *marooning* myself out here—God, I hate that word now because that's exactly what Ellie said—was a deliberate attempt to escape what happened in London.

I reassured her that it had absolutely nothing to do with that and everything to do with the fact that the time was right for us to move on to the next stage of our lives. She has her new post. I have the renovation of Frost Lake Manor. We were both sick of living in the city anyway. Moving made sense.

And so, it's taken us a while to get here. The bridging loan I needed to acquire the manor turned out to be more complicated than I originally thought because of the amount involved. Alright. It was more of a nightmare. Then English Heritage seemed to drag their heels which made me think they no longer wanted to sell. Weird. They just kept telling us that the abandoned property wasn't ready, and yet when we visited back in the summer, apart from looking like humans hadn't inhabited it for over a decade, it seemed more than ready.

So, yeah, it's been a stressful few months. Still, I eventually managed to sink almost all of the money I have into a dilapidated mansion filled with junk and extend the credit I can't afford in the form of a bridging loan with an interest rate high enough to pay off third world debt.

Still, buoyed by Sarah, who insists that this is my time —which I still don't fully understand beyond sounding like a *Celine Dion* song, I embraced my new life. I signed two seriously life-changing leases in addition to everything else.

One of which befits my new status of a foolhardy property tycoon. And that's a shiny electric BMW SUV. Brand new model. Just out. I did manage to get a fantastic twelve-month offer on it, though.

I've never owned a brand-new car in my life. I didn't even know what they smelt like until I rode in my father's Maserati and then David's Porsche. I was literally shaking as I climbed into the driver's seat of that thing. Sweating like a bloody pig.

Marco Battista in a brand-new Beemer. I still can't believe it— even now—and often look out of the bedroom window to check it's still sitting in the driveway and not another figment of my imagination.

It isn't. It's real and a thing of beauty. Fully loaded. This means—if I allow myself to look at this from a positive perspective for just a moment—that when it all goes to shit like, I don't know, the place is swallowed up by a sinkhole or something, or the bank forecloses because I'm unable to sell the property for whatever reason. I don't have a brass razoo left to my name, and both Sarah and probably even the dog have left me; I'll at least be able to drive off a cliff in style.

Fuck.

What the *actual* fuck have I done?

WHAT HAVE I DONE?!

I sweep back the quilt because it's suddenly hot and stifling in here and hear Buddy groan.

"Sorry, mate," I say, peeling the covers off his sleepy head.

Sarah had to go to work on a Sunday, so the dog has obviously decided to take her place as usual.

I swing my legs over the side of the bed and breathe deeply while placing a hand over the thump in my chest. *You're okay. You're alright. Calm down.*

Buyer's Remorse is a thing, apparently. It's a crushing sense of regret and anxiety after an expensive purchase, like a car or property.

Yeah, I googled that too, about a day or so after I signed the lease for the car and then again when the house sale went through, and I literally started having palpitations, like now.

At first, I researched because I was quite literally looking for a way to cope with my feelings. However, when I started digging a little deeper, I discovered that it's actually a form of *cognitive dissonance,* which, of course, as a therapist, I know all about.

If you haven't spent the best part of four years reading and writing about this stuff, cognitive dissonance relates to how we view ourselves. We all have a perception of who we are. In my case, I'm Marco Battista, the bloke you already know who has spent most of his life living from hand to mouth, looking through the shop window at other people's fortunes. Then, suddenly, overnight—relatively speaking—that all changed, I became a millionaire. Now, while this didn't quite come as a shock, say the same way that winning the lottery might, I still acquired two major things—the house and the car—that, at least on an unconscious level, still do not jive with who I am since in the world I'm used to, I could never afford anything like that.

This is consistent with psychologist Art Markman, PhD's theory that buyer's remorse is the by-product of two motivational systems that guide us; *the avoidance system* that deals with preserving our survival and helping us avoid negative things, such as debt as it may ultimately, at least on a psychological level, cause us harm. And *The approach system* that deals with our wants, needs, and desires.

During the purchase phase, *the approach system* is in control, urging us to satisfy the compulsion. Then, the moment it has been satisfied, we're abandoned in favour of the *avoidance system* that seeks to protect us from self-destruction.

Bit bloody late now!

Cue a severe case of buyer's remorse, where after enjoying the car for a couple of days, I started thinking of fanciful excuses that would enable me to return it to the dealer.

The reality is, I can't. I've signed the lease now. I am committed. The house, well, that's a different story.

Yes, it's all as convoluted as it sounds, but that convolution is, somewhat ironically, helping me deal with this because I understand what's happening. And sometimes, part of solving the problem is understanding it.

Sarah just says I deserve it. I, on the other hand... Well, that's a whole different bundle of neurosis.

I hear Buddy whimper on the bed behind me, and I turn to see that he has one side of his head resting on the plushness of the quilt, and the other is observing me with a sleepy eye. "I'm alright, Buddy. I'm okay. I've just bought a multi-million-pound property and signed leases on several thousand more."

Oh, is that all? I imagine the dog says as his eye blinks a few times before he dozes off once more.

"Yeah," I say, collecting my breath. "Good talk. Thanks, pal." I roll my eyes and then reach out and pet him.

By the way, I don't normally allow him to sleep on the bed—that's still part conditioning from Ellie—because he has his own perfectly good bed on the floor next to us. And I mean, bed. It has its own mattress and everything. It was a move-in present to him when we first got here. So, he really doesn't need to be taking over mine, which is exactly what he is doing right now.

Have you ever seen a dog starfish on a bed? Well, he doesn't do that. Obviously. Because, well, he doesn't have the dexterity, but he certainly tries, lying on his back, furry belly in the air.

Commotion draws my attention to the window. Or, more specifically, the glass wall with that view over the back lawn and the lake where a gaggle of geese is migrating from one side of the water to the other with an obnoxious display of flapping wings and loud honks.

It's moments like these that I'm reminded why I had that moment of madness and needed to be here. Like the soft, velvety feel of Buddy's fur beneath my fingers, the view from the snuggling comfort of my bed is mesmerising.

If only the *old man* could see me now.

I mean, this master bedroom is the same size as the lounge. It's massive, wide, and spacious. And the super king-sized bed is on a raised platform, reached by two steps. Strategically positioned so that whether I sit or lie here, the view will always be the same. Right now, it's a cerulean sky that still has its corners dipped in the dregs of marmalade dawn. It's admiring itself in the lake's mirrored surface framed by verdant trees and what looks like a smattering of multi-coloured marbles but are birds. A gigantic moving canvas that can be enjoyed from the comfort of my pillow, scored by the morning avian opera.

Then, beyond the lake, sitting stoically, like a jilted bride, is the silhouette of Frost Lake Manor. The building that quite literally holds my fate in its walls.

So, you may well be wondering why we didn't just move in there while the refurbishment takes place. If you are, I have just one question for you? Weren't you there during our last terror-filled sojourn at Dolce Vita? If not, perhaps you should familiarise yourself with that story first and then come back and tell me if, after everything that happened, you'd be in a hurry to move into another place just like it.

No, thank you.

I may have a few screws loose, but I'm not insane. No. I have altogether different plans, and they don't include sharing some 18th-century dusty old mansion with assorted families of insects and God knows what else.

No.

Besides, Frost Lake Manor isn't habitable. Not yet anyway. It's getting there, but there's still a lot of work that needs to be done first.

I never did have any intention of moving into the manor regardless of its condition. It's only when we took the *ghost house* tour that I thought there was no way we could move in there. That's when Kal told me about this place, and, well, you've seen it, it's like something out of *Lifestyles of the Rich and Famous*. Lucky for us, it had just become available for lease, fully furnished. It's a dream home. And I've signed a twelve-month lease on it. I figured that would give us enough time to complete the works on the manor and decide what we will do next. We may even decide to stay. Who knows, maybe even make an offer.

And so, yes. This is the other thing that I've been *buyer's remorsing* about. But I keep telling myself that the deed is done. The right decision was made. Now we just need to focus on enjoying it.

Well, I do. Sarah seems to be having the time of her life.

I enviously leave Buddy snoring, slide out of bed, and to the bathroom, which is twice the size of the bedroom at Dolce Vita and, yeah, well, not even going to mention the B&B we were living out of.

It is separated into zones. The first with hanging space, storage, cupboards, vanity dresser, large mirror, and seating because, of course, we all love to hang out in the bathroom.

I open the glass cabinet and take out the orange vial of pills while side-stepping another dollop of guilt that insists on presenting itself every bloody time I look at these things.

What happened is in the past. You're fine. Just a bit stressed. You're perfectly fine.

I shake two pills into my hand and return the container.

The next section is the toilet, bidet, and twin basins with large wall mirrors. I drop the pills into the toilet, pee on them, and then flush.

The next zone is the wet room with an alcove in the corner and a giant freestanding bath with a spectacular multi-view of the lake on one side and out over the canopy of trees on the other. The thing I love about this beyond the obvious is that you can tell by the position of the bath that the bathroom experience here was meticulously thought out, and that just impresses me. I know it sounds sad, but my life, like most, has always been about the bare necessities, things that are functional. It just feels so bloody exciting to experience something that is a pure unadulterated indulgence, as arrogant as that may sound.

Privacy is not an issue up here since the only *peeping toms* are likely to be of the feathered variety, but for the churlish, the windows feature special filaments that frost over at the touch of a button or voice instruction to Holt.

Ironically, while this room is one of my favourites, it's also the one that often makes me feel like I don't belong in this lap of such luxury. But, as always, I get over it by wiggling out of my shorts and walking over to the shower that features an astounding backlit living wall.

You know what that is, right? Of course, you do. I was the only imbecile who didn't have a clue. I could never have imagined that there are plants in existence that thrive on you, drowning them in hot water and shower gel.

The best part is being able to instruct Holt to—get this—*start the shower*. I know I shouldn't be that surprised because my Beamer can do that via the app on my phone, but still, it's bloody impressive.

A circle of water at least two feet wide appears in the ceiling in the middle of the room, raining a perfectly circular waterfall onto a raised stone platform.

A bloody platform to perform your shower in the morning like it's a stage. It doesn't get much better than that because those who know me will know I've had bad experiences with showers before. Enough said.

I can tell you, stepping under this thing is like literally stepping under a waterfall. If *it* doesn't wake you up, nothing will.

Of course, my eco-warrior girlfriend did question the water use, but that was until the estate agent told her that much of the water used at Holt is a specially filtrated derivative of the lake. Which is something that both excited and terrified me in equal measure because, well, I'm me, always looking on the practical side. This technology is all fabulous when it works, but when it breaks down, it's like, shit, thousands of pounds a pop. And that's fine for a zillionaire but not someone like me.

But Kal reassured me that everything is included in the lease. Much of this technology is made by Carson's own companies and comes with a lifetime warranty. And no, I didn't ask if that included a call-out and labour fee because, well, that just sounds cheap.

Ten minutes later, I'm refreshed, wide awake, and–

What was that?

"Holt, turn off the shower."

The waterfall ceases immediately.

I listen carefully.

Birds chirp. Water gurgles.

I'm sure I heard something. It sounded like Buddy.

Seconds drift by.

"Buddy?" I call, although I don't know if the dog will even hear me from back here. So, how did I hear him? Is he in the bathroom?

"Buddy?"

Dripping water is the only response.

I listen and wait…

Wood pigeons coo. Falling leaves tap on the glass-like fingers before cartwheeling down to their eternal rest.

Then it comes, slicing through the muffled birdsong, echoing around the wet room, and yanking at my heartstrings.

Buddy! Wailing pitifully as he was in the woods that day when the fox was trying to drag him back to its lair.

I'd recognise that sound anywhere! He's hurt!

"Buddy!" I yell, jumping off the shower perch, racing out of the wet room, through the bathroom, bare feet slapping and squeaking loudly as they slip and slide on the floor tiles.

I burst into the bedroom and come to a skidding halt on the wood floor when I see the hound casually lift his head from the quilt and languidly flick his one and half ears up to gawp at me, sleepily.

Where's the fire? Blink. Blink.

I look around the room as if the dog has suddenly adopted a twin.

There's nothing in here but us.

Shit.

I heard him. I definitely heard him wailing as he was that day. He even sounded different, not like a puppy but like a dog. A dog that was being hurt, tortured. A dog in excruciating pain.

And yet, *that* dog, as if bored with the sight of me, dripping and hanging all over the place, lets his head fall to the quilt once more while keeping a cautious eye on my naked form.

Bong. Bong. Bong. Marco. There is someone at the front door. Would you like to see who it is?

Bong. Bong. Bong. Marco. There is someone at the front door. Would you like to see who it is?

So, we all know about my misophonia and how I feel about repetitive sounds. Well, as much as I would love to tell you that this other quirk of mine has faded, the reality is, it hasn't. In fact, I think our stint in London only made it worse. This is precisely why I love living out here.

And yet, bong, bong, bong.

Bong. Bong. Bong.

The rising notes keep repeating, unaffected by the fact that I'm still trying to reconcile what I think I heard with the reality that the dog is perfectly fine and has now deigned to lift his head at the prospect of an early morning visitor.

Bong. Bong. Bong. Marco, there is someone at the front door. Would you like to see who it is? Bong. Bong. Bong. Marco, there is someone at the door. Would you like to see who it–

"On screen!" I yell into space.

"The ten-inch LED display next to the bed springs to life and beams a high-definition image of someone wearing a wax jacket and flat cap standing at the front door. The figure appears to be looking at the front garden and is facing away from the camera, but by the profile, I can tell that it's a man.

Okay. No idea who that might be. Hardly anybody knows we even live here. And that's the way I like it.

When Buddy sees me slide into shorts and a t-shirt, he groans as if complaining, *so are we really doing this? Are we really waking up now?*

"Get up, sleepyhead," I say, leaving the bedroom and padding barefoot down the stairs because I can. Unlike Dolce Vita, the wood underfoot is warm.

I know Buddy is following me because I can hear his nails clicking on the floor, but I'm still startled when he starts barking as we make our way up the corridor.

"Really? So, now you have something to say about it, eh? Shush," I tell him as I pull the door open.

The stranger still has his back to us, and if I were paranoid, I'd be thinking that the man is trying to conceal his identity. "Can I help you?" I say irritably.

Buddy, ears back now, fires off a warning bark and then chases that up with a growl. I hold out my hand to him. "Stop," I say. I'm serious, and he knows it because he heels instantly without taking his eyes off the intruder.

When the man finally turns to face us, lead sinks to the bottom of my stomach. That's because I recognise him. He looks much older than I remember. The toll of the past two years etching lines under his grey eyes and colouring the tufts of hair sprouting out of the sides of his flat cap a shade whiter.

Heeding my warning, Buddy opts for a frustrated growl and whine as I stammer, "Um, ah, Mr. Stevenson."

"Good morning, Marco," the man responds, looking me up and down with those judgemental eyes of his. Yes, I'm in my shorts and a t-shirt. Perfectly acceptable attire for someone who was minding his own business in his own home. And yet, I find myself unconsciously straightening up, feeling underdressed and somewhat awkward in the presence of this man. Just as I always have.

"Wow. What a surprise. It's been a long time," I add.

He doesn't answer but instead makes a show of standing back and looking at the building as if he hasn't already done that. Then he glances back at the BMW—again like he's seeing it for the first time. *Yes. I've leased a new car. I don't have to explain myself to you anymore.*

And yet, I suddenly feel bloody embarrassed.

Of course, responding as if he's just read my mind, the man nods at the car and says, "Looks brand new."

I nod like a child. I want to say something, but words fail me, so I just stand there like a tool watching his beady eyes rove over the car and building before he whistles under his breath and adds, "Quite the place you have here." He speaks the words but doesn't bother looking back at me. As if I were unworthy of his gaze.

"Thank you. I, um. Would you like to come in?" I ask.

"No, thank you. I won't be staying long," the lawyer says, finally turning and then scrutinizing me as I imagine an alien might before whipping out its laser beam to obliterate me.

Okay.

Seconds sail by on a chilly breeze. I can feel it playing with the hairs on my legs, reminding me that I'm wearing inappropriate attire to be receiving my visitor, who appears to have nothing else to add to the conversation.

So, I say the first thing that pops into my head, "Um, Mr. Stevenson…" yes, I call him that because we've remained formal for the totality of the time I was married to his daughter. In fact, I remember the one time I joked about calling him dad, the glare he shot me may as well have been a punch in the face. "…It's been a while. What, um, what can I do for you?"

"What can you do for me?" he echoes, forcing a chuckle. It's bitter, like the cold out here, and it disappears as suddenly as it appeared before he growls, "Oh, I don't know… you could give me back my child, I suppose. Remember her? My little girl. You could return her to me. Can you do that?"

My stomach lurches, and the chill that dribbles down my spine has nothing to do with perspiration and everything to do with the way those cold eyes are now burning with disdain. "And while you're at it, perhaps you'd be so kind as to resurrect my grandson too," he adds facetiously in that clipped accent of his.

Buddy growls suddenly as if he understood those words that appear to have knocked the stability out of my legs because they suddenly feel like they're going to buckle beneath me.

Toby.

…warm summer breeze. The pier. Toby is laughing. That thing descending from the sky. That look on my son's face. The loss. The guilt. Toby!

"Can you do that, huh? Can you do that, *Mr. Therapist*? Or is it property developer now?" he mocks.

I squint at him because that's all I can do. I'm unable to find words. Unable to articulate. It seems that the harder I try to find the right thing to say, the more it keeps hiding under my tongue, which is suddenly thick and heavy.

Eventually, I manage a pitiful, "You, you know I can't do that."

"No, you can't, *can you*?" His voice cracks on those last words, which is the most emotion I have ever seen this man express in the whole time I've known him.

"Look, Mr. Stevenson, I can't begin–"

He holds up a silencing hand. "Quiet. Just be quiet. Don't speak. Just don't speak. I am not the least bit interested in hearing what you have to say. Quite frankly, I don't even wish to hear your voice. The one and *only* thing that I am interested in is *making you pay*," he growls through gritted denture-like teeth. And then, with a narrowing of his bushy salt and pepper eyebrows and a raising of his bible-thumping fist for agonized emphasis, he says, "And you *will* pay. By the lord almighty, while there is still breath in my body, you will." The words are spoken with such vitriol that I can almost taste it contaminating the once fresh air blowing about me.

I'm shaking now, and I don't know if it's from the cold or the prophetic way he just delivered those words.

Buddy's growl metamorphoses into a bark. If Stevenson is intimidated, he doesn't show it, but that could just be because he's locked in his stare-off with me until I break it by dropping my gaze to my bare feet. I think they're turning blue; I'm not sure.

Okay. So, let's just get this out of the way. I know you're expecting more of me. Maybe kick the old fart in the balls. Perhaps chase him back to his car, but for some reason, I can't. I don't know what it is about this bloke, but every time I am in his presence, I revert to being that kid that stole his daughter from him all those years ago. The same one who is, albeit indirectly, responsible for her losing her life.

I feel *guilty. Ashamed.* And because of this, it seems that all appropriate responses to the man's angry onslaught have run off to hide in the woods somewhere, leaving my tongue paralysed and seemingly happy to let my dog stick up for me.

This man, like me, is grieving. Not just for the loss of his grandson but also that of his daughter. And this is a particular brand of pain that I, of all people, am familiar with. That's why instead of trying to put the bloke in his place, my instinct is surprisingly the opposite.

I want to help him.

I want to invite him in for a cup of tea so that we might talk about this calmly and constructively. And if I thought for one second that he'd take me up on that offer, I'd be extending it to him right now.

"You took our daughter and our grandson from us..." He swallows, wrestling no doubt with the lump in his throat. "They were everything we held dear. *Everything*," he emphasises, thumping his chest with that clenched fist as tears bubble and spill from his eyes. "And now I... I am going to do the same to you."

In one swift movement, he swipes the tears from his cheek and reaches into the inside breast pocket of his jacket, and I won't lie, for a split second, I think he is going to pull out a gun, but instead, he retrieves a brown manila envelope and shoves it at me.

I instinctively take the thing from him and turn it around in my hand. "What's this?"

"You've been served," my father-in-law says with a satisfied smile, "see you in court."

With that, he turns and heads back to his car, leaving me standing there.

4

THE RETURN

WEDNESDAY. EARLY MORNING.

Guess where I'm travelling to.

That's right. London.

It feels like I've only just managed to get shot of the place, and yet here I sit as the train clatters its way back towards the capital.

Why am I visiting London? Oh, nothing important. Just meeting with a firm of lawyers specialising in *tort* cases.

That's right. I scanned and sent copies of the legal documents very kindly delivered to me by my father-in-law over the weekend to my lawyer. I then video-conferenced with him to discuss. After reading them, I watched his face crease into one of those pained expressions people adopt when they think of or, in this case, read something they know you aren't going to like.

Apparently, this case is so serious that my lawyer declined to have anything to do with it because, quote, *this is serious shit, Marco, not something that I can help you with, mate.*

Admittedly, I've only ever known the bloke to deal with my property affairs.

Instead, he recommended a top London firm of lawyers, assuring me that they may be *a bit pricey* but are highly rated.

Great.

Then, thanks to the fact that he knows someone who knows someone, he was able to squeeze me in at the earliest availability, which was first thing today. Handy, because I had to be in London for something else anyway.

Oh, God. I loosen my tie. I don't know why I decided to wear a suit. It just felt right, but it's ridiculous! I'm behaving like I'm already in the dock or something.

It's stifling in this compartment. Summer may be over, but it isn't going without a fight. It must be at least twenty-three degrees in here. The train is crammed with commuters. Sweltering. And I feel like I'm going to throw up.

Calm down. You're working yourself up into a state.

So, now I wish I had taken the car instead, but that's a rubbish idea. I have enough on my mind without having to battle through London traffic too. If there's anything I've learned in the past two years is to try and deal with one bloody challenge at a time.

So, I let Sarah have the car. She has a few days off in lieu and plans to visit her mother, whom she hasn't seen in months. I was going to brave going back to Porthcove too before the merchant of grimness, Stevenson, decided to visit me.

Sarah offered to stay so she could come with me today, but I told her there was no point as I'm a big boy. She rarely gets to visit her mother. Thankfully, she's not planning to stay over and will be back tonight.

Isn't that weird? All this time we've been together, I don't think I've truly had the chance to experience what it's like to be without her, and I have to say, it's crap. And I truly hope that's because I care for her, and it has nothing to do with the fact that I just hate being alone.

God, that thought just made me sound like a right prick! Of course, it's because I care about her. What a fucking stupid thing to think.

I take a deep breath.

Calm down. Calm. You know what this is about. You're

allowing yourself to become overwhelmed by your environment and your thoughts. Think of something nice.

Calm. Cool. Calm. Cool. Breathe in and out. In. Out. In. Out.

"Excuse me, Sir." I feel a hand on my shoulder and am instantly irritated, but I turn to look over my left shoulder to find a sweet little boy with blonde hair, brown eyes sitting in the seat behind me. It's weird because I am instantly reminded of my son, although this boy looks nothing like him.

My stance softens immediately. "Hello," I say with a big smile.

"How are you?" the boy asks.

I grin at his maturity and respond, "Very well, thank you. How are you?"

"I'm okay."

"Are you off to London for the day?" I ask.

"No. I'm stuck here."

I cock my head. "Here?"

"Yes. Here... alone."

"Oh, alone?" I look around the carriage. There are couples talking, a man reading the paper, several other people staring at their phones, a sleeping young lad with a hoodie, and this little guy. "Where are your parents?"

He shrugs. "My dad's gone, but my mum's still here."

"Oh." I scan the train again. "Where is she?"

"She's under the seat," he says casually.

I laugh. "Under the seat?"

He nods. So, I indulge him by making a show of folding down to look under my seat, but, as expected, I see nothing but scuff marks on metal and a discarded polystyrene cup.

I look back up at the boy with a smile. "Nope. There's nobody under here."

"Not that one, silly. The one in front of you."

"Oh right," I say with a nod. Then, I swivel around and slowly look at the seat in front of me... and recoil in horror when I see Ellie's contorted body folded underneath there like a macabre pile of laundry. Her glassy dead eyes gazing up at me.

I jerk awake, sputtering and panting. The action startles the lady sitting next to me, who first shrinks away from the window and then scowls unhappily.

"Sorry. I'm sorry," I say, holding out an apologetic hand. Then, I turn and look over my shoulder at the seat behind me. No little boy, just some bloke wearing a hoodie and giant headphones.

I sigh with relief and then, as casually as I can, check under the seat in front of me.

Empty.

***

There are people everywhere. You wouldn't have thought that the world had been through a major pandemic. But then again, I suppose this is how it's always been. Panic at first, and then, as soon as a vaccine is developed, we go back to our usual intransigent complacency.

I really don't like London anymore. And it has nothing to do with the city itself. London is beautiful. It's just the memories that are conjured every time I come back here and how they make me feel. And I'm not just talking about the memory of Ellie and Toby but also, somewhat surprisingly, how much this place reminds me of me. Or, more specifically, of how I used to be.

I used to go around repressing all the crap from my past, and the by-product of that was that it made me tougher. More impervious to emotional vulnerabilities. Admittedly, it came at a price. A hefty one that almost cost me my marriage. Although, some would argue that it was doomed anyway. Others, well, they'd point out that my behaviour back then didn't help.

Whatever your opinion, I could still function in some capacity before Doctor Holmes opened my eyes to all the putridity from my past. My dysfunctional relationships with females, my emotional unavailability, and of course, who can forget the bizarre and somewhat sadistic relationship I enjoyed with my mother, which was undoubtedly the catalyst for the above. By *enjoyed*, you realise I'm being sarcastic. Right?

Anyway, as we know, after Ethan ungraciously opened my eyes

to my past, I've become more self-aware. More *sensitive* to the sensitivities of others. The result is this somewhat pathetic shadow of the raging bull I used to be. And this in and of itself could be the focus of a whole battery of therapy.

Using anger like armour to function and go about life obviously wasn't good. Walking around like a simpering idiot? Not much better either. A happy medium would be nice.

Therapy may have helped me understand my past and identify the reasons why I developed all my idiosyncrasies, of which we know there are now many, but it doesn't necessarily mean that it was able to heal them.

People often make this mistake, but therapy doesn't work that way. It's like an onion. You peel away the layers to get to all the stuff that's festering beneath, and then once you've had a good rummage around in all that shit, you have to clean it up, air it, and then put those layers back in some shape or form.

This takes time.

Not unlike an addiction, you've got to keep doing the work to ensure that you control your peculiarities so that they don't control you.

Shit.

Why am I babbling about all of this right now? Well, that's what happens when you have too much time to bloody think. Your mind wanders over all topics and not just the ones you feel you should be focussing on.

That, and the fact that I've decided to take the underground rather than jumping into a taxi. Why? I have no idea. It's just something that popped into my head. After being on the train for the best part of three hours, it just made sense to take the underground rather than a bus, which I've been doing for the past year.

And there is a good reason for that. One that, oddly, today I chose to ignore.

Now I feel like I need another bloody shower. And no, I'm not talking about the great unwashed down there, nor the fact that I had to stand for the whole journey between St Pancras and Holborn with my face buried in the armpit of some bloke with dreadlocks down to his arse. No, it was that other thing. That thing that I do that I hate. That thing that makes me feel like a pervert, and yet I do it each time I descend into this place.

Nothing has changed.

Fuck.

It all starts perfectly fine, but then I see her. A brunet. Hair cascading out of her red beret and over her long black coat.

She crosses in front of me just as I am about to join the escalator, and I know I need to do it. Palms hot, sweat beading, I hold back. I hold fucking back and watch her fiddle with her phone for several seconds before I surreptitiously draw in a deep and long lungful of air through my nose and savour it like a fucking crack addict. Only this *hit* isn't some derivative of the coca plant, hydrochloride, and God knows what other shit; no, my reward is jasmine and honeysuckle with a woody undertone.

I can't work out if it's a fragrance or a shampoo, but it's fucking sublime. So, I inhale again. Only this time, there's nothing discreet about it. This time, I inhale like a cokehead inhales a shitty line.

And it's bloody orgasmic. Delicious. Arousing.

Now I feel ashamed.

Dirty.

Oh, God.

It takes all the willpower I can muster not to about-face up that escalator in the wrong direction. Instead, I board the train until the next stop and then hurry out of here like the bloody devil is chasing me.

Shit.

Even after all this time, that compulsion is still there. And I hate it! I hate how just the thought makes me feel both turned on and soiled in equal measure.

So, I tell myself to get a grip. Get a grip. It's a relatively innocuous thing. After all, isn't that the whole purpose of a scent, for it to be appreciated? For it to invoke feelings of sensuality and desire?

Yes, but you wanted to fuck her, though, didn't you?

Oh, piss off!

I flag down a cab. I need the time to pull myself together. The last thing I want to do is arrive at this meeting flustered and rattled.

It's over now. You're okay. You're fine. You are fine. Just don't think about it. In the scheme of things, it is unimportant.

I pay the taxi driver and step out into the din of the city with its inimitable chilled carbon monoxide air and look up at this place with its glass façade and the words PETERS, THOMAS AND HARDY etched in giant lettering over the entrance.

Thomas and Hardy? Really? Am I the only person seeing this?

Oh yeah. Now I know the true meaning of your *legs turning to jelly.* Mine have turned to bloody mush just looking at the outside of this place, which I know is the whole point, to project professionalism. Strength. Expertise. But the only thing I'm seeing is *expensive.*

Oh, Christ! Is this really happening? Is this really happening to me? I'm being sued. I could lose everything!

My heart is thumping. Palms are sweaty, again. My face is flushed. I feel like I'm going to double over and vomit right here on these shiny steps, but I fight it. I fight it and straighten myself up.

Come on. You can do this. You're just rattled by what happened on the underground. Breathe. Pull yourself together, man. Breathe!

I do. For a minute or so, and then, reluctantly, I push on the door and step inside.

5

THE SUIT

WEDNESDAY. 10:25.

As soon as that glass door pulls itself shut behind me, it feels as if I've stepped into another world. The bustle and roar of London are instantly muted and replaced by hushed voices, subtle telephone rings, and some kind of woody fragrance. Designer, no doubt. Molton Brown, maybe?

After presenting myself at reception, a petite-looking girl, who must be on some kind of work experience, directs me to the third floor via the lifts with a sweet smile which is completely lost on me right now.

The ride is short, and when the elevator doors open, I'm immediately presented with a large mahogany reception desk and am reminded, via giant silver lettering hammered high on the wall above it, that I am in the offices of PETERS, THOMAS, AND HARDY.

The receptionist, a mature lady with a serious perm and a comfortable air of superiority, tells me to take a seat and that someone will be with me shortly.

Shortly is five minutes later when a young man with an overenthusiastic demeanour escorts me through a desk pool buzzing with office activity and then down a corridor of glass doors stencilled with names I don't recognise before stopping in front of CONFERENCE *ROOM 1*.

He knocks, opens the door, and ushers me inside.

There, I'm presented with the rear view of a woman clad in a figure-hugging black dress, pinched in the middle with a leopard print belt and matching heels. Her perfectly straightened black hair is long and spilling over the back of her shoulders.

"Oh, I'm sorry," I say, glancing back at the now-closed door behind me. "I'm looking for a Mr. Wilson. Geoffrey Wilson?"

That's when she turns around to face me, and I think my mouth falls open. At first, my mind tells me that it's because she's attractive. Milliseconds later, the fluttering in my stomach suggests a different story.

I recognise her.

"El? Ellie?" I croak.

"It's actually Amanda now. I go by my middle name," the beauty responds with a sultry smile, "it's good to see you, Marco."

"You too. I, um, you've changed your hair. It's dark. What happened to the blonde?"

"This is my natural colour," she says.

I nod, stalling for time, then instinctively glance around the room for cameras because it feels like I'm being set up for some sadistic TV show.

"What? How? What are you doing here?" I garble.

I watch the dimples on her face magically appear as her thick painted lips open to reveal a commercial-worthy set of white teeth, "I work here," she says.

"I um, I, I..." *Spit it out, Woody Allen!* "I had no idea. I, um, I had a meeting with Woody, I mean um Mr. Wilson."

"Yes. Sorry," she says, making a pained face. "Geoffrey's been detained out of town. He was due back this morning, but there was a last-minute thing, and he had to stay behind. So, when I saw your file, I agreed to do the preliminary consultation rather than cancel your meeting. I hope you don't mind," she says, gesturing to the chair in front of a large frosted-glass desk. And I'm about to take a seat when she says, "Actually, on second thoughts. Let's just go to my office. We'll be more comfortable there."

"Are you sure? I mean, I, I don't mind meeting here."

"No. Follow me. It's just down the hall," she says, walking out of the door with all the grace of a catwalk model.

I follow her like the simpering fool that I am, but then, what do you expect? I'm still in shock here.

The walk is short, as promised. She stops by a glass door and ushers me through. As I comply, I snatch a glimpse of the name stencilled on it.

Amanda Stapleton

SENIOR LITIGATOR

Okay. I can't decide if I'm aroused or intimidated by that.

I watch her close the door behind us and then confidently take a seat in the leather swivel chair behind a polished desk. No doubt solid wood. Unlikely the brainchild of some Swedish flat-pack furniture maker.

"Please, Marco. Take a seat," she says, pointing to the chair opposite the desk.

"Thanks." I assume the position of a vulnerable client and marvel at the impressive display of awards, plaques, and accolades for excellence no doubt strategically affixed to the wall behind her to project her prowess as a lawyer.

"So, how have you been?" She says, picking up a pen and tapping on a manila folder in front of her.

"I, um, well, I've been okay. Thank you." And then an incredulous laugh forces its way out of my lips. "I'm sorry, but I'm still in shock. You know, to find you here."

"Why? Didn't you think I was smart enough to be headhunted by a firm like this?" She nods at the plaques behind her.

"Oh, no, no. Of course not. Nothing like that at all. I just didn't expect to find you here. I thought you'd gone back …to Chester."

"I did. And I thrived. Won a few cases," she rocks her head and smiles coyly, "and a few awards. The next thing I know, I'm being offered Senior Legal Counsel."

"Here?"

"Well, we have offices all over. So, I pretty much go where they need me."

"That's amazing," I say, looking around the lavishly furnished room. Leather divans. Chrome. Glass. More trophies for I don't know what, and a large window with views out over the city. "You've done really well. I'm really happy for you," I say.

Those dimples make a reappearance when she responds with a smile. "How about you? I hear you're a bonafide therapist now."

"You heard?" I cock my head.

"Yes," she taps the folder in front of her, "It's in your file. Along with property development. Amazing."

"Yes. I got there in the end. It isn't as highbrow as what you do, but I like it."

"Helping others or making money?"

"Um, helping people."

"Why do you like it?"

"What do you mean?"

"Why do you like helping people with their problems so much?"

Actually, I would rather talk about property development. How I've made something of it. Of myself. How I'm no longer living hand to mouth. Well, I am, just in a different way.

Nonetheless, I think about the question. "I don't really know. I suppose I just like to help people feel better about themselves," I offer. Where the hell did that just come from? Did you hear how lame it sounded? I can do better!

My cross-examiner obviously isn't impressed either because she looks at me for the longest time with those almond-shaped hazel eyes and then suddenly says. No, correction, she doesn't say, she more like emits a rather disappointing, "Huh."

So now I want to do some cross-examining of my own. What the hell is *huh* supposed to mean?

Calm down, you fool. Remember why you're here.

"So, Marco," the lawyer jumps in, "I only have a limited amount of time because I have another client right after you. So, I think, if it's okay with you, it's best we dive right in," she says, looking down at the folder in front of her. Jesus Christ. I've already become a folder on someone's desk.

Don't you keep a dossier on your clients? I remember Ethan asking me that question when we first met and me scoffing.

Not so funny now, is it, mate? Successful property developer! I want to talk about that. Shut up!

"Oh yes. Of course. Sure," I say as I watch her read the content of the folder, but something tells me that's just for show. There's no doubt that she will have studied that thing way before I got here.

So, I push her along when a spark of irritation flares up out of nowhere. "I suppose you could start by explaining what this all means. I don't even know what the hell this suit is about. *Reckless endangerment*? How does that even apply anyway? To me, that's someone driving a car without due care and attention. None of this makes any sense to me," I ramble.

My lawyer, substitute lawyer, or whatever she is looks up at me and says, "No. It wouldn't. But, for the record, reckless endangerment can pretty much be applied to anything where the plaintiff is able to make a case."

"But he can't, can he? Make a case, I mean. Can he?" Wow. That anxiety has made a reappearance. I can feel it squeezing my chest.

Relax, you fool. You're letting your emotions get the better of you. Focus. This isn't about you two; it's about the bloody lawsuit!

"Well, in my extensive experience, I think this case is without merit, but I won't be the one sitting up there deciding this. It's someone else who will have their own thoughts and interpretation of the evidence in this case, and he or she will most likely be wearing a wig."

"A trial? You think this thing will actually go to trial?" My heart's thumping again, and I can feel that tell tail tickle of sweat on my scalp. "Shit. I can't believe this is happening. *What* is happening?"

"Right, okay. Why don't I walk you through this, and then if you have questions after that, I'll do my best to answer those too, okay?" she says calmly, glancing at that bloody folder again, which is another way of telling me that although that sentence was structured like a question, it wasn't.

"So, the plaintiff, in this case, is your wife's estate," she continues glancing up at me and then back at the papers, pen swinging casually between fingers. "It is suing you for recklessly endangering the life of one Elisabeth Stevenson Battista. Your wife," she says, pointing the pen at me. "It asserts that you knew that the property formerly known as Dolce Vita was a danger to life, that it was at risk of subsidence, and yet you still forced your wife to join you there. A decision that resulted in her death."

"That's fucking ridiculous!" I rage, jumping to my feet and moving over to the window as if I can get some bloody air from it, but I can't. "I didn't *force* her to do anything. It was a mutual decision."

"Did you know about the subsidence?"

"Of course I fucking didn't!" I snap, "the first I knew was when the estate agent called me and told me about it."

"But you did know that there was some danger, right? I mean, didn't you say…" she breaks off to refer to the magical mystery folder once more, shuffles some papers around, and then continues, quoting an extract, "You *hoped that it [the property] had been reclaimed by the fucking sea*?"

"How the hell do you know that?"

"Says so. Right here. Your father-in-law claims that his daughter told him what you said during a meeting that resulted in you punching a man in the face in front of at least eight witnesses."

I shake my head in an effort to dispel the rage that is bubbling through me like hot lava. "You don't have to be a lawyer to know that is hearsay."

I watch the lawyer rock her head. "His testimony might be, but not that of the other witnesses, and if a jury hears–"

"A jury?" I echo. "You keep saying that, but I thought you said this case was without merit?" I say quickly, more heavy slabs falling to the pit of my gut.

"I did. I do believe it. But it isn't up to me. This is the very reason why I thought I should take this meeting. Whatever we may think, this is a serious complaint, and as such, it should be taken seriously. Especially as we have little time to prepare."

"You think I'm not taking it seriously?"

"No. I'm just saying that—"

I screw my face up. Thoughts rushing all over the place like bloody headless chickens. "Are you telling me that my wife told her father word for word what was said at our meeting?"

"Well, we don't know that with any degree of certainty, but it would appear she did. Is it true? Did you say that?"

I hesitate. "It is. But it's not what it sounds like."

"And what about the part where you punched that man?"

I nod once more. "Again, though, it isn't how it seems. Besides, what's the relevance?"

"Well, there's a lot of subtext here. It reads very much like you're prone to violent outbursts—"

"Violent outbursts? Jesus Christ," I run my hands through my hair and pace the room.

"The prosecution may well be able to build a case on the allegation that your violent outbursts are the reasons why your wife followed you to that place. Like she didn't have a choice, that she was afraid of you."

I force an incredulous laugh. "Of me? She was afraid of me? That's fucking rubbish! If anything, the facts show that it should have been me afraid of her! These claims are baseless. You know that." I instinctively move closer to the desk and add, "You know that. You know me," I say, somewhat imploringly.

"Do I?" she quips enigmatically.

I stare at her for a few seconds then the words finally leave my lips. "What's that supposed to mean?"

"It doesn't matter," she says dismissively, looking back down at that file which she's obviously using as a fucking barrier, and I just want to reach over and rip that bloody thing to shreds.

"No. I want to hear it, Amanda. Please. What do you mean by that?"

She rocks her head and then meets my gaze with an impassive lawyerly one. "There are many things I thought I knew about you, Marc, but none of them turned out, did they?"

Seconds tick by as a swarm of thoughts rush at me, each buzzing for the same attention.

Eventually, I croak, "Is that what this is about?"

"Forget it," she says, "it doesn't matter. It's history."

"I was married, for Christ's sake, Amanda. I had a son."

She forces a laugh. "Funny it took you the best part of a year to work that out before you ditched me," she says with a bitter smile. And it's the first time that she's allowed her professional mask to slip. And I recognise her now. I recognise her as the woman that I had an affair with. The woman I thought I loved. The one for which I risked losing everything in the world that mattered to me.

And just like that, I feel wretched. Sick to my stomach. All of the rage, the tension, repressed emotions punched out of me like a deflated balloon.

I collapse onto a divan by the window. How the fuck did I allow myself to get into this situation? Isn't the shit pit I'm already drowning in bad enough? Did I fancy more of a challenge by allowing myself to be dragged down memory lane too?

A minute or so must tick by, filled in by the grumble of traffic outside, the industrious mind-jangling drill of a ubiquitous city jackhammer, and chatter in the corridor beyond the door.

She joins me by the window and takes a seat in the chair opposite.

"I um," I say eventually, "this obviously isn't going to work."

"Marco. I'm sorry," she says, the lawyer, my former lover, the person I had been having nightmares about, "that was inappropriate. Unprofessional. I really don't know where it came from."

"It's okay. You're right."

"No. I should never have raised that here of all places."

"It's okay, Amanda," I say, standing up and looking at her with a smile. "But I think it's best we wait for, um, Mr. Wilson to return to carry on."

The lawyer stands and speaks quickly, "Oh, of course. I mean, we can, but I really think you would benefit from–"

I step closer to her. And I don't know if it's what just transpired or the fact that my eyes have just been opened to who exactly I'm standing in front of, but I can see now that she looks tired behind the makeup. Behind the power dressing and the demeanour, I can see the person I once thought I would leave my wife for.

"I think it's best I speak to Mr. Wilson when he gets back," I say decisively.

I watch her eyes dart back and forth like she's eager to say something else but instead, her shoulders relax, and she nods. "Of course. I understand. Mr. Wilson is an excellent lawyer," she adds with a faint smile, "he'll do an excellent job."

I nod and force my own smile. "Well, thanks anyway. It was good seeing you."

She nods. "You too."

With that, I leave the room without looking back.

6

CARRINGTON'S

I could not get out of that place fast enough. The underground was just metres away, but given the emotional state I was in, the last thing I needed was more angst.

So, I grabbed a cab and asked him to take me to the station, but when I got there, I realised that I was in the wrong place and had to have him turn around and take me across the city instead.

Now, I'm handing over my credit card while trying not to react to the figure the driver just read out to me.

Shit. My heart is still thumping, and the worst part is that I have no idea if that's a reaction to this lawsuit that is most likely going to destroy me or to the fact that Amanda—as she likes to be called now—is back in London.

So, I know what you're thinking. How the hell did I end up having a relationship with two women with the same name, marrying one and cheating on her with the other? I have no idea. Sounds like me, though. I was probably attracted to the name as people are attracted to accents.

If I'm perfectly honest, when this stunner of a lawyer was in my life, I wasn't thinking too straight about much, but one thing. So, she could have been called Minnie Mouse for the difference it would have made.

Oh, I sound like a complete prick! It wasn't like that. Just… back then, I wasn't like I am now. I didn't feel things as deeply. Back then, things were easier. Or at least they seemed that way. Not as heavy as they feel now.

But it was *heavy*. I almost left my family for her.

Toby.

Oh, God. I feel sick. I'm going to puke. I'm going to puke right here on Saville Row's swanky pavement, which you may know is a street in Mayfair, central London. It's best known for its traditional bespoke tailoring for men. What you may not know is that it was once also the headquarters for the Royal Geographical Society from which many historical expeditions have been launched.

See what I'm doing? I pluck out this crap and focus on it so I don't have to focus on the things troubling me. Not least the fact that I've just spent a fortune travelling all the way over here to throw up on the pavement of this notorious street.

I'm just negotiating it now. The turning stomach, the tightness in my skull, the sweat on my brow, the thickening of my throat, the rising bile and….

"Ellie?"

It's her! My wife! I'm sure it is. On the other side of the road, watching. Judging me.

Marco. Get a grip. You know that isn't possible.

No. It's her. She was standing behind those people at the bus stop. Black coat. Blonde hair.

My legs buckle, but I catch a nearby lamp post and hold on.

Her coat collar is pulled up, and someone is blocking a partial view of her, but I'd recognise that face anywhere.

"Ellie?"

She's staring right at me as if she knows exactly who I've just met with!

Oh, God.

I wait for a gap in the traffic and am just about to launch myself into the street when–

"Dude. What are you doing?" The hand on my shoulder startles me, and I realise that I must look like I have some kind of mental deficiency, holding onto a lamppost gawking at the opposite side of the road.

"Marco, mate. Are you alright?"

It's my best friend, David.

I look at him but am momentarily unable to speak. Eyes wide. Face awash with sweat.

"Marco?"

I glance across the street. Wait for a van to trundle by.

She's gone. The person who was blocking her is still there, but Ellie, my dead wife, is gone.

My *dead* wife!

I take a deep breath and then a few more. Oh, no, what is happening to me?

What's happening is that this is exactly the reason why you should be taking your pills. It's stress-induced psychosis because of Amanda and all that shit you've just stirred up.

"MARCO!" David yells, startling me. I look at him. "What's going on?" he demands.

I shake my head. "N… nothing. Nothing. I'm good."

"Are you sure? You're looking a bit green around the old gills, mate?"

"Yeah. I'm good. I'm fine."

"Okay. Alright then, well, let's get ya inside, eh? We've been waitin' ages."

"I know. I'm sorry. I'll explain when we get inside."

Inside is through an immaculately painted green door of a handsome brick building.

I've barely walked in when a smartly dressed man with preened silver hair and scrubbed complexion intercepts me.

I'm just fumbling for the words when a voice behind me says, "He's with us, mate." Then to me, he adds, "so, what happened? Did the meetin' overrun?"

"Kind of. I went to the station," I say between breaths because I'm still recovering from almost puking outside.

"The station? I thought you had a meeting with the lawyers this morning?"

"I did. But then I was so bloody flustered when I left that I just got into a cab to the station. It was only as I was getting out of the thing that I realised I needed to be here."

"Hey, Marco," it's Aaron walking up to us, "you okay?" he adds, scrutinizing my face.

"Bloody hell… do I look that bad?"

"Um, well, you do look kinda pale, yeah."

"And sweaty," David adds.

"Thanks, mate." I nod.

"And awkward in that suit—"

"Yeah, alright. I get the point."

David gestures to the silver-haired man who's still hovering nearby. "Can we get some champagne over here, mate, and some water, please, and do you have some snacks? I think my friend here could do with something to eat."

I look at him and then around the place as if I'm only just realising where I am. A cosy little room kitted out with plush seating and racks of suits in an array of conservative colours. And yet, my friend just ordered beverages and snacks like we're at a bloody wine bar.

But then this isn't your average department store, and these aren't your average off-the-peg garments.

Carrington's of London is one of the city's finest dressmakers. They've been tailoring menswear for celebrities and the occasional royal since 1849. I know that last bit because it's emblazoned on the blue plaque with silver lettering hammered on the wall outside.

"Was the meeting that bad then?" David asks.

"No. It was worse," I say, looking at both men. "Ellie was there." When I see their blank faces, I correct myself, "I mean Amanda," I say, shaking my head.

Aaron pulls a face. "Amanda?"

"The woman I cheated on Ellie with," I say in a frustrated hushed tone.

"Fuck me! Amanda?" David says loudly as the silver-haired *maître d'hôtel*—because that's what he looks like—returns with a tray of drinks. If he heard David, he didn't show it. Nonetheless, I feel better when my friend leans in and lowers his voice before adding, "You mean the bird that you were–"

"Yes, her," I jump in, not wanting to relive the detail out loud.

"You've lost me," Aaron says, leaning in also to the point where we must look like a trio of housewives gossiping over a garden fence. Of course, I could make a stereotypical quip here about the gays, but I won't because, well, I've seemingly become a reluctant gossiper.

David explains to Aaron, "Amanda is some bird he was shagging for the best part of a year while he was married–"

"Sir?"

The silver-haired bloke is back, and I close my eyes and cringe because he definitely heard that.

"Would you like me to go ahead and pour?"

"Yeah, cheers, mate," David says, unwilling to unglue his eyes from me for fear that he might miss something.

"And are you ready to get started with–" the man continues.

"Yeah, mate. Yeah," David says, waving distractedly at the man.

Instantly, like posh ninjas, a trio of suited men seemingly appear out of nowhere armed with measuring tapes and hover beside us.

"I had no idea you cheated for that long with one person," Aaron says way too excitedly.

I turn slowly to look at the trio of shop assistants and then at my best friend's fiancé. Yeah. I love my private business shared with complete strangers. Thanks.

"Sir?"

It's Silverhead, and he's offering me a flute of champagne which I force myself not to inhale.

"I, um, thought you'd stopped drinking?" David remarks with a frown.

"I had," I say, trying not to burp with the spectators nearby. "But you ordered it."

"Well, just for us, really. You're supposed to be drinking the water," he says slowly.

I can't tell if he's joking or not. Either way, I shoot him a glare.

The boys have barely sipped their drinks. I'm just starting my second glass as the trio takes a step forward and starts shadowing us like bloody footballers on a pitch—if footballers got close enough to breathe over you while gently turning you to face full-length mirrors.

Oh shit. I look worse than I thought.

Then, they proceed to extend measuring tapes in perfect synchronisation. Over and under our right arm. Then the left.

David, who is now at least six feet away and separated by Aaron, proceeds, "So, what's that bird doin' at your lawyers anyway?"

I hesitate since a, I'm presently being garrotted by measuring tape, and b, I have no interest in resuming this conversation now with this lot listening to our every word.

And yet... "Marc, what was she doing there?" David asks, a tone louder.

I look at the man in front of me who must be in his early sixties, perfectly turned out in some kind of morning suit with two tar brush slashes for eyebrows and a propensity to breathe heavily but skilfully and mercifully not over me.

"She, um, she works there," I say discreetly as if the person right up in my grill can't hear my every word.

"But I thought she went back up north."

"So, did I until I saw her standing there. Apparently, she's been promoted and decided to come back to London."

"What for?"

"Oh shit. I forgot to ask her that while busy worrying about the bloody lawsuit that could ruin me and the fact that I was broadsided by her being there at all," I retort sarcastically and then turn to force a smile at the bloke who is way too intimate for my liking.

"Yeah, alright, don't have to get arsy," David says, then adds quickly, looking down between his legs, "Easy down there, mate, most people buy me dinner first. Besides, my fiancé is standing right here."

The man crouching down and measuring David's inseam has a bald head that quite visibly turns scarlet in the overhead lights.

"So, this chick," Aaron chimes in, "that you were fu... um, having an affair with just shows up out of nowhere at the law firm that just happens to be handling your case?" Aaron asks mysteriously as if I hadn't already contemplated that.

I turn to him and nod with a grimace because these two insist on discussing my business in front of a bunch of strangers, and, um, it's my turn to have my inseam measured.

Aaron whistles. "Dude, you don't do simple, do ya," he says with an incredulous widening of the eyes while casually assuming a starfish pose for the bloke between his legs.

"So, is she going to be handling your case?" David asks.

"God, no. I've asked for the original lawyer to be assigned."

"Why's that?"

Both Aaron and I turn to look at him.

"Alright, alright, keep your 'air on. I was just checkin'."

"How did she take it?" Aaron asks.

I think about this. "Good, I suppose."

"Oh shit, dude. I hope for your sake that's true because the last thing you need right now is for that bitch to go all *Glenn Close* on ya."

I've no bloody idea how my best mate has this knack for not only stating the bloody obvious but also reinforcing my insecurities.

"Glenn Close?" Aaron asks.

"You know. Fatal Attraction. Bunny boiler!"

"Oh right, yeah."

Several minutes go by before the invasion of our personal space is over. And amen to that. Can't say I enjoyed it much.

Now, we're looking through racks of hanging suits for fabrics to get an idea of preference. Well, the happy couple is. I'm just standing here finishing my second glass of champagne and already wishing I had something to eat when I find myself lifting the tag attached to a navy-blue suit jacket that I quite like.

"Fuck me! Three and half thousand for a suit!" The last part of that sentence is subdued when I notice that the first part drew the attention of nearly all eyes in the store. "Three and a half thousand?" I repeat in a loud whisper.

David smiles in that condescending way he does. "He's adorable, ain't he?" he says.

"What?"

Aaron responds with a smile, "Not for the suit, buddy. That's the price of the jacket."

The blood must drain from my face or something because

David feels compelled to put an arm around my shoulder. "Don't worry, mate," he says, squeezing me and then planting a slobbery kiss which he knows I hate, "it's my treat! Now, tell us everything about this bloody trial. Will you at least be able to come to the wedding before gettin carted off to prison?"

"Not helping," I say.

"Oh, come on, mate. We're gettin' married!"

"Finally!" Aaron contributes.

And I think about this. "You're right. You are. Let's stop talking about my shit, and let's talk about something else. Like, why the hell are we being refitted for suits again when the wedding is just weeks away?"

"Because I wasn't feeling the other ones we tried on."

"What, wrong shade of blue?" I say sarcastically.

"They were black, actually," my friend retorts. "These are blue."

"OK. I still don't get why you just don't ask people to dress up. You're getting married on Halloween! It's the perfect opportunity."

"Not by choice. That was the only day the Royal Crescent had available this year," David says.

"Then why not go somewhere else?" I say with a shrug.

Both men gasp, deliberately and dramatically, but it's David who elaborates in his unique way, "Because it's the Royal Crescent, you doughnut! That place books years in advance. Celebrities get married there."

"Fair enough. So why not ask people to wear a costume?"

"Because it's our wedding, and I don't fancy pictures of *Buzz Lightyear* walking 'im down the aisle. You know what Americans are like. Halloween's just an excuse to put on a stupid costume."

"Yeah. And my mom, she's already threatened to squeeze herself into a *Wonder Woman* costume. When you meet her, you'll see why that's an image nobody wants on their wedding day," Aaron says with a shudder.

David laughs. "I'm going to tell her you said that."

"I wouldn't worry about it. She knows already."

"You two are bloody awful," I say with mock seriousness.

"No, your idea was awful!" David laughs, but several seconds later, he looks at his fiancé and adds soberly, "I just can't believe that this is finally happening. Can you?"

Aaron shakes his head. "Nah, after all of the talkin' and postponing and...stuff. It's hard to believe that in just four weeks, I'm gonna have to start being monogamous."

"Oi, you!"

The boys should have been married a year ago, but for some reason, neither felt that it was right to go ahead with the wedding just months after what happened at Porthcove. I tried to convince them that they should. That we could all use a happy occasion after everything, but they just weren't feeling it. This is why David keeps fussing and continuously changing everything. The venue, the season, and now even the suits.

I may be wrong, but I have a sneaky suspicion it might be because they're both feeling a little superstitious after what happened. As if my bad luck might have in some way rubbed off on them. Neither has said anything; this is just me being my usual paranoid self.

I'm very happy for them both, and I, for one, am really looking forward to it.

7

THE RELICS

FAWNDALE· 18:36·

It's almost dusk by the time the taxi is driving me through the trees and into the multicoloured world that is gradually being reduced to the monochromatic outlines of an old photograph.

Brockenhurst train station is located roughly in the centre of the New Forest. It's a couple of hours train ride straight into Waterloo Station in London and about a ten-minute ride to our tiny hamlet of Fawndale. And when I say tiny, I mean it. I used to think Porthcove was small, but it's a metropolis compared to this place that consists of just a few cottages and a village-store-cum-post-office.

I'm disappointed to find the driveway empty. Sarah messaged me to say that she would leave Porthcove a bit earlier, but she still isn't home, so I make a mental note to check in with her once I've changed out of this ridiculous suit and let Buddy out.

I had lunch with the boys after our stint at Carrington's. Thank God because I very quickly discovered that abstaining from alcohol for long periods also turns you into a bit of a lightweight the moment you choose to resume, which meant that, on an empty stomach, those glasses of champagne were already making me a little tipsy and very mouthy. I don't even want to imagine what might happen if I started drinking again as I used to.

Yeah. I know. Pathetic.

During lunch we talked suits, of course, and about this swanky new venue for the wedding reception and all the supposed celebrities that frequent it. It meant nothing to me, but the fact that they had managed to find an available slot seemed to excite them both, so I made a conscious effort to share their enthusiasm.

I'm really looking forward to the wedding. I know Sarah is too. It's been a long time coming, and God knows we could use the festivity.

Of course, the mind being the sadistic shit that it is, the more we celebrated the imminent union between those two, the more I was reminded of how my seemingly idyllic life has taken a dramatic turn for the shitty in the space of a few days.

But I was determined that I wasn't going to let that spoil the moment for the lads, so I ploughed in to actively participate in the finer details of the planning since I am the best man after all.

Oh, if you're wondering... of course, I had it all down and memorised. I take my best manly duties very seriously. But then they decided to change everything, which in hindsight, was a good thing because it distracted me from the mind-trip of bumping into Amanda. Scratch that. I didn't exactly bump into her. It felt more like she was waiting for me. Lying in ambush like a trapdoor spider.

But I'm okay now. That's behind me. I'm back, away from the anxiety and the cacophony of the city that rubs against my misophonia like fingernails on a chalkboard.

But this place...it's like a different world. Here, the only sound is coming from the avian stragglers who have their usual natter before bedtime. Otherwise, it's quiet enough for me to hear that low whistling sound of the blood rushing behind my ears. Everything is still. The countryside equivalent of a library, melting away the tension from my shoulders with the rays of the setting sun. I love my sanctuary here. I don't want to lose it. *I'm not going to lose it.*

The moment I leave the car, the floodlights prematurely fill in the shadows already stalking the building, and a runway of small

LED lights illuminate the pathway to the front door.

I think of Ellie, of course, and how she used to complain that Dolce Vita didn't have any external lights—that worked! —and how she would often have to *feel her way* to the front door.

Plenty of light here. Not that it's needed just yet. I reckon I have just about enough time to let Buddy out to do his business before the land is smothered in darkness.

At the front door, I can already hear him barking, and I interpret that as either a greeting or a complaint. *Where the eff have you been? I've had my furry legs crossed for the best part of an hour!*

The thought of seeing him brings a smile to my face.

I frisk myself for keys before realising for the hundredth time that I don't need them and push on the door. Sure enough, it rotates open.

Welcome home, Marco. Hope you've had a nice day, the disembodied voice says as the corridor lights spring to life and the giant golden wonder launches himself at me in a flurry of kisses.

Instantly, I'm feeling better. "Oh, I've missed you. Yes, I have. I have."

I consider changing, but this boy probably needs to go desperately, "Pee-pee? Do you need pee-pee?"

I have my answer when he bounds out of the house only to stop suddenly and turn to me. *Are you coming, or what?*

So, I pull the door shut, and we make our way around the side of the building as a breeze picks up out of nowhere, bringing with it the musky dankness of night.

We've been here the best part of a month now, and I still can't get used to the sight of that lake quite literally in my back garden. Feels like I've stumbled on this mystical place in the middle of the national park and that I need to go home sometime soon. But the beautiful thing is, I am home. That reflection of the luscious green trees and fiery red sky in that stillness of the water is mine. As is that building on the opposite side of the lake that, despite all its challenges, remains nonetheless the key to our future.

Life here in the middle of the woods isn't anything like how I imagined it. For a start, there's no incessant chorus of crickets chirping in the background. There are a few, yeah, but nothing like the obligatory trill you hear in Hollywood movies. And as for life by the lake, there's the occasional ripple, boing, and pop of fish coming up for air. And now, even the occasional frog performing its nocturnal serenade for a potential mate, but it's not overworked or intrusive, but delicate and in a strange kind of way more impactful on my senses.

Yeah. See? That's what being immersed in nature will do to you. You get all philosophical. I won't stretch to poetic because anybody who knows me knows I am anything but.

The only thing here that I'm struggling a little bit with is the fact that the back lawn is immediately flanked by trees. This means that any forest animal can easily wander back and forth and up to the house without a care.

You could argue that such is the whole point of living among the trees. And I like it; I do, especially if it means getting to watch the wildlife from the comfort of our balcony. But, at the same time, I don't know. There's something about this freedom of access that gives me the odd pang of vulnerability, especially in moments like these where twilight is still squeezing orange rays from the fruit of the sun and irradiating the land but for that blockade of trees. The light stops there as if it's too afraid to venture over that threshold, creating an inky black demarcation line beyond which all kinds of evil may flourish and watch as we go about our daily lives. Just waiting for the ideal time to strike and....

Okay. We'll have enough of that, thanks very much.

Maybe I'd make a good writer after all. What do you think?

Oh, you don't know about that, do you? I've been so wrapped up in everything else that it hadn't even crossed my mind until now.

I think it was the day after that fateful Christmas Eve. Some of us hadn't even left the hospital, and already the reporters were showing up, demanding to speak to me. Bribes were apparently offered to anyone who could get them access to *the survivors*, which, which we became known as, like—like a bloody rock band.

To be fair, the hospital staff did a pretty good job at keeping the vultures at bay, but once we left, it became a bloody feeding frenzy which was no doubt fuelled by that bloody ill-timed newspaper article. The *House of Horrors* headline had them all clamouring for juicier details, especially from me.

I've never experienced anything like it. I mean, I've read about it, of course, seen it in films but to experience it, it's something else. There were times when we had reporters quite literally camped outside the B&B. They accosted us at work, at school, in restaurants, and on the street. One bloke followed me into the fucking toilets and started quizzing me at the urinal, and I'm standing there with my dick in my bloody hand!

Agents called me, offering their services. It was insane!

One of them, a cheeky cockney geezer who loved the sound of his own voice, did give me a tip, though. He said that part of the *hard-on* that the press had for me was that the story was not only current but that it had *mass appeal*. All the *best ingredients. Mental illness, spooky stuff, and death of your missus, no less!* And that they were all jostling for the exclusive. He told me that the moment I secured my first interview, it would let the steam out of the story, and things would get easier. He added that if I signed with him, he'd easily be able to secure me a six-figure deal. Which I have to say, in the interest of full disclosure, did give me a few seconds pause, but then I surprised myself by telling him to Foxtrot Oscar and disconnected the call.

I was already struggling with guilt as it was. There was no way I could have agreed to that and be able to live with myself no matter how financially dire things were at the time.

But I did take his advice, though. I returned a call to one of those national daytime talk shows. I've no idea which now because they all seem the same to me. But you know the kind, sitting on a couch with two normally over-enthusiastic presenters acting over sympathetically to my tale of woe. They even made those pained faces at intervals. The lot.

Can't say I enjoyed spilling my guts on national TV, but it did work, though. The vans left, the calls calmed, and people didn't pose as bloody waitresses just to get my bloody story.

I did a few more shows after that, often with some of the other survivors, and then that was it. We became yesterday's news.

If I'm perfectly honest, it did have a positive impact on my fledgling new career. On the shows and in print, I became known as

Psychologist Marco Battista. In the gutter press, I was known as *the nutter turned psychologist.* Either way, people wanted to be treated by me because, as one of my assessors kept telling me, *I have a uniquely empathetic set of skills.* I was the bloke who had been through it and so was able to understand their brand of pain better.

And so, I started booking my own appointments while I was still undergoing supervision which, as it turns out, expedited my becoming fully certified.

Battista Properties was also taking off. Things were looking good. That's when I received a call from a publisher who wanted me to write about my experience. I thought it was a joke at first, but he gave me his name, told me to ring the company switchboard and ask for him. I did. And he offered me a generous advance in exchange for a *no holds barred* account of everything that happened at Porthcove.

Can you believe it? Me? Marco Battista. A bloody writer?

Well, you can imagine my reaction. I just laughed. I laughed and laughed until I started crying, and then I hung up on him.

I now realise that I was quite literally hysterical, overwhelmed with grief and remorse at the mere suggestion of profiting from what happened there.

Doctor Ethan Holmes, on the other hand, held no such qualms. He said it would be cathartic. He would. I tell you, I'm sure that man gets off watching me wallow in the abject misery of my history.

Sarah thinks I'm perfectly capable of writing a book if I put my mind to it. David laughed at first, then shrugged and asked, why not? *There are plenty of people, especially celebs writing crap. Why not you?* Yes. Thanks, mate, I'm not sure that's much of an endorse–

"Buddy. Shush!" The dog is barking again now. He's finished fertilising the far side of the garden and is now yapping at the demarcation line of the woods.

"Buddy! Stop! Oi! Buddy!"

But he's not listening. So, I follow his line of sight to the periphery of darkness. It's obviously an animal or something. Hardly surprising since this is woodland, after all. This is their territory. We're just lodgers here.

I scrutinize the blackness to establish what exactly has got

Buddy's furry pantaloons in such a twist but can't see anything until a flicker catches my eye, and I turn towards the house.

Ugh. Bats. Skittering out from beyond the roof of the building to fly sorties over the lake where a creepy mist is rolling in like something out of a bloody *John Carpenter* movie.

Creepy. Mist. Bats. Darkness. Why does every bloody thing have to become spooky with me? I've watched way too many horror flicks in my lifetime. Did I mention that–

Oh, Sarah must be back. The light just went on in the lounge, although… I can't see anybody in there. Weird.

Meanwhile, Buddy is still barking at…nothing.

"Come on, you, let's go. Sarah's back, and I need a comfort break of my own. Come on! Let's go!"

But the hound isn't listening. Instead, he's moved closer to the edge of the trees and is bolstering his barking with the occasional growl.

The dog's deep baritone rumble is unsettling, and it's hard to believe that this giant bundle of joy is the grownup version of that tiny little thing I wrapped in my top that morning.

"Buddy! Come on. Let's go!" I say, walking up to him. And I'm just about to speak again when a loud snapping of a twig slices through the air. It is closely followed by the hissing, clicking, and scuffle of leaves.

Something is moving around in there.

Okay. That's it.

"Buddy, let's go," I say, touching the dog's back but instantly snatch my hand away when he flicks his head around to growl at me. "Hey, you. It's me! What's wrong with you?"

The growling stops instantly. That was new. And a bit unnerving. He's never done that before. Nearly bloody peed myself! "Come on, there's nothing there," I say, but I don't know if I'm convincing the dog or myself. "Let's go! Now!" I order, eyes reluctantly scanning the blackness but seeing nothing.

The mist is drifting closer now. It's less than twenty metres away. It's devoured the lake, the jetty, the barbeque station and is now creeping up the lawn towards us.

I've no idea why but there's something about its relentless

motion that unsettles me. That and, well, I must be imagining it, but it seems to have a greenish hue. I've never seen anything like it, and, for a few seconds, I'm entranced.

It's truly freaky, but there's bound to be a scientific explanation for it, like the dying light distilled through all the greenery or some shit. Either way, I don't like the idea of us being smothered by it.

The demarcation line between lawn and woodland has taken on a sinister appearance now. The inky blackness is thick and impenetrable.

A chill scuttles down my spine as one of those unhelpful thoughts presents itself to me. Anything could be hiding in there; an animal, an alien, a stranger skulking in the shadows, observing, scrutinizing us, and plotting creative ways to…

"Okay, Buddy! Let's go!" I shout, cheerily even if that isn't how I'm feeling.

Finally, the dog complies.

I hurry us around the house and back to the front just as the misty gloom swallows up the back lawn.

The driveway is empty. Sarah isn't home. Not unless she walked.

Shit. Maybe her car broke down. I pull my phone out of my pocket. No messages. No missed calls.

I hurry to the front door but pause when I realise that Buddy isn't following again. Instead, he's stopped and is sitting on the lawn, staring at the archway that leads into the woods, one and a half ears up and erect as if he's listening to something that I can't hear.

"Buddy?"

No response. Not a glance in my direction nor a wag of the tail. Again, totally out of character for him, and shit, that's starting to worry me.

"Buddy. Come on, boy. Hey Buddy! Come on! Buddy!" My voice bounces off the house and back at me, but the hound isn't budging again. So, I move to walk back and grab him by the scruff of the neck but jerk back when a blood-curdling scream rushes out of the trees to punch me in the face. "SHIT!"

The world stops but for my thudding heart. And I mean stops. No nocturnal creatures. No crickets. Nothing, just the memory of that sound resonating in my ears.

What the hell was that? It sounded like someone, a woman, maybe? Screaming? I'm not sure. It sounded different. An animal? I've never heard any animal make that sound. A fox? No. I'd recognise that cry anywhere. No. it sounded like a woman screaming, only not as high pitched but deeper.

My heart's still knocking. Eager to get back into the safety of the house because visibility out here has worsened. I can barely see a few metres in front of me, and I won't lie, that's starting to creep me out a little.

Then Buddy starts growling again, and I'm done. "Buddy! Oi! Buddy! Get here right now!" I yell angrily.

This time, the dog snaps out of his trance almost instantly and turns to look back at me. *But there's something out there...* "NOW!" I reiterate, pointing to my leg so that he understands I want him to heel.

Just like a sulky child, he complies. "Let's get inside right now," I say through gritted teeth. And with frequent glances back at the blackness, we make our way indoors.

Welcome back, Marco.

My instinct is to lock the door behind me, but I remember that I don't have to. Holt auto-locks the front door, and only designated residents can open it from the outside. Right now, that's just Sarah and me. And amen to that.

Now that darkness has fallen, Holt has entered night mode. LED lights are dotted throughout the building, which means no room is ever in complete blackout, which is perfectly fine with me.

In Porthcove, I had to invest in night lights. It's not because I am afraid of the dark per se. It's more that I am afraid of what thoughts the dark may conjure. Which probably doesn't make any sense, but it does to me. So, of course, when I found out that Holt featured low-level lighting as standard, well, I was a little excited.

Right now, the wall lights spring to life, illuminating the entrance hallway in an amber glow.

I hurry down it, Buddy at my heel. "Sarah? Are you home?" I call out, but the subtle echo of my voice in the hollowness of the corridor is the only thing to reply.

"Holt?"

Yes, Marco.

"Page all zones," there's a beeping sound. I pinch my nose and put on my best plummy supermarket announcer voice. "Sarah Collins, please report to the main entrance hall. Sarah Collins, please report to the main hall. Thank you."

My voice rings out from the various rooms as we make our way to the lounge.

In the doorway, lights obediently spring to life in my presence. It's empty.

So I listen. Nothing. Not an owl hoot beyond the glass, nor the creak of timber, and certainly no footsteps alerting me to the fact that there's someone else in the house.

Just silence.

And it's times like these when I miss that perpetual rumble of the ocean in the distance, but then I'm reminded of the racket it made that last night and, well… enough of that.

Here, the emptiness of night is filled with just occasional sounds. Owls, foxes, the odd insomniac of a bird, and other weird noises that I'm yet to identify. Like that bloody thing out there!

Oh, God.

"Holt?"

Yes, Marco.

"Turn the lights on, everywhere."

Of course.

I know. And I'm sorry, planet, but this is an emergency. I promise it's just until I get used to the place.

I pull my phone out of my pocket and consider dialling Sarah. I'm starting to feel just a tad anxious now. There's been no sign of her, and according to my phone, no message. But I don't want to dial her because she hasn't quite worked out how to sync her phone to the car, and if she answers, she may be driving and–

"Fuck!"

The lights in the lounge flicker and die, erasing my reflection in the glass wall and offering a faint yet visible view of the fog outside. It's pressing on the glass now as if it were a sentient being eager to find a way into us.

Ebbing. Flowing. Searching.

"Holt! Turn the lights on in the lounge."

As you wish.

But nothing happens.

"Holt?"

Yes, Marco.

"Lights on. Lounge. Now!"

Of course.

Still nothing. So, I move over to the nearest wall panel. Access the lights menu and tap *lounge*. The lights spring back to life. The view outside disappears and is replaced by my reflection in the doorway, which startles me for a moment.

"Bloody hell!"

What's going on? I've been here over a month and have never felt like this, not even when we first moved in. I mean, I kind of expected to, but I just didn't get that vibe from this place. It feels so sound, robust, and secure.

And yet tonight... Well, even Holt's losing his bloody marbles, and that's all I need. "Don't you start," I grumble under my breath as I make my way down the corridor towards the toilet because I'm at serious risk of peeing myself. "Already have a creepy dog and don't need a creepy AI too–"

Front door open. Welcome guest.

The words drag a curtain of shivers down my spine. That is not supposed to happen. I programmed it that way.

Things get worse when I slowly turn on the spot just in time to see Buddy pad over to the hallway junction, sit on his hind legs, and stare towards the front door. Ears up and scanning at one and half-mast. Although he doesn't seem to be reacting to any–

That guttural growl of his sends a rising and electric current of panic through me, jumpstarting my heart into a frenetic thump that worsens the moment I feel a cold breeze on my face.

The front door is definitely open. Someone is in the house.

The fog drifts languidly in and out of the overspill of the night lights. It's just mist, and yet, despite the breeze, it moves like it's self-aware, surveying, exploring, searching, and tasting this new frontier like a snake would a new habitat.

I glance at Buddy. He's just staring at the thing like he's never seen fog before, but we both know he has. At Dolce Vita, we saw something just like this, and it turned out that it wasn't the fog he had a problem with but what was inside it.

Oh, God.

I can feel that spider leg tickle of sweat on my scalp again, and I hate it! I hate it because it's the trigger for every hideous, unexplained event in my miserable–

What's that? *There!* There's something in the mist. A shadow! I can barely make it out, but it's there, backlit by the floodlights in the garden. Something or someone is standing at the bloody front door, staring at me!

Good evening, beautiful. Hope you had a lovely day.

Holt's voice booming through the house may as well have been a bloody hand on my shoulder because it makes me quite literally yelp.

"Marc? What's this in aid of then?" Sarah's cheery voice asks as Buddy barks happily before trotting over to greet her. "Hold on, Buddy!" she says quickly, "hold on!" She's carrying a box, and it wouldn't be unlike the dog to knock it out of her hands.

"Holt, can you close the front door for me?" she says to the walls.

Of course, Beautiful.

"Marc, have you been fiddling with Holt's settings again?" she says with a laugh as she sets the box down on the dining table and then turns to make a fuss of the dog.

She continues for several seconds before looking up to find me gawking at the front door, which is now closed.

"Hey, you know there are hugs over here for one more handsome boy, you know?" she smiles.

I finally unstick myself from where I'm standing and walk over to her.

"Are you okay?" she asks with a frown.

"Yeah. Why?"

She shrugs. "I don't know. You just look, um, weird. Like you don't recognise me or something."

I laugh, "Oh, I recognise you," I say, pulling her into a tight hug.

"Hmm. This feels good. Traffic was horrible. There was an accident on the way back. Constant stopping and starting, which, of course, was a breeze in that car."

Breaking the embrace and looking at her, I ask, "I did wonder. You said you were going to leave early."

"I know. Sorry. I did. Just that accident, and then every time I thought about texting, we'd start moving again. Still haven't worked out how to properly pair my phone for messages. Anyway, I'm glad to be back here in the lap of luxury," she says, rubbing my arms. "Especially with a reception like that. Did you see the car coming or something?"

I go with it and nod, "Yeah."

"Oh, you're so sweet," she says, pecking me on the mouth. Then she turns to the dog, puts on that affected voice, and starts rubbing his face, *"And so are you, yes. And so are you!"* The dog laps up the attention with his usual dopiness like he didn't just scare the shit out of me.

"What's in the box?" I say, stepping over to the table, but my girlfriend jumps to her feet and intercepts me.

"Uh-uh, all in good time," she says, standing in front of the table and making sure the flaps on the box are folded down. "All in good time. But first I need the loo, then you're going to make us one of your signature cappuccinos and tell me exactly how it went with the lawyer today."

"That was today?"

She rolls her eyes and moves to leave the room, but before she does, she turns and adds, "No peeking in that box."

"Alright," I say, holding up my hands, "no peeking."

Half an hour, two cappuccinos, and a comfort break later, I had shared everything about my day.

Oh, alright... maybe not everything entirely. I skipped that whole bit on the back lawn and, of course, the weird shit at the front door while making a note to check Holt's configuration.

It's weird. Kal said that the sensors built into the house react to biometric, motion, and heat sensors. And yet, Holt opened the door for a bit of fog and then spoke to it like it was a bloody person. That can't be right! Although, by that same token, I'd need to check the hound's programming, too, because he also reacted to it.

That's the first time that's happened. I hate the idea of having to call tech support. Yes, there's tech support for the house. Well, for Holt at least, and I don't know if I can take it offline.

"Hey, mister!"

Sarah's face comes into focus.

"Where were you?"

"I'm here. Right here."

"It didn't seem like it. What's up beside you being sued by some nasty, vengeful toad?" Sarah replies, rubbing my arm affectionately.

"I'm okay. Sorry. It is all just a bit. You know, overwhelming. And I think Holt's is on the blitz too."

"Why?"

"Oh, nothing serious. Just, I think he's going deaf in his old age."

"Technology, eh? Can't live with it, and you can't live without it," she says with a wink.

"So, anyway. Are you going to show me what's in that mysterious box of yours, or what?" I ask.

She thinks about this.

"Okay. Should I be worried?" I ask, trying to read her face because it has suddenly lost its shine.

She sighs and nods. "After you."

"Okay… that doesn't sound ominous at all."

The lights fade up as we enter the dining room like actors onto a stage, and the lonely box on top of the long, empty table has now taken on a life of its own because we've talked way too much about it.

Sarah steps in front of me again, and it suddenly feels like an enactment of *Seven*. "*What's in the box, Sarah? What's in the box?!*" I ask, putting on my best Brad Pitt accent. She laughs, but I can tell it's with her mouth and not her eyes. She's nervous about something, and that, in turn, is making me nervous.

"So," she begins, "as you know, I was at Mum's today who sends her love, by the way."

"I know. You told me. We've already talked about that,

remember?" I say, squinting at her curiously.

"Yes. Right. Course. I have some stuff in here from the house."

"Your mum's house?"

"No, yours."

"Mine?"

"Dolce Vita."

I don't know why but that just made my stomach flip, so I glance around her.

"After what happened," she continues, "people, well, some of the workers sent from the council, you know, to secure the...*debris,*" she speaks this word slowly, softly since she's obviously very much aware that one man's debris is otherwise my stuff. "As you know, much of it wasn't salvageable, but some of the things the workers thought you might want to keep. And, as you know, being the main store in the village, the place is also a bit of a lost and found. The men also know Mum, so they went to her for advice. And, well, they recovered some of your things.

"Mum actually told me about them a few months back, but I suggested that we wait, you know, until you were settled in a new place somewhere."

My heart is tapping on my ribcage now. It's eager to find out what exactly has been recovered, especially after this presentation. I, on the other hand, well, I'm just staring at the innocent cardboard box like it's unexploded ordinance.

"Much of it was water damaged, luckily not saltwater," Sarah continues, turning to the box, unfolding the flaps, and retrieving something.

Then, she slowly turns to show me. Photo frames. Eight by ten inches, just like the many black frames that had been hanging in the gallery at Dolce Vita.

I thought they'd all been lost. I have this vague memory of seeing them sink to the bottom of the ocean. "Some of these were still inside the house," Sarah continues.

I catch my breath when she hands me one of the frames. It's the image of me as a little boy with that mop of curly black hair, running on the shingled shore. My mother behind me. Beautiful. The black Labrador puppy nearby.

Tears prick my eyes, and I don't even know why. I'm just suddenly feeling overwhelmed with emotion, although I don't know what kind exactly. Anger? Nostalgia? Sadness? I have no clue. I am without a doubt reacting more to the image itself than to its content which would look innocently happy to most, even to me, because I don't truly remember that day. I do remember what my mother tried to do to me since, and I think it's this that I want to react to. The thing that's been haunting me ever since my sessions with Doctor Holmes.

I want to scream!

But instead, I take a deep breath, snuffing out the flame of anger in my chest.

It's just history. It's all history. It's history.

Good or bad, this is my history, and it is all I have, which is probably the very reason Marjorie chose to preserve it for me.

I glance up from the photo frame and force a short smile. "Thank you." Which Sarah interprets as a prompt for more. So, she hands me another one of the frames. This is a photo of my mother, brown eyes, wide smile. She's holding a pair of short pasty white legs in tiny shorts while a distinguished-looking man with grey hair, bushy dark eyebrows, and a salt and pepper beard, my father, holds the other half of the little boy, whose face is contorted in a fit of laughter.

It's weird because this image stirs something in me, but I don't know if it's a genuine connection to the memory or something I'm artificially projecting on it.

My father, Roberto Battista, wasn't the prick my corrupted mind had remembered him to be. In fact, he was the best father he could be. And he died in Dolce Vita. Alone. And the thought of that for anybody, not least him, fills me with abject sadness.

I look up, and by Sarah's reaction, I can only assume that she must read something etched on my face because she pulls me into a soft embrace before kissing me on the cheek and then stepping aside, allowing me full access to the rest of the box.

"I hope it's okay," she says softly, wringing her hands together. "Mum had some of the photos restored as they had water stains."

I want to say something reassuring to her and express gratitude, but when I speak, I realise that there's a lump in my throat, so I wrestle with that instead.

Inside the box, there's another familiar framed photo. It's a moody black and white shot of a shingled shore being ravaged by an angry white surf. Behind it, out of focus, is a giant cave, then a ragged cliff face, and high above that, perched on the peninsula, is Dolce Vita as it once was, silhouetted against a tempestuous sky.

Something brushes against my leg and startles me. But then I look down and see that it's Buddy nuzzling against me.

It's because I'm cute and I say cute things.

Toby.

I can hear my son's voice in my head as I distractedly rub the dog's ears.

It's been over a year, but these photos feel as raw and real now as they did then. Then, I spot something else sellotaped to the side of the box. Something that shoves an emotional dagger into my chest so deep, I can barely breathe.

"Oh...G...od," I rasp as I am engulfed by a tidal wave of emotion that instantly drowns me.

It's a USB stick.

8

OLD FRIENDS

HOLT· EARLY MORNING·

I stop running through this expensive yet magnificent woodland that I temporarily own and rest up against a tree, sucking in the dank air while allowing my pounding heart to recover.

Buddy comes bounding back, tongue hanging, tail-wagging and sits next to me.

"I… I'm alright," I say to the hound that is cocking his head as if to say, *What's your problem now, lightweight?*

I look around me and breathe in the earthy aroma of moss, the pine-like scent of wood bark, and the musky smell of leaves.

Quiet.

Seclusion.

Tranquillity.

It's as palpable as the fresh air. All my anxieties carried away on the wind like feathers. You can't put a price on that. At least not until your in-law shows up and shits all over it.

The lake on my left winks at me through the trees as I start walking the rest of the trail, slowly picking up the pace until I'm jogging once more through pools of sunlight, over roots, around branches.

About ten minutes into the run, I can see the light at the end of the track and eventually emerge to a wide-open meadow. Beyond it is a sprawling lawn, the formal gardens and then Frost Lake Manor itself, perched on its rise overlooking the land, its dark façade and slate roof glistening like dragon scales under the early morning sun.

It's taken us a while to get here. And there were several times, of course, when I thought we never would. And yet, here we are, already a month into a three-month schedule. It's behind, of course, not to mention the fact that it was supposed to start in the summer and now we're well into autumn and, if we're not careful, this thing is going to drag well beyond deep winter. By then, the bridging loan will have matured, and... well, I'm not even going to think about that.

Let's just focus on the fact that we're here. Things are happening. We're making progress. And that's good. That's bloody good.

If you told me that I would head up quite literally a multimillion-pound operation like this a couple of years back, I would have laughed in your face.

If you asked my father, he would have... well, I don't truly know how he would have reacted because my memories are unreliable here. I had him down as the villain of my history. The womanising prick who didn't give a shit about his first family and moved quickly to secure himself another. But then, at Porthcove, they all loved him. Everybody I spoke to said he was forever talking about and heaping praise on me. Going on about how proud he was. And yet, even now, I still can't reconcile it. I don't know what I would give for him to see me now so that I might find out once and for all how he truly feels about me.

But he isn't. It's just us.

We have our own Antiques Roadshow later this week. Who knows what hidden gems are buried inside that place? With a bit of luck, we might find some long-lost Monet or something, undiscovered all these years and worth millions. The thought brings a smile to my face because that's just too good to be true, but hey, you can dream… it would certainly be a load off.

Kind of.

I don't know what's wrong with me today. Something feels off. And no matter how much I try to dismiss it, I keep coming back to the same bloody thing. Each time, I feel like an ungrateful shit. And yet, no matter how much I try to rationalise it, my feelings remain the same. I wish Sarah hadn't brought that little box of memories home yesterday.

Yes, I know, I'm awful. But I do. I just wish she'd left them there at Porthcove, where they were discovered instead of bringing them back here. This is supposed to be a fresh start for us. A new beginning, but the moment I laid eyes on those things, I was instantly transported back to everything that happened. And I mean everything. All the shitty stuff that I've spent the best part of two years trying to process, discharge, and move away from, but now, everything just feels off.

I mean, for fuck's sake, they even salvaged that Perspex box of bloody toy dinosaurs. Why the hell would you do that? I could have gone out and bought a bloody new collection if I was that way inclined. If I fancied opening a fucking vein! Oh, God… Just the sight of those things. They really threw me. I was pulled right back to memories of Toby and, most hideously, that agonizing feeling that still carves through me every time I am confronted with the reality that he's gone forever.

Last night was no exception. After plucking that container out of the box, I had a moment. Oh, alright, I had a full-blown meltdown again in front of Sarah for crying out loud. No, it's not like she hasn't seen me cry before; shehas. A couple of times since Porthcove, but I don't think she's ever seen me like that. Bereavement has its own unique brand of agonized expression that is fully dependent on the emotional specials of the day.

And, if I'm perfectly honest, because it's just you and me here, I would have much preferred it if Sarah hadn't been there to witness that. No, not because I looked weak and it diminished my masculinity in any way, but because I just feel like that pain is my own from a different time before her, and it's personal.

Something else for Doctor Holmes and I to pick apart.

Joy.

Anyway, you'll be pleased to know that I didn't express any of this to her. Instead, I played the role of the grateful boyfriend. I told her that I was overwhelmed by her mother's gesture, evidenced by the snotty snail trail I was leaving over her shoulder after she threw her arms around me.

Well, it lightened the mood.

When she asked what I planned to do with the photos, I stopped short of telling her that I wanted to burn them. Instead, I suggested that the study might be a good place, and that's where they are now. Sitting on my desk, in the box.

I pushed the Perspex container as far as I could to the back of the wall unit in the study, behind stationery and anything else I could find that would place a barrier between the past and the present. I plan to keep them for a while, and then I'll conveniently lose them in a skip one day. With my eyes closed, of course.

I know that sounds ungrateful, but let's not forget, those toys were mine and not my son's. His are still in storage, along with all the other stuff from the flat in London, which is a task I know I need to get to but can't. Especially since I'm paying good money, I don't have for that mausoleum of relics.

By that, I would just like to stress that I'm talking about the things from my life with Ellie and not those that I shared with my son. Again, I know that sounds weird because I should and often do perceive them as one and the same but, curiously, ever since that night at Dolce Vita, well, you'll appreciate that I am now automatically making the distinction in an unconscious—alright conscious—effort to separate the two. Toby is the only reason I can't bring myself round to sending the lads around there for a good clear-out. That's something only I can do in time.

Yeah, I *do* sound like an ungrateful shit. Don't I?

It's okay. I know I do. Just, I had no idea until now, until that stuff was presented to me, how much it would affect me. And it's odd. I don't even recognise this reaction, but I do understand it. It's obvious.

Those objects are a trigger. They're loaded with all this negative energy. Painful. Hurtful. Emotional. And being exposed to them in that way was like a cattle prod to my senses! Especially when I saw that thing taped to the box.

I have no effing clue how that USB stick even survived Dolce Vita and why those people felt compelled to save it. I mean, what did they do? Did they watch it or something?

Mercifully, I didn't have to explain it to Sarah because the moment I unpicked that thing from the box and held it in my hand was the moment the waterworks came.

Shit.

Made worse by old magic paws and his uncanny ability to make me think of my little boy every time he's close.

Speaking of which… "What now?"

Buddy has stepped in front of me and is barking at the manor in the distance.

"Really? Shush. What's the matter with you?"

But the dog's only reaction is to take a few more steps forward and continue his rant that echoes loudly in the open space.

"Stop it!" I say, touching his fur. "Stop!"

And yet, he persists to the point where I start to feel conspicuous standing here on the edge of the woods like I'm surreptitiously checking on the boys to see if they're working. Although now that I think of it, I can't see much activity. Those windows are dark, lifeless, and filled with foreboding.

Really?

"And you! You're the worst!" I say to the dog, "come on! Let's go! Come on." I pull at his collar until he finally turns away from the house. And, in his usual style, he instantly flicks back to his usual self, trotting forward into the undergrowth without a care in the world.

I swear that dog has A.D.H.D.

Oh, he heard that because he's stopped and is now looking back at me. *Are we running or what?*

"Seriously? Just like that? I can't take you anywhere."

If my dog feels castigated, he doesn't show it. Instead, he scampers forward, sniffing his way as he goes.

I roll my eyes but take my cue. "Fine."

Of course, the hound that also has delusions of being my trainer is always a few steps ahead as if to challenge me to keep up the pace which, to be fair, I do… for about five minutes, but then… what's that?

There! In the clearing. A few yards up ahead. Something glinting in the trees. I don't remember seeing them before.

So, I jog to a stop and walk over. Heart thumping. Recovering breaths coming fast and shallow.

It's… it's some kind of natural hanging pendant, made of string and I think some kind of coloured glass or gem with a hole crudely bored through it. Not the prettiest thing I've seen. Looks like something a child would make, but it's hanging on a branch at about my head level, so that's around six feet. A child wouldn't be able to reach that far.

I look around as if I'm going to find the artist nearby, but there's nobody here but me, the birds, and a giant golden retriever who's finally made a U-turn and decided to come and see what the delay is.

What's that? There. Another one, but on the opposite side of the trail. Then another and another. They're hanging at intervals throughout the woods.

I'm assuming that the sun has shifted, and that's why I haven't noticed them before, but now they're all blinking in the gloom of the forest like fireflies.

Crows caw as I stop at another a few yards up and notice that these aren't individual pendants, but are part of a whole twig-constructed mobile of the kind you normally find hanging over a baby's cot. Cheap dreamcatchers straight out of the bloody Blair Witch.

Ugh. Maybe I should take one down. Show Sarah. Rocks. Crystal. Mysticism is more her thing than mine. She might be able to identify them or something.

No. I don't even know why. I just don't want these things anywhere near the house. So, I snap a couple of pictures on my phone instead.

Magpies chatter nearby. And I'm not sure if they're encouraging me to take the shiny thing home or telling me they'll have it if I don't.

"You're welcome to it!" I shout out before I resume jogging, gradually upgrading that to a run, and it feels good. Tendons stretching, fresh air pumping, pulse rushing.

Several minutes later, Buddy and I explode out of the mottled shade of the trees and into the sunlight, where I punch both hands in the air. This has got to be a personal best. Tomorrow I might try running around the lake in the opposite direction.

I consider this and start plotting the potential route as I double over, hands on knees, to recover.

Buddy has collapsed, tongue wagging in front of me. "I... I nearly... nearly... caught up with you this time, bud," I say with a grin, but the dog doesn't seem impressed. Instead, he rises to his feet and starts sniffing...

Hello. Where did that come from?

There's a white Porsche Cayenne parked in the drive behind the Beemer. Not a car I recognise. The driver's seat is empty.

Buddy sniffs all around the vehicle. Then, as if tracking the driver, he slowly pads up the garden path.

Hands-on-hips, as I still haven't fully recovered from the run, I follow him around the garage corner and pause when I see the back of a tall, slender body wrapped in a rusty-coloured coat. Female this time. She has her back to us, seemingly inspecting the house.

"Can I help you?" I call out.

The visitor turns immediately, and when she does. "Amanda?"

"Hello Marco," she says with a big smile. Those eyes are now chestnut in the sunshine.

For a few seconds, a wood pigeon has more to say than me before I eventually manage to stutter, "Amanda. I, um. What are you doing here?"

"I'm your eight o'clock."

"I don't have an eight o'clock."

"Good. Because you do now," the lawyer says, hunching her shoulders against the morning chill.

I force a laugh because I can't find words. And, despite the not-so-subtle body language hint, I'm torn between asking her in or to leave, which I know sounds discourteous given how far she must have travelled but, well, you've met her, you know our history and—

don't read too much into this—I don't trust myself around her. Okay, I just made that sound worse.

"So…" she says with a smile, "are you going to invite me in?" just as I imagine a vampire might ask if vampires existed, of course.

I hesitate. "Um, yes, of course, sorry," I say and lead her to the front door.

Her heels sound unusually loud as she enters the house. A bit like the alarm bell in my head.

Because I have a history of being a duplicitous prick, I take a furtive look outside before pushing the door shut behind us. I have no idea why. Just being in this woman's presence. My heartbeat's elevated, and I, um. I don't know why.

Welcome, guest, Holt chips in, unhelpfully.

Amanda looks around herself, trying to identify the source of the voice.

"It's, um, a smart home," I offer because I have no clue how to introduce this woman to the artificial intelligence that runs this place. Then I try to casually stuff my hands in my pockets, but my shorts are way looser than I remember; wow, that running must be working. And I don't know if I imagined it, but I'm sure my visitor just copped a look at my midriff.

Okay. I take my hands out of my pockets and swing them awkwardly in front of me like I've just been reduced to a child.

Luckily, my guest is already distracted by the house. "Oh wow… this is incredible," she breathes, clicking those unusually high heels around the entrance hall. I imagine Sarah wearing those and suppress a chuckle. It would be the equivalent of me walking on stilts.

Sarah's never been one for heels or to dress up, for that matter. It's not like she doesn't when the mood takes her, but she much prefers Converses and trousers to heels and dresses.

Meanwhile, just having this woman in the house makes me feel like I'm doing something illicit. And it's with a deep sigh and a throbbing pulse that I watch her gaze out of the window while I contemplate changing into something *less* comfortable.

Having somehow identified our guest, Buddy has given up the act of a scary guard dog and is now sitting halfway down the entrance hall, watching as if he plans on recording everything he sees and telling on me later. Then he groans and flops to the floor.

I don't know what it is with that hound, but his mannerisms always have a way of telling something without saying anything. In this case, it's *seriously, dude? Are you bored and looking for more trouble?*

"This place is amazing," Amanda says, looking through the archway into the dining room as birds tweet happily beyond the window.

"Yeah. It's something else," I say, scratching the back of my head and generally not knowing where to put my hands now. "So, Amanda. Um. As much as it's good to see you… what are you doing all the way out here?"

"If I told you that I was in the area, would you believe me?" she asks, stepping by me and into the dining room.

"It's almost a two-hour drive from London. Um, not really."

"Okay. No point lying then," she says, pulling off her hat and unleashing a waterfall of chestnut hair over her coat. It's much longer than I remember, and the thought has barely been processed before a snapshot of what it looked like hanging over her naked skin presents itself to me.

No. No. No. Shit.

"You've really done well for yourself, Marc. A bit different from when we last saw each other, eh? Therapy must pay really well," she says, eyes roving all over the place before settling on me.

"I, um, well, actually–"

"And you. You're still looking good. Maturing nicely with age," she says, stepping closer. "But then you men are like that. Don't have to worry about crow's feet, cellulite, and the saggy bits like us women, do you?"

No. No. Ears, don't you dare start burning! Don't! But it's too late. I can feel the heat radiating the back of my neck and upward.

For God's sake, get a grip, man! I seem to spend my life telling myself that.

I watch a smile form on her face. "Oh, I see your ears still go red when you're embarrassed."

I shake my head as if that's going to dispel the colour from those traitors. "No. Not really."

"Are you not going to give me a tour then?" she asks, looking out into the hallway.

"Amanda, well, actually, I've just been running, so I could do with a shower."

"Oh, that's no problem. I can wait. Or join you if you like."

"Well, if you—I'm sorry. What?"

She allows herself an uncharacteristic giggle. "Relax, handsome. I'm just teasing you. I could murder a coffee, though. Maybe use your loo?"

I observe her, neat eyebrows lifted, inquisitively, a mischievous grin on parade.

I nod. "Of course."

I lead her down the hallway, where she notices the large arched window on the stairs and then the view of the lake.

"Oh, this is gorgeous, isn't it?" she breathes. "No wonder you didn't want to leave her. Fuck, I wouldn't have left her either if I knew I was going to end up with this," she says with a wry grin.

I feel like I should put her straight, but then, on the other hand, I know her. I know how she operates. This is exactly what she does, and it's probably why she's so successful in the courtroom. She's an astute observer of people. She knows which buttons to press and when to press them to get the reaction and thus the information she needs.

"The toilet is at the end of the corridor," I say, pointing. "I'll be through here. In the kitchen." I smile at her and then make my way inside. I'll have to shower later. No. I'm not being churlish, far from it. This is me we're talking about. I'm being cautious.

I open the swing door to find Buddy sitting up, expectantly like a disappointed parent.

"Bloody hell. Stop doing that, ninja," I say and then add in a hushed tone, "Don't bother with judgemental looks. She's just having a coffee."

The hound groans and collapses to the floor as if fatigued by my erroneous ways.

"Yeah, thanks for your support," I say, filling the Sage coffee machine with water. Yes. Carson was obviously serious about his coffee and amen to that.

I thought it was going to be difficult moving in here and living amongst other people's stuff. But oddly, it hasn't felt that way at all. It was actually brilliant. We were moved-in in a couple of days. A bit like people do when they go away to a self-catering holiday home. Everything we needed was right here. All we had to add was us, a deep clean, and groceries.

Sarah was so excited. Her enthusiasm for moving out of the city matched mine. I can't believe I agonised over that for so long.

Amanda being here while Sarah's at work feels weird though on so many levels, but then I suppose I only have myself to blame for that since I've only known her as the embodiment of adultery and betrayal, among other things. There's a lot of history. And, if I'm perfectly honest with myself, she still looks great. Something about her. She's ruinous, dangerous, and bloody sexy.

There. I said it.

And it isn't just a physical thing before you write me off. I'm a man. And yes, of course, I'm cursed with the same compulsion of most hot-blooded heterosexual males (if we can put aside my addiction for a second). But this is different. This is more than the way she looks, the danger she exudes, her sexuality. This is about intimacy. About the voracious way we went about discovering everything there was to know about each other when our relationship was still new, illicit. The antithesis of the apathy that often thrives in the confines of a marriage or ongoing relationship where discovery ends, and complacency often sets in like dry rot unless you work at it.

What the fuck am I talking about? Who am I even talking about? Ellie? Sarah?

I realise now, at this moment, that Sarah and I never went through that. There was none of that. We were just friends who shared a traumatic experience, became lovers, sponsors, and co-dependents.

Oh shit. Where's this–

"Wow. Just when you thought this place couldn't get any better," Amanda says, coming through the door and gazing up at the skylight in the kitchen.

"Yeah. It certainly has a wow factor," I say.

Buddy growls and barks, startling our uninvited guest out of her daze, but if she's affected, she doesn't show it. Instead, she says, "I can't believe you've actually got a dog now." She side-steps Buddy and comes around the island to where I'm busy pouring milk into a metal jug.

"Yeah. I know."

Her perfume announces her arrival before I sense her proximity that shocks my heart into an unauthorised frenzy.

"What about you?" I ask.

"Pets? No. I'm allergic." And as if to prove it, she sneezes.

"Bless you. There are tissues in the drawer," I say, nodding at the island.

She looks at me expectantly for a few seconds, then sniffs before opening the drawer and fishing a tissue out of the box. I know this might be my cue to take Buddy to another room, and I consider doing so for a few seconds. But *no,* this is *his* home too.

Instead, I proceed to steam the milk, pour in a couple of espressos, and then rather than handing it to my guest, I turn and place the cup on the island, making the act look natural rather than a blatant attempt to put some space between us.

"Thank you," she says, tugging at the belt around her coat and then shrugging it off to reveal a tightly fitted, cream woollen jumper and mink high-waist trousers. She places the coat on one of the stools at the island before taking a seat next to it.

I, now nursing my own Americano, remain standing on the opposite side.

She nods at the large blackboard imitation frame hanging on the wall over the coffee machine. It's titled *the anatomy of coffee.* And has a series of chalk coffee cup designs illustrating various types of coffee shop beverages. "Wow, a barista too. Is there no end to these new skills of yours?" she asks, "and you remembered how I like my latte," she says, nodding in my direction.

I rock my head. I could explain that this stuff was already here but instead opt to dispense with the small talk and get straight to the heart of the matter. "So, you were in Cheshire but decided to move back to London. How come?"

I watch her take a sip from her beverage and smile before asking, "Are you deposing me?"

"No, just wondering."

"Well," she begins, brushing lint off her trousers, "as you know. After we…" she gestures between us but leaves the sentence hanging as if she's unable or unwilling to find the word. "I moved back to Cheshire. Was offered a position at a firm there. Shortly after met Jeffrey, he's one of the managing partners. It's not a big firm, but you know, renowned for what we do. Enough to have offices around the country."

"And you were posted here, to the London branch?" I ask.

She takes another sip from her cup with immaculately painted rosy lips and nods, "Uh-huh."

"I thought you said you were headhunted and offered the position here."

She pauses and squints at me as if she's spotted that I'm trying to catch her in a lie. "So, you *are* cross-examining me. I said I was headhunted from *within the firm*. And since I had already worked in London, they offered me the position, and I took it. Jeffrey travels a lot. He has a place in the city."

"So, how's it going?"

"What? At the flat?"

"No, with this managing partner bloke, Jeffrey?"

"Good. Great, in fact. You know what it's like. New relationship, he's all enthusiastic. Younger than me. All sorts of hopes and ambitions for the future."

"And you?"

"I don't really know. I can't say I've thought about it," she says, taking another sip from her cup. "Hmm, this really is a good beverage," she says.

There's silence. Kitchen appliances hum. The woodland fauna sings. Somewhere in the distance, a woodpecker drums for his morning breakfast.

"I was sorry to hear about Ellie, by the way," she says suddenly as if she'd just remarked on how sorry she was to hear that I had caught a cold.

I feel a shiver scuttle down my spine at the mere mention of

Ellie's name. Not least because they are spoken by *this* woman whom I know is lying. She hated my wife for obvious reasons.

"You heard?" I ask.

She shrugs. "Well, read, listened to, watched on television. You and that place became a bit of a national celebrity after what happened. You looked good, by the way. Credible."

"Credible?"

"Oh, you know. Suitably sympathy-worthy in the court of public opinion."

"Right," I nod sadly.

"Must have been scary."

"It was," I say grimly as the ever-present flashbacks use my visitor's words as the trigger to shoot memories into the back of my eyes. *Collapsing roof. Screaming. The terror in the eyes of those washed over and into the abyss. Someone pushing me into the pits of hell, that sense of finality....*

"...But still, you survived."

I shrug because I'm momentarily unable to find words.

"And managed to snare a new, younger girlfriend in the process." She laughs, "every cloud, eh?"

I must have frowned at that because she holds her hand out and says, "Oh, I'm sorry. I didn't mean to sound insensitive."

I shake my head dismissively as if none of the words that are still hanging in the air, like toxic fumes, are having any effect on me. I'm fine. I've worked through this, processed it all with Ethan. I'm fine. I'm okay.

I'm fine. I'm okay.

And yet. "Why are you here, Amanda?" I vomit.

She looks up from her cup, seemingly surprised by my perfectly rational question but hesitates as her neatly painted face creases into a frown. "I wanted to apologise for the other day. How I behaved. And I suppose we should probably tack on just now, too." I shake my head, but she continues, "No, I was out of order. I should never have said those things. It was completely unprofessional of me. My words were insensitive. I should know better."

I shrug. "It's okay. I understand."

She rolls her eyes and shakes her head. "God. You haven't

changed."

"What?"

"This whole, *it isn't you, it's me,* "humility thing. It's disgusting and really irritating, and it takes me right back. Can't you just let me fucking apologise without making me feel worse?" she snaps, eyes blazing under the skylight.

I hold up my hands, surrendering to the ordinance of her words.

"I'm sorry. I don't know where that came from," she says, looking out of the window. She swallows hard as if fighting back the tears and chortles. "You know… just like all of those perfect little heroines in those romantic films, I gave myself *the speech* on the way over here. I promised myself that I would not do this. That I would just walk in here and say what I had to say. I'm a fucking professional! Oratory is my speciality, for Christ's sake. And yet, every time I see you…" she leaves the sentence unfinished.

I say nothing. Partly because I want to give her the chance to express herself since that's no doubt the real reason why she drove out here and partly because I haven't got the foggiest what to say to this woman that I unceremoniously ditched the moment I finally came to my senses and realised that my wife and son were the most important things in my life. Unfortunately, as you've already heard, it took me the best part of a year to come to that conclusion. Sadly, what we had agreed was going to be just a bit of uncomplicated fun had become something more. At least it had for the person in front of me.

Me? Well, I'm just an insensitive prick. We've already established that.

She turns back to me, and I can see that her eyes are shimmering with repressed tears. "I want you to see me," she says seriously, quietly. Almost like she doesn't want to articulate the words and, again, my face must have reacted to that because she quickly adds with a disarming laugh, "No, not like that, of course. I know you've already replaced your wife, but I mean as a client, a patient, whatever the term is."

Okay. I wasn't expecting that.

I shift on my feet, frown, and put my cup down. "Amanda I–"

"And don't give me any crap about it being a conflict."

"Well, that's exactly what it is. You know that."

She cocks her head. "I don't understand."

"Amanda. Come on," I say, hanging my head because I'm pathetic and can't hold her gaze for fear that my traitorous body might reveal something I don't want it to.

"You mean," she forces a laugh, "you mean because of what happened?" She laughs again as if to press home the point. "Are you telling me that you haven't moved on?"

"A lot has happened since then," I croak.

"Exactly. We've both moved on. You're with a much younger model, and me too. I'm happy with a very handsome, successful man. See? We've both moved on. There's no conflict."

I hesitate. My feathered neighbours fill in an awkward silence before Buddy lets out another loud groan as if he's been hanging on our every word and is not enjoying where this conversation is going.

Then, "So, what's she like?"

"Who?"

"The new girlfriend."

"Amanda–"

"Oh, come on, don't be coy. I'll show you mine if you show me yours," she says with a mischievous smile, "does she make you happy?"

I think about this and then say, "Yes, she does, actually. She makes me very happy."

"Happier than I did?"

"Amanda–"

"Well, you can answer questions, can't you? It's not an official state secret, is it?"

I muse on this too. "It's different."

"Different, how?"

I force a laugh. "Are you deposing *me* now?"

I watch her shoulders relax, and those lips drink from the cup before they move to laugh and say, "I'm sorry. I get like this sometimes. Conversations turn into interrogations. Occupational habit."

There's another long pause, and I'm just about to say something when I hear her utter, "So, will you?"

"Will I what?"

"See me."

"Amanda, I've already told you that I don't think–"

"You owe me."

"What?"

"You fucking owe me," she growls, looking me straight in the eyes. And suddenly, I'm reminded of how much I do.

9

THE DARK

Alright, so, given this fascination you seem to have with my car crash of a life, I assume you have an opinion. You know, the whole Amanda thing? You might think that, given the history involved, you would have handled the whole thing differently.

Well, if that's the case, hold your judgement. You haven't heard the worst part yet. Yeah, even I have no idea why I do half the things I do sometimes.

So, given that everything is perfectly innocent, that there was no premeditation on my part since Amanda just showed up at my doorstep and broadsided me the way she did, you would have thought I'd have no problem telling Sarah about it.

Yes. As I said, hold your judgement. It's not because I enjoy sneaking around and withholding information; it's more because I was quite literally unable to articulate the words. After all, it sounded so bloody fantastical.

Think about it for a second.

Hello Sarah, did you have a nice day? Remember my trip to

London? It turns out that the lawyer who was going to handle my case is the woman I cheated on my wife with for the best part of a year, but I chose to omit that detail when you asked me for specifics about the meeting. And today, well, she, the lawyer slash bit-on-the-side, showed up at the house and wants me to see her as a patient and, guess what, I, because I'm now a pathetically weak excuse of a man, have agreed to do so especially after she decided to raise the whole subject of…

Um. Yeah. I think that's more than enough to be getting on with for now.

Bloody hell.

I don't even want *you,* my judgmental psychological hitchhiker, to know the sordid details. I can't, however I stretch my imagination, find a way of telling Sarah that doesn't make me look like a complete knob-end.

And yes, of course, I can see it. Humans have been behaving this way for centuries. I'm not so concerned with the actual content of my words but more about how they will *make me appear.* Disloyal. Spineless. Secretive, and like I have something to bloody hide. I don't. I just have a knack for getting myself into these situations, and even I don't know how.

And there goes another flare of anger, but I chew it down by grinding my teeth.

"Are you okay?" Sarah asks.

We're sitting out on the lounge balcony watching the sortie of bats skitter to and from the woods on one side and the glassy glowing embers of the setting sun on the other.

In Porthcove, I used to think that the moving canvas of the ocean was an unrivalled spectacle. And yet, here we are, snuggled under our throw, enjoying our hot beverages while taking in another exclusive and unique performance of nature's majesty that includes the silhouettes of birds retiring for the night into that creepy looking mist that has materialised at the far end of the lake again, smothering the manor.

"Yeah. Why do you ask?" I respond casually.

"I don't know. You just seemed quiet at dinner. Like you have the weight of the world on your shoulders. Are you worried about this lawyer?"

My ears prick up. "Eh?"

"You know, the trial. Do you trust your lawyer? You haven't really said much about him."

"Oh, yeah. He's good. He's fine," I say with a dismissive shrug.

"Are you sure?" she asks with a scrutinizing squint.

I smile. "Yeah. I'm sure. It's not just the trial. It's everything else, you know."

"Like what?"

Amanda! Amanda! Is the first bloody thing on my brain, so now I'm scrambling to find something else, but luckily, she continues, "I know the trial is scary, but even the lawyer said it's without merit, right?"

Worried about the lawyer.

"You're right," I say with a smile. "It's just that things are finally looking up, and I don't want anything to happen to change that," I say, which is the closest thing I can find that isn't an outright lie.

Sarah reaches over and squeezes my hand. "Nothing is going to spoil it," she says earnestly, "as you said, things are even coming along with the house. Uncle Irvin and the lads will have that place finished in no time, it'll sell, and then you'll truly be ready to take on the world."

"Oh yeah? How do you know? Have you been consulting your crystals again?"

She shrugs. "Kind of." And I can't help but notice a twinkle in those green eyes of hers.

"Right. What do I need to know?"

"Oh nothing," she says coyly, settling back into her chair and pulling the throw up around her. It is getting chilly out here.

I laugh. "Go on, spill it."

"It's nothing important," she says, looking out over the lake. "Only, Martin called me into his office today."

"Oh right. What is it?"

She turns to me. "He said that the way things are going, he can't see any reason why he wouldn't consider me for a permanent placement."

"What? Sarah, that's fantastic news!" I say, patting and rubbing her leg since it's the closest thing to me.

"I know… right? I can't believe it."

"Well, I can."

"Yeah?"

"Of course. They're lucky to have you. You're great with animals and people. They've obviously seen that."

"Oh, thank you." She leans forward and kisses me on the mouth. And then sits back again.

"Why didn't you tell me sooner?" I ask.

She shrugs. "I don't know. I was more interested in your news. In hearing how things are going with the manor. I know it's important to you."

"It is. Of course, it is, Sarah. But this is a partnership, remember? And this is big stuff. You've worked really hard, and I'm so proud of you."

"Thanks, babe. It *is* great news, and it'll help keep the wolf from the door while we wait for you to make your next million, which won't be long." She cocks her head and gives me a knowing smile.

"Yeah. Fingers crossed, we don't find any problems. We're progressing in stages too. Irvin's idea. One side of the house first and then the other. That way, we could technically start showing people around if we need to. So don't worry. It's all good. Especially now. Looks like I can just send you out to earn the dough, and I can sit on my arse and do nothing," I add with a grin.

"That's fine by me. You can be a stay-at-home dad," she says excitedly, and then I watch her smile slowly ebb like the fading light, presumably because of the look on my face.

Shit.

**

Morning arrives way too soon. And when it does, it brings with it another beautifully warm summer's day musically scored by the ever-cheerful birdsong.

Last night's awkwardness is nothing but a distant memory, and if Sarah was in any way affected, she isn't showing it.

Children are not something we've discussed. The thought hadn't even crossed my mind. My girlfriend, on the other hand, has over a decade less life experience than me.

But I'm not going to think about it. No. Not today. Today, I'm busying myself with cleaning out the barbeque station, which obviously hasn't been used in a while because there's an abandoned bird's nest in here. And yes, I spotted that metaphor too. It's the very reason why I boarded this train of thought again while mindlessly scrubbing to clear away all the desiccated leaves and insect corpses that are ingrained into this thing. It's spattered onto the bricks, welded to the so-called stainless-steel griddle, and filtered through the fat drainage hole.

I don't know what the hell Carson cooked here last, but the crimson, black blood caked on this thing won't come off; it. It seems stuck to it like tar.

Shit. I'm working up a sweat here. I could murder an ice-cold drink right now. If only–

"Buddy! Buddy!"

Oh, it's Sarah. Who's obviously going all out today because she's *actually* wearing a dress. Blimey. A yellow dress, no less. And she's cut her hair into a curled fringe with two giant folds on top fixed in place by a matching polka dot hairband. Wow. Normally, she harnesses her hair into a practical ponytail. Sometimes, she'll even put it under a baseball cap but not today. Today, even the converses are out, replaced by black pretty-bowed pumps.

Goodness. I barely recognise her as the lady of the house.

Lady of the house.

She's carrying a tray. Lemonade, by the looks of it, with slices of lemon competing with her dress for oversaturated attention.

Although, I suppose I'm one for talking. I'm wearing rusty-red chequered shorts and shirt ensemble that I don't even remember buying. I look like one of those blokes out of a fifties clothing advert. The kind of look you'd find in an episode of Mad Men.

Mad Men.

Oh, that must be it. That must be the theme for this barbecue, fifties summer.

"Buddy!"

Sarah keeps calling out to the dog on the other side of the garden. So, I follow her line of sight and freeze when I see Toby, my son, standing opposite, waving and smiling back at her.

"Toby?" My stomach summersaults at the sight of his gold hair, hazy in the glare of the sun.

Sarah calls to him again, and he responds. Or at least I think he does. I'm not sure because when he opens his mouth, instead of the beautiful sound of his voice, I hear the harshness of a dog bark instead.

My son is barking like a dog!

"Toby? Toby!" I call out to him, but he isn't hearing me. "Sarah! Sarah!"

But neither of them is listening; instead, they both turn their backs to me and look towards the forest, towards that black demarcation line. Sarah points at it, and Toby, my baby, my pride and joy, starts walking forward.

"No! Toby. No! Sarah! No. Don't let him go in there. Don't!"

But she isn't listening. Instead, she looks back over her shoulder at me, smiling. Smiling like she knows something I don't. Something I don't know but can feel.

"NO! Sarah. Please! He's my son! He's my baby. Please! Stop him!" But instead, my girlfriend turns back and watches my little boy move towards the boundary, towards the darkness. And I can sense it; I can feel it beckoning him inside. Calling to him.

"NO! TOBY! DON'T! Don't go in there!"

I'm running now in slow motion, soapy water bucket toppling over, water and suds washing over my feet. Only, when I look down, it isn't water, it's blood! My son's blood!

He's running now at speed, barking like a dog as he makes his way towards the black, but I can't stop him. I can't reach him. The blood is sucking at my feet, solidifying glueing me to the spot.

He's inching closer now.

Woof! Woof!

Closer to the darkness.

Woof! Woof! Woof! Woof!

"TOBY, NO!" I wail. "PLEASE DON'T GO IN THERE!

TOBY!"

Woof! Woof!

But it's too late. Without even turning to look at me, my son steps out of the sunshine and into the inky darkness, and that's when I see it. "Oh, God." I see it! Just a snapshot. A flicker. "What is that?" A grey gnarled, veiny claw is reaching out of the gloom and tugging him inside.

"NO!"

I jump awake into a sitting position, arms outstretched in front of me, reaching into the dark of the room. Panting. Sweating. And I've barely gathered my bearings when I feel a hand on my shoulder that startles me.

"Fuck!"

"It's me. It's just me!" Sarah says, urgently staring at me.

"Shit. You scared the shit out of me," I gasp through breaths.

"I'm sorry. But you were. I think you were having a nightmare. You were screaming."

Woof! Woof!

I think it's still the dregs of my dream at first, but then I tune in, and Sarah validates it.

"…Buddy. He's really unhappy about something and won't stop barking," she continues.

The bark sounds distant. He must be downstairs.

"I'll go and check," I say with a sigh, "you go back to sleep."

"Back to sleep? Do you want me to come with you?"

I smile at her. This woman is nothing like Ellie. I sigh and run a hand through my hair, "I'm not that much of a wimp, you know."

Her only response is to smile at me and squeeze my arm, but she doesn't settle back on the pillow. Instead, she sits up against the headboard, which isn't really like her. She's not easily rattled, and yet there's something in her eyes, but I think that has more to do with whatever I was screaming in my sleep than the dog's uncanny late-night serenade.

Late night. It's more like early morning.

It's 02:03.

I leave the bed and shiver. Ew. The cold sweats are back. Great. I pull on a t-shirt which is something I wouldn't normally have to do. Holt isn't like that place by the ocean. There, I'd have to layer up before venturing downstairs. But here, we enjoy climate control bliss. No erratic temperature fluctuations.

Normally, no matter the weather, I can walk around the house in my shorts and not feel a thing, and yet right now, it feels cold in here. Chilly. To the point of compelling me to pull on a pair of jeans before making my way out of the room.

The landing is bathed in subtle blue light, thanks to the *strip LEDs* built into the base of the wall and at intervals on the stairs, making it easier to move around the place in the dark.

I cautiously make my way downstairs.

Buddy's bark is much louder now, ringing up from what I think is the lounge. And, wow, the thought of that just sent a chill through me. I've no idea why. He's never done this before.

Until now.

To make things worse, the house is supernaturally quiet, which isn't unusual out here. But, if there's one thing that I've come to learn over the past month is that the woodland never truly slumbers. The opposite. It seems to come alive at night. Especially since we happen to live in the only area of England where Cicadas are putting up their last stand before extinction from this country. Otherwise, this is the time when grasshoppers, owls, frogs, toads, deer, birds, and a whole host of *other* creatures come alive.

But seemingly not tonight.

I pause by the giant arched window on the stair landing and attempt to peer out into the back garden. But it's a moonless night. All I can see is a sheet of impenetrable blackness on which my reflection is being lit by the runway of nightlights leading down the stairs and up the hallway to the front door.

Everything is deathly still but for the dog's midnight rant. Empty. Echoey. That bark is drilling right through the dregs of my stupor.

I look up, and I have no idea why, but I address Holt with a whisper, "Holt, confirm the status of doors and windows."

All doors and windows are locked and secured; Marco, the disembodied voice responds in an equally creepy whisper that makes me cringe.

Despite the confirmation, I still feel vulnerable, like I should be carrying a conveniently located baseball bat or something, because I suddenly and inexplicably feel like I'm not alone. Like there's something else skulking in the shadows, waiting, watching.

Yeah. That'll be enough of that.

I make my way down the rest of the stairs and then turn left into the doorway to the lounge.

From the loudness of his bark, Buddy is on the opposite side of the room, and I have barely crossed the door's threshold when dazzling light from the overhead chandelier both blinds and startles me. "Holt, lights off! Fuck!" I yell.

Of course.

I squeeze my eyelids shut and wait a few seconds as floaters drift on the sea of orange seared onto my eyeballs before reopening them once more.

Okay. So, turning the lights off again didn't make much sense since it's dark outside. I can't see anything beyond the glass anyway.

"Holt, turn on the side lamp."

Sure.

The lamp, a few feet to my right, magically springs to life, bathing part of the room in a tawny light that scares the darkness backwards into pools, behind furniture, and into the corners of the room.

I can see him now. Buddy is standing in front of the glass wall. He's adopted tactical hunched shoulders, swishing tail mode, and is growling at something out there.

"Buddy? Hey! Buddy? What's up?"

The dog is so deeply focused on what's out there that he doesn't respond to my voice. And I'm getting tired of that. He's normally so responsive. In tune with my every step, but recently, I don't know what's got into him. And it's unsettling.

"Bud?" I say, slowly, making my way across the room. And yet, even when I reach him and place a hand on his head to rub his floppy ear, the guttural growl remains.

So, I follow his gaze. But I can't bloody see anything. Just the pitch blackness of the glass and the projected reflection of the dim-lit room behind me.

I imagine how I must look from outside the building. A tall silhouette standing next to that of a dog. Both of us peering out of the one-way mirror into the night and whatever it is out there observing us like specimens inside a dome.

Shit. I have this knack for creeping myself out without even realising it.

I shrug the tingle from my spine, rub the raised hair on my arms and pat the dog's head, "Come on you. Stop being silly. There's nothing out there; otherwise, the security lights would have come on," I say lightly. And yes, I do realise that I'm saying that more for my own benefit than the dog's because, well, he's a dog.

Had we come here straight from the city, I know I'd be finding all of this particularly disturbing. But this place isn't so different from that one by the ocean. Although, to be fair, that place at least had the village and lights on one side. Here, it's just us. We have become the lighthouse on the ocean of infinite darkness. And that takes some getting used to. Especially after a stint back in the city where, ironically, much never sleeps.

Interestingly, I still prefer this. I prefer the distinction between night and day. Not the bastardised version that the city has to offer.

And yet.

There's something about this blackness that unsettles me. It feels tangible. Palpable. And I know I must be imagining it when it appears as if the glass wall in front of me is yielding to it, bowing inward. Reaching for me.

Buddy's growl brings me back to the moment.

"Yeah. This is you, isn't it? This is you being you... creepy Buddy. You're always doing this creepy stuff to–"

The dog's sudden bark at the inanimate wall startles me, and I feel a flare of anger. "Jesus! Stop it now. You're starting to scare the crap out of me!"

But the dog ignores my outburst. Instead, eyes still fixed on the night beyond the glass, he folds back his ears, squats down, and emits more ominous growling.

My heart is pounding now. Something about this new side of my big friendly giant is truly unnerving, and I'm ready to retreat to the safety of wherever as long as I'm not standing here feeling like

I'm being scrutinized by something I can't see.

"Come on, buddy. It's just a deer doing what... they do at night. Come on, mate, let's go back to bed," I say, petting the dog's back, but I'm rewarded with a snarl so vicious that I'm forced to snatch my hand away.

"What the hell is wrong with you, eh?"

But the animal isn't listening.

So then, as if to prove a point—I don't know to whom because the dog doesn't care, presumably to myself—I take a step forward in front of him, towards the black glass. But even squinting, I can't see anything but the reflection of the room behind me.

So, I take another step closer, and as I do, I realise that it is... shaking. It's subtle, but now that I'm closer, I can see that the reflection of the lamp, sofa, and the rest of the furniture is vibrating, and the sight of this shifts my heart into a higher gear, especially when I realise that it isn't the glass. It's me! I'm shivering. And I've just realised why. It's bloody freezing in here! The climate control appears to have taken on a life of its own and plunged the room into arctic conditions. That or I'm losing my bloody mind.

And yet, I take another step closer. My nose is just inches away from the thick glass now. So close that I can smell its composition, feel the coldness emanating from it and eradiating my face.

Then, I watch as each of my exhalations fogs a patch of the glass-like frost that melts and reforms faster and faster as my heart bangs louder and louder as it seemingly wants to burst out of my chest and hide behind the sofa.

Slowly, gingerly, I lift shaky hands and cup them around my face as I press it against the smooth cold blackness of the glass, and I can see...

Nothing. I can't see a bloody thing!

Buddy growls softly behind me as I turn away from the freeze that, like a parasite, had already started crawling over my hands, through my veins, and up my arms. "There's nothing there, mate. There's nothing out there, just you, having another one of your–"

Thump! Squeak!

"SHHHHHIT!" I twist and leap back, away from the wall and gawk at it.

"What the bloody hell was that?!"

Something just hit the glass. Something big. Something really big. A stone? No. It would have been sharper. This sound was smooth, heavy. Organic. A bat? A HAND sliding and squidging down the outside of the glass?!

Oh shit.

Buddy emits another grumble. Head lowered. Eyes up.

I follow his gaze, now dreading what I might see out there, suppressing the bloody image of what could suddenly materialise out of the dark. *A pale face! A tentacle-endowed alien!*

Instinctively, I take another step back and watch my normally mild-mannered golden wonder of a dog square up and snarl at the glass, specs of saliva spraying and glistening over it.

Oh, God. I just… I don't even recognise him. In all the time we've been together, he's been pissed off several times but not like this. Never like this. Now, he seems to have worked himself into a frenzy. Fur bristling. Teeth baring.

He's intimidating, *me*.

Breath ragged. Heart pounding. Sweat forming, I am now officially afraid. I don't know why or how, but something has just pushed my terror button, and suddenly, I can feel it. No. I can sense it. That *thing* beyond the glass. Somehow and I don't know how, but I can feel its eyes on us.

That's just your imagination!

"No. That's it. Buddy. Come on. Come away from there. Come on, mate. Come away from the glass."

I take another step back, and as I do, I feel a hand on my shoulder. The touch sets me off like a firecracker!

"OH! JESUS CHRIST!" I spin around. "SARAH! What the hell? You scared the bloody shit out of me!"

"What's going on?" she asks, ignoring my outburst, scrunching herself up, and rubbing her arms against the chill.

I gawk at her, breaths thick and fast, hand over my chest as if to stop the bird of my heart flapping frenetically against my ribcage. Then I try to swallow, but the tide's gone out in my mouth.

Eventually, I turn the dog. "I don't know… there's… there's something out there. Buddy's having a bloody fit."

Sarah follows my gaze. "Any idea what?"

"No. But whatever it is. He isn't happy about it."

"Hey Buddy," she says cheerily. "What's up, boy? Hey, handsome…."

The dog glances back at us, and I suppress the urge to roll my eyes. Thanks, bud. Won't turn around for me, but as soon as a pretty girl is in the room.

"It's probably just a fox or something," Sarah says, stifling a yawn. I keep forgetting that she's a country girl. "It's freezing in here. Did you turn the heating down?"

I pull a face. "Really? You nearly made me crap my shorts, and you're asking about the heating?"

She smiles and puts on the affected voice she normally reserves for belly rubs with the dog while patting my arm, "Aw, you poor thing. I'm sorry. Are you going to be okay?" Then she reaches up and plants a kiss on my cheek.

"So, why did you call me? *Were you afraid to wander the house alone?*" The last bit is in that baby voice again.

I roll my eyes at her. Then, "What? What do you mean?"

"You called me."

I shake my head. "No, I didn't."

She cocks her head, places hands on her hips, and then studies my face. "Haha… stop messing with me."

"I'm not messing with you."

"Marco, if you are, I–"

The rest of her sentence is cut short when Buddy restarts his barking, only this time it's much louder. Angrier. Vicious.

And I can feel another tingle down my spine as I watch my normally languid companion rush to one end of the glass and start snarling and growling before chasing that up with bare teeth barks that are now filling the room with palpable rage.

Sarah and I can only watch the intimidating spectacle as the dog slowly make his way from one side of the glass wall to the other, clearly mirroring something on the opposite side.

The scene must have Sarah worried too because she grabs my arm, startling me again. And I'm just dealing with this when–

Perimeter breach in rear garden! Perimeter breach in rear garden!

Holt starts bellowing before an ear-splitting sound, I can only equate to an air raid siren, fills the room.

Intruder alert mode has been initiated. Please remain calm. Authorities have been notified. To cancel, please enter your pin in 40 seconds.

Then, we both flinch as grey metal shutters unfurl loudly over the glass wall.

"Shit!"

Sarah, hands over her ears, yells, "Do you know what the pin number is?"

30 seconds.

"Pin number? No. I was supposed to change it, and I forgot!"

Scanning perimeters. Please address your attention to the nearest display.

Like obedient humans, both Sarah and I, hands over ears, look at the wall-mounted display, which is now projecting a series of black and white night views of the front door…back door…back garden.

They all seem empty. There's nothing out there.

"What was that?" I yell.

"What?"

"Did you see that?"

"What? Did I see what?"

"On the back lawn, I just saw… Holt, show back lawn!"

Please enter your pin in 20 seconds.

"Holt!"

"I think Kal said the default code was written on the back of the control panel latch."

I race out of the lounge and down the corridor.

Lights spring on overhead as I make my way to the front door.

10 Seconds.

I'm scanning the latch for the bloody code when the display panel on the wall, currently cycling through live images of the building and a zone schema of the house, pauses on the schema, and Holt starts bellowing.

Perimeter breach, front garden!

Perimeter breach, back garden!

Perimeter breach in zone 1.

Perimeter breach in zone 2.

Perimeter breach in zone 3.

Backdoor open.

Front door open.

Kitchen window is open.

Then, the siren wails louder. The forest that was once slumbering springs to life in panicked chatters. Sarah starts screaming, the house phone—I'd forgotten even existed—starts ringing, and our once peaceful home descends into complete pandemonium.

10

ROTTWEILER

HOLT. 10:36.

I don't even know where to start with last night. It all seems so surreal. Especially now, in the cold light of day.

I have to keep reminding myself that it did happen and that it wasn't one of those shitty dreams as much as my exhausted brain keeps trying to pass it off as one.

The whole time we've been here, nothing. Then, in the space of a few days, Holt suddenly turns into a creepy version of *HAL* from *2001*.

At least it did in my mind.

Sarah wasn't the least bit phased. Once she got over the whole air-raid siren thing and the fact that we'd been jailed in our home, she was ready to get back to sleep.

Me, on the other hand, I don't think I slept much more than an hour. Eventually, I just decided to get up as there was no point lying there cogitating about the whole mind fuck!

And it is just that. I mean, this stuff just pisses me off because it's hard enough keeping my shit together every day without all this weird crap fuelling my imagination. No. I'm not having it. I'm not fucking having anything ruin what we have here. And that includes my spiralling! I will not allow myself to spiral back. I won't!

Breathe Marco. Breathe.

There's got to be a rational explanation for all of this. There is. That's why I've set about debunking the whole thing.

First thing this morning, since I couldn't sleep anyway, I started doing some research because it's occurred to me that as much as we've become accustomed to some of the sights and sounds of our new habitat, we don't truly understand them.

I found this interesting BBC report on what happens in British woodland after dark. The journalist spends a night in the forest and, while he's there, he very helpfully records all of the flutters, snaps, cries, hoots, groans, and squeals, including, and this is the best part, the rather chilling and somewhat horrifying *call of a muntjac deer*.

Have you ever heard one of those things?

Specifically, a buck. Apparently, they roam around at night, especially during mating season. Their bark, or more like their shriek, is so otherworldly, it sounds like something out of *Jurassic Park*.

Now, I can't be one hundred per cent sure, but I'm confident that this was the thing that screamed at Buddy and me from the woods the other day. And, already, I'm feeling much better. Mystery number one, solved.

Last night, one of the things freaking me out was the fact that if there was something on the back lawn, then why the bloody hell didn't it trigger the security lights? I say *if,* but you'll appreciate I'm using that word loosely. I know something was out there because Buddy corroborated it. Yes, I know he's a dog, but still. He was obviously pissed off with something out there.

I *did not* imagine that.

And yet, upon close inspection this morning, I couldn't find any obvious evidence of what it might have been. Muntjac deer? No clue. There was no handily flattened grass, no obvious hoof, or footprints of any kind. Not even a horrifying, bloody handprint on the glass.

Nothing.

What I did find, however, is a broken lightbulb. Yes, convenient, I know. And if I was so inclined, which I am categorically not, it would be easy to think that something or someone deliberately smashed that bulb to disable that light.

Now, who or what would do that? And why?

Nobody and nothing is the answer. We're in the middle of a bloody forest. Woody debris is falling, things flapping all the time in the breeze.

So, I'm not even going to think about it anymore. Sarah didn't seem fazed when she left for work this morning, and I am going to take a leaf from her book for once.

So, yeah, the lightbulb is being replaced. End of.

"Er, Mr. Bat... Batty."

Really? Batty? Dude, you're just begging for a slap. The mood I'm in right now. "Battista," I help out, "but Just call me Marco."

"I'm all done in there."

Here's explanation number three in the form of a young man. Probably still in his twenties with over-waxed spiky blonde hair and beard. He's wearing a uniform of navy-blue cargo paints and a short-sleeved polo shirt that proudly showcases the sleeve tattoo he has on one arm of a girl with flames for hair.

I'm standing on the front lawn. The sun is out, and the birds are quite literally singing. The air smells as fresh as it did the day we arrived here. It's another beautiful day in the woods.

And yes, I'm feeling quite relaxed as I take in the distilled rays of the sun over treetops and the verdant vitality of this natural world. I'm content and full of resolve. Holt is quite literally the definition of my dream home, and I will not allow it to become something it is not.

I join the *boy with the girl tattoo* by his small blue van with a logo on the door of a dog in a suit standing on its hind legs with folded arms and the disgruntled expression of a nightclub doorman on its face. Underneath it are the words *Rottweiler Security Systems,* underscored by a small print that reads, *a CARSON COMPANY.*

"That was quick. What did you find?" I ask.

The boy, because that's how he looks, he even has acne to prove it, shrugs and pulls a face. "Nothing really. Everything seems to be working fine."

I force a chortle. "Well, we know that can't be. Right? I mean, the security company was out here in the dead of night trying to disable the alarm that I think must have scared half the wildlife off," I say, exaggerating a little. The reality is that they arrived relatively quickly, found the code on the panel, and disarmed the alarm for us before asking for identification. You would have thought I'd learned my lesson with this one, given how things went down at Dolce Vita a couple of years back, but the less said about that, the better.

The boy, whose ID tag is hanging from a lanyard around his neck, shrugs again, which, of course, makes me want to use that thing to strangle an altogether different expression on his face.

"Um, Damon," I say, reading the badge, "that thing said that all of the doors and windows were open last night when they quite clearly weren't."

"Yeah, I know, you said," the boy responds flatly. "But there's no record of that in the audit trail."

Now it's my turn to scowl. "So, are you saying we imagined it?"

"No. I'm saying that there's no record of it in the audit trail. You see, every time the alarm is tripped, it records the action in the audit trail, and that information is stored then fed back to us and the security guys as a record. You know, time-triggered, time reset, and all that. In case it needs to be used in court or something."

I stifle an outburst by running fingers through my hair. "I get that. But the alarm *was* triggered. We didn't dream that. Your people responded. That proves that–"

"Well, it only proves the alarm was triggered, which in this case, it was because you didn't enter the code in time. That *is* recorded. We're obliged to respond to those false alarms just like any other."

"Damon, I know how it works," I say, mustering all my restraint, "what I am telling you is that there must be something wrong with the sensors because it was telling–"

"Yeah, you said. I don't really know what to say, mate. From what I can tell, everything's working as it should."

That's right. Interrupt me.

"So, what about Holt? Did you check *it*? Maybe it's the problem. The other day it just opened the front door of its own accord for no reason. Anybody could have just walked right into–"

"Let me just stop you there, mate," the boy says, holding up a flat hand.

"Marco. I said my name is Marco."

"Marco. Mate, we don't deal with any of that stuff. You'll need to speak to the guys at tech. We don't get involved in any of that. We can go as far as rebooting the system for ya, which I did as part of the review, but we don't have anything to do with smart systems."

"What do you mean? Aren't they both the same thing?"

He forces one of those patronising smiles where the lips curl at the sides like sad sandwiches, and now he's just received an upgrade ticket from a slap to a punch in the face. "Um, no. They just interface with each other, but they're two completely separate pieces of software. If you want to talk about Holt, you'll need to speak to the boffins over there. We don't deal with any of that stuff."

"So, basically, what you're saying is that you're as useful to me as a bloody chocolate fireguard," I retort.

He looks at me for the longest time, and there's a moment when I think he's finally affected by something, but instead, he shrugs like I've just told him his shoelace is undone. "Well, I'm sorry you feel that way. Now, if you can just sign here, mate, to say that I've checked your system, run diagnostics, and confirmed that everything is working as it should, I'd appreciate it as I have another ten rounds to do before my shift is over."

I am just about to come back at him when Buddy's bark interrupts us both.

I look over and watch as a taxi makes its way up the drive and rolls to a stop in front of us.

11

MAJA

HOLT. 11:03.

Given recent events, it would be easy to think that I've forgotten the one thing that I've swotted, sweated, and—Ellie used to tell me—alienated my family for, my degree as a bonafide psychologist.

When we left London, I also left the clinic where Ethan had secured me a position as part of my dissertation. As it turns out, and try not to fall off your chair, but my paper on how childhood experiences affect adult relationships even had good ole Doctor Holmes conceding that I had a unique set of skills for dealing with affairs of the mind. No. My own mind doesn't count. It doesn't work that way.

Anyway, Ethan and his cohorts were so impressed that I was offered a position as a junior psychologist. Under his supervision, of course. Something that, as you'll know by now, I'd normally equate to having one of my molars pulled.

And yet, turns out that things weren't anywhere near as bad as I had anticipated. In fact, if you'd told me that I'd end up discussing the merits of cognitive behaviour therapy for obsessive-compulsives with a man who, during the most hideous chapter of my life, appeared obsessively compelled to make my life a misery, I'd say it was you who needed a good shrink. And yet, here we are, one degree and a seemingly interminable number of hours spent listening to the angst of others—primarily so that I could forget my own—later.

Of course, just before I left the clinic, I did tell the Doctor that it might pay for him to discuss the fascinating story of how the dynamics of us changed once he started treating me like his equal and not something that needed to be tortured and studied.

His response? The usual. You know I always appreciate and value your input.

Dick.

Of course, like everything with me, it wasn't all plain sailing, but if it's alright with you, I'd rather not get into that right now.

So, anyway, here I am. Like the proverbial housewife, all dressed up with nowhere to go. I've moved into my dream home while also doing myself out of a job.

Yay!

David doesn't get it. In a few months, I managed to make more money turning over properties than I would make in a lifetime as a psychologist.

True. But then David didn't grow up as I did. And hasn't experienced life as I have. If he had, not that I would wish my former life on anyone, he'd probably see things differently.

Brace yourself for a cringe because that's how I feel each time I think this way, but for me, therapy is no longer a living but a calling.

I know. I can hear that too. Try not to vomit. As much as people droning on about their problems while stubbornly resisting changes can be depressing, frustrating, and often unfulfilling—if mismanaged—I like it.

I need it.

That's why when we arrived here in the middle of nowhere without much prospect of me landing any patients beyond the local passive-aggressive badger, I did what any self-respecting psychologist does to win new business.

I printed up a batch of business cards and paid the local village store the grand sum of 5.99 for one whole month of prime position on their noticeboard.

It was Sarah's idea. The best money I have ever spent. I can't even beat away the new business with a stick. I am booked out weeks, almost months in advance, and the money just keeps rolling.

You believe that, right? Of course you don't.

There's been one response so far. And I think she just rocked up in a cab.

"I am Maja Szymanski. And I look for the Doctor Battista," are the stranger's opening words. I don't bother correcting her on the title because I realise it's futile.

My visitor has an accent that I've heard before. Eastern European, although I can't quite place it. She's a diminutive thing. Maybe late sixties. Five-foot something and wrapped in a coat and headscarf. The only thing on display is a pale-looking face with dour grey eyes, thin lips, skin wrapped over sharp cheekbones, and not a scrap of makeup. She has got to be the school's headmistress or something like that.

There's the sound of someone clearing their throat, and I turn to see that the boy with the girl tattoo is still here. He offers his device up to me. I want to offer a fist back.

But instead, I sign the screen with my finger because, this just in, my first patient is standing nearby listening to our every word.

I give the little shit a sweetly smile.

"Thanks," he says.

No. Fuck *you* very much. I make a mental note to call his boss and Holt's tech support as soon as I get a moment alone because it appears that, right now, I have a booking.

Thanks, Sarah.

I turn to my visitor. What the eff am I going to do with you?

When we arrived here that day, my first thought was how perfect the study would be for therapy. And I mean that literally. It has comfort. The duo stunningly relaxing perspectives as well as quiet and privacy from the rest of the house.

Perfect.

However, it has since become a hangout for the boys. Buddy and I love going into the space at every opportunity for a read and a good snooze. Well, I read, he doesn't because, well, he's a dog.

Anyway, it's been our den for the best part of the month now, so you'll appreciate just how strange it feels to be ushering a stranger into our sanctuary with a smile on my face.

Even the hound isn't impressed because he groaned when he caught sight of the intruder and then refused to even enter the study in protest, opting instead to flop down out in the hallway.

Where else am I going to put her, mate? Can't exactly use the dining room or the kitchen. Wait. The dining room might…

No. This makes sense. Just feels odd.

"I wasn't expecting it to look like dis inside," my visitor says with all the wonder of a Roald Dhal character.

"Yes. It does take some getting used to," I say, forcing a big smile.

Luckily, I've got this thing about keeping my spaces tidy, so she gets the full impact of the room at its best. Not that I am looking to impress her in any way. I just want to get this session or whatever it is over and done with.

And yes, I did think about sending her away, but I felt guilty. She obviously paid for the cab here from God knows where, and she doesn't exactly look like she's flush with cash. The headscarf. The practical shoes are scuffed and have seen better days. The ill-fitting coat—at least two sizes too big—in garish bright green. Most likely from a second-hand store.

And anyway, there's something about the lady. I feel like she's in need. She could probably use some positivity.

So, I know this is going to sound weird. Especially since it's coming from me, Sarah gets it, of course. But then, she's into that mystical stuff. But, well, there's something about the study. Something I can't quite place. But believe me when I say that this room seems to be channelling its own energy. What I mean by that is that if hugging the oak tree at Dolce Vita that eventually laid down its life to save ours made you feel as good as hugging a loved one, then this, well, this is one step further.

I've discovered, and please try not to roll your eyes, that it doesn't matter what mood I'm in, the moment I walk in here, everything starts to change in me. It's like some kind of spiritual reset button where the default setting is warmth, calm, peace and tranquillity.

And the light in here; well, it's an artist's wet dream, perpetually shifting and morphing with the sun's movement.

Yeah. I know what that sounds like. Either way, I've concluded that even if it is in some way psychosomatic, the result remains the same, so does it really matter?

I direct the guest to one of the cream couches in the centre of the room. Today's view over the lake is so vivid through the self-cleaning glass that it feels like we're floating over it.

"*Mój Boże*," I hear my guest breathe as she takes a seat. "You have a beautiful home."

See?

"Thank you. It really is something else," I say, taking a seat in the black wingback chair opposite her.

"You must make lots of money with your job," she declares, moving over to the glass and looking out through the trees.

I'm not sure how to answer that, so instead, I just smile, inanely because, well, I haven't really received much external feedback, and I realise I'm feeling just a little bit embarrassed.

How about that?

"Please," I say.

My visitor turns to me, looks at my outstretched arm, and, horror of all horrors, the couch.

"You not live here long?" she asks, walking over to the couch and unbuttoning her coat. I notice now that there's a hole on the sleeve.

"No, not long," I respond.

She takes off the coat and holds it aloft while looking around the room. "You not have, what you say, stand for coat, though."

I smile. "No, now that you mention it. I don't. But there's a closet in the hallway. I could gladly hang it in there for you," I say, standing up.

"No, tis okay. I put it here next to me," she says, shaking, folding, and then carefully placing it on the sofa like it's the most valuable thing she owns, "Tis okay?"

"Oh yes. Of course," I say, retaking my seat just as a waft of that coat-shake reaches me, bringing with it a cloud of musty air like damp clothes that have been sitting in the laundry basket for too long.

"My boss, she no like it when coats are brought into the house. She say it bring diseases from outside?"

"Your boss?" I ask as I watch her take a seat opposite me.

"Yes. My boss. I work for one of those country houses down by the Beaulieu."

"The river?"

She nods, still distracted. Perhaps somewhat intimidated by her surroundings.

Okay. Maybe the room hasn't quite worked its magic on her yet.

"Can I get you something, Maja? Water or something?"

"No. I'm fine. Thank you," she says in that clipped accent that manufactures words from the front and not the back of her mouth. Then, she proceeds to untie her headscarf, folds it, and then places it on top of her coat. I can see now that she has dark hair. It must be long because it's braided, then coiled tightly on top of her head.

She touches it to make sure it's still in place before brushing invisible creases from her skirt, which I imagine is part of her uniform of blouse and grey cardigan.

She continues frowning at those creases for a while before allowing those curious eyes to rove around the room once more.

She has a hard face with many more creases than I first thought and not many laughter lines around those eyes.

"Tis your family over there?" she asks suddenly.

She's referring to that photo of me on the beach with my parents. I left it on my desk next to the box containing the other relics from Dolce Vita since I couldn't decide what to do with them.

I told Sarah that I was thinking of hanging them over the side unit in here, but when I offered them up to the wall, they seemed out of place. Didn't belong.

I don't even know if I want them here, but I also don't want to seem ungrateful. Maj thought she was doing a good thing. She wasn't to know that I'm still psychologically scarred for whatever reasons.

They're just bloody pictures, for Christ's sake!

Anyway, I left them on the desk. And now, I'm going to have

to justify it.

So, I force a smile. "Actually, that one is of my parents and me. At what used to be our holiday home," I say, feigning fondness at the memory.

Then I move quickly to the other photo sitting opposite, which is of Toby and me. It was a random image that I have no clue how but somehow, presumably directly from my phone at the time, had backed itself up to my cloud account. One beautiful solitary photo of my boy and me. I was thrilled and queasy when I came across it because the moment my mind registered the image, I was absorbed by it. Instantly transported back to that morning.

It's a selfie. Taken by the river. Toby, eyes wide and chestnut brown, sandy blonde hair gleaming in the early morning sun, is holding his first catch of the day up to the camera while I arm wrapped around him, fingers folded into a shaka sign, am grinning proudly, and sticking my tongue out.

Shaka sign. You know what that is, right? It's when you fold down all your fingers on one hand but your pinkie and your thumb and then turn the palm of your hand to face the recipient.

I know this how? That's right. My adorable walking encyclopaedia of a son. He informed me that the shaka hand gesture symbolises *reverence, solidarity, and friendship*. I just did that sign because it's the kind of thing blokes do when having their photo taken, but it was my son who enlightened me to its actual relevance in that moment.

My lovely boy.

Anyway, if you look closely, you can see there's a certain sheen to my eyes.

Toby.

"That's my son, Toby," I declare with a smile.

She nods knowingly.

Small talk. My guest is feeling nervous. Unsure. Eyes looking every which way. Grabbing onto the family photos like a drowning person does a life raft. Yes, I heard that analogy too.

Ocean. Drowning. Ugh.

Shit. I didn't even realise. Maybe it isn't my guest who's nervous but me projecting onto her.

No. She's definitely looking for signs of my humanity. Wife. Children. Family.

"So, he's the one?" she says suddenly.

"I'm sorry?"

"I mean to say, he no live here with you?"

That was phrased like a question, but it sounded more like a statement, and she must see this in my face because she adds, "No toys, very clean."

Curious question. Live? Not quite. "What about you?" I ask, heading off the topic because I'm already starting to feel that stifling prickle of sorrow creeping up on me, even in here, and quite frankly, I don't fancy talking about my son with a complete stranger.

"Me? I have no family."

"Nobody?"

I watch her wring her hands together. "No. just my parents. But they live back in Polonia. You been there?"

I shake my head. "Poland? No. I can't say I have."

"I know Kraków is famous for one thing, but 'tis actually a beautiful place, especially when it snows. What you call? It's like a fairy tale."

"Yes. I've seen the castle and the square. It also used to be the capital of Poland. Is that right?"

She smiles. "You know your geography, Mr. Battista."

"I'm no expert. Just a few things I've caught on travel shows. And please call me Marco. My father was called Mr. Battista."

"Oh, you have a different name?"

I laugh. "No. It's just an expression. Something people say when someone addresses them formally."

She nods, but from the squint in those grey eyes, I'm not sure she actually understood.

I give her a few seconds to see if she offers anything further to the conversation, but she doesn't. So, "Maja, you mentioned your boss earlier. Not liking it when coats are brought into the house. What exactly do you do?"

"I'm housekeeper," she says confidently.

I could probe her more about work, but I want to know more about her family history since I don't have any information about her. I need to get organised if I'm going to start seeing people. I don't even have a notebook. I'm totally unprepared for this.

"So, what about you, Maja? Any children?"

"No. No children," she says in a much softer tone. "I wanted but, um, Brian...he..." she trails off.

"Brian?" I prompt.

She hesitates then, "My husband."

"He's English?"

"With a name like that? Yes. We don't have many Brian back in Polonia."

I smile. "You met him when you came over here?"

"No," she smiles at the memory, "we met in Poland a very long time ago now."

"Oh, right. What was he doing there?"

"Work. He driver. Was there with some other colleague."

"Right. So that's where you met?"

"Yes. We met at a bar in Kraków. I work there as a part-time job." I watch her face crease into a smile as she recalls the memory. "I serve him drink, and he buy double and ask if I want to drink with him. Of course, I said no, I was working, but he was, what-you-say, um, very insistent."

"Did you drink with him?"

"No. I lose my job. My boss there. He was very strict. But Brian, he come back the next night. He told me story that he was leaving soon to come back in England and that I couldn't send him away without at least one, what you say now, date."

"And you went?"

Another pause as she considers the question. "Well, he make such a fuss in the end that I had to say yes just to shut him up. I mean, I need money, and I didn't want to lose my job."

"Not because you liked him then?"

She thinks, shrugs, and then smiles once more before making pincers with her thumb and forefinger. "Trochę. A little bit."

"Just a little bit?"

"At first, yes. He wasn't, what you say, my kind, but he keep coming back again and again. Bring me chocolate and flowers. I still not sure." She smiles, but it's an empty one.

We pause here as there's a flutter of movement beyond the glass, closely followed by the honk of a trio of geese as they flap their way from one side of the lake to the other.

"It really is beautiful here," Maja says dreamily, looking out, "peaceful. You're so lucky with view of lake too. I used to have view like dis."

"Yes? Where in Poland?"

She doesn't answer. Instead, she continues gazing out of the window.

I give her a while before turning to her and asking, "So, what happened?"

Eventually, she turns her attention back to the room. Her face emotionless. Like we've just been talking about the brickwork of the house and not her courtship with her husband. There's no nostalgia there. No wistful smile of reminiscence.

"What do you mean?"

"Your husband. Did you talk to him?"

She shrugs. "I don't know. He come back in England."

"Oh. Did you miss him?"

Another shrug. "No time. I was busy working job and taking care of my mother. She been sick most her life. I take care of her from young age."

"You don't have any brothers or sisters?"

She shakes her head, and I can see melancholy behind those eyes, but I'm not sure if it's because of the thought of not having any siblings or the memory of her youth.

I decide to move the subject back. "So, Brian, I'm assuming he stayed in touch because he became your husband."

"Yes. He visit sometime, you know, with work."

"So, things started to get serious?"

"Kind of."

"Kind of?"

"Well, it was not like young people of today if that is what you expect," she says, dismissively, like she's now regretting the subject.

Which only makes me more curious. "So, you came to England to be with Brian?"

She hesitates and then nods. "Yes. Yes."

"And it's good? Your relationship is going well?"

She nods. "Yes. Brian's nice. You know, charming. He was good at that. Good at making people like him. Very, what you say, cheeky Englishman when he's in the mood."

"Only when he's in the mood?"

She thinks about this. "Well, you know what you English are like sometimes; you can be, how you say, grumpy."

"And Brian... he's grumpy?"

"Yes. That I no like."

There is a seriousness to her tone. But then, almost as if she notices that she's overshared, she follows it up with the familiar, "But he can be very nice most of the time." She pins a smile at the end of the sentence, but it's one of those that garner the interest of the lips but not the eyes.

I consider whether or not to press the subject right now but conclude that it's probably best to circle back to it.

"So, Maja, earlier you mentioned your job. Tell me a bit about that. Have you worked there long?"

"Oof. Many years."

"What's it like?"

She rolls her eyes. "It's okay, but the lady... she's... what you say..." she flaps her arms around in the air and adds, dramatically, "bah bah bah bah bah bah... very dramatic. You know, difficult. Like one of those actress and very, what you say, eccentric. Just like in that book?"

I think about this.

"You know, Great Expectations."

"Mrs. Havisham?"

"Yes, her."

"You like Dickins?"

"Of course. Who doesn't?"

The question was posed with a furrow of her bushy eyebrows.

I nod. "So, she was jilted by her husband?"

"No. He just drop dead."

"Oh, right. And now she's angry that he left her?"

"Why would she be angry? He left her all the money. Or so she think. Pah!" she says with a smirk. The first emotional reaction of any kind since she arrived here.

"Oh, it's just you mentioned Mrs. Havisham. I had this image..." I trail off here, "never mind."

"She's Mrs. Havisham because she live alone and is mad all the time, not because she likes to walk around in her wedding dress."

Okay. That told me. "Right. I understand now."

I give her several seconds as I've just noticed that the wildlife outside has either taken an early night or is busy eavesdropping.

"Brian," she says, suddenly, breaking the silence, "he says we need the money. So, I had to find a job as soon as I get here from Poland. And there's not much in the village, so I take a full-time job nursing home in the next town."

I must have frowned or something because she quickly qualifies that with, "That was before I took the job with Mrs. Havisham." She turns to look at the door. It was a fleeting movement but obvious.

I cock my head.

"What is it?"

She laughs and shakes her head. "It's nothing."

"Really? Please. I'd like you to finish the thought," I say with an encouraging smile.

But she just gives me another shake of the head and looks away once more. "What was I saying?"

I glance at the door and then back at her. "You were telling me about your job at the nursing home."

"Yes. So, Brian say we need money, so I take job, but I no drive which mean I get bus there and back every day."

"What was it like working there?"

She shrugs. "It okay. I care for my matka most of my life so..." another shrug, "but Brian, he no like it."

"Why not?"

"The money not good and getting there, it difficult. No, getting there was okay but getting home not okay. You see, when Brian not in country, tis good, but when he is in England, not so good."

"Why is that?"

"Well, you know, you're a man. You come home, and you expect dinner on table, no?"

I smile at the thought of Sarah donning an apron with slippers in one hand and a pipe in the other. I rock my head from side to side. "Well—"

"Exactly," she continues after clocking the look on my face. "Well, the bus, it has its own timetable, I no control that, but Brian…" she pauses and sighs, "he come home too many times to empty house and no food. And that make him unhappy.

"So, I ask him, what do you expect me to do? We need money. And he say he no care… you're gonna have to find another job. So, I tell him, there is no job in the village. No job. And so he—" she stops abruptly, brushes her hand over her neck, and then touches her hair like it might suddenly have escaped the shackles of the braid before resettling in her seat once more.

"And he?" I prompt.

She looks at me for a long time. Dark eyes scrutinizing mine before saying calmly, "Well, he no like it."

"So, what happened?"

She thinks about my question and presumably her answer before coming back with, "Well, one day, I'm in the shop. You know it?"

I nod. "Yes. Go there regularly."

"Well, I in the shop to buy bread and I overhear this woman talking. Well, no, not talking. She was, you know, very mad. She was like… *that lady, she's unbearable. I don't care how rich she is. I don't care about the money. I'm never going back there, never!*" she mimics the woman's words in an angry whisper. Then continues, "She was, how you say, very hot, you know, angry. Her friend try to calm her down, but she not care. She complained the whole time she was in shop, and she no care who hear her.

"So, I wait. I wait until they are going, and I go over to the lady behind the counter. She is still watching them out of the door, and then she look at me and roll her eyes. And I ask her; I ask who was that lady talking about? And she tell me.

"She say this Mrs. Havisham lady how she live alone and how she never leave the house. How workers no last there because she, what-you-say? Impossible. Nobody like her. The pay is bad, and, she is a… *czarownica*. How you say? A witch?

"So, I ask. Where does this woman live? And she is about to tell me, then she stop and say. *Oh right...* and she look at me."

She pauses on that note, clutches her hands together, and starts wringing them, and I realise now just how dirty her nails are. I saw that a couple were broken and ragged earlier, but the ones that aren't look stained brown, or is that dirt?

Focus.

"What do you think she meant by that?"

My guest shrugs and pulls a face. "What they always mean. We Polish always do the jobs that English people no like."

"Did that offend you?"

"Me? She brushes those fingers under her chin. "No. I not offended. I'm used to it.

"So, anyway I go home, I make Brian his dinner and then, on the next day, I tell work I am going to be late. I walk up the hill to the house."

"And was it the person at the village store who gave you directions?"

She nods.

"So, you weren't put off by her or the way she looked at you?"

"Who? The serving lady at the shop?"

"No. The one you overheard, complaining."

She lets out a short laugh. "Of course not. She's English. No? You English are always complaining. On front page of newspaper, about money, your jobs, your life. You're never happy unless you're complaining. Besides, I live here for long time now. I know how nasty some of you are. Also, I worked in care home. I think, how much worse can this old lady be? Besides, to me, I only care about the money and that she live ten-minute walk from my home.

"So, I arrive at this house, I ring the bell, and who do you think answer the door? That Englishwoman."

"The one from the store?"

"Yes. Barbara or whatever her name is. The one that complain, the one that say she never go back. She open the door, take one look at me and says, *oh, I suppose you're here for job then?*"

"She knew you were there for the job?"

"Yes."

"How did she know?"

She shakes her head. "I have no idea. I assume that she hear my accent and automatically think that I am there to take her job. That is what most English people think, no? They think that we come here to steal their jobs. They not realise that the only jobs we take are the ones that they don't want, don't like, or cannot be bothered to do."

I rock my head, pensively, as I think she may have a point, but I don't want to get into that.

"So, what did you say to her?"

"I said yes. You don't seem to want it."

"Right. And what did she say?"

"She get, what do you say, in my face, snarl like dog and say, *you people are all the same, aren't you?* I ask, what you mean, hard-working?"

I can't help but smile at that clap-back. "How did she respond to that?"

"I don't know because just as she was about to say something, the woman with the posh voice interrupt us. She wants to know who was at the door."

"Who does?"

"Mrs. Havisham."

"Right Mrs. Havisham. Maja, I have to ask, why is it that you haven't used her real name? I noticed that since you got here, you haven't mentioned her name once. Why is that?"

She shrugs, "I just don't think it's right. You know, appropriate."

"Okay. What happened next?"

"This woman, Barbara, look back into the house then at me and with big pig eyes says to me, *"Fuck you, fuck her and fuck working my notice!* And walk off."

"Just like that?"

"Just like that. And, that's how I get the job."

"Wow, Maja. That's some interview. You handled it really well, though, I have to say."

She shrugs as if it was all in a day's work.

There's a commotion through the glass as a pair of giant wood pigeons seemingly stage an enactment of the story I just heard. Maja notices it too but appears as unfazed as she seemingly was by her encounter with her predecessor on that doorstep.

"So, you've got the job. It's closer to home, making it much easier to get to, and you're back on time for dinner. Brian must be pleased. Right?"

Another shrug. "He likes the money. Yes."

"But not your boss?"

"Not really. It's fine most of the time, but he no like when she ring the house in the middle of the night."

"She does that?"

"Oh yes. All the time."

"What for?"

"Lots of reason… from wetting the bed to hearing noises. And it's okay when Brian no home because I stay at the house with her but when he's back, and I go home for the night then she no like."

"I see."

I think about everything I've just been told. And one thing's for sure, Maja's a bit of a hard nut. Which, for me, translates as someone who's been through the mill. Much of that is obvious. And yet, something tells me that we haven't even scratched the surface. But this is a good start. This is a fantastic start and a good time to ask that all-important question.

"Maja. I think we've made a very good start. A great start. But we're almost out of time, and there's one question I normally ask my patients that I'd like to put to you if that's okay."

"Okay."

"Why exactly are you here? What is it that you feel I can do for you?"

She hesitates, eyes flicking to the door once more as if she wants to do a runner.

I sit forward in my chair. "Maja. It's okay. You can tell me. What is it?"

Her response is so chilling that it brings tears to my eyes.

12

HOUSE OF TWO HALVES

FROST LAKE MANOR. 13:50.

So, you know supernatural movies where the main character drives up a long-gravelled driveway of potholes and puddles left behind by the previous night's rain when, suddenly, a dilapidated mansion peeks through the gnarled limbs of trees? Well, that's what the drive over here is like.

Frost Lake Manor is classed as a Grade 2 Tudor Victorian mansion nestled in 50 acres of its own rolling parkland. Featuring a formal garden, large copses, and attractive mixed woodland. It measures 17,000 square feet over two floors, plus a tower and cellar. It's constructed from chisel-dressed (cut) ashlar (grey stone) under a pitched slate roof. Now, this may not sound like an important detail but, apparently, it is when it comes to property valuation.

I drive the car onto the walled courtyard and stop behind Irvin's battered truck.

I've suggested that he might want to trade it in for something new. He asked, *what like Battista Properties?* I told him that it didn't sound too shabby, but he hasn't quite taken me up on that yet.

I step out. Crows caw a begrudging greeting. Wood pigeons coo, birds tweet happily, and the rest of the world, well, it just doesn't exist.

"Come on, Buddy," I say, barely opening the backdoor in time before the gold bundle leaps out. "Okay, easy," I say in between laughs as the dog nearly knocks me off my feet before trotting around the courtyard, stopping only to sniff the occasional weed.

I look up at the large promenade balcony about ten, fifteen feet above. Behind it, dominating the centre of the house, is an octagonal stair tower with a ragged-looking flag flapping cheerlessly in the breeze. The emblem it carries faded long ago.

There's no doubt that Frost Lake Manor has seen better days, and I imagine that back then, it would have been quite impressive to arrive here and be greeted by his lord and ladyship standing on that balcony and waving like royals welcoming their subjects. Now, it's just the hound and me, and the balcony is grey, weatherworn, flaky, and scarred with veiny desiccated ivy.

Yes, this building is impressive at first impression. It's only when you look closely that you can see the cracks in the wall, the rot in the window frames, the courtyard overgrown with weeds, and the rusty, moss-riddled wrought iron gates leading to the sides and rear of the building.

The main entrance is via part-glazed double oak doors located inside what is commonly known as a Porte-Cochere. Which I was told is French for *Carriage Porch*.

"Come on, Buddy," I say, looking at the dog that was following but has now decided to stop and stare instead. "Well, come on then," I prompt. But he doesn't move. He just remains seated on his hind legs with one and a half ears up, scanning. "What's the matter with you?" I ask. The dog simply cocks his head and stares around me. "Wow. Okay, well… if you're not coming in, you need to wait here. Alright? STAY," I say loudly, holding up the palm of my hand. "STAY."

He twitches his ears back and forth, which I accept as acknowledgement.

OK. So, you know that stereotypical drive up here? Well, allow your mind, if you will, to venture beyond the doorway to every haunted mansion fable you've ever heard. This place looks just like it.

This is just one of the reasons why I refused to move us in here.

Don't get me wrong. It's a beautiful place. I mean, the entrance hall alone is a sight to behold with one of those impressive split part cantilevered staircases directly in front of you as you enter the building with no less than eight bedrooms arranged around the arcaded gallery landing featuring two theatre balcony-like archways that overlook the hall.

Four doors lead off to various rooms. To the left, as you enter, is the billiard room (aka the study), then the library. And to the right are doors to the drawing room and dining room. To the back of the hallway are two other doors to the kitchen and service areas.

The space is beautifully lit, thanks to the waterfall of natural daylight cascading in through the giant glass lantern roof.

Or so the marketing PDF had us believe. When we first came here, the reality was that most of the glass had been smothered by black sludge and vegetation that had reduced the light to patches of distilled gloom. The only area that wasn't covered was a section where the glass had been smashed through, allowing the elements to have their wicked way in here, causing the timber staircase to rot in sections. The place looked miserable with flaky plaster and wallpaper like blistered skin, a collection of oil lanterns scattered about the place that we've since discovered is because of an issue with dodgy wiring, and, somewhat surreally, weeds sprouting on the dirty, bird-poo smeared floor. It stank too of dust, decay, mould, and I can't be sure, but maybe even a rotting dead animal.

Montgomery Parker-Cohen—or Monty—is every bit the stereotype. To the point that when he first showed up at Frost Lake Manor in his sage green vintage Citroen DS, I started laughing because, for a split second, I thought he was a prank somehow set up by the lads.

I soon learned that the man with a dandyish demeanour, an awfully posh accent, dressed in an immaculate blue pinstripe suit, mustard cravat, and brown brogues was the antique dealer I'd been so eager to meet.

It turns out that Monty may well come across as a mild-mannered, scatty character, but he is, in fact, a shrewd businessman with several antique parlours and a global operation trading and exchanging artworks.

My plan was to install him at the manor for a while before the restoration began, but we missed our window thanks to the delay in exchanging contracts which meant that I lost him to a sabbatical slash festival in Kathmandu.

This has led to the lads having to work around all the junk, I mean valuable artefacts, by removing paintings from walls and storing them in the drawing room along with the smaller pieces of furniture in anticipation of Monty's arrival.

The plan is simple. Monty will value all the tangible assets and will then assign them to three separate categories. *High Value,* items a grand or more which will be removed from the manor and sold at auction to raise desperately needed funds for this hair-raising endeavour. *Medium,* items less than a grand but more than three hundred. These are items that will most likely be left at the property. Their collective value will be added to the total of *fixtures and fittings* and thus the overall valuation of the property. *Low*-value items are hardly worth anything and can be either scrapped or added to the tally of fixtures and fittings.

"Good morning, Monty," I say, pushing aside the dust curtain that is now hanging over the door to the billiard room.

"Marco, good afternoon, it's so good of you to join us," the valuer says, from his workstation made from three wood crates stacked atop of each other crowned by a tiny notebook. I have to say, I was surprised when I saw him whip out the computer to build his spreadsheet inventory. I half expected the man whose wardrobe *du jour* is a linen suit with yellow polka dot cravat to use a quill and ledger.

This bloke has such a dry sense of humour, though, that I often find it difficult to work out if he's making a joke or having a dig. I'll assume it's the former since I'm supposed to be the boss around here, although sometimes I wonder.

"Well, some of us have got to work for a living, Monty. Not unless you've found a few pieces worth a couple of million each," I say with a grin.

TONY MARTURANO

"All will be revealed in good time," he says flatly, peering down his round spectacles at his computer screen. "Did I mention that the power keeps cutting out around here?" he asks without looking up.

"Yep. A couple of times now. I'm expecting someone to come out soon."

"I can't be certain," the man replies casually, "But I believe that's what you said *last week*," the last bit is delivered as a sing-song which I've come to learn is Monty's way of saying *same old song* without just saying it.

I smile at the man who should, by nature, irritate me but doesn't. I can only assume that's because I'm unconsciously aware of the fact that he's about the only one around here that is working to generate cash from trash. "Always a pleasure, Monty," I say with a smile.

I leave the Billiard room and step back into the entrance hall, which is already one step closer to being restored to its former glory. Gone is the gloomy, leaky glass ceiling. In its place is now a plain—in comparison—yet expensive replacement. It looks much bigger and brighter in here now that the space is flooded with glorious natural light.

I'm still torn between being excited about the repair or depressed that the extent of the water damage is now much more obvious in the cold light of day.

Irvin thinks that some of the damage to the stairs and banister isn't as bad as it looks and that it can be restored. I have my doubts. But hey, what do I know.

The debris, bird excrement, and fertilised vegetation that had a residence here has also been evicted. The place is looking more like a mansion and not a rundown stable.

Frost Lake Manor is now officially a house of two halves. Irvin's plan to refurbish one side of the building and then the other to facilitate early viewings is underway.

It isn't a perfect solution because anybody who knows about home improvement knows that it's a process that follows one basic order:

Strip out and removal.

Structural Fix—floors, ceilings, walls.

First Fix—plumbing, heating wiring.

Plastering, flooring.

Second Fix—plumbing, heating, wiring.

Bathroom, kitchen fit-out.

Decoration.

We're a bit of a hybrid of those things now, with step one being subject to Monty's progress.

But things are happening, and while we're still at least a couple of weeks off from anything near presentable, it looks like Irvin may well be pulling this off. Have I mentioned how much I love that bloke?

I follow the tinny sound of the radio through one of the back doors and into the pot-marked disaster zone of what I think was the kitchen. I find Irvin yanking an old dresser away from the wall along with Drew and some other bloke I've never seen before.

"Afternoon, boys."

It's warm in here. Dusty and sweaty, so just as well, I didn't come empty-handed.

"*Deeth Daa*, Marco mate," Irvin says, stopping what he's doing, removing his flat cap, and mopping the sweat from his balding scalp. I keep forgetting the bloke is from the Southwest, and now and then, he enjoys throwing a word at me. This one I know is Cornish for *Good Day*.

"Looks like dirty thirsty work in here?"

"Just a tad, yeah."

"Just as well, I picked this up from the store," I say, rummaging in the bag I'm carrying and handing out bottles of fizz and water to each of them.

"Where are the other lads?" I ask.

"They've made a start in the dining room. Taking stuff down for Lord Monty."

"You know, I think he'd probably like that nickname."

"He doesn't," Drew chimes in after taking a swig from his bottle. "Dean tried it on him, and he just shot him a look."

I don't know why but that makes me smile. "I see you installed him in the east wing," I say.

"Well, it made sense, that way he can get on with 'is bit and we can get on with ars," Irvin says flatly. I don't think he has much time for Monty, although there's an element of professional respect there.

"Oh, please tell me Sparky's coming out soon. He just mentioned the electrics to me again," I say.

"The bloke's already been out. Says he can't find nout wrong," Irvin says, after taking a swig from his bottle.

"We know that can't be right. These people had oil lanterns all over the place for a reason."

"Well, as you know, he thinks the only other thing it can be is a problem with the board. It needs replacin', but he can't get out to look at it for a few weeks because he's got other urgent jobs on."

"Do we need to find someone else? I know he's a mate of yours and everything–"

"It ain't about us being mates, Marco. The bloke was ready to start work; it ain't his fault we dragged our 'eels in making a start."

I nod. "Fair enough. But–"

"If I find it's holdin' us up, I'll get someone else in. As it stands, he's due out in a couple of weeks. Sooner if he can."

"OK. It's just when I saw the cellar door open in the hallway. I thought the man had actually made an appearance."

"Nah."

"Have you been down there then?"

"Nope. We've got enough gettin' on with."

"Oh right."

"Hey Marco, come take a look at this." It's Drew, and he's aiming the light beam from his mobile phone at the wall where that dresser must have rested for decades, maybe even hundreds of years.

"What is it?" I say, walking over to him, careful not to stumble on some of the chunks of mortar and plaster on the floor.

I peer around the cobweb strands hanging like scarfs from the dresser, but instantly snap my head back when I see hundreds of tiny spiders scampering away from the light.

"I just saw big mamma spider disappear into that crack in the floor next to your foot," Drew narrates. "And she's a beast!" he adds with a note of excitement.

I leap backwards, nearly stumbling over some of the debris on the floor. Muscles taut, jaw clenched, and breaths instantly coming

CURSED

quick and shallow.

"Oh, Drew, what the ell is wrong with you? You know Marco ates spiders," Irvin grumbles.

"It's actually a phobia," I add, taking another step backwards while scanning the space around me. "There's a difference."

"Sorry, Marco, mate. I didn't realise."

Something tells me that he did. Now I'm considering how much he might be able to claim in damages from a tribunal after I've punched him in the face.

I circumnavigate Irvin, make my way out of the door and into the courtyard. It's cooler and fresher out here, and I breathe deeply, allowing both the shock and the irritation to subside. *Forgive him, Marco, for he knows not what a dick he is.* That or he doesn't care.

The boring grey-slate sky is starting to drizzle.

"Miserable day, ain't it?" Irvin says, joining me out in what appears to be a courtyard. Kal told me that this used to be the herb garden. Not anymore. Now, it's just a square courtyard studded with wild ferns and stone troughs full of weeds.

"Sure is," I say, squinting into the miniature precipitation.

"On the radio, they were sayin' we might get some freakish early snow this year. Somitt to do with global warming."

"I'll believe it when I see it," I say glumly.

"Sorry about im," Irvin adds.

I force a smile. "It's fine. I know what he's like, remember? Besides, even I know it's ridiculous. But then, that's the very definition of irrational fear; it's *irrational*, even for grown men like me. That doesn't mean I didn't want to punch him in the face, though."

"You already did that once, remember?" Irvin says with a knowing grin.

"Oh yeah." The memory brings a smile to my face as I look out onto the back lawn and gardens. That's when I spot him. A man I've never seen before, wearing green overalls and a cap, wandering around the place. "Who the hell's that?"

"Oh, that's the gardener," Irvin says casually.

"Gardener?"

"Yeah."

My heart skips a beat. "So, you *can* see him then?" I ask.

My foreman turns to me and squints, curiously, as if it's me now playing a practical joke. "Yeah. I can see him. Why?"

I'm just about to respond when my mobile phone starts ringing. I pull it out of my pocket and look at the screen. It's David.

"Alright, mate?"

I soon discover that he is not.

13

A FRIEND IN NEED

HOLT· LATE AFTERNOON·

Rather fittingly, a band of marauding rain clouds had devoured the dregs of the afternoon light triggering premature dusk when Holt announced David and Aaron's arrival.

Now, the three of us are sat in chairs out on the lounge balcony, watching blanket lightning like gunfire backlight the manor in the distance. Not unlike my friend's mood, the air is thick and charged with the birthing pains of a rainstorm.

"Okay," I say, holding up my hot beverage. "We're all sitting comfortably. Tell me what the hell's happened?"

"Where's Sarah?" David asks flatly.

"She's still at work, David. Now, stop stalling and tell me, what's wrong?"

"I'm tryin'. I just can't bring meself to say the bloody words. I'm so fucking mad," he seethes. Open-taxi-door ears scarlet even in the dim light.

I look at Aaron, who steps in, "It's the venue. They've cancelled the wedding."

I frown at him. "What do you mean *they* cancelled the wedding? Why?"

"For *circumstances beyond their control*, they've had to close shop. At first, they didn't wanna say why but then, when I insisted, they explained it was due to some kind of infestation. The whole place has gotta be treated, inspected, and then re-certified before they can reopen."

"How long will that take?"

Aaron shrugs. "No fuckin' idea. Weeks. Months even. Either way, it's useless to us because my folks, my friends, they're flyin' in next week."

"Shit," is all I can say to that.

"We're not the only ones they've let down. There are others. Some of the places I called told me that they had already been contacted by other couples looking for alternative venues."

"That's crap. How does this stuff even happen?"

"That's exactly what I asked?" David says, staring off over the lake.

"I've already told David that we should sue their fuckin' asses," Aaron says angrily.

"Well, what's the bloody point of that, Aaron?" David retorts. "It's not gonna help us now, is it? Your mates, your family ain't gonna have refundable tickets, are they!" David counters.

It's odd because I've seen him angry more times than I can remember in all the years that David and I have been friends. Often at me. But today, today is different. He's angry, yeah, but there's something else there. It's what comes after the rage, that kind of weary sadness, like an outnumbered soldier who has accepted his fate. This is nothing like him, and that bothers me.

"Okay. Okay," I wade in. "So, what have you done so far? You've tried to find somewhere else?"

"I was on the phone most of yesterday," Aaron responds, "it was me who got the call. Dave was in meetings most of the day. So, I tried to fix it before I had to tell him, but no luck," he says glumly.

"And that was sweet of you," David responds, touching his fiancé's arm.

"You knew yesterday?" I ask.

"Yeah, but he didn't tell me until this morning," David adds.

"Right. But you should have told me. I might have been able to help. I don't know how exactly but, still," I say thoughtfully.

"I know. And I thought about it, but I figured that you kinda have your hands full with the trial, the house, and… well, I didn't want to unload all this shit on you too."

It would be easy to think that the guy was trying to fob me off, but I genuinely believe he was trying to solve the problem without burdening us.

"Hey, this is exactly what best men are for, isn't it?" I say with an encouraging shrug.

Aaron nods. And I can see that he, too, has that look of a defeated warrior. In his case, literally, it's like he's failed in the most crucial mission of his life. I imagine that for an ex-marine, that's got to be tough to swallow.

"Okay," I begin, setting my cup down as thunder rumbles in the distance. "So, let's work the problem," I say like I'm somehow assuming control. "We have just over a week to go until the wedding of the year–"

"The century," Aaron says, winking at David and then looking back at me.

"Of the century… that's right… with a bunch of guests but no venue. You've called most of the obvious places but no joy at such short notice, and let's get real, David, anything less than a grand country hotel is going to have you whining like a little bitch, isn't that right?" I say that with a grin, but he just watches me pointedly. "Okay. Tough crowd. The reality is that it's your wedding day, so you're understandably going to want somewhere that is picturesque. I know you're keen on somewhere like that too, Aaron. Old country house. And I mean this place you'd chosen; it didn't come cheap. Just goes to show, sometimes, it isn't all about the money."

Oh, shit, I'm waffling like I have some kind of climax solution to this problem when I haven't got the foggiest. The reality is, trying to find a decent place at such short notice right on the tail end of summer is going to be nigh on impossible, not unless it's some kind of shit hole.

"At this stage, I'd settle for a hut in the middle of a field," David says desperately.

"Yeah, you say that, but if I found you a hut, you'd probably want to get that lot from *fabulous,* or is it *fairy makeovers*? What was the name of that shitty program you and Ellie used to watch all the time?"

I trail off because if looks could kill, I'd be keeled over by now. David's not in the mood. And who can blame him?

"Shit. In a different world, if we hadn't been delayed as much as we have, I'd gladly offer you the manor, but as you know, it's still pretty much a building site right now. I mean, you could have it here...."

Wait. What? I look up at both men hoping that I didn't just say that out loud, but judging by their expressions, I think I did! So, I do what any self-respecting best man would do. I try to backpedal because, well, that's just a ridiculous idea.

"Yeah! That's a fantastic idea," Aaron says breathlessly, turning to David for validation.

"Actually, well, I, um. Of course, I don't know if we can accommodate everyone. I mean, how many guests did you say there are? Forty-nine?"

"*One hundred* and forty-nine," Aaron says.

"One hundred and forty-nine people, here at Holt. Yeah. Piece of cake. We can easily accommodate them here."

No, we can't.

"Wow. That would be awesome, but are you sure?" Aaron asks.

Nope.

I look at David. His eyes have widened. His ears flushed again, but I'm assuming for a different reason this time which I'm hoping is good.

"Seriously though, this place is beautiful. It's perfect. But we couldn't ask you to do this, though. Could we?" Again, Aaron turns to David, who appears to have been rendered mute, unlike me and my verbal diarrhoea.

My friend, who always has an answer for everything, is gawking at me like I've just told him to go and take a run and jump off the jetty out there. I don't even know if that thing can hold one person, let alone two, three with the officiator person thingy. Will they be having one of those? What about facilities? Do we even have enough for all those people? Isn't there some kind of law about how many toilets you're supposed to have?

Stop overthinking!

Fuck.

"David? Are you alright, mate? You feeling as queasy as I am right now?" I ask with mock trepidation.

I watch my friend's bottom lip quiver. Okay. Not what I was expecting. "Um, so. Good, bad, rubbish idea?"

Several seconds pass. Thunder rumbles. A panicked nightingale flutters off into the woods. He's obviously as gobsmacked as the rest of us.

Then, "With everyfin you've got goin on, you wanna take on our weddin' too?" David says with such seriousness that I'm starting to think I may have offended him somehow.

"Well," I cock my head, "now that you put it like that. Sarah?! Where's Sarah!" I make a show of looking back inside the house. "She's normally my voice of reason. I'm obviously no good without her."

David launches himself out of his seat and pulls me into a crouch-like awkward hug. "Yeah, right. Okay. Is that a yes then?"

Several seconds drift by, and I'm not quite sure what's happening. I look at Aaron through my weird stronghold, and he just claps his hands together silently and mouths, *Thank you.*

"Dave? Everything alright, mate? You fallen asleep or something cos we've got plenty of perfectly comfortable couches inside," I say.

Eventually, my friend emerges from the weird hug thing, and I can see that his eyes are wet. That's major because my friend is from tough stock. He didn't have the easiest childhood because of his sexuality, but he's always refused to wear it as a badge. Consequently, he's learned to repress his feelings, often wrapping his emotions in wit and or sarcasm.

"Yes, mate. That's a grateful yes. But if you don't mind me asking…how the fuck are you gonna fit everybody in this place?"

And there he is. I put a big grin on my face. "I have no idea, but you let me worry about that," I say with as much confidence as I can muster, "in fact, I want you both to do that. This whole wedding thing has obviously worn you down. Let me deal with everything from now on?"

Wait. What? No! Don't say that!

"What do you mean?" David asks.

"Do you trust me?" Both men make a dramatic gesture of looking at each other. "Hey, come on, seriously. You trust me, don't you…? *Don't you?*"

It's David's turn to rock his head. "Kind of, yeah, but dude, you're talking about a wedding for a bunch of gays and hillbillies."

"Hey!" Aaron protests then thinks about it. "Yeah. I think that's fair. That's fair."

"Oi. Haven't you heard? I can turn over multimillion-pound mansions; you think I can't handle your wedding ceremony slash reception?" I watch their blank faces. "Okay… don't answer that. So, just one question before I tie myself to this thing. When you say gay wedding, you're not expecting floating rainbows and waiters with their arses hanging out, are you?" I deliver that last bit with an exaggerated disgusted face.

We laugh. And as the rain starts to fall, so does the reality of what I am offering to do here.

It's clear that this isn't just about helping a friend in need. It's so much more. These are two of the most important people in my life. Their happiness is paramount, especially on their wedding day. I have just made myself instrumental in that.

But then, Holt has fast become one of my favourite places to be in the world. I can't think of a more fitting location for these two men to tie the knot.

How am I going to coordinate, transform, and host a wedding here in just eight days?

I have no idea.

14

NIGHT LIGHTS

HOLT. 02:03 AM.

7 Days until the wedding. ♠

Have you ever seen lightning over a lake? I can tell you that it's truly spectacular. Watching that light show streak across the sky mirrored by the surface of the water is unlike anything I have ever seen. Add to that some freakish green and blue hue, and you're left with a natural performance seemingly conceived by a visual effects team.

We must have sat out on the balcony for at least another hour or so, planning the revised wedding. Then, after Sarah came home and as the rain fell in sheets, I left them chatting to rustle up toasted sandwiches and tea, which we ate while enjoying a front-row seat to autumn's tempestuous dual with the remnants of summer.

Now, several hours later, I'm sat up in bed after yet another of those bloody nightmares. This time, I felt a pair of cold and craggy hands around my throat. I don't know if it's my imagination, but I'm sure these bloody things are getting worse, and there are no prizes for guessing why.

In Doctor Holmes' patronising words, it would be because you're under a lot of pressure. Immense pressure.

Taking over the planning of my best mate's wedding will not have helped any, mainly because David is a bloody control freak. He must be desperate if he's letting me take over the planning of his big day.

Sarah disagrees. She thinks it's because he recognises how competent I am. You only need to look at how much you've accomplished in such a short period.

Yeah, get myself into a world of debt is what I wanted to say, but I held my tongue. She was being supportive, and I didn't want to reward her by being a miserable git.

So, now the boys have gone, and I am sitting up in bed with that familiar icky cold sweat, panting like I'm trying to imitate Buddy after he's been on a long run.

I look across at Sarah. She's sleeping soundly for a change. Normally, I disturb her sleep too when I start screaming in the dead of night. And I mean screaming, by the way, so you can imagine what that must sound like.

The rain has stopped by the sounds of it, but it remains a moonless night. One of those where if you sit still long enough and allow your hearing to tune in, the woodland comes alive with assorted night dwellers and, if I'm perfectly honest, I tend not to linger on that because–

"What the hell is that?"

Circular lights, like torch beams, slicing through the dark and gliding across the bedroom wall like miniature UFOs.

What… the… hell? There's somebody on the back lawn!

I glance over at Sarah, and in the faint blue LED light of our phone charger cables; I can see that her eyes are still closed. I consider waking her but dismiss the idea as I want to see what we're dealing with first, and I don't want to panic her unnecessarily.

I watch the beams. They're like searchlights, roaming all over the ceiling and walls, seeking out furniture and gradually drifting towards me.

How are they even doing this at this angle? We're at least two storeys above them.

I slide out of bed and onto the floor with a thump. My heart has already cranked up the nerves in my body, which are taut and ready for action. Slowly, I make my way over to the glass wall, and, like a soldier over the parapet, I carefully peer out.

Nothing. It's just dark out there.

I snap my head around. Scan the walls. The lights are gone.

I turn back to the glass—just darkness.

"Marco?"

"Oh! Bloody hell, Sarah."

"What are you doing?" my girlfriend asks sleepily.

I glance outside. "I, um. Nothing."

"Holt," she begins.

Yes, Sarah.

"Turn on the la–"

"No!" I interrupt.

Sorry. I didn't quite catch that.

"Cancel," I say.

Cancelling.

"What's going on?"

"Nothing. I just… I just had a bad dream." I lie because I don't want to tell her I've got this horrible feeling that we're being watched. "And I just wanted to stand here for a while with the lights out."

"Are you sure? Can I do anything?"

"Yeah, I'm sure. No, I'm fine. Go back to sleep," I say as calmly as I possibly can. Right before movement catches my eye, I turn back towards the glass just in time to see a light bob from the lawn across the boundary into the woods, illuminating trunks and branches.

"What the fuck?" I breathe.

"What is it? What's wrong?" Sarah is alert once more.

"I think there's someone outside."

"What?" There's alarm in her voice, and I want to tell her not to worry, but at this stage, I have no bloody clue who's out there.

"What are you doing?" she asks when she sees me slide into jeans and fleece.

"Marc, you don't even know who's out there."

"That's exactly why I need to find out."

"Maybe we should call security."

"It's a security company, Sarah. Not security."

"Then let's call the police."

"We don't even know who it is."

She thinks about this. "Then, I'm coming with you."

"Oh no, you're not."

"Why not?"

"Because, because, um, this is man's stuff."

"Man's stuff?" she echoes, "are you serious?"

"You know what I bloody mean. And we can discuss sexism in tense situations when I get back."

"But Marc–"

"Sarah, seriously. Just wait here. It's probably just horny teens who have probably done their business and already gone by now," I say, moving towards the door as she slides out of bed and pads across the room.

"Stay here with Buddy," I whisper before leaving the room and pulling the door shut behind me.

The house is eerily still. I've just realised that the whole bloody night is after the din of the rainstorm. Once again, I'm thankful for the night strips on the stairs while whistling that Happy song— which I hate—but I've concluded is much better than that two-tone piano chase theme from the Halloween film, which is otherwise following me down the stairs.

I consider turning on a light, but suddenly, I'm aware of the fact that we live in a glasshouse. At night, it's hard for us to see outside – without the floodlights. But easy for whoever is out there to see inside. It's the basic rule of lighting.

And I hate that detail right now, just like I hate the questions that keep introducing themselves with every step I take closer to putting myself in danger.

What are those lights searching for? Why haven't the safety lights come on? Why wasn't the perimeter breach triggered? Why didn't Buddy sense anything? He normally senses a bloody nit pissing, and yet tonight….

At the foot of the stairs, I approach one of the wall panels.

"Holt, confirm security system is armed."

The security system is disabled, Marco. Would you like me to enable it?"

My stomach lurches, winding my heart up into a thumping frenzy. That's impossible. I remember asking Holt to enable it last night. He, it confirmed my instruction. I'm sure it did.

Would you like me to enable it?

A bit fucking late now. "No."

"Holt, check for perimeter breaches."

There are no perimeter breaches.

"Holt, cycle all security cameras."

Okay.

The screen in front of me springs to life, and a black and white image of the front door materialises. Then the front garden, the side of the house, the back garden, and so on. I wait, pulse racing, mouth like sandpaper, for something to appear inside one of the frames.

It doesn't.

There's nothing out there according to this.

Yet, "What the hell was that?!"

A shadow. A bloody shadow just passed in front of one of the hallway windows. There is someone out there! "Holt, turn on all external security lights."

As you wish.

There's a whiteout of light on the monitor as all the external floodlights spring to life, filling the house with light. I imagine it looking like a football stadium out there, scaring whoever it is back into the darkness of the woods.

I take over the display panel and use the arrow keys to cycle through the various security cameras, but each frame looks exactly the same.

Empty.

Someone definitely walked by the corridor window. It was just for a split second, but I saw it, I bloody saw it!

Bong. Bong. Bong. Marco, there is someone at the front door. Would you like to see who it is?

That familiar and dreaded rodent of terror scuttles down my spine. What the actual eff is going on? It's nearly two-thirty in the bloody morning.

Slowly, I step back and look up the corridor towards the front door as if I can see through it.

BANG! BANG! BANG!

Someone or something has given up ringing the doorbell and is now hammering on the front door, instantly transporting me back to those nights at Dolce Vita. And suddenly, I'm afraid.

Bong. Bong. Bong. Marco, there is someone at the front door. Would you like to see who it is?

No. I don't want to see! I don't!

The security lights buzz and flicker, creating a strobe effect inside the house for added terror.

Just answer the door! Just ANSWER THE FUCKING DOOR!

I yelp when the dining room light suddenly glows to life—filling the empty hallway with light.

Oh my…

Bong. Bong. Bong. Marco, there is someone at the front door. Would you like to see who it is?

I realise that I am holding my hand over my mouth to suffocate a scream. And yet, slowly, shakily, I remove that hand, and with a trembling voice, I utter, "On screen,"

A bolt of terror surges through me when I see that the front door light is somehow horrifyingly inconveniently disabled, but the security and path lights perform a shockingly good job at highlighting the humanoid silhouette of someone or something standing out there. It's in profile to the camera, staring at the front door, eyes glinting like cat eyes in the dark.

Oh my God. What is that?

I bite on my fingers to suppress the noise that is drifting out of my mouth.

Then, I find myself asking the questions I learnt both during my rehabilitation and my training designed specifically for situations like this.

Could this really be happening here and now?

Yes.

Is anybody else affected by it?

No.

On balance, how likely is this to be real?

Most likely.

15

THE ROT

HOLT· 10:35·

By the time Buddy and I return from the morning run, I've already taken my first shower of the day. Running through the rain-washed trees probably wasn't the best idea, but I wanted to perform *casual* reconnaissance on the property.

By casual, I mean that I wanted to have a look around the place for obvious signs of intrusion while at the same time feeling like I wasn't indulging my neurosis. A run, under dripping branches, through soggy leaves, and over the muddy trail seemed like the only way to do that.

Of course, I didn't discover any damning evidence and have concluded that if I were to base last night's mind-trip on evidence found, then it never happened. But then, I never did complete my training as a Navaho scout, which means it's doubtful I'd notice anything other than a giant yellow arrow pointing at a set of muddy footprints.

Shit.

I'm fine. I'm okay. Obviously, it was all just another hideous nightmare. Now seemingly upgraded to noctambulation. From the Latin word *noct* as in nocturnal and *ambulare,* to ambulate. In other words, bloody sleepwalking.

Having waited ten or so minutes for my return, Sarah left the safety of the bedroom to investigate my disappearance only to find me sound asleep on one of the couches in the lounge. It was Buddy, apparently, the traitorous hound who led her straight to me. Then, when all attempts to rouse me failed, she opted instead to cover me with one of the throws and let the dog take my place in our perfectly comfortable bed.

"Thanks, mate," I say to the hound who, fresh from his own shower after our run, is now dozing on the bedroom floor.

Don't worry. I'm not quite ready to accept that last night was all a dream. No, my neurosis would never settle for that. That would be way too easy. Nope. Thankfully, I live in the one building that was seemingly designed to deal with the likes of me.

Holt is kitted out with that whole Rottweiler thing which that pimple-faced prick said was working fine. So, if that's the case, it would mean that last night was all caught on Holt's hard drive, wherever that may be, I think it's up in the loft or something in its own *Blackbox* kind of thing to safeguard it from fire or flooding. And I, as king over this dominion, plan to review all the footage from last night to establish whether or not I am indeed losing my marbles again.

That's right, just as soon as I've returned the one call from my lawyer, the two from Irvin, and made a head start on planning the wedding reception, which is due to take place here in just a week!

But first, important stuff. Milk. We're out. I tried using Sarah's soy milk this morning as a substitute and nearly threw up.

Now, I'm playing hunt the bloody car keys, which is weird because there's a key station right by the front door, and I always leave the keys there. But they're gone.

"Holt, where are my bloody keys?"

Sorry, Marco, I don't understand. Could you repeat the question?

"Help me find my car keys."

No problem. I am going to ring the keys now, so you may want to turn off all background noise.

I listen. Birds tweet noisily outside.

Buddy groans and flops to the floor in the corridor. Dude, you said we were going out, now you're frozen like a fart in a trance.

Hold on. What's that? I can hear tinny electronic music playing. But it seems far away, nowhere near the front door. I hurry back down the hallway. Lounge? No. I think the sound is coming from the… study!

I rush down there before the thing stops ringing and fling the door open. Oh okay. The keys are on my desk. But I don't remember coming in here yesterday. The boys were coming over. I went straight to the kitchen. Or did I?

The wildlife seems much louder today. And, as always, the view from this room gives me pause, especially after last night's meteorological douche. Everything is bursting with oversaturated colour.

And yet, something is off.

Yeah. You're imagining things again.

No. It's something else.

"What the…?"

Buddy, who has followed me into the study, whimpers as if he too had noticed that the cardboard box Sarah brought home that night is now sitting on the floor next to my desk and that the photographs it contained are now set out neatly on the sideboard.

Why would Sarah do this? I told her that I hadn't decided what I was going to do with them.

Looking at those images now, all I can see is Dolce Vita. All I can remember is that we nearly died there. All I can feel is alienation. There is no glow of fondness nor any of the nostalgia that these things are supposed to invoke. Instead, there's just anger bubbling through me like boiling water.

I want to react. I want to grab that fucking box, throw those bloody frames in it, and ditch the whole lot. No, actually, I want to stomp over there and sweep those things off the side with the back of my arm with a dramatic flourish!

Well, not, really. Because, well, that would be messy, and I'd probably end up with an injury knowing my luck. Besides that, I'm preoccupied with something else.

The photo of Toby and me by the river; it's gone. All of the other shitty ones are here except for the one I actually care about.

I look around the room. Scan the walls.

Nothing.

What's she done with it? Did she take it out? Why? Why would she do that without saying anything? She knows how much it means to me. She knows how excited I was when I found it.

"Come on, Buddy, we're leaving."

I leave the house, load the dog in the car, and drive away.

I'm steaming.

I consider messaging Sarah. No, I'll ring her. Messages are slow and subject to interpretation. No. She's at work. Probably has her hand stuck up a cow's backside. I'm not going to get a decent answer from her, which will probably piss me off some more.

"Fuck!" I yell, thumping the steering wheel, which causes Buddy to whimper again.

"It's alright, mate. It isn't aimed at you." I just can't believe Sarah would invade my space like this. I want that photo. I *need* that photo back. I need to see it.

I consider reaching for my phone to see the original.

You're driving. Pull yourself together.

I sail past the tiny stone house with the red post-box outside, otherwise known as the village store. Probably just as well. I need to clear my head.

Why? Why would Sarah take it?

I press the button on the steering wheel, and after the beep, I speak to the cabin, "Call Irvin."

There's ringing on the line then. "Allo," is my foreman's cheery reply. The sound of hammering, talking, and laughing surrounds me as if I'm there.

"Morning, Irvin," I say, doing my best to sound calm and collected.

"Marco, mate. Mornin', how's it goin'?"

"Yeah. Good. I'm just returning your calls. Sorry. It's been busy this side."

"Oh right, yeah," he says, lowering his voice as if he doesn't want the others to hear. Then the background noise fades like he's moved to a quieter part of the building, and suddenly I'm nervous.

"Marco?"

"Yeah, I'm here."

"Sorry, mate. Just wanted to move somewhere quieter."

"OK. You're starting to sound a bit ominous, mate," I say with a smile that I'm not feeling. "What's up?"

"Well, we've hit a bit of a snag."

I hold my hand to my belly, but I don't think it's butterflies, but more because I'm trying to stifle a scream. I am so fucking sick of this sensation. It seems I can barely go one day without being bloody soiled by this sickly fairground-ride feeling of dread, and I've had enough of it!

"Snag? What kind of snag?" I ask in an artificial upbeat tone, grateful that I happen to be in the car now, driving through winding country roads surrounded by green fields.

"Work started on the attic this mornin'."

"The attic? I thought we were going to focus on all the main rooms first."

"Yeah. We were. We are. But we came across a damp patch in one of the rooms upstairs, so I got one of the lads to go investigate the source, you know. And they found a massive hole in the roof."

Shit. "Right. Well. We expected that. We had the same problem in the entrance hall, didn't we? You sorted that."

"No. Well, it wasn't just that. The hole ain't the problem. See? It's just the fact that while he was up there, one of the beams, it collapsed, and when he tried to right imself, he ended up comin' through the ceilin' in one of the bedrooms. He ain't hurt or anyfin', but—"

"Shit. How bad is it?"

"Well, the whole thing's gonna need fixin', screenin' and paintin'. But that's not it, ya see? The problem ain't just the load-bearin' stuff, but it's in the wall too. I think we've got a case of rot up there."

It takes me a few seconds to process that because I don't know which part chills me the most; the hole in the ceiling, the bit where

Irvin tells me that the building that I've sunk all my money into is riddled with dry rot, or how he delivered the news. Grave. Sombre. Reluctant.

When it comes to building work, Irvin has always instilled me with confidence. Even when there have been problems, there were always ways to solve them. Today, he's stopped at problems only.

"How the hell was this missed by the surveyor?" I demand in a repressed growl.

There's a pause. The sound of him clearing his throat then, "Well, these blokes don't tend to do more than they 'ave ta. For somethin' like dry rot, you need to look deep in the corners. I imagine this bloke just stuck is ed up in the attic and ticked the box on is form."

"Great. Good to know that I'm paying him to tick a fucking box! And what about you, Irvin? You've been there all this time. You would have thought you'd taken a bloody look before now!" I explode.

"With all due respect, Marco, you don't pay me to check the surveyor's done his job properly–"

"Then, what do I pay you for?" I rage. "I don't know the first fucking thing about dry rot, but you do. Jesus Christ!"

I run my hand through my hair. The road rumbles beneath the wheels of the car, and then I hear Buddy sigh. I can't see him, but it's enough to take the sting out of the news I just knew was coming in one form or another.

FUCK! FUCK! FUCK!

Yes. I know. I'm being a dick.

"I'm sorry, Irvin," I say with a deep sigh, "I'm taking it out on you. I know it isn't your fault."

"It's okay, Marco, mate. I know this place is a lot of pressure," the man says softly. It's the same tone he used that day at Dolce Vita when we talked about my son's death.

Toby.

And just like that, I feel a crushing sense of sadness.

Somehow, Irvin must read the silence, so he fills it. "Look, Marco, mate. We don't really know enough yet to make any sensible decisions. Right now, what we need do is get a specialist out 'ere to take a look. They'll be able to tell how far this thing goes. It might just be restricted to the timber in the loft. If it is, that's no bother because we would replace part of that stuff anyway to fit the skylights. If it's spread to the brickwork…" he trails off here before adding, "well, we'll just have to see what they say."

I nod as if the man can see me because that makes perfect sense. "Okay. That makes sense. Did you have someone in mind?"

"Well, I've already called em. They're sending someone out tommorra. I just wanted to make you aware."

Of course.

"Thanks, Irvin. I appreciate that," I say, pushing on the brake as I spot a group of vehicles up ahead.

"Okay. I best get back then," he says.

"Okay. Yeah. Um, Irvin?"

"Don't worry about it, mate. Try not to stress," the man jumps in, presumably anticipating my apology for being a shit.

"Thank you so much. Please keep me updated."

"No problem. See ya."

"Bye," I say, bringing the car to a rolling stop.

Up ahead, parked on the grass verge of both sides of the road, are several cars and a couple of media vans, each with a giant satellite dish mounted onto its roof. There are also at least a dozen people scattered on and off the road. Some chatting in groups, others looking in the same direction across the fields.

"Okay. What's going on here?" I mutter to myself as I pull the car over to the side of the road and engage park.

I consider letting Buddy loose but decide against it since I don't even know what's going on. I turn and look at the backseat to find that he's already sitting up, expectantly.

Walkies?

"No, Buddy. You're staying here. I'll be right back." He cocks his head; *you can't be serious.*

I am.

I look across at a group of people congregated around a BBC News van. Some are looking into the back of the vehicle; others are gazing up at the sky over the nearby cornfield. I look up but see nothing but a cloudless expanse of pale blue.

I set the car to *comfort,* so the climate control keeps running for Buddy, then I pull on my jacket and step out into the chilly air, laden with the husky scent of vegetation.

"Stay," I say, seriously to the hound before closing the door.

I make a beeline for the BBC truck. Curious now because whatever is going on, it's interesting enough for nobody to notice me.

As I draw closer, the hubbub of excited voices grows louder. I turn and lean in such a way to get a peek over the shoulder of a blonde ponytailed man who's one of those people that refuses to let go of summer; he's wearing shorts and a t-shirt with gloves and a scarf.

The inside of the news truck is, as you'd expect, kitted out with an array of monitors. All are flickering with footage, presumably live feeds from different channels. But, the largest monitor, mounted in the centre of them all, is beaming something altogether different. It is gradually revealing a wider aerial view of the field next to us.

Instinctively, I look over but can see nothing.

"Oh my God, it's amazing," a girl says breathlessly.

"Unreal," says another.

Although I have a good line of sight into the van, my view is partially blocked by the ponytail guy, which means I can't see the whole screen. What I can just about make out is the image of a small circle. Then, as the camera travels higher, the picture pans wider, I can see another larger circle linking into it.

That's when I realise.

I look across at the group of people who are still squinting—hands held flat as shades over their eyes—into the sky. Now, to the backdrop of a clutch of giant grey clouds, I can just about make out the quadcopter. It's climbed so high above the field that it's become the size of an insect. Its buzz diluted by its distance from us.

Pressure on my shoulder startles me, and I hear a female say, "It's incredible, isn't it, Zach?"

I don't turn around; I just nod my head.

Then, I turn back to the van. This time, I move left of ponytail man for a much better view. The drone's elevation is transmitting a stunning symmetry of the kind I have never seen before, at least not outside a YouTube video. It's etched into the cornfield right next to us, yet sprawled so far and wide, it's pretty much indistinguishable from the ground.

"It must be something like eight hundred feet long, and, what, five hundred feet wide?" someone says, voicing my thoughts.

"Nah, more than that," someone else says.

"It's hard to tell."

"Shit, have you ever seen anything like it?" Ponytail man asks the woman next to him.

"No, never," she gasps, eyes glued to the monitor in front of her.

They are, of course, talking about a crop circle. I mean circles, plural, crop fucking circles! A whole series of them. Identical in shape and pattern but different in size. A daisy chain that starts small and grows to form a semi-circular sequence that eventually doubles back on itself like a claw.

"Okay, Paul, let's have you back on camera," a bushy blonde-haired man says to ponytail boy, "and Clare, we'll have you doing a piece with the field in the background."

The ponytail guy shifts immediately, leaving a gap between me and the van, and it feels like my cover is blown, so I instantly turn and hurry away from the scene.

I climb back into the car and pull the door shut behind me.

Buddy observes me with a whimper. *You left me here.*

"I'm sorry, mate," I rasp, blowing air out of my mouth as I watch the reporter perform her piece to the camera. "Shit. Buddy. We may not be alone. What've you got to say to that?"

His only response is to groan, which I interpret as a roll of the eyes.

I rub his chin. "Really? I probably would have felt the same a few years back, but now… I'm not so sure." Now, I'm prepared to think that anything's possible. But then, I guess you could argue that I would when you consider my propensity for seeing things that aren't there.

"What do *you* think? Genuine or hoax?" I ask the dog, who's looking across at the reporter like he's interested in what she has to say.

"Fancy that, eh? With the infinity of space, aliens have decided to visit the outer reaches of the southwest of England, I say, starting the car, making a U-turn, and taking us home once more.

16

THE UNINVITED

HOLT. 12:35.

It's gone lunchtime by the time I make the turning into trees towards Holt.

Where the hell did the morning go?

As we approach the house, I sense Buddy move to the opposite side of the backseat and start barking out of the window.

"Bloody hell, mate. You can't be that desperate to go, surely," I say, looking over my shoulder. But the dog isn't looking at me. He's looking out of the window towards the woods.

"Okay. I get it; when you've got to go, you've got to– "SHIT!" I yell, stomping on the brakes. The act almost launched Buddy into the front seat with me. "What the bloody hell?" I breathe.

In front of us, seemingly appearing out of nowhere, is… Maja.

Buddy starts barking. He's obviously as pissed off as I am that he nearly ended up through the bloody windscreen of the car while I'm still reeling from the fact that I almost ran over her.

I yank on the door handle and step out. "Maja, I nearly ran you over," I say, doing nothing to mask my irritation.

"I need to see you," is her only response.

"What?"

"I need to speak with you."

I gawk at her. "Maja, did you hear what I said? I nearly hit you with the car. Where did you just come from?"

"I take taxi like last time."

"No, I mean just now."

"Oh, I was in the forest. I take a look around while I wait."

"You've been waiting?"

"Yes, for almost one hour."

"Maja. No, this isn't on. This is not how it's done. You're supposed to make an appointment. I told you this when we met last time."

"I know, but tis an emergency."

I gape at her for several seconds. I don't think she's even listening to what I'm saying.

Something has changed about her demeanour today, though. She looks older somehow and sporting some serious dark circles around her eyes like she hasn't been sleeping.

Buddy is still unhappy. He's now moved to the front passenger seat and is barking through the windscreen at the uninvited guest.

"*Proszę,* Mister Battista, I promise I no take much of your precious time," she says, clasping her hands together, the plastic supermarket carrier bag in her hand rustling as she does.

She's wearing the same clothes as last time, and there's a desperation in her eyes that instantly reminds me of someone else. Someone I realise I haven't thought much about since escaping the city, and now I feel guilty.

"Please," she continues, hands still supplicating.

I look at Buddy, who, by his barks up against the windscreen, isn't in a forgiving mood.

"I go if you wish," she adds forlornly.

"No. It's okay," I say, "but this is the last time. In the future, you must book an appointment, do you understand?"

"Oh, bless you, bless you," she chants, hands still clutched together, which is making me feel awkward.

"I just need to park the car properly," I say.

I park the car on the drive and let Buddy out, but the first thing he does is turn around and bark at the woman. "No, Buddy! Stop! Stop!"

If my uninvited guest is intimidated, she doesn't show it. She doesn't even blink. She just keeps staring at him with dark lifeless eyes, which is probably what's pissing him off.

"I'm sorry about this," I find myself saying, "I don't know what's got into him today." Lately, he seems unhappy with everything.

I watch a smile appear on her face. I'm expecting one of those polite smiles that you wear when your neighbour's dog starts humping your leg, but I don't get that. This one is shorter, more mild amusement than tolerant courtesy.

"I'm just going to drop him off," I say, struggling to pull the dog back by his collar and leading him off towards the house. "Come on, you. Come on! If you can't behave, you can wait in the utility room" —which has been designated as his *timeout* room, not that he's had to use it much since we arrived here, until now.

I love you, mate, but with everything else that's happening, I can't risk another lawsuit because my dog bit one of my patients. That wouldn't go down well on so many levels. Not that she had paid. I told her not to worry last time as she said she didn't have her purse. I wonder if that's going to be a pattern.

A couple of minutes later, I emerge from the kitchen through the lounge and into the corridor to find the front door still open and my visitor standing outside like she's afraid to cross the threshold or something.

"Maja?" I call, walking up to her, "it's okay. He's in his den," I say, as evidenced by the fact that he's still barking.

I watch her hesitate. Eyes shifting at and around me like she's never been here before and needs a bloody invitation.

"Come in," I say, masking my impatience. Partly because I don't need this right now, and I think the other part is because I realise that I didn't enjoy leaving Buddy in that utility room. It felt like I was locking my boy in a closet or something. I should know better. It felt alien. Wrong.

My uninvited guest finally steps over the threshold with muddy flat shoes, but she does so like she's crossing a bloody minefield which only adds to my irritation. She didn't even seem affected by the dog. Now, she's acting like she's terrified of it.

I stop short of asking her to take off her shoes. I have a hard enough time getting Sarah to do it, and she comes back with muddy wellingtons full of shit, literally. That's the one difference between her and Ellie. And I wonder if my dislike of dirty shoes in the house results from the conditioning I received from my wife.

My wife.

"We'll be in the study," I say. Leading the way down the corridor, "where we were last time." But when I look over my shoulder, I see that my patient – who was desperate for a chat earlier – is now taking her time, languidly walking down the hallway, arm outstretched, dirty fingertips and broken nails trailing over the hallway walls.

What the hell?

"Maja?" When she doesn't respond, I yell, "Maja!" This does the trick and snaps her out of her daze. "Are you alright?" I ask. She doesn't respond but instead observes me with those dark eyes of hers. "Maja?"

"Yes. I'm very good."

"Shall we?" I say, gesturing down the hallway to the study.

Inside, I offer my guest some water, but she declines. And I can't help but wonder if she's even eaten today. Judging by her withered frame, revealed to me the moment she takes off and shakes that green coat of hers, I'd say she doesn't eat much.

Yeah. She's definitely wearing the same clothes from the other day. Only today, she's looking much more dishevelled. And that dank, musty odour that emanated from her last time has worsened. Stagnant. Ripe. To the point of making me want to open a window.

At least Buddy's stopped barking. I'm grateful. The more I heard his muffled protests at being locked in that place echoing down the hallway, the guiltier I felt.

I won't be doing it again.

"Okay, Maja." I force a smile, "what's been troubling you?"

She doesn't reply. Instead, she folds her hands on top of her legs and looks around the room as if checking to see if everything's still in its place.

"Maja?"

She finally looks up at me.

"How are you today?"

"I'm fine, thank you. How are you?"

"I am good, thanks. Maja, are you sure everything's alright? You seem a bit off today? And you seemed quite desperate to see me at the door."

She simply gives me one of those short smiles of hers like she knows something I don't, and, of course, it's starting to annoy me.

Yeah. Really professional.

"Maja, if you don't mind, I'd like to start where we left the session the other day."

"Of course."

"As you'd expect, I'm particularly interested in what you told me just before you left." I watch her face for a reaction, but there isn't one. So, I continue, "to be perfectly honest with you; I was somewhat troubled by what you said. And, if it's okay, I would like you to tell me a bit more about it."

My patient looks through the glass over the lake, towards the manor. And after a few seconds of watching the trees sway in the breeze, she says, "I love days like today. You know, where the sun is bright, and there are big black clouds in the sky." Her voice is flat, distant, like she's left this room and is already drifting away on one of those clouds.

I take a deep breath, force a smile and myself to calm the bloody hell down because I am a professional, and I am in session. "I know what you mean," I say, "when I lived by the ocean, I could gaze at the sky for hours. And I loved how changeable the weather was there."

"English people love to talk about the weather, don't they? I don't think I ever talked as much about weather before coming here. And in Poland, the weather is much more what-you-say, bad. It always make me laugh when we have a bit of snow here. In England, tis always the wrong kind of snow. It stop bus, train, the whole country." She sniggers. "English people have no idea. In Polonia, many people, especially in the countryside, are snowed in their house. So bad that they must bury, you know, dig their way out of home in the morning," she says, turning her hands into excavator claws. "Have you ever been to Polonia?"

I shake my head. "No. I haven't."

"Well, you should. My country is beautiful no matter what you may have heard."

"Do you miss Poland?"

"Yes, of course. Tis my country."

"Then, why don't you go back? You've had ample opportunity. Why not go home?"

She observes me for the longest time as if I've just insulted her. And I realise how that must have sounded. "Oh no, I don't mean it that way, of course. What I meant was–"

She holds up a calming hand. "Tis okay. I understand what you mean. I know a racist person when I hear one. I've hear them plenty of times."

"I'm sorry if it sounded like that. That wasn't my intention," I continue to bumble as if I haven't already made enough of a tit of myself. Jesus. Whose idea was it for me to go into this business?

Don't answer that.

"I'm just curious. You talk about Poland so fondly, but you've never talked about going back."

"This is my home now," she says decisively. But it sounds very much like someone who's been coached to say it rather than someone who genuinely believes it. And there's something behind those dark eyes of hers. Just the way they keep shifting around the room. There is more to this. Much more. And I want to push her, but I don't know if that's a therapeutic decision or simply because I want her to get to the point of why she just showed up here today, unannounced.

Oh, well. "Maja, I would love to talk some more about what you told me at the end of our last session."

I watch her thin lips curl up at the sides like those of a mischievous cat. "We all say things in anger, Marco. Don't you?"

I think about this and nod. "Of course, I certainly do. Only, Maja, you weren't angry."

"How do you know? How do you know I wasn't angry?"

I shift in my seat then shrug. "Well, I don't know. Not for sure.

All I know is that I was speaking with you for the best part of an hour. You appeared perfectly calm, rational, articulate. Frustrated perhaps. But not angry."

"Frustrated?" she lets out a short laugh that soon turns into another of those sniggers, only this time it goes as far as making her shoulders judder.

And I wait. I wait until she has the whole thing out of her system, and the moment begins to fade to normality when suddenly she cuts back to seriousness and an uncharacteristic narrowing of the eyes. "You have absolutely no idea, do you? No idea."

"Well, why don't you tell me? Tell me, Maja. I really would like to know."

"I spend most of my life being angry. I'm angry right now. I am furious that people like you think you know me after just a few hours in your fancy room. You don't know me," she spits, eyes blazing now. That anger she just alluded to fully on display. I know this because I recognise that look. I've seen it on my wife's face enough times. Although, while I suspected that this diminutive woman before me might have something lurking behind those passive dark eyes of hers, I didn't think it was this volatile.

Good. We're making progress.

I wait and watch her gaze out of the glass, which I also believe isn't so much about the view anymore but more about having somewhere where her mind can retreat from me.

And so, I'm just contemplating my next move when, suddenly, she speaks without turning. "Something is coming, mister Battista." Her voice is low. Impassive. Ominous.

I cock my head. "I'm sorry?" I think I've misunderstood her because it looks like she's referring to the manor across the lake.

"Something is coming."

"What do you mean by *something*?"

She looks at me, but her face is different somehow. Ashen. As if she's taken leave of her body and left a cold shell in its place. As if she wants no responsibility for the words she's about to speak.

"You know what I mean," she says with a wry smile.

"I'm sorry, Maja. I don't–"

"Yes, you do. You experience before," she says.

"Experienced what? I'm sorry, Maja, you seem to be talking in riddles," I say, keeping a smile on my face although I'm starting to feel uneasy. *She,* my patient, my client, is making me feel uneasy. "You keep looking across the lake, Maja. Are you referring to Frost Lake Manor?" I ask, "have you been there before?" I say, pointing out of the glass.

"I talk about the place where you used to live, by the sea. But it's nothing like this," she says with a vacant smile.

A shiver ripples through me, and this time, it isn't because she's talking about Dolce Vita, but it's the way she spoke those words. Assertively. Knowingly. As if we both share a secret, when I have no fucking clue what she's talking about, and I feel like I've just been played.

Oh. Hello. Where did that come from? I'm suddenly rattled in session. What's that all about?

Is it a session, though? She fucking lied to your face! She knows about you!

I shift in my chair. Swallow. "You know about me, Maja? You know about my past?" I ask with as much self-control as I can muster.

She doesn't respond while I continue processing what I've just heard.

She chose you! She knows all about you!

My heart is already protesting by thumping on my chest.

Okay. Calm down. You know what this is about; she pushed multiple buttons simultaneously, and you are reacting to everything single one. Now, relax, you fool. Relax. You're supposed to be a professional. Act like one!

I shift back in my chair and wrap my need to suck in air—that's now pungent with the stench wafting at me from across the room—in a casual sigh. The act looks as if I'm simply making myself comfortable.

That's right. You're in control here.

"Maja. I don't know what you think you know about me, but—"

"I don't think, mister Battista, I know."

"What do you know?"

She leans forward—eyes wide like saucers for the first time since we've met—and whispers as if the walls have ears, "I know that you see things in that place. Bad things."

"Hang on. That isn't—"

"And now you'll see them here too."

I force a smile. And when I say force, I mean it because my instinct is to tell her to fuck off! To get out of my house because she's making *me* feel uncomfortable.

"Maja, the article and everything that came after was just the media overhyping things to sell more papers. It wasn't real."

"I need you to help me," she says urgently. Desperately.

"I am trying to help you."

"Not like this!" she snaps angrily, "talking in here is not going to give me what I need."

I take a deep breath because my heart is still thundering like the hooves of the wild thoughts in my mind pulling against their mental restraints and wanting to gallop off into all places that I shut down long ago.

"I know it may not feel that way. But more than often, the two are related," I say, keeping my voice steady.

My guest-slash-patient-slash- home-invader lets out a chortle. "You think I'm crazy? Like you?" she asks.

Fair enough.

I shrug. "Well, maybe not like me, perhaps. But there could be other things about your life. Other unresolved psychological scars that haven't healed and are now manifesting themselves in other ways."

My visitor glances at the closed door as if she's expecting someone to come bursting through it. That, or she's considering a rapid exit which would be fine by me.

"Maja?"

She doesn't respond. When I call her again, I startle her into looking back at me, and I can see that something's changed. Her whole demeanour is different now. It's like this thing, this secret of hers – that she's been keeping to her chest like a captured bird – has been liberated and is now free to flutter wherever she chooses.

She's looking every which way but at me now. Eyes wide. Top lip chewing.

"Maja. Are you alright? Can you tell me how you're feeling right now?

No response.

"I couldn't help but notice that you keep looking at the door. Do you need to be somewhere else?" Which is code for *what the fuck is wrong with you, and who are you expecting to come through that door?*

"Can you hear that?" she asks suddenly.

"What?"

"That sound."

"What sou–"

"Shhhh…" she holds up a finger in my direction, and we both pause to listen.

Bird's chirp. Wood pigeons coo. A magpie chatters.

Nothing else.

After several seconds of listening to nature, I finally say, "I can't hear anything. Maja?" But she isn't looking at me. Now, she seems focused on the desk behind me. Again, to the point of making me want to turn around.

I move in my chair so that I'm in her line of vision. "Maja, I would like you to tell me what you're thinking right now."

There's another chortle before she finally turns her attention back to me. "You keep asking me to tell you how I'm feeling. Why? You want to know if I have any bad thoughts in my head?"

"I'm interested in any thoughts you may have."

She leans forward in her chair and says with a ragged breath, "Bad thoughts are the *only* thoughts I have, Doctor."

Another chill runs through me.

In London, I've sat in on and led many sessions with people with all types of mental illness. From manic-depressives to people with schizophrenia, none of them creeped me out the way this woman is now.

"I can't help you in any capacity if you don't talk to me. So, how about we start with that?"

Wait. Do you still want to help her? She's off her rocker, mate. She knows all about you.

You're responsible for her now.

"Maja?" She's looking at the door again, and I have to say that, oddly, it isn't irritating me but is starting to spook me to the point where I have to suppress the urge to get up and reassure myself that there's nobody on the other side.

There *is* nobody on the other side.

How can you be so sure?

"Maja?"

She tunes back into me.

"Maja, can you please tell me why you keep looking at the door?"

"There's something out there," she says in a hushed tone, "listening to every word you say."

"Every word *I* say?"

I point in that direction. "Who's out there, Maja? Who's on the other side of the door?"

She doesn't respond. She just keeps staring at the bloody thing, the act raking up the tiny hairs on the back of my neck.

Now, the atmosphere in my once comforting, reassuring, relaxing room is inverted. It feels unwelcoming. Unpleasant, like damp clothes on cold skin.

"Maja. Would you like me to check what's behind the door?" I ask, but I don't wait for an answer because as much as I may not want to admit it, the action is more for my benefit than hers.

I rise from my seat, walk over to the door, and yank it open. Then, I step out into the corridor, turn around and look at my houseguest, who is now perched on the front of the sofa, eyes wide with curiosity.

"See? Nothing here," I say, holding out my arms.

I look left through the window at the end of the corridor to leaves trembling in the wind. Their dry red and orange colours glow and fade as clouds drift across the sun.

Then, I look to my right at the stairs and hallway steeped in shadows. There's nothing up there either.

So, I turn back to my visitor, who is still watching with eager anticipation, before rising from her seat and heading towards me as if to inspect for herself.

"See?" I say brightly, stifling a grimace as a stench grabs my throat and tickles my gag reflex. "Nobody... um... nobody out here."

"I need *toaleta*," is her only response.

I look at the woman for a few seconds. "Oh, toilet. Yes. It's at the far end of the corridor, second to the last door on the right."

I watch her shuffle up the hallway like she's suddenly become an old lady before I walk back into the study and look out over the lake, longing for some fresh air.

Even the water has been smothered with a monochromatic veil. Its colours muted as a flotilla of ominous black clouds slowly absorbs the sun. The Manor has already disappeared into the gathering gloom on the opposite side of the lake.

I think of Irvin and the boys and of what I learned today. We've been lucky with the other houses, but I know dry rot is serious not just because of the damage it can cause but because of the underlying damp problems that it represents. It could cost thousands to repair the damage as well as delay the project even further. Something I know I can't afford. That bridging loan will become due regardless of where we're at with getting that place sold, and if I don't have the funds....

I watch the clouds prophetically burgeon closer, wider, transforming day into night. It's going to rain again, and it's going to be bad.

Buddy's bark breaks into my thoughts, and it occurs to me that the utility room is close to the downstairs loo. Shit. He's no doubt sensed our uninvited guest's proximity and is throwing a fit.

I hurry out of the study and into the hallway, which is much darker now to the point of triggering the nightlights, completely transforming the house's atmosphere. It feels bigger now. Hollow, and....

Fresh air. It's rushing down the hallway to greet me. I welcome, yet I'm surprised by it.

At the stair junction, I look up to the front door. *NO.* It's bloody open again! What the hell is going on with that bloody thing?

Did she leave? The house feels peculiarly quiet. Empty, but for Buddy's occasional bark.

I remain motionless, listening as my hair is ruffled by the breeze rushing at me, bringing with it the *petrichor,* also known as *the smell of rain.* How do I know that?

Higher humidity is experienced before it rains, and the pores, like those on human skin, of rocks and soil, becomes clogged with moisture, forcing them to release oils.

Toby. My walking encyclopaedia of a beautiful boy. Oh, I miss you.

What was that?!

Shadows. All around me. It's like something just flew in front of the stair window; something big swooping over the house.

Get a grip. You're just reacting to everything that's happened today, including the creepy visitor that's locked herself in your loo doing God knows what.

Ugh.

I look down the hallway and the toilet door, which is closed, but no sounds are coming from beyond. But for Buddy's occasional disgruntlement, the whole house has descended into the typical calm before the storm.

"Holt."

Yes, Marco?

"Close and lock the front door."

Of course.

I watch the dregs of daylight fade, and then the loud thud of the lock rattles off the walls and down the hallway to me.

I approach the toilet carefully as if there's a rabid animal trapped inside because I don't like the idea of her coming out of there and clocking me, standing here like a bloody perv. So I call out, "Maja? Everything okay in there?"

Crows caw. A gale rumbles around the building, but there's no response from the toilet.

"Maja?"

I wait. Nothing.

I'm right outside the door now. Gingerly, I raise my knuckles and tap on it.

"Maja? Is everything okay? Could you please answer as I'm starting to get worried?"

Tree branches sway back and forth. Leaves scream and flutter to their death.

"Maja?" I tap harder on the door.

Nothing.

"Maja, can you please answer me?" I say forcefully. "Otherwise, I'll have no choice but to come in." My mind unhelpfully projects a series of potential discoveries beyond the door, all of which tickle that gag reflex again.

I grab the door handle and rattle it loudly. "Maja?! Maja, I'm going to have to come—"

The door just opens. It isn't locked from the inside as anticipated, and now I'm freaking out. I look around me, expecting to see the woman elsewhere in the house, but it's just me here.

I push on the door, it slowly creaks open, and the light comes on.

The first thing to hit me is the foul stench of excrement. It wraps itself around me like toxic gas, burrowing its way into the fibres of my clothing and forcing its way through my nose to the back of my throat. I throw and clamp a hand over my face in an attempt to block the stench and stagger backwards until I feel the wall against my back.

I cough and gag several times before allowing my eyes to drift back to the toilet because I saw something there, something that fired a surge of panic through me.

Oh, fuck! I didn't imagine it. It's true! There's something in there. Something scrawled on the mirror; one word that I can't be sure about, but I think is actually written in... in shit!

SIEDEM

Terror grips and then paralyzes me as the reality of this starts to sink in. This woman, whoever she is, this disgusting human being with some kind of axe to grind, has infiltrated my home to make some kind of protest. And for all I know, she's still here, biding her time, waiting to slice and dice me with a knife or something.

Oh, God.

Calm down. Calm the bloody hell down! You don't even know if this is real.

The stench is pretty fucking real!

Pull it together. Could this really be happening here and now? Come on, breathe. Breathe. Could this be happening?

Yes.

Is anybody else affected by it?

No.

On balance, how likely is this to be real?

Most fucking likely!

Yeah. That didn't help.

"HOLT!" I yell, looking around myself because it feels like I am being watched!

That's your paranoia.

It isn't. Look at what she did!

Yes, Marco?

"Where is *guest*?"

Searching...

"Huh? What do you mean fucking searching? HOLT?"

Yes, Marco?

"Where is guest?"

Searching...

My face is so wet with sweat that I can feel it pooling to become a rivulet on my forehead. I swipe the back of my hands over it. Oh no. I'm hyperventilating. Teeth clenched. Muscles taut. Head pounding. Breaths, coming shallow and fast.

Calm down, Marc. You need to calm down. You're inducing a panic attack.

I jolt sideways when I hear sound travel up the hallway and crawl into my ears.

What the hell was that?

It's so dark in the hallway now that all the nightlights have sprung to life. Day has turned into night; fear has clamped its jaws around and is shaking me in an attempt to devour me whole.

Come on. Move! Move!

I'm at the junction with the stairs now, and I'm comforted by the fact that the front door is still locked, but something still doesn't feel right. I don't feel like I'm alone in here.

"HOLT!"

Yes, Marco?

"*Where* is guest?" I say slowly, angrily.

Searching...

"Stop searching. Why do you keep search–"

Another thud draws my attention to the arched window on the stairs. It's as dark as twilight out there now. I can't make out what that was.

I look at the front door. Consider leaving. But not without Buddy. Maybe I should go and get him. Free him.

Marc! Pull yourself together. It's just some woman protester. What's the matter with you?

I don't know. I don't even know.

Oh, SHIT! I crouch down as a giant shadow appears and then scampers across the wall in front of me. "Oh, Jesus!" My phone is in the study.

You don't need it!

"HOLT?"

Yes, Marco?

"Dial the police?"

Is this an emergency?

"Yes!"

What kind of emergency?

"CALL THE FUCKING POLICE NOW!"

Dialling.

There's ringing on the line.

Police. What is your emergency?

"There's an intruder in my house. Please send someone."

Sorry Sir, it's a terrible line. I can't hear you. Did you say, intruder?

"Yes! Yes, a fucking intruder. Please send someone over now!"

Sir? I'm going to need you to calm down, please. I am going to need you to tell me your name and address. Can you do that, Sir? Can you hear me?

There's another thud. It's coming from the study. Slowly and reluctantly, I make my way down there while Buddy is wondering why I didn't free him because he's barking loudly in the background, and I consider going back for him. I consider retreating up the corridor, but I can't no matter how hard I try because I am drawn down the hallway into darkness, towards the study, towards the sound that is growing closer. Louder.

I swipe my sleeve across my face. My muscles are screaming from the spasm of terror they're locked in, and yet, through clenched teeth, I still manage to methodically chant at nowhere in particular, "My name is Marco Battista. I live at Holt, High Street, Fawndale. I have an intruder in my home and am in fear for my life. Please send someone. Please send someone now. HOLT, end call," because I can't think straight with her asking me any more questions!

I've reached the threshold of the study. Outside, the claws of branches reach for, tap, and then shy away from the window at the end of the hallway with such violence that I expect them to smash their way through at any time.

I run my hand through my damp hair and peer into the study, half expecting to find the demented Polish lady standing there with an axe in her hand.

She isn't.

The room is empty. It is its usual innocuous self. There's nothing in here but the stench of the intruder. This is a momentary comfort until I spot something on the glass wall. Something that wasn't there when I left the room. Something that I cannot identify from over here. So, after looking around me, I step forward to make sure nobody is stalking the shadows

The side lamp springs to life as I pass it and makes me jump out of my bloody skin.

I can see it. It's a stain on the glass. As I draw closer, it grows bigger, clearer. It's a yellow, orange splodge about the size of a hand.

Closer.

There's something in it. It's tiny but big enough for me to identify it as a... feather. It's a bloody feather glued there by a sinewy goop.

Oh shit. It's a bird. A bird has flown straight into the glass! "That's not supposed to happen," I utter, reciting the estate agent's words as if explaining myself. As if I'm in some way responsible.

This has never happened before. At least not while we've been here. The windows are specially treated. Opaque from the outside during the day. And yet–

My sentence is cut short when there's a loud *SNAP* on the other side of the glass! I yelp and leap backwards but notice a dark shape slide down the outside of the glass.

"OH SHIT!" I can't be sure, but I think that was another bird.

I step forward to investigate when there's another loud *THUMP!* Right in front of me.

I jump away, this time tripping over myself and crashing to the floor.

THWACK!

Another.

THUMP!

And another.

Marco, I have found the location of guest.

I look around myself like she's going to come charging at me from behind the sofa. "WHERE IS SHE?" I yell.

There's a long pause, and then comes the AI's casual yet chilling response; *she's everywhere.*

I crawl backwards on all fours and watch in horror as two more blackbirds seemingly kamikaze at the glass, leaving a series of multicolour splodges in their wake. Then another and then another.

Before long, the wall that offered a spectacular view of nature's beauty is transformed into a macabre tableau of blood and feathers.

17

SIEDEM

6 Days until the wedding. 🔔

Do you know that *siedem* means seven in Polish? No. I didn't either until I looked it up.

Seven birds. Seven black birds, from what I could tell, flew into the glass wall overlooking the lake.

My so-called patient, you know the one, the stinky lady who had her fun creeping me out by making me think that someone or something was stalking the house, listening to my every word. The same one who then revealed that she had a screw loose, literally spouting all that crap about Dolce Vita and me. Anyway, she scrawled that word, presumably by using her finger, with shit on the mirror of the downstairs toilet. And I mean shit —as in human waste.

I suspected it was that when I first clapped eyes, or more specifically, nose, on it, but I just couldn't believe it. And yet, when I went back later with rubber gloves, a bottle of bleach, and disinfectant, there was no mistaking it.

She never did show up anywhere in the house—yeah, thanks for nothing, Holt! She must have done the deed and then followed that up by doing a runner. Most likely by disappearing just like she had appeared from the forest.

Joy.

I just loved cleaning up after her, along with contemplating the prospect that the weirdo is still at large.

Jesus Christ. I'm sorry. I'm sorry, but I really am out of adjectives to express how I'm feeling right now. Don't get me wrong because I'm trying not to overreact here, but WHAT THE FUCK?! WHAT THE ACTUAL FUCK?!

Am I imagining this, or are things starting to take a turn for the bloody Dolce Vita? Alarms going off. Doors spontaneously opening. Birds divebombing the glass, and crazy lady—yes, I should know better than to refer to her this way—seeking me out and doing that.

I mean, who does that? WHO?!

Anyway, the police finally arrived about thirty minutes later. It's a good job she wasn't wielding a bloody axe because she would have had me diced and bubbling on the range cooker by the time they showed up.

Not that they were of any help. All they did was ask a bunch of stupid questions. How long have you known her? Do you have any idea why she would write something like that on your mirror? Did you see which direction she went in? What is her address? That's pretty much when the stupid questions stopped because suddenly, it was all about me being unprofessional. I had taken on a client but didn't even have any basic contact information for her. So then, I'm rewarded with one of those condescending looks. No sorry. I got that anyway because, generally speaking, policewomen (and men) tend to assume that air of superiority anyway. Only this time, it was exacerbated when they saw the house. It was then that they seemed more interested in what I did for a living than the woman who pushed her way into my home under false pretences, then took an artist dump on my toilet mirror.

Yeah, just call me Blow-Lord Battista. No, I don't deal in drugs. More's the bloody pity!

Anyway, I managed to encourage them to at least take my statement, which they insisted on reading back to me in a fantastical way like I was a child before I signed it. Then, thanks very much for nothing, and they were on their way, asking me to be sure to contact them if she showed up again. What for? Are they thinking of asking her for one of her fancy autographs?

Anyway, so then I did what I'm sure most home invasion victims do after such an experience. I took pictures of the offending graffiti for posterity and evidence before sterilising the hell out of the room.

Then, after scrubbing myself down under the shower, I dressed and sat at the computer to do the research and found out what siedem meant. Along the way, for added excitement, I also discovered that in Poland, the number seven is bad luck. A bit like our equivalent of thirteen. That's because of the number's uncanny resemblance to a scythe which we all know is the must-have accessory for any self-respecting grim reaper.

Fancy that, eh?

I'm still none the wiser as to what could have possibly motivated her to do that. I can only assume that it's some kind of jinx based on what I've discovered thus far. But why? Why would she want to wish me ill? We don't even know each other. Was my therapy that bad?

It's ridiculous.

I had considered not telling Sarah. I know that sounds awful. I just didn't want to worry her. But then she got back and smelt that the place reeked of bleach and disinfectant and wanted to know why.

She seemed to take it quite well, considering. I don't know if that was genuinely how she felt or if she played it down for my benefit. She just widened her eyes as expected and then said that given the amount of publicity we've had since Dolce Vita, it was only a matter of time before something like this happened.

Something like this? Really? You were expecting some nutjob to scrawl some foreign word on the loo's mirror with her faeces, were you?

You know what I mean.

Actually, I didn't. It's been over a year. Why now? It doesn't make any sense.

Regardless, Sarah, unsurprisingly, seemed more interested in the kamikaze birds. She listened carefully as I recounted the story and then went on to casually share a selection of possible reasons why the birds would have divebombed the house, including avian flu. However, she quickly explained that although there have been a few infections and even deaths in humans worldwide, most of the strains do not pose a threat, especially if we avoid contact with the corpses. When she spotted me looking at Buddy, she also added that there's minimal risk to dogs, providing they steer clear too.

I felt an overwhelming sense of pride at that moment. I mean, Sarah's been doing this for a while now, but it was only right then in that moment that I appreciated and respected her knowledge. And I think that's because it quite literally made me feel better, which reminded me of that morning I took puppy Buddy to her and how she made me feel then. Calmer. Reassured. She has a knack for that, my girlfriend.

So, I kissed her. She kissed me back and, you know, without even thinking, I'm locking all doors, windows and telling Holt to set the alarm. This time I asked him to confirm the instruction back to me. Twice. I had to be sure. Then, we retired for an early night, if you know what I mean.

And we took our time with it. The intimacy. The pleasure. This meant that I was suitably and blissfully exhausted before succumbing to restless sleep—all thoughts of that woman erased from the forefront of my mind.

Mercifully, I only had one nightmare last night. I had the usual hands around my throat, only they weren't craggy this time but just faceless hands, still female, I think, pushing on my windpipe so hard that I woke up coughing.

I couldn't get back to sleep after that. And since dawn was already signalling its imminent arrival by lighting a bonfire beyond the horizon, I slipped out of bed, sat at my computer, and began a session of extensive and well overdue research for the wedding.

Chair hire, catering, decorations, provisional decking, raised platforms, PA systems, officiators, bar staff, ushers, favours, and I also came up with a quirky idea featuring the golden wonder himself. If I can pull it off, that is. I have no idea.

I and the laptop then migrated to the kitchen to enjoy coffee during my bleary-eyed activities without disturbing Sarah.

I was still tapping at the keyboard when she came down, dressed for work. Then I made more coffee, did more research, and made more notes since it was too early to start calling people.

I considered skipping the morning's run, but then I looked at the hound who met my gaze with his judgemental cock of the head. So, off we went, ensuring the door was locked behind me. I avoided the woodland today. I just wasn't feeling it. I wanted us to stay in the light.

Then, I showered, made a multitude of phone calls asking for quotes, and then before I knew it, it was lunchtime.

So, now, guess what I'm doing....

That's right. I'm relaxing, feet up, telly on, can of lager in one hand and pizza in the other.

Believe that?

Of course you bloody don't! I'm standing out on the back lawn, freezing my nuts off because even the good weather has decided to pack up and get the hell out of here. The sun is still making the occasional appearance, but there's a northern chill driving into my bones that's making me wish I pulled on a fleece or something before coming outside.

In front of me is a woman in uniform, holding a clipboard and ticking boxes. Her colleague, whom she identified as John – wearing a white jumpsuit and mask – is hunting down bird corpses with a pair of giant tongs in the I'm-too-ashamed-to-even-admit-it long grass of the meadow that is my back lawn and placing them in a plastic bin.

Fear not. I called Irvin this morning and asked about the gardener that I saw that day at the manor. I figured that if he can take care of those formal gardens, he can do this place in his sleep. I also want to pick his brains about our options for having the ceremony and reception back here. There's plenty of space, but I need to think about how we're going to arrange everything.

"Okay, I think we've got all of them," the clipboard lady says, walking up to me.

According to the ID badge hanging around her neck on a lanyard with the words DEFRA (Department for Environment, Food and Rural Affairs) printed on it, her actual name is Joanne Tate. And I'm assuming that the slender-faced female in the photo with black hair down to her shoulders is undoubtedly a younger facsimile of the sun-bleached ponytailed ruddy-face I see before me.

"Any ideas of what could have caused this?" I ask.

"Could have been anything, really," Joanne says with a subtle northern accent, ticking yet another box on her seemingly endless clipboard form.

I thrust my hands in my pockets and try to cop a peek at the document she's filling out in the hope that it might give me some insight into what they've discovered so far.

"Should, I, um. Should I be worried? I noticed that your guy's all suited up."

"It's just precaution, really," she says, glancing at me before returning to more ticking and scribbling.

"Bird flu?" I ask. And I'm no expert, but I know it can be passed on.

"We'll know more once we've carried out some tests," she says unhelpfully.

"But have you seen anything like this before?"

"Aye, it's not that uncommon. Especially when you stick a giant building smack bang in the middle of their habitat." She follows that up with another sideways glance.

Okay. So now I'm feeling guilty. "Well, I didn't design the house, but as far as I know, it's supposed to be bird-friendly."

I watch her lips curl up, but she doesn't say anything. Not that she needs to. She's just assumed I'm one of those rich arseholes who doesn't give a shit. I want to tell her that I do. Especially if it's going to bring me more bad luck—yes, birds flying into buildings is considered bad luck too, fancy that, eh? – I've already got plenty of that.

I'm being flippant, of course. If I don't try to make light of all this shit, I'd be taking her snooty little smile way too personally, and right now, I want answers, not another argument.

"So, um, Joanne. In your extensive experience, have you ever witnessed several birds fly into a building at once?"

She finally looks up at me. The Battista charm strikes again.

"In my extensive experience, I have seen all sorts of things. Whole flocks of birds suddenly dropping dead, often without reason.

Electromagnetic changes in the Earth's surface or giant buildings reflecting the rest of their habitat. And each time, we're still none the wiser until we've carried out those tests."

Okay. So maybe I'm a little rusty after all. And yet, undeterred, I'm just about to go in with another question when we're all interrupted by the dulcet barks of one giant golden wonder as he comes bounding, fur jiggling, floppy one and half ears flapping, over to me.

"Hey, you! Hey," I coo, steadying myself against the weight of the dog as he nearly bowls me over. "Did you have a nice day with mummy, eh? Did you have a nice day?" I ask as I kiss and rub the dog's head and am rewarded with a series of slobbery licks.

Wow. I think the sight of the hound has even thawed the northerner standing next to me as she looks up from her clipboard and actually cracks a smile.

Sarah, in wellington boots and jeans, joins us.

She pecks me on the cheek when Buddy finally releases me and then turns to our visitor, who greets her with a nod of the head.

"Hey, what's going on?" Sarah turns to me and asks.

"Hey, you're home early."

"Yeah, I was a bit worried this morning, so I managed to get a few hours." Then she looks at our not-so-chatty guest.

I'm about to explain when John—mask hanging around his neck now—joins us. He nods at me and then looks at his colleague. "All done?" she asks. He nods again. I think he must be a mute as I haven't heard him speak once since he arrived.

"Okay, Mr. Battista. As I say, we'll run our checks and will let you know."

"How long will that take?" I ask as we start to make our way back to the front of the house.

"Not sure, really. That's all down to how busy the lab is, but it's normally around two to three weeks."

"Two to three weeks? What if it is something serious? We live here, after all. If something is affecting the wildlife, then we need to know."

"I appreciate that. All I can say is if you do discover any more dead animals, please don't touch them and give us a call."

"Marc?" It's Sarah who's suddenly looking alarmed.

"I'll explain in a second. Buddy!" He's snooping around the back lawn. I may be overreacting, but I just don't want him out here more than necessary. "Come on, boy."

At the front of the house. "Joanne, is there any way we can expedite the tests? I'm concerned for my dog," I say.

She opens her car door too eagerly for my liking considering that I'm obviously concerned. "We'll do the best we can. In the meantime, this is my card; feel free to call if anything else happens."

I take the card and watch the mute, now free of his jumpsuit, climb into the passenger seat of the small van before Miss unhelpful starts the car, reverses it off the driveway and away.

"Marc?" Sarah prompts.

"How did it go today?" I ask.

"Yeah. Okay."

"Is Buddy alright? Did he get his shots?" I add thoughtfully, eyes still on the diminishing red taillights of the van.

"Yes, he's perfectly fine. Why? What did she say?"

"It isn't what she said. It's what she didn't say that worries me."

18

THE RAVENS RETURN

5 Days until the wedding. 🐚

You know how, in the movies, morning arrives, and you get a close-up of the character's face sleeping soundly on a pillow as sunshine, and then the morning chorus fills the room and gently encourages them to open their eyelids with a flutter?

Well, that's not me. Me, no, I don't wake up drooling, although that has been known on the odd occasion. No, I spring up like Count-bloody-Dracula rising from his coffin generally because I've been dreaming about something hideous.

But not today. Today is a good day. Nope. Today is a *great* day. Sarah has taken leave so that we can go to the beach. Admittedly, it isn't my first choice, but given that we now live in a forest, I suppose that makes sense.

The warm summer breeze blows at my face and brings with it the delicious smell of…fried onions?

"Sarah, where have you brought us?"

When I turn to look at her, I realise that she isn't there and that I am standing on a deserted pier.

The pier.

"No. Sarah?" I call.

I can hear people talking. Buddy barking in the distance, but there's nobody here. The hot dog stand is empty, as is the pink cotton candy kiosk with that giant picture of a grinning child stamped on the front.

Seagulls call overhead, but when I look up, the deep blue sky is empty.

No.

I'm alone but for the breeze caressing my hair.

"Sarah?"

Who said that? I look around. Somebody said that, but it wasn't me. And yet, I'm the only one here.

"Can we have an ice cream now?"

Toby. "Toby?"

But there's no reply but for the haunting organ music of the carrousel, which is lifeless.

A flutter draws my attention to the pier's railing, where a group of ravens has appeared. All symmetrically aligned like soldiers on parade. I watch their heads bob up, down, and sideways. Black marble eyes swivelling. Large, curved beaks snapping.

No. No. Not again. This isn't happening. This isn't real.

"Can we have an ice cream now?"

I turn on the spot, looking in every direction. "Toby? Toby, where are you?!"

That's me. Only, I didn't make that sound. I can't open my mouth. It's stuck. Glued shut. I touch my lips and then try to pry them apart with my fingers, but they won't open. They're sealed together.

"Marc?"

"Sarah? Sarah, is that you?"

I spin around again, but the only things staring back at me are the ravens.

My movement spooks them, and they all fly off, but for *seven*. They remain. Cawing and pecking each other. Cawing and pecking. Cawing and pecking before they suddenly freeze. Like a movie within a movie, they've been put on pause until, one by one, they start falling backwards off the railing, plummeting to the rocks below.

"NO! NO!" I cry, but the words push against and bounce off my lips as they continue to fall…

One… two… three…

I rush toward the railing.

Four…

I'm trying to move fast, but I can't! My feet are sinking into the wooden decking.

Five….

"Marc?"

"Who is that? Who's calling me?"

Six…

"Siedem!"

I reach the railing, climb up and look over, down at the jagged rocks bathed by the frothy white peaks of the ocean like saliva over the serrated teeth of a rabid dog.

"Marc?"

I snap my head to the left, and fear pulls at the muscles in my body. Oh, God. There's my wife. There's Ellie. She's climbing onto the railing.

"NO! ELLIE! NO!"

She turns to me and opens her eyes, but instead of two beautiful sapphires, there's nothing there, nothing but empty black sockets. *"Yo…u… le…ft me… ther…e to die!"* she garbles as saltwater dribbles out of her mouth.

"ELLIE, NO!"

Then she lifts a withered, clawed hand, points at me before screeching in a voice I do not recognise, *"SIEDEM!" "SIEDEM!" "SIEDEM!"* And then allows herself to fall backwards.

"ELLIE! NO! ELLIE!"

I climb onto the railing after her. It creaks and groans under my weight. I move to step off again, but it's too late! It collapses under me, and then I'm falling, limbs flailing, mouth open, rocks beckoning until…

I wake, gasping, spluttering, coughing as if I've just emerged from the deep.

Rain spits heavily at the glass wall of the lounge.

Sarah is fast asleep on the couch across from me. We're both sharing a blanket. It takes me several seconds to get my bearings. We must have dozed off here while watching the light show of another storm, which is in the middle of an encore by the looks of it.

Thunder cracks then rolls away as if to confirm that.

I tap my watch. 02:03.

It's dark in here. So, "Holt, turn the lights on in the lounge."

Thunder rumbles.

"Holt?"

A power cut? This place is supposed to have a backup battery. That's one of the reasons why there are solar panels on the roof.

"Shit," I hiss and tap my watch a few times until a bluish hue dazzles me. I aim my wrist at the floor where Buddy is slumped. One eye observing me like a parent does a playing child. He no doubt heard me in my sleep. Yes, I know that sounds odd, but if you were here last time, you'd know that this dog has a knack for sensing my moods.

"I'm okay," I whisper as I watch those big doe eyes blink in the miniature spotlight of my watch before they suddenly look past me and around the sofa.

I turn slowly, following his gaze, training the beam of the light in that direction. There's nothing there but an empty room.

Lightning flashes, highlighting the skeletal features of the furniture.

"What have I told you about doing that?" I mumble at the dog, turning the light on him, but he simply blinks into the glare and moves away.

And I'm just about to follow him with the beam of light when.

"Marc?"

The voice startles me, especially as it's scored by a loud clap of thunder.

I turn to Sarah but am surprised to find that she's still sound asleep.

"Sarah? Hey?"

No response.

"Hey, come on. Let's get to be–"

"Marc?"

A bitter draft of panic blows through me. I am looking right at Sarah, and her lips did not move. That voice. It seemed to be coming from…

I don't finish the thought, but instead, slowly pan the light up in the direction of the sound, and–

Jump backwards, off the couch, crashing to the floor.

There's something in the hallway! Backlist by the nightlights, something is standing in the bloody hallway!

Something?

"Fuck! Sarah! Sarah! Wake up!" I scream, shaking her leg and shining the light in her face. But she doesn't stir. She doesn't respond.

"Sarah!" I yell, whipping the light back to the doorway…only to discover that the sofa is now in the way.

Shit!

Slowly, reluctantly, I bend forward on all fours, crawl across the floor to the edge of the sofa and peer around it, training the tiny light beam in front of me like it's a weapon. It drifts over Buddy's shiny gold fur and then to the doorway – there's nothing there now.

But I saw something.

What was it?

I don't know. It was tall. Much taller than me. Skinny and withered.

Like a tree!

No. Yes. No. Maybe. But it was bony with legs!

"Oh, sweet Jesus… I'm really starting to lose–"

A loud clang and swishing sound makes me yelp when the metal shutters slide, loudly, down over the glass wall.

Thunder booms overhead, and I duck instinctively. My heart is thudding. Temple throbbing. Muscles taut. What the hell is going on? I didn't do that! Who's doing that?

Scuttling. Behind the sofa.

It's that thing. It's in the room! I crawl around the opposite side of the sofa as Buddy's growl fills the air.

I close my eyes. "No. No. No… no… this isn't happening. This isn't real," I chant through ragged breaths, afraid to reopen my eyes.

Afraid of what I'll see. And yet…

I reluctantly reopen my eyes. The room remains steeped in blackness. I shine the light beam in front of me, then slowly, cautiously move to peer around the sofa, but before I do, I hear a strange chittering sound. I turn the light in that direction, invoking an abrasive screech from something I can't even describe: a giant insectoid, tree-like creature with quivering extrusions crawling over Sarah.

Buddy barks and lunges for the thing causing it to screech and rear up onto the back of the sofa before falling onto the wood floor, where it scratches, skids and eventually clicks its way out of the room.

"Oh… My God…." I tremble, running fingers through my damp hair. What on earth was that thing?

"Marco!" I yelp! A voice. Right next to me, but there's nothing there. There's nothing bloody there! I just felt the cold, smelt the fetid breath on my left cheek

"Marco!"

"Leave me alone!"

"MARCO!"

"LEAVE ME ALONE!" I jolt awake. The sun is shining. The birds are singing, and I am hyperventilating, gulping in air as if I've just emerged from the bottom of the lake.

"Hey… hey… are you okay… are you alright?"

In an ugly scene way too reminiscent of my life with my wife, Sarah is standing over me, holding a mug of coffee.

I'm sweating. My heart is still trying to escape my nightmare, and it takes several seconds for me to absorb my surroundings.

I'm still in the lounge.

"You spent the night down here," Sarah narrates as if reading my thoughts while I sit up and push the throw that's draped over me away as if it's made of hot coal.

"I um," I swallow, "um, why didn't you wake me?" I say with a croak, gratefully taking ownership of the mug as Sarah perches on one of the sofa's armrests. "I tried, but you seemed adamant that you wanted to sleep down here, so I left you to it."

"Oh," is all I can muster because my head is still fuzzy.

Shit. I seemed to be trying for a hat trick last night. I groan, "I had the shittiest nightmares," I say, sipping the hot, bitter liquid.

"Yes, I could tell."

"What do you mean?"

"What were you dreaming about?"

"I, uh…" I run my hand through my hair, "just a load of shit."

"Yeah?"

"Yes. I can barely remember any of it."

"Really?"

I squint at her. "Yes, really."

"So, you weren't dreaming about Ellie then?"

I sigh. Shit. "Well, dreaming is not the word I'd use exactly."

"You've been dreaming about her a lot," she says casually.

I rock my head. "Well, she is my wife," I say flatly.

"Was."

"What?"

"*Was* your wife," she repeats.

"Well, technically, she still is."

My girlfriend nods and looks away from me. "Right."

"Oh, come on, you know I didn't mean it like that, but I am still married to her. What do you want me to do? Pretend that I'm not?"

"I don't want you to do anything."

"Good. Because for a second there, Sarah, you were making me feel bad for dreaming about my dead wife," I say with an incredulous chuckle.

She takes a few seconds before sighing and allowing herself to slide off the arm and into a seat so she can be closer to me. Then she runs a hand over my shoulders in a semi rub. "I'm sorry. I know you've got a lot going on right now. Is there anything I can do to help?"

I look across at her and reach over my shoulder to touch her hand. "Thank you. But you've been working just as hard."

There's a pause. Those lake inhabitants who haven't already migrated for the winter make themselves heard while I take another sip from my cup.

"Marc, should I be worried?" Sarah begins, "your nightmares, they're–"

"I'm fine," I interrupt. I'm not. I know that. These crappy dreams are back with a vengeance. And you don't need to be a psychologist to understand that these are a manifestation of something else. Most likely stress. Physically, I'm coping but mentally… well….

I blow air out of my mouth and stare through the glass to the lake that is its usual glorious self under the early morning sun. That, coupled with the mini massage, is already rubbing away the dregs of those nightmares.

"I'm okay. Just a lot's been happening. I just need to get through this latest stuff. You know. Like organising the gay wedding of the century."

"You do realise that, at this stage, the boys will just be glad to be married. They've even said as much."

"I know," I say, watching a trio of geese take off from one side of the lake and land on the other. "But that's precisely why I want it to be special. They've had to postpone this so many times, and now, with this latest run of shitty luck, I don't want to let them down."

"You're not going to let them down."

I turn to her. "How can you be so sure?"

She continues rubbing my shoulders. "Because you're Marco Battista and," she sighs, "I may not have known you as long as your wife, but the Marc I know doesn't do things by half."

I close my eyes and bow my head. "I'm sorry about that. I know how it must have sounded."

"No, you're right. Really," she says with a reassuring smile, green eyes sparkling in the morning light, "it's just strange. You know I'm not like that, how pragmatic I am when it comes to, you know, affairs of the heart. But you dreaming about her, that's something I can't compete with. It's personal. Intimate."

I scoff. "Yeah. Well, if it's any consolation, my dreams about her are anything but. Seriously. You have nothing to worry about."

"It sounds so petty, doesn't it?"

"No. I get it. Really."

"You do?"

"Of course."

Never one to be left out, Buddy pads over and collapses onto the floor next to me before resting his head on my thigh. "Oh, good morning to you too," I say, rubbing his furry ears.

"Well, I need to get to work," Sarah says, standing up.

"Yeah, us too, mate. We've got a ton of calls to make, paperwork, and emails to deal with. Then, we need to stop by and see how the boys are getting on."

Sarah crouches down to make a fuss of the dog before planting a kiss in my hair. I smile at the action, although I feel like grimacing because my hair must be damp and sweaty. "I'll see you boys later then."

I look up at her. "You sure will," I say because it's starting to feel like one of those awkward moments. You know, like when you bump into someone you haven't seen in a while and have made your small talk, and then things go a bit quiet. This is odd because we're not generally like this, and I realise that it's probably because my girlfriend still has more on her mind.

I look at her, and when she doesn't move nor add anything more to the conversation, I smile, "What?"

"I'm still worried about you," she says thoughtfully.

"I told you, Sarah–?"

"Yeah. I know, but all that romantic stuff aside. With everything that's happened, I'm worried you're taking on too much on your own. The manor, the wedding, this other stuff."

"Other *stuff*? You're worried I'm *cracking up* under all the pressure?" I ask with a half-smile.

"I just know how you get when you start something."

"Well, my father used to say, if you're going to do something, then do it properly."

"Yeah. He also died of a heart attack," she says curtly, wiping the smile off my face.

"Oh, okay."

"I'm sorry. I didn't mean it like that," she adds quickly.

"It's okay. It's alright. I'm alright. You don't have to worry."

"Are you sure?" she asks earnestly.

I cock my head and gaze up at her curiously.

"I spoke to Ethan yesterday, and he said you haven't talked to him a while."

I frown at that and then nod knowingly. "Right. Well, he's not my warden anymore, Sarah. I don't have to check in with him, you know."

"No, but I think it would be useful for you right now."

"Right now?"

"You know what I mean–"

"Sarah, look, I'm fine. Okay? Has it been a stressful week? Of course it has. But I'm fine. Really. And I know you two are pals and everything now, but I'll talk to Ethan when I'm good and ready, alright?"

"He saved my life, Marc. Of course, we talk. I remember you telling me that he saved yours too. I just thought that–"

"Sarah, I said I'll speak to Ethan when I'm ready." My words are much sharper than I intend.

"Okay," she says suddenly. "I'll see you later then." With that, she turns and leaves the room.

19

GOSSIP

FAWNDALE. 10:15.

Fawnham has a population of 30,000, and it's what I like to refer to as civilisation since there are an array of shops, supermarkets, pubs, eateries, charity stores, and, um, more charity stores. What can I say? The people around this neck of the woods generally tend to need nothing and thus make themselves feel better by regularly donating to those who do.

Fawndale—note the theme here—is tiny by comparison. It's even smaller than Porthcove. There are less than one hundred dwellings, comprising a whopping crowd-making population of around three hundred. Many years ago, it wasn't even classed as a village. It was just a tiny hamlet of cottages that served as dwellings for the hired help that served the aristocrats around here.

There's no pub, church or much else but for the village store slash newsagent slash post office; a quaint stone building attached to the owner's home.

I quite like our quaint little nothing village consisting primarily of trees, sprawling fields, brooks, bridges, and streams sprinkled with the occasional fuck-off giant mansion.

So, anyway, I'm in the village store right now, and I've managed to wedge my six-foot-something-frame down the goodie aisle as my shopkeeper-cum-parish-counsellor member, Mary, loves to refer to it when I hear the bell ring. Yes. A cowbell, and yes, that's obviously a village store thing.

Am I like a rat in one of those experiments, reminded of Porthcove every time I hear the sound of that thing? Of course I bloody am. And it's just occurred to me. This is almost certainly one of the reasons why Sarah loves this place so much. It probably reminds her of home.

Ah, Sarah! Chocolate biscuits. I also need vegetables for the casserole I'm planning tonight. This place has a whole selection of fantastically organic produce that actually tastes like what it's supposed to be.

Can you hear this shit? My conversion to house-bloody-husband is almost complete.

So, anyway, plain or milk chocolate? With or without reduced sugar....

Wow, that *Carol? Karen?* I've forgotten her name – the village busybody – has just wandered up to the counter and is loud. She's barely entered the place and has already initiated compulsory village gossip, which begins with the enthralling topic of the weather, moves onto the fact that Mary's son called her from Africa last night where he's thoroughly enjoying his safari with his wife of three years, and then descends into the scintillating recount of last night's parish meeting.

Time for a sharp exit.

Oh...no...wait...Gossip... Apparently, Ken – presumably another parish council member – was very unprofessional at last night's meeting. He kept talking over K, which was undoubtedly a point of order, especially since a decision was already made to demolish *Frost Lake Manor*.

My ears prick up instantly.

Apparently, the big-city developer has been dragging his heels with the refurbishment of the place, and now there's a serious concern that they might be deviating from standard preservation orders. She, K-whatever-her-name-is, believes English Heritage should be notified.

What the fuck?

On the other hand, Ken —who in her opinion must have made some kind of investment in and or received a backhander from the developer, given his behaviour—was incensed. K then argued that the hotel chain was a much better choice. They may well have dragged their heels, but it was through no fault of their own. Ken disagreed. An argument ensued, some insults traded, and then it all descended into a farce.

…but that isn't the worst of it, Mary. Did you hear that somebody called the police out there yesterday? Two patrol cars, no less. Sirens blaring, the works. I can't say for sure, but there is talk of him being, you know, a bit quick with his hands. Nobody's seen her. She tends to run off to work first thing, but they think, you know, that he might have a violent streak on account of him being, you know, mentally deficient. And now we've got him living here right in our back yard.

Wow. I'm a wife beater and mentally deficient. There's no doubt David could make a joke out of that last bit.

So now I'm stuck.

Especially since, well, you know where I described the so-called *goodie section* as an aisle? Well, it isn't really. It's more like a shelf for dwarfs, really. And there's only so long you can stand there and agonise over the biscuit selection, which is only three from the leading brands with a couple from the discount brands that most avoid like the plague unless absolutely desperate.

Shit. Awkward.

Maybe I should slink out and get the veg before–

"Everything okay over there, Marco?" comes Mary's cheerful voice.

I look up and smile. "Yes, all good, thanks, Mary. Just, you know, deciding the fate of the world over here," I say with a big smile and a wave of my *quick* hand. I resist the urge of conjuring a nervous twitch for the old battle axe.

I'm good at that now. I'm well trained at public performances, thanks to Porthcove.

K, clearly wishing to dispel the vitriol of her recount, which is still hanging heavily in the air like a poisonous vapour, decides to do my favourite; initiate small talk.

"Oh, morning, Doctor. I didn't see you there," she says, projecting an overenthusiastic smile, clearly just for me.

"Oh, good morning, K… um," oh shit! "how are you today?"

Like I don't already know.

"Oh, wonderful, just wonderful," she says in a clipped English accent, which I'm starting to get a distinct impression is just for best around here since most of the people I've heard don't have any genuinely discernible accent. Maybe the occasional vowel sounds a tad country-like, but beyond that, it's just general stuff.

K, for example, sounded just like that until she shifted demeanour and greeted me because she thinks I'm a successful doctor from the city. Not that I wish to diminish her intellect, of course, but I don't think she genuinely appreciates the fact that *Doctor* Battista and the *big property developer* of Battista Properties are one and the same.

"How are you settling into Holt?" she asks—all smiles.

"Oh, very well, thank you," I respond with my own proper accent.

"Oh, that's wonderful. And how's business?"

Code I'm interpreting as who else is mental in the village and perhaps gossip about next. "Business is very good, thank you so much for asking. How are you feeling?"

"Oh, I'm fine. Just fine. Well, I best get going," she says, lifting the newspaper she just purchased.

"It was a pleasure to see you again," I say, beaming a fake smile as I watch the woman retreat out of the door then hurry down the cobblestone path.

Mary, who, by the way, reminds me of the countryside edition of Joanna Lumley with a well-kempt appearance most becoming of a woman who must be in her early sixties, waits until the sticky wooden door has shut before offering, "Karin."

"I'm sorry?"

"Her name is Karin."

"Karin. Of course." I smile, smacking the pack of biscuits

against my temple.

"And *how are you* settling in?" The question is posed genuinely based on the inflexion she injected into her words and the smile on her face.

"We're fine," I say, "and by the way, it was just the one patrol car, not two. And they strolled to the front door. There were no sirens and no flashing lights," I say.

The shopkeeper gives me a knowing smile, and because I know she represents the heart of the village, I add, "We're having problems with our alarm lately. It keeps going off, and it's connected to the station," I lie.

"What you do in the privacy of your own home is your business," she says, offering no further comment except, "did you say you need some vegetables too?"

"Yes, please. Some carrots and potatoes. I'm planning on making a casserole tonight." Yes. Even I can small talk when the situation calls for it. But it doesn't feel that way with this lady who reminds me a little of Sarah's mother, although they don't look anything alike. I can only assume the similarity has nothing to do with appearances and everything to do with the fact that she stands behind the counter in the same oracle-like way most people do in such tight-knit communities.

I watch her pull out some brown paper bags from under the counter and make her way over to the front door. "Oh, I can do that, Mary."

"Nonsense. We're all about service around here, you know," she says with a wink as she pulls the door open and then proceeds to make a fuss of Buddy, who's been patiently waiting out here.

"Kilo of each?" she asks, nodding at the wicker baskets of vegetables sitting on shelves just outside the front door.

"Yes, please," I say and then watch her put potatoes into a bag.

After several seconds, I venture, "Mary?"

Without stopping what she's doing, she pre-empts me with, "I know. I'm sorry you had to hear that. Karin does work herself into a bit of a state sometimes. I've told her, I've said, Karin, why bother being on the council if it vexes you so? Those men are forever getting on her last nerve. But she insists that it's her civic duty. Although," she looks up and touches her nose, "between you and me. I think it's more about keeping her finger on the pulse than it being a so-called *calling,* if you know what I mean."

I smile conspiratorially. "Well, actually, Mary. There's something about what she said that did interest me."

"Oh?"

"Yes. The hotel chain she mentioned, the one that was going to buy Frost Lake Manor, do you know why they didn't in the end?"

She thinks about this, then, "No. Not really. I know they were particularly keen at one point, wrote to us detailing the plans they had for the place, how it was going to create jobs, and all that nonsense. And then the next thing we know, they'd withdrawn their offer, and the property was back on the market again," she says, handing me the paper bag full of potatoes.

Then, shaking out the next bag, she makes a start on the giant carrots that I can see still have earth clinging to them. "Of course, there was all that bother with the so-called tenant who still lived there at the time. Maybe that scared them off."

"Tenant?"

"Yes. Well, not really a tenant per se. More like a squatter. She used to work there; had for many years. Then Lady Emmerson died with no family, so she was out of a job. Everybody thought she'd just gone back home, but instead, months later, they found that she was still living in the house."

"But I thought the house had been abandoned for some time," I say.

"So did everybody else," she says, giving me a knowing look and handing me the bag of carrots.

And just like that, the sun disappears behind a big black cloud.

"That's what the parish council are up in arms about," Mary continues unabated, "some members, I, for one, just want to see the place restored to its former glory. Others, well, let's just say that they're more possessive."

I follow Mary back inside to the till. Buddy sighs with boredom and flops back down.

Meanwhile, my mind is a hive buzzing with a swarm of thoughts, but there's one in particular that keeps bothering me, but

I don't want to address it for fear of getting stung by something else.

"Is everything alright?" Mary asks.

I don't even know how to process this. It doesn't make any sense whatsoever.

"Yes," I say, "of course."

"You don't need to worry, you know. Most of us are glad you're there. I, for one, cannot wait to see what you do with the place. How are things coming along?"

I nod vacantly. "Great. Yeah. It's all progressing well," I lie.

"Marvellous. That's just marvellous," she says, ringing up my goods while I consider whether or not I even want to ask the question.

No. Don't do it! Don't!

And yet, "Mary. Can you tell me a bit more about this woman?"

"Lady Emmerson? Didn't know much about her, really. She was a bit of a recluse. Kept herself to herself. I don't think she was very well towards the end. Bedridden for some time until the day her help found her."

"No. Not her. The woman who worked for her."

"Oh," the shopkeeper says, handing me my change. "Don't really know much about her either. They were well-matched. Rarely saw her in here. Just the once, really. Years ago."

My stomach starts griping as I ask the question. "Did she happen to be looking for a job by any chance?"

The shopkeeper looks at me sideways. "Why yes. How did you know that?"

I shrug because she's the weirdo that made a complete tit of me before smearing shit all over my toilet mirror. No wonder she was pissed off. I bought the house she was living in. Rent-free.

Fuck.

Of course, me being a masochist, I ask, "Did this woman have an accent by any chance?"

Mary makes a show of thinking about this. "Well, it's been a while now, and I wouldn't normally remember such detail, but this lady. There was something about her, you know? She also made a smart remark that I didn't think was appropriate at the time. No idea where she might be now. Probably gone back home with a bit of luck."

I can't quite work out if Mary is racist or if she's just pleased to be shot of the woman. I'm going to go with the last one. Then, I force a smile, thank her for everything and bid her a good day before hurrying back to the car and starting the engine.

It all makes perfect sense now. She was quite happy squatting at the manor until I came along. So, I suppose she got her revenge. But that wasn't my fault. I didn't even know she bloody existed!

Shit.

Back at Holt, I pull up on the driveway, kill the engine and then listen to it tick over.

Gradually, the chorus of wildlife fades in like the orchestra at the beginning of a performance, and I'm reminded of where I am. *Home.* This is *my* sanctuary. And I've decided that if I manage to pull this sale off, I will make an offer on this place because I'm not going to let some bitter old bint scare me away from where I belong.

I, we belong in Fawndale. She did not.

I close my eyes, pinch the bridge of my nose and breathe deeply. Oh… my skull feels like it's slowly inflating like a bloody balloon!

Calm down. You're okay. Calm down. Breathe…. That's it.

On the bright side, this latest news means that there's nothing supernaturally creepy about any of this. It's just a simple case of a psychopathic squatter taking her revenge.

"That, of course, is much better."

Shit.

Buddy obviously doesn't care for my sarcasm because he's getting antsy in the backseat. Like he wants to be out of the car. He keeps grumbling and tapping at the door until I'm forced to open my eyes and turn to him. "What's the matter with you, eh?"

The dog just looks at me, doe eyes blinking innocently like, *what? Do I need to explain it?*

"Oh, sorry, mate. Do you need pee-pee? Is that it? Alright, but don't go running off. I don't think I have the mental capacity to play hide and seek with you today. And we still don't know what happened to those birds."

The birds? Freaky coincidence?

I reach over and tug at the door handle. No sooner has it swung open and the dog jumps out and runs off, barking as he goes.

"Buddy! No! Buddy! What did I bloody say?!"

But the hound isn't listening. He's bounding away from the car down the side path toward the back of the house.

"Buddy! Wait!" I jump out of the car, slam the door shut and give chase. As I do, I can feel my anxiety growing because, for all the bravado and hard talk, these things, these events are starting to take their toll and–

What the hell?

I skid to a halt in the tall grass as I watch Buddy trot down the lawn-cum-meadow towards the jetty but stop twenty or so feet away and start barking.

Fear yanks at my stomach muscles and pulls them into a tight knot. A man is standing on the jetty! He's wearing a flat cap, a shirt with rolled-up sleeves, and a grey waistcoat, like something out of bloody Peaky Blinders.

"HEY! EXCUSE ME!" I yell angrily. No, it isn't anger. It's red-hot rage. Another intruder on my back lawn. Another bastard stranger is invading my castle, and I'm not bloody having it.

I start forward. Fast. Half running. Half slipping as cold wetness wraps itself around my ankles yet does nothing to cool my ire.

Oh hello. The scariest beast of all appears to have made a comeback. The one that speaks with its fists and not its words. The same one that sent Aaron crashing onto a diner's dinner table, demolishing half of the room in the process. The dark passenger that I believed Ethan Holmes had exorcized months ago.

But then, you know all about that already, don't you? My psychological hitchhiker. Eagerly devouring each calamitous episode of my life with voyeuristic voracity. See? Now I'm taking out on you.

"Excuse me," I rage disdainfully, "this is private property! What are you doing here?" I demand as I reach Buddy, who's still barking at the stranger. The man moves a few steps closer, removes his hat, and holds it up in a surrendering gesture to the hound.

"I'm sorry. I didn't mean to scare you, I'm–"

"Who the fuck are you?" I demand in my human bark. "What are you doing here?"

"I'm, I'm Bernard, the gardener," he says in a soft lilt.

"What?"

"Bernard, Bernie, the gardener," the man offers again.

Buddy, who has obviously accepted the man's word, has stopped barking now and is looking at him, brown eyes on full, flirtatious display because *he's* a bloody tart!

You're way too trusting, I want to school him, but I don't. Obviously. Because, well, there's a time and place for that, and this is not it.

"Irvin sent me," the man offers, "he tells me, you're thinking of avin' a weddin' here in a few days."

"Hopefully," I say and watch his bushy wild eyebrows furrow, so I qualify, "yes. We're hoping to. It's just all a bit last minute, so I've been running around like a headless chicken trying to sort everything."

"Aye. Well, you'll need to be careful if you're thinkin' of using the jetty. Those two wood struts in the middle there," he turns and points, "are a bit loose. I think someone's hit em with a boat or something. They could do with a bit of tightening. You wouldn't want the appy couple to end up in wa-er."

"No. God, no. That's the last thing we need," I say, running a hand through my hair because I just got a snapshot of that. Any other time that might even be funny, but not on David's wedding day.

I've calmed down a little now. I think that's in part because this man gives off the same vibe as Irvin. Calm. Unpretentious. Knows his craft. He's exactly the type of person I need around here right now. As it is, I've had to ask Irvin and the lads to help set up for the wedding. That's taking them away from working on the house, which is equally time-sensitive, but needs must.

The gardener is chuckling. "You're a beauty, ain't ya?" He is, of course, referring to my floozy of a dog who, when not busy scaring the shit out of me with his spooky ways, enjoys throwing himself at the first stranger that'll rub his ears.

"What appened?" the old man asks, noticing that one of the dog's ears is permanently wilted.

"Ah, he had a run-in with a fox when he was still a puppy," I explain.

"A fox?"

I nod. "Yeah. Long story." Because I haven't got time to go into it, I sigh. "Look. I'm sorry about the greeting. It's just that...." I don't want to get into that either.

Luckily, the man must pick up on that because he says with a faint smile, "Oh, don't worry. I understand. A man's home is his castle."

I shrug. Couldn't have put it better myself.

"I've missed this place," he adds.

"Yeah? You used to work here?"

"Oh aye, it's been a while now."

"And you live around here?"

"Yeah. In one of the cottages in the village. You 'ave to drive by my place to get ere," he says, giving Buddy a second round of head rubbing.

"So, how long have you lived here?"

"In Fawndale?" he smiles amiably, "pretty much most of my life. My folks owned a farm a few miles away. I grew up there until I met the girl of my dreams, and we moved in together. We had many a happy year until she fell sick, and, well, as you can imagine... everything changed."

"I'm sorry. What was her name?"

"Charlotte," he says with a wistful smile.

"So, you knew Mrs. Emmerson?" I ask, eager to steer the conversation away from any personal stuff.

"*Lady* Emmerson. Oh aye. And, of course, the Carsons after that."

"The Carsons too?"

"Aye. I've been here pretty much since this place was built. Handpicked apparently. Mr. Carson had heard good things about me," he says with a chuckle, "yeah, it's comin' on five or so years if I'm not mistaken."

"So, you knew them well?"

He nods. "As well as anyone can know their boss," he says with a wry smile, "they were decent folk. Not that I saw much of em. He was always away on business. Lady of the house was often here alone. Aye, we've had many a chat out here. She was a kind soul. Would bring me tea and biscuits. Lemonade in the summer. Lovely lady.

Always respectful, you know. Considering who she was married to. She didn't have any of those airs and graces. But Lady Emmerson. She was different, more like Mr Carson."

"How so?"

He looks at me. No doubt starting to feel interrogated.

"I'm sorry," I say quickly.

He observes me for a few seconds. Then, "Well, you know what these successful types can be like. They hire help to do a job. Not socialise. And I'm fine with that. You just tells me what you needs doin', and I'll make sure it's done."

Oh okay. I consider pushing him on the other stuff, but I'm not sure this is the time and place… I may just circle back to it. "Well, as you can see," I say, holding out my hands to the meadow in front of us, "this place is in need of some TLC. And you mentioned the jetty. Do you think you could take a look at it? I was hoping to use it as part of the ceremony, but now I'm worried," I say, turning around to look at the offending thing.

"Oh, aye. No problem. I can sort that. The brackets probably just need tightenin' and maybe add some more reinforcement."

"Oh, great. That's brilliant."

"And, I can have the rest of this place restored to how Mr. Carson liked to see it, stripes in the lawn, the lot. Just need a couple of days."

"Well, that's the thing. I need it done like yesterday as we need to start prepping for the wedding."

"Well, I'm supposed to be working at the manor–"

"Yeah, this supersedes that."

"Okay. Well, I promised my neighbour, she's a bit frail, bless her heart, that I'd be over to do her lawn, but I can come over after that. So, if not tomorra, then the day after."

"Oh, that's fantastic. Thank you so much, Bernard," I say gratefully.

"Call me, Bertie."

"Bertie," I say, proffering my hand to shake his, "I'm Marco. I realise I didn't even introduce myself."

"So, what happened?" I find myself asking. Partly because I'm feeling brighter and partly because I'm an idiot and the words just slipped out of my mouth. Anything so I don't have to think about just how much I have bitten off here.

Bernard frowns at me. "What do you mean?"

"Well, you knew the Emmersons from the Manor. The Carsons from this place. What's their story?"

"I really should get going. I've taken up enough of your time," the man says, putting his cap back on. "As I say, I'll be over as soon as I can to make a start on this," he says, looking around the so-called lawn and then glancing furtively up at the house as if he can't even bring his eyes to look at it.

Then he's gone. But not up the lawn to the front of the house, but across it and into the woods.

20

TROUBLE

HOLT. 15:30.

4 days until the wedding. ⚖

Slumped over the laptop, clutching my mobile phone. That's how Sarah found me last night.

She said I scared her to death. Code I interpreted as she thought I had a heart attack but obviously stopped short of voicing that after yesterday's little chat.

Anyway, no coronary, just more phone calls to more companies so that I could hear how they wanted to laugh at me, some even did, when I said I needed their product and or service for a wedding that I was looking to stage this week.

This bloody week!

Oh, look. More palpitations. Maybe Sarah's going to get that heart attack after all.

None. I repeat, none of the companies involved in the original wedding has been able to change the date at such short notice, which means I've had to call far and wide to find others with last-minute availability, otherwise known as cancellations. E.g., I found myself deliriously happy with the news that somebody else's dream of lifelong marital bliss had been crushed.

Yes, I'm despicable. But I'm also desperate.

On the bright side, I have a vague recollection of Aaron calling last night to inform me that all the guests have been sent the change-of-venue information. Some have confirmed, but the others will probably need a progress chase. Then he repeated for what feels like the hundredth time to let him know if I need help with anything.

Guess what I said?

Oh, God. I don't even want to think about it. I don't know who I'm trying to impress with this thing, but, well, they're definitely going to be unimpressed.

I couldn't sleep last night either, no doubt, thanks to that lovely nap I didn't intend to have deep in the arms of my keyboard. That, and the usual clutch of bad dreams. Last night's episode featured a special guest appearance by Bernard. He was mowing the lawn in his boots and a wedding dress complete with billowing train and his white hairy rug of a chest on full display, thanks to the dress's plunge neckline.

I woke up, gagging; that's all I can say.

I concluded at 08:33 this morning, while on hold for at least thirty-five minutes and being brainwashed into believing that your call is important to us, that the one upside of all of this is that I've been so busy fretting over this wedding that I've barely had time to process much else, which is good. On the other hand, I shouldn't have to induce a nervous breakdown to avoid thinking about and even dealing with certain other things. Including what the fuck has Sarah done with that picture of Toby and me? I kept glancing over to look at it for comfort while on the phone yesterday, and each time, I felt its absence like a lost limb.

I even looked at Sarah for the longest time yesterday evening.

What? she said, but I couldn't bring myself round to talk about it. I was physically and thus too emotionally exhausted to deal with it in a diplomatic way that was more subtle than a please just stay the fuck away from my stuff, will you?

So yeah. It wouldn't have been my finest hour. Now, I can see much more clearly in the cold light of day, like an alcoholic after a drunken stupor. And by default, I'm feeling bloody guilty just at the thought of that. Yeah, jump on in. The water's warm.

Now, Buddy is sitting at my feet while I nurse a mug of hot black coffee and take a breather from my tele-solicitations to gaze out over the mirror of the lake that has wrapped the colourful majesty of autumn in an early-morning veil of mist. Through it, I can just about make out the outline of Frost Lake Manor—the property that now directly reflects the key to my financial salvation. Even with its problems.

A sigh pushes its way out of my lips. This is a lot. Even I can see that, and if I carry on like this, repressing everything, it will only come out in other ways. I had the foresight to avoid that confrontation with Sarah last night, but they'll come a time when that red mist will descend, and God knows what will happen.

But I can't talk to anybody. David. Well, this is supposed to be about him, not me. Sarah. It's complicated. I don't want to burden her. Ethan is the most logical person, but I hate talking to him because I feel like I'm right back there, in therapy when I do.

But then, maybe that's where I belong. Perhaps I'm going about this arse about-face. It's like a cycle. I go to therapy, get better and then stop because I don't want to feel like I'm still in treatment and then I get overwhelmed, start seeing shit and then agonise about going back into therapy. If I could just bring myself round to submitting to Ethan's fucking condescending ways, all of this, this shit, would be so much easier.

"SHIT!"

Buddy whimpers.

"It's okay, mate. That isn't aimed at you either. It's aimed at me," I say softly, looking down into those chocolate eyes observing me with interest.

"I'm cracking up, mate."

The dog groans and puts a paw over his eyes.

The sight makes me chuckle. "Yeah, thanks for your support."

I know I'm starting to unravel because now that I am no longer in a heightened state of anxiety, I can see that it was me who rang the doorbell the other night.

When what I believed was some kind of entity dissolved into

the so-called silhouette of my dead wife, which then dissolved into the mist drifting in through the front door, I ran over there. I ran over and stared out into the night, calling her bloody name like a lunatic, like she was going to come skipping back to me.

She didn't. Obviously.

But then, like the twisted fool that I am, I started ringing the doorbell for some obscure reason, testing the thing as if the action would, in some warped way, validate what I had just seen.

Of course, it didn't.

Would you like to know how I know that for a fact? Because this morning, I had the presence of mind to go through Holt's video logs. There were no entries for that night. None. No videos of anybody ringing the bell or banging on the door except one person. Bet you can't guess who that was.

Shit.

Buddy jumps up from his seat and, for a split second, I think he's going to do his soothing magic paws thing, which interestingly, I'm happy to welcome for once, but instead, he trots out of the lounge and into the hallway where I can just about see that… "Oh hell no. Don't even think about starting your creepy–"

I'm cut short by the ominous sound of that low guttural growl that never fails to set me on edge.

I don't know what it bloody is about this place, but he was nothing like this before. Even in the pits of London, he was never like this. Here, everything seems to piss him off.

"Buddy, mate, you aren't helping with all of this–"

"…it would seem that residents of this sleepy village are divided on what to make of the crop circles and the uninvited attention that they have brought on their community."

The TV has just sprung to life and scared the crap out of me! A news bulletin. And it's loud.

But before you start reading into that, I can tell you; it's happened before. Nothing creepy going on here. I think it's something to do with Holt. Of course. Which reminds me, I need to call those people out here to check him, it over.

"Holt, turn the TV off."

TV is not responding. Please check the power supply and try

again.

"Holt! Turn the bloody TV off!"

I'm sorry, Marco. I didn't quite hear that. Could you please repeat the instruction?

"Oh, forget it."

I hunt around the couch for the remote.

"…well, why not? Considering the size of our universe, is it really that much of a leap to think there's another intelligent life out there attempting to communicate with us?"

"Then, they should pick up the bloody phone like normal people," I mutter, picking up the remote and prodding the off button.

Nothing happens.

"SHIT!"

The household phone that I keep forgetting even exists startles me by shrilling, loudly, tugging at my last nerve.

I snatch the thing up from its charging cradle on the wall unit. "Hello?"

A cacophony of loud static and what sounds like scraping metal sounds blare out, forcing me to hold the receiver away from me like a wriggling wounded rodent.

Scowling at the thing, I yell, "I can't hear you! Try again!" then slam the contraption down on its cradle. Who the hell even has a house phone anymore anyway?

"…so you don't believe beings made it from another planet? Nah, not really. Just some bored kids, ennit, with a stick and a piece of string."

"Holt, turn off the TV!"

TV is not responding. Please check the power supply and try again.

"Not responding, eh? I'll give you not bloody responding!"

The sixty-something-inch screen is sitting on its own dedicated solid wood wall unit along with an array of other entertainment equipment, all of which I've just realised we barely use.

I stomp over to it and lean over the back to turn the thing off at the switch but freeze when I notice that it's already switched off.

"What the…?"

I yank the plug out of the socket and stagger back in disbelief.

"…local authorities have confirmed that there have been multiple reports of mysterious lights in the night sky, most of which have been explained away by the fact that there's a military airfield just several miles away."

I'm gawking at the TV now. Not because of the reporter's image standing by that field but because, apparently, that electrical device is working without power, but I barely have time to register this when the phone starts ringing again. Then the nearby lamp glows on and off as if someone is messing with the dial.

I take another step back, hand clamped over my mouth, half expecting the TV to jump off its stand and start chasing me around the room.

"Holt…!" I've barely started the sentence when all sound is suddenly silenced, and a claw of terror scrapes down my spine. There, in the dark reflection of the now extinguished screen, I can see the shadow of something standing behind me.

I yelp and whirl around; there's nothing there, but I saw it! I bloody saw it! I saw the distorted outline of… I don't know what it was, but it was standing right behind me. Watching me!

I rub the back of my neck in an attempt to stem the chills trickling down my spine.

There's nobody here. I look all around the room; it's empty.

"Okay. Calm down. Calm yourself." I run reassuring fingers through my hair.

Is this possible?

No.

Is anybody else here seeing this?

No.

The rest of the process is interrupted by more growling. Buddy hasn't moved from his spot in the corridor.

"No," I snap, walking out to him. "What is with you and this creepy shit? Why can't you just bark like normal dogs?" I ask, much louder than I need, as if my voice might scare away the sense of unease that's still smothering me.

Oh shit. Suddenly I'm afraid. Scared to be alone in this house, and I have no fucking clue why.

You've worked yourself up into a state. That's why. Pressure. Guilt for being a dick to Sarah. But you're okay. You're alright.

"We are alright, aren't we, mate?" I ask, massaging Buddy's head and drawing comfort from the warmth and softness of his fur.

My formerly sweet dog does not respond, though. He's still staring at the front door as I suddenly become aware of a chill in the air. And I don't know if it's cold in here or if it's symptomatic of how I'm feeling.

"Holt, set the temperature in all zones to 20."

Yes, Marco.

I look right, down the corridor towards the study. Tree branches sway in the breeze casting shadows like wagging fingers over the walls. I didn't like the hall at Dolce Vita because it was gloomy. Here, I don't like the windows. They feel too low. Too accessible.

I glance to my left, up the other end of the corridor. Same wriggling patterns and green blur of the forest beyond.

No shadow walking into view, though. That was obviously all in my head. Still, these corridors. Something about them. Stark. Hollow. Cold. Gloomy.

Buddy is still staring, so I walk past him and up towards the dining room. That's right. I'm not giving in to any of this crap this time. There's nothing at the front door but the neurosis of a canine. For which, in case you're wondering, I accept full responsibility. After all, they do say that pets become their owners.

Before entering the dining room, I look back to find Buddy hasn't moved but is observing me.

"You're not satisfied unless you've completely creeped me out, are you?"

Blink blink is the dog's only response to that. "Yeah, we need to have a chat about—"

Bong. Bong. Bong. Marco. There is someone at the front door. Would you like to see who it is?

The sound of the doorbell startles me and causes Buddy to bark.

I look at the dog. "Bit late now," I grumble.

There's nothing wrong with this house, Marc. It's all in your head.

I take a deep breath, shrug, then address the panel on the wall.

"On-screen in the dining room."

The screen springs to life, and I'm both relieved and disappointed.

"Shit. Is that today?"

***

"You really have done well for yourself, Marco. This view is incredible. How much did this place cost you anyway? Oh, sorry. Don't tell me. It's none of my business. So, where do I sit, here?" Amanda asks, gesturing at the couch in the study.

Yes. I'd completely forgotten that I had agreed to a therapy session with my stunning-and-still-bloody-sexy ex today of all days – it's not like I don't already have enough going on – but it seemed like the right thing to do at the time.

No. I don't know how I get myself in these situations either. Well, I do.

Anyway…I watch Amanda place her handbag on the floor by the couch. It's Y.S.L, by the looks of the letter motif decorating the outside. I know this, you'll understand, not because I'm a fan myself but because Ellie was.

Then, she shrugs off her coat, revealing tight-fitting oatmeal rollneck top and figure-hugging black trousers punctuated by impractical yet very sexy black heels.

She dumps the coat on the sofa and then takes a seat next to it with a sigh.

"You must love it out here. So peaceful."

I smile at her. "It's a bit different to the city," I say.

"Do you miss it?"

"The city? No."

She smiles but doesn't say anything.

"What?" I ask.

"Nothing."

"No. Go on. Please finish the thought."

"Well, you used to say you loved the city and that you hated it when your wife raised the subject of moving to the country."

"I did?"

She nods; I shrug like I don't remember. I do. But I don't want to talk about that right now. I don't actually want to talk to her either because I know this is dangerous territory, but, oh well, I'm committed now.

It's just one session. How bad can it be?

Don't answer that.

"The house I'm renting is right next to this pub," she continues. "It's called the Hare and Hound. Landlord's a right slimy git. Anyway, the pub must be at least eight, maybe ten houses away, and I can still hear that racket on a Friday night. It's worse than actually living in London. I hate it."

"You're renting a house?"

She nods, "Yes. Why?"

"No particular reason. Just the other day, you said you were staying at your boyfriend's place. I forget his name. Jeffrey, is it?"

"I said that?"

"Yes."

"No, you must be mistaken."

I shake my head. "I don't think so. You said he had a place down here and that you were staying there."

"Does it make a difference?"

"Well, I was just wondering why you would say that."

"Jeffrey's place is in London, but I didn't want to stay in London. Is that alright?" she snaps, "Jesus, you're like one of those hounds. Is this what it's going to be like? You hanging on my every word?"

"Well, that's kind of the point," I say with a smile.

"Picking me up on everything I say isn't, surely. Trying to make me feel like a bloody fool can't be part of the process. Can it?"

"Is that how you feel?"

"Now I do. Yeah."

"Why is that?"

"What do you mean?"

"Why do you feel like a fool? What, specifically, was it about my sentence that made you feel that way?"

She glares at me and then shakes her head. "I knew this was

going to be a mistake. This is a mistake."

"Amanda. We're just talking."

"We're not just talking."

"No?"

"No."

"Then what are we doing?"

"You're analysing me. Judging."

"Is that what you think I'm doing?"

"Aren't you?"

She holds my gaze for a while, but I say nothing. I remain impassive because I know anything I say right now is only going to make things worse.

Eventually, she breaks away and turns to look out towards the lake. "This place really is something else. You do nesting well, Marc."

"Nesting?"

She turns to me. "Yes. Nesting; making a home with your new little girlfriend. What's her name?"

"Sarah."

"Yes. Sarah. How old is she anyway?" she asks with a curious lift of an eyebrow and a shaking of her right leg, dangling over the other. The heels of her shoes that are no doubt designer must be at least five inches long, and yet I watched her glide into this room with the grace of a catwalk model.

I don't respond to her question because I know where this is going.

"...What, twenty, twenty-five? She can't be much more than that, can she?" I maintain my silence. "What? You don't want to answer that?"

"I'd rather not for fear that it may incriminate me."

She lets out a short laugh. "You're already guilty, fella," she says with a narrowing of the eyes and a reptilian smile. Seconds drift by. Woodpeckers drum.

"Why don't you want to answer the question?" she prompts.

"We're not here to talk about me."

"No? How do you know what I want to talk about?" she asks, leg swinging as she observes me for the longest time before she allows it to slide with a loud swish of her trousers to the floor.

"You know my assistant, Chloe – she's twenty-five – spends most of her time sexting her boyfriend. She thinks I don't see her behind that desk, but I do. Christ, what it would be like to be twenty-five again, eh? Young. Firm. Carefree. When I was that age, I remember I felt like I held the world in the palm of my hand. My mother used to make me think that. She used to encourage me to believe that I could be anything. Do anything. And I did."

"You don't anymore?"

"What do you think?"

"I don't know. I'm asking you."

"Well, anything seems possible at that age. It's only as you get older that you realise that life may not be as easy as mum led you to believe because reality gets in the way."

I cock my head. "Reality?"

"Yes. Reality. School and all of the shit you have to endure there. College. Disappointment. Sexual harassment. Glass ceilings. Chauvinism. Love. Heartache. Abandonment. Self-loathing. Disillusionment. Midlife crisis. You know, the usual stuff."

"Wow. That's a lot of emotionally eventful stuff. Is that what you think? That you're going through a midlife crisis?" I say, shifting in my chair.

She laughs. "No. I was talking about you. At least that's how you seemed when you first met me. Disillusioned with your life, dissatisfied in your marriage."

"That's how you saw me?"

"Um, from what I can remember, that's how you viewed yourself. Isn't that why you kept coming back?"

I don't answer. Instead, "You know, Amanda. I'm curious. I couldn't help but notice how everything appeared to be in chronological order in that life summary you just gave me. You know, school, college, and then… disappointment."

"Shit. You got stuck on that?" she says with a sneer, bending down to her bag and pulling out a packet of cigarettes. "Is it okay if I have a quick one? I can open a window or something?"

"I'd rather you didn't," I say quickly.

"Oh, come on. You won't even notice it."

I squint at her.

"Wow. You really are a stickler, aren't you? Then I'll go and smoke it out on the balcony."

"Amanda, I'd rather we focus on the session. Could you please wait until the end of our session? Besides, I thought you'd quit."

Okay. No idea where that came from, but it isn't a good sign. And if I have any sense, I'd pack this vixen up and send her home with strict instructions never to return.

"I did. But then I started again not long after we split up."

"Is that how you felt? That we broke up?"

"Of course, that's how I fucking felt!" she snaps, crossing her legs once more, heel pointing angrily in the air and jiggling up and down like a wagging finger.

"Amanda, we were never together, remember? That was our agreement."

"It was; before you kept coming back to me for the best part of a year. Are you telling me it wasn't more for you? Are you seriously saying that I was nothing but a fuck buddy for a whole fucking year?" Her eyes narrow to slits once more. Blazing.

I've seen this behaviour so many times before in patients, in me, but this particular brand of volatility appears new. Unpredictable. Raw. Still.

"I'm just saying that we both agreed that we didn't want anything serious," I respond softly. "We talked about it. Remember?"

"Yeah. But that's before I…" she trails off here and then, realising herself, quickly adds, "are you really going to be a prick about me smoking in here?"

I nod slowly.

"Fine. How long have we got left? We can't have long now."

"I look at my watch. We still have a few minutes."

Lips pursed, my patient, former lover and if but for a few minutes lawyer, gazes out of the glass at the lake. I give her several seconds before asking, "What are you thinking about?"

"Oh, you don't want to know what I'm thinking about."

"Of course I do. That's why you're here, isn't it? To get me to sit in the same room as you, to hear you finally. Isn't that why you grabbed my file the moment it arrived at your office, swapped the meeting room for your office that morning so I could see all your awards, achievements? To show me how well you're doing without me?"

I watch the contours of her slender neck move as she swallows, and I know she's internalising what I'm saying.

"How do you do that anyway?" she says without looking at me.

"Do what?"

Turning, she asks, "How do you set up home with someone else just weeks after your wife dies?"

Oh okay. That hurts. Her words slash at me like razors. I don't think I considered my relationship with Sarah in that context. I mean, I was aware of it, but there didn't seem to be anything wrong until this moment. Perhaps that's because I've managed to successfully ignore it all this time. But we're good together. And I love her.

Yeah, but do you love her?

She's still watching me, and I'm searching the back of my head for some kind of casual quip to bat back those words that are still stinging.

It wasn't like that, I want to say. Of course, I was conflicted about Ellie. I still am. She was my wife. Admittedly, she was a fucking psychopath towards the end there, but I loved her. I still love her in some weird and warped way. She was the mother of my child. My boy.

Toby.

"What, no smart quip? Glib response?" she prods.

"I get the feeling that however I answer that question, Amanda, you'll find some spin because that's what you do. You are, after all, an excellent litigator," I say with a smile.

"And you an excellent bullshitter. You're a typical man-ape. You don't let go of one branch until you've latched onto another. It's what you do."

"I don't follow."

She nods at me with a wry smile. "Yes, you do. You know exactly what I'm saying. But you still aren't over her, are you? Ellie. What was it about her? What made her so special?"

I shift in my chair. "You mean besides her being my wife?"

"No. It wasn't that. That's just a piece of paper barely good enough to wipe your backside with. Jeff's a good example of that." She sits forward in her seat now, eyes wide, lips pursed in what I imagine is her cross-examiner mode. "I mean in your own words; you used to say how things had changed between you. How you barely had a civil word for each other and how if it weren't for Toby, you wouldn't even have stayed with her. So, what made her special, huh?"

I can almost feel the heat of her breath from across the room, and I imagine what it must be like facing her from the witness stand. I can already feel that familiar tickle of sweat on my scalp.

No.

"Jeff. That was his name," I say, "what did you mean by that?"

"By what?"

"You said Jeff was a good example of that. Of what?"

"You're deflecting, Marco. Why won't you answer the question?"

"Again, I thought I already had. I can only tell you now what I told you then. She was my wife. Mother to my child, Amanda. I couldn't leave my family. I explained that to you at the time."

"You also couldn't wait to fuck me every chance you got either," she says with a dismissive hiss before settling back into the couch and looking out of the window once more.

I give her a few seconds. Swallow casually on the dry sand in my throat while checking everything about my demeanour for fear that she will read me like the bloody book I am. Then, I casually attempt to deflect with, "What did you mean about Jeff, Amanda?"

"Why do you want to know?"

"Because it's relevant."

"You don't even know what it is, and you think it's relevant?"

"Everything's relevant. You're a lawyer. You know that."

I watch her shoulders relax as her resolve dissolves, just like a small cloud that just passed in front of the sun.

"What is it with men and me anyway?" she says, shaking her head.

"Is Jeffrey married?" I ask.

She laughs. "With two point four kids." Then she looks at me.

"After you, I found it hard to forge any meaningful relationship... because they weren't you."

I nod. "I'm sorry."

"So, what do I do? I go and repeat the same mistake all over again. Only this time, he's the opposite of you. He says that he's going to leave his wife, that he's going to tell his children."

"How old are they?"

"No fucking clue. Not that old."

"Almost a year later. And I realise that I'm still waiting for him to talk to them." She holds her face. "Fuck! What is wrong with me?"

"There does seem to be a pattern here. You see that, right?"

"My penchant for married men? You'd have to be blind not to see it. But is it so terrible? I mean, really. If these men are with me, then it means that they aren't happy at home. I'm the one who makes them happy, yet I'm also the one who ends up paying for it."

I rock my head.

"You disagree?"

"Well, you're simplifying it."

"That's because it is simple."

I rock my head again as I consider that.

"Are you denying that you enjoyed your time with me?" she asks flatly.

"No."

"Didn't you get hard just thinking about me?"

"Amanda..."

"What? That's what you said. Do you deny that too?"

"No. I do not deny it."

"Isn't that why we had sex at your work? You used to love being spontaneous. You remember that, right?"

"Of course, I remember. That's how I know that it wasn't my idea to have sex at my work, but yours."

I watch a mischievous smile creep across those lusciously painted lips. "But you enjoyed it."

I nod. "I did. Didn't quite enjoy being caught and then sacked, though."

She shrugs. "You didn't belong in that shitty place anyway."

"No? Where did I belong, Amanda? With you?"

"Yes. Is that so bad?"

"No."

"Was it so wrong?"

"No."

"Then why do you keep talking like it was?"

"I was married," I say slowly. Pointedly. More like I'm impressing it on myself than on her.

I watch those slender shoulders lift casually once again as she offers me her profile to glance at the beauty beyond the glass. I've noticed this about her. She seems to retreat to the view to deal with the byproduct of our interaction.

I join her for a few seconds before continuing. "You know, Amanda. It was interesting what you said earlier, about finding it difficult to form meaningful relationships since me."

"How so?"

"I don't think you've ever forged what you would term as meaningful relationships, have you?"

She rolls her eyes, folds one long leg over the other, and starts to jiggle it. "Oh shit, is this the part where you tell me that the reason why I don't form meaningful relationships is because of my parents?" I watch her neat eyebrows arch. "Or more specifically because I had an absent father who was working all hours when not busy fucking his secretary. A little cliché, don't you think?"

I pull a face. "Kind of. I was referring more to the fact that your father was ruthless, and he, by your own words, often took his small daughter to the office where you witnessed him at his worst, including how he domineered his subordinates and then went home and did the same with your mother."

I watch her face crease into an angry frown, and she growls, "You don't know anything about my parents."

I nod. "I think you told me enough for me to reasonably suspect that one of the real reasons why you don't seek out meaningful relationships and are attracted to married men is power. Control. By soliciting these interactions with men who are already committed, you ensure that they have everything to lose, and you don't. Isn't that a fair assessment?"

She blinks giant lashes at me for the longest time. Wood pigeons coo. Ducks quack in the distance. Then, she spits, "You're a prick!"

I smile at her. "Well, as my therapist would say, I'm always interested in your opinion."

"So, what happened between us was all about my power and nothing to do with you?" she counters.

"Of course, it was. It had everything to do with me. I was an adult. Fully responsible for my actions."

"Good. Because I've already got one lying prick in my life, I don't need another."

"Amanda, I'm not in your life," I say clearly.

"Figure of speech, Marc. Calm down." She makes a show of looking at her watch. "Shit, anyway, our time must be up now."

"We still have a few minutes."

"Keep em. I have another meeting I need to get to. You'll send the bill to my secretary, right?" she says, sliding into her coat and putting me back in my place. She is the one paying me. I am the hired help.

I nod. "Sure."

At the door, she suddenly stops and turns to me. "Do you think we can carry on doing this?"

I cock my head. "Doing what?"

"Seeing each other."

I smile. "Amanda, we agreed that—"

"Why?"

"Why?"

"Yes, why?"

"Because that's what we agreed. Given our history and all. There's a potential conflict here which is the very reason why you've removed yourself from my case."

She doesn't say anything and instead opts to fiddle with the buttons on her coat.

"Amanda?"

"Okay. I heard you," she says, starting forward.

Woof!

Buddy, who was waiting outside the study door, barks once at her loudly, causing her to scream.

"Buddy," I admonish.

"Jesus Christ! That bloody thing almost gave me a heart attack!" she says, holding her chest.

"I'm sorry," I say quickly and then glare at the hound who sticks his tongue out at me like he's just come back from a run. I wag a finger at him, but he counters it with a yawn in my face.

Meanwhile, Amanda has already retreated up the corridor and is heading towards the front door.

"Amanda, wait!" I say, catching up with her.

"I told you I'm going to be late for my meeting," she says without stopping.

But, at the front door, I catch her hand. "Amanda!"

"What? I told you—"

"You have removed yourself. Right? You did tell them about us? Right?"

Now it's her turn to rock her head. "Not exactly."

My heart skips a beat. "What do you mean not exactly?"

"You stand a much better chance of winning with me."

"Okay. So, putting aside just for a second how conceited that just sounded, let me just ask you this question… Have you lost your fucking mind?" I demand in a hushed tone as if the house might overhear us, "this is my life," I say seriously. Desperately.

"Exactly. That's why you need me. You need the best, and I am the best." She pulls on the door, and it swings open effortlessly. "What are you afraid of anyway? Worried that you'll fall for me all over again?" she asks, deliberately batting her eyelids once more.

"There's no danger of that," I say dismissively, running my hand through my hair as I consider my options.

"What? You think I haven't noticed how you've been looking at me. Especially that first day at the office. Couldn't pick your tongue up off the floor," she says, stepping forward so close I can feel the heat of her body. And my traitorous pulse quickens, triggering all sorts of involuntary reflexes.

Shit.

I take a step backwards, but she pinches my shirt and pulls me towards her. "Amanda, stop."

"Stop? I haven't even started… yet," she says with a wink and is just about to take a step closer when I hear.

"Hello."

I turn and look down the path to see Sarah, hair scraped into a ponytail, scrubs hanging baggily off her body and disappearing into muddy, wellington boots.

"Oh, hello. You must be Sarah! It's so good to meet you," Amanda says overenthusiastically, extending a hand. "I've heard so much about you," she adds with a big smile.

Sarah returns an awkward smile and then glances at me for further clarification, but Amanda sees this and steps in. "I'm Amanda," she states happily, like that should mean something to my girlfriend. "I'm an old friend of Marc's. Now his lawyer and his patient," she adds with an uncharacteristic giggle.

Sarah frowns as she looks up at the woman who must be a good two, maybe three inches taller than her, thanks to those heels. "His lawyer? Oh, do you work with Mr. Wilson?"

"Not exactly. Wilson reassigned the case to me due to my intimate knowledge of the subject," she says in a breathy voice I don't even recognise on her.

"Well, I've got to dash. I have another client meeting, but it was wonderful finally meet you." Then she turns to me. "And I'll see you soon, Marc." It isn't a question but a statement before she turns and clicks her way down the garden path leaving a cloud of perfume in her wake.

Sarah and I say nothing, each wrapped in our own thoughts as the Porsche Cayenne reverses and then speeds off through the trees.

Great. And the hits just keep on coming.

21

THE CRACKS

HOLT· EARLY EVENING·

So, how exactly am I going to hold a wedding ceremony at Holt?

Well, at first, I just wanted to stick my head in the lake and hold it there since I'd clearly already lost my mind. But then thought about it, and I concluded that the obvious way was the most logical, with a spreadsheet.

Yeah. I know, sounds shite, but it actually makes perfect sense. How else do you think I managed to pull together the thousands of tasks and components that go into *flipping* a house? Yeah, I learned the hard way with house number one. Pen and paper didn't quite cut it.

So, I've created a spreadsheet with multiple tabs. On the first tab is the running order of the event, right down to individual five-minute segments. All of the other tabs contain the various tasks, products, components, services, and costs that fulfil everything in the first tab.

Simple right? It is. The most complex parts are the tangible moving parts of that first tab. By that, I mean sourcing all the bloody stuff and then quite literally physically placing it at Holt.

When Kal showed us around that first day, he told me that the size of the back lawn, not including the trees on either side, is 120 yards which just happens to be the length of a football (soccer) field. The width—that is, the distance between the house to the jetty—is about half that.

A red double-decker bus is 80 feet long. When you convert the above into buses, I have the grand total lawn space of 4.5 buses back-to-back wide by 2.2 buses deep. It may not seem like much when you consider the total number of guests coming to this wedding. Still, it turns out that I have more than enough square footage to accommodate 160 clear polycarbonate *Napoleon Regal Chiavari* chairs with interwoven white organza, gathered at the back with silver bangles. These wonderful chairs only take up a wonderfully frugal footprint of 0.5 square feet.

Yay!

Fuck. Can you hear this shit? I, Marco Battista, now bonafide organza queen, for Christ's sake.

Every day's a school day.

Anyway. The chairs are sorted. They'll be sitting on temporary decking—reclaimed wood, of course, because that's what Holt is all about—and will be positioned to form an aisle down the centre. It will line up perfectly with the jetty that I have established is easily wide enough to accommodate both men and the officiator.

Big tick.

The sit-down reception is something altogether different.

The weather forecast insists that it will be blue skies with scattered clouds otherwise lots of sunshine. I've been religiously checking the app every single day since I chained myself to this event.

Assuming that the boffins at the Met Office aren't lying to me, I could risk interlinking a series of tables to create three or four massive ones to one side of the lawn and have everybody sit at those, bugs and all. Or I can choose the sensible option to try and wedge a marquee big enough to accommodate everyone and relevant tables.

I'm opting for the latter because I keep getting these visions of overweight women in flimsy rain-soaked pastel dresses running for their lives, slipping and sliding on the decking, boobs and fat jiggling and flapping all over the place. Panda eyes. Makeup running….

Ugh. No. I don't know how my mind works sometimes either. The bottom line is, I'm not sure I want to take the risk, so I've opted for a marquee, but who would have thought that those things come in such a variety of shapes and sizes.

Shit.

Luckily, I managed to chat-up a lovely lady called Rosemary, explained my plight to her, and she was more than helpful in assisting me in making a decision.

And it's done now. The full price was paid with money I didn't think I had until I checked my bank account to find that I was thirty thousand richer. When I checked with Aaron, he said to let him know if I needed more.

More? What the hell are they expecting? Cirque de bloody Soleil?

Shit. Weddings are expensive! I didn't realise just how much until I started doing this. Ellie and I got off lightly since ours was understandably done with a minimum amount of fuss at a registry office in Islington, primarily to spite her parents. At least that's what she wanted.

Anyway, focus. Here. Now.

I don't want to speak too soon, but I think I'm almost there.

I had considered hiring a boat and have the lads board on the Manor side of the lake, sail along to Holt and then dock directly at the jetty, but I chickened out because a, it seems a bit poncy and funny-enough that isn't David's style, and b, knowing my luck, there'd be some kind of disaster like them ending up stranded on the lake. Or worse, they somehow end up in it. Nope. They can arrive by car and walk down the aisle like ordinary people.

The remaining big issues are logistics, accommodation, and transportation. Initially, many of the guests were going to stay at the venue where the wedding reception took place. They can't stay there now, and I can't accommodate them here, not unless they fancy sleeping in a tent in the woods—there's an idea—so that's one of the remaining thorns in my side along with the most important thing of all. He is currently trotting off to Sarah, who is standing opposite me about thirty feet away with her back to the woods. That is roughly the length the aisle will be before the jetty.

The sun's weary fiery fusion of reds and golds is still eradiating the land it slowly slides into its pyjamas behind the manor on the opposite side of the lake.

I've noticed the temperature is dropping faster now, but I don't know if that's because of the fading light or because Sarah has barely said a word since Amanda left an hour or so ago.

"Are you sure you want to do this?" Sarah shouts in the distance. Her voice rebounding off the house and out to us.

"Yeah." I shout back. "I think it'll be a nice touch. Don't you?"

She doesn't respond but shrugs before bending down to make a fuss of Buddy standing in front of her.

"Are you ready?" she calls.

"Yep. Ready. Okay... Buddy... come to daddy... come on, boy... come to daddy."

The dog instantly turns to look at me. Thinks about it and starts trotting over... "No! No! Buddy," I say, holding out my hands. "Remember how we're doing this... slowly. Come to daddy. *Slowly.* That's it. Walk.... Walk." I watch the dog pause, cock his head. *Make up your mind. Do you want me to come over to you, or not?*

"Yes. That's it. Slowly. Slowly. Walk to daddy. Slowly."

I watch the dog tentatively walk towards me. Stop, look back at Sarah and then walk towards me some more.

Sarah sniggers in the distance. "Okay, alright. So, it needs a bit more rehearsal," I say.

"A bit more?" she asks sarcastically.

"Yeah. Not helping."

Eventually, the dog reaches me. I pet him and make a fuss of him. *Good boy! Good boy! Who's a good boy?* Then take a treat from my pocket and reward him with it.

"Over to you."

"Buddy. Hey. Come on. Come to Sarah!" Sarah says brightly.

Buddy looks up at me as if seeking permission. "Yeah, off you go. Go on." The dog turns and saunters back. *Good boy. Good boy.*

I sigh deeply and turn to see a trio of bats flap and jitter from the house to the woods and back again. The lake is still. The air is woodland dank as it cools from the warmth of daylight. Our neighbours are having their last natter before retiring for the night while, around me, desiccated leaves flutter like exhausted butterflies to the grass.

And here we are, training our dog. It's an idyllic scene. Or at least it should be, even though it doesn't feel like it.

Sarah isn't one for overt bouts of passive-aggressiveness, but then she has this other habit of going quiet. Speaking when spoken to. Polite yet conservative with her words. Now, I can run with that or tackle this head-on, which is – frustratingly – more her speed.

"So," I start loudly, "are we going to talk about it?"

"About what?"

"Sarah," I groan.

"Oh, you mean talk about the fact that your solicitor isn't a man but a pin-up model you used to be *friends with*?" She makes air quotes with her fingers. "What's to talk about? I suppose we could talk about the fact that she's now also your client. Which isn't weird at all."

Okay, this may well be worse than I thought. "It isn't like that, Sarah," I say.

"No?"

"No."

"Well, maybe you should tell me about it, Marc, because it would seem that for some reason, you chose not to."

"Buddy. Come on. Come to daddy!" The dog looks at me and then back at Sarah, who I watch say something to the dog because, shortly after, he reluctantly starts moving in my direction.

"How did you know this woman anyway?" she calls out.

Oh shit.

Buddy, who is now about halfway to me, stops and looks back at Sarah as if to say, *you really don't want to know*. In fact, he must be so scandalised with what's about to come because he emits a loud groan and collapses on the grass, head alternating between looking at me and then at Sarah behind him.

Yeah. As always. Appreciate the support.

I take a step closer to both the hound and my girlfriend because, for some reason, I feel that this is the kind of stuff you don't want to yell across the back lawn.

"Um, well, we used to see each other," I say sheepishly, "For about a year."

"See each other?" she echoes, "what, across platforms on the underground, over the toolbox at the garage?" Sarah asks sarcastically because no doubt she already has a theory.

So, I take a couple more steps forward and just get on with it. "She's the woman I was seeing," I say. A gaggle of geese honks loudly in the distance, and somehow, it sounds like incredulous laughter.

"*She* is the woman you were seeing? The one you cheated on your wife with?"

I nod slowly while hoping it's imperceptible in the fading light.

"But I thought her name was Ellie, too."

Obviously not.

"Um, it is, was. She goes by Amanda now. That's her middle name. I think she changed it after we broke up."

Sarah shakes her head slowly.

"Now, Sarah, this isn't what you think," I say quickly, taking a few more steps forward to the point where I reach my traitor of a dog that I've noticed has been witnessing this whole exchange like he's watching a game of tennis. "Thanks for nothing, mate," I whisper to the hound, who responds by sticking his tongue out at me.

"How do you know what I'm thinking," Sarah says petulantly.

"Well, I can't be sure, but for once, I think you're thinking the worst, and you shouldn't, really, I promise. It's nothing like that," I say, taking a few more steps forward.

"Marc, the woman you were cheating on your wife with for the best part of a year, has returned looking, well, looking like some, some," she struggles with the words. "…she shows up and is not only representing you in a very serious case, but you've also chosen to take her on as a client. What the fuck am I supposed to think?" she says evenly.

Which is fair. "Sarah. I know you must be miffed–"

"Miffed?"

"Alright… angry."

She frowns. "I'm not angry."

I cock my head and lift my eyebrows.

"I'm not angry," she insists, stepping toward me, "I'm not. I know that's what you're expecting, but I'm not. That isn't who I am, and you should know that by now, especially after what happened. Life's too bloody short," she says, making a show of looking at the majesty that surrounds us. Then adds, "I'm surprised. Definitely disappointed but not angry. That's your wife, and you keep assuming that I am going to behave like her, but…."

I pull another face.

"Okay. Maybe you have a point. But Marc, really? What the hell are you doing?"

"I know," I say, stepping closer to her. "It's an error of judgement. I get that."

"Error of judgement?" she echoes, "I'm no expert or anything, but lawyer, patient person, who, judging by her performance at the front door, is still hot for you–"

"She is not hot for me–"

"She's still got the hots, Marc. Again, I'm no psychologist, but that's got to be one of those boundary things. And then that overenthusiastic introduction. Come on. She was trying to get me to react exactly the same way that you're expecting me to. And the fact that you're choosing to ignore it only validates my next point: this has somehow got to be a serious conflict of some kind. No?"

I don't say anything because… well, what can I say?

"Marc?" she prompts.

"I know it looks bad," I begin but pause when my girlfriend scoffs. "I know it looks bad and that it's a shitty idea, but it really isn't what you think. She kind of inserted herself into the case, and as for the session, I owed it to her."

"You owed it to her? Marc, relationships end–"

"It isn't just that," I say, looking around us as if the words are going to flutter down to me like those leaves from the trees.

"No?" she says, interested, "then what is it?"

"I, um, can we not talk about it anymore. I've had a bloody long day and–"

"*What* do you mean?" she insists.

I think about this because, you know, there are times in life when you're presented with a choice. Choose one way, and you're sure of a certain outcome, choose another, and, well, it's anybody's guess.

Of course, me being me, I choose the one most likely to rain down devastation on this once peaceful setup of ours.

"When it ended, she was upset. I felt bad."

"Marc, you were married. If you had any sense of duty or remorse, it should have been to your wife and not her.

"It's not that simple."

"Seems pretty simple to me."

"Well, it wasn't."

"No. Why not?"

"Sarah, as I said, I really don't want to talk about it now."

"Well, that's too bad, Marc, because we are talking about it!" she snaps. "We need to talk about it because you've turned this thing into something ugly, which apparently has become your M.O. I mean, for Christ's sake, we've barely moved in here, and you're already sneaking around."

"I'm not sneaking around!"

"No? What do you call lying to my face, Marc? You met her in London, and you told me that your lawyer was some old man called Wilson. What's that if it isn't a blatant lie?"

"I didn't lie, Sarah. His name is Wilson. And he is my lawyer. Amanda just happened to come across my case."

"*Happened* to come across it? Seriously? I know you're not that naïve. But let's just assume for a second that you are. Having her as a patient?"

"That's different."

"Different how?"

"It's just different."

"Well, why don't you tell me about it? Come on."

"Sarah, I told you I don't want to talk about it."

"And I don't give a shit what you want, Marc! Now I can put up with your past, your weirdness, but what I can't put up with is you flat out lying to my face."

"My weirdness? What the fuck is that supposed to mean?"

She doesn't respond. And she doesn't have to. I know exactly what she's talking about. And, oddly, I'm not offended or anything because it's true. I *am* bloody weird. I'm riddled with peculiarities, neurosis, and, well, you've already witnessed everything else. Most people would run a mile from that stuff, but not her.

And yet. I nod. "Well, I'm glad you've got that off your chest."

"Oh no, you don't get to do that."

"Do what?"

"You know exactly what you're doing, Marc. You're avoiding by deflecting this onto me."

"I'm not turning it on you. If I was turning it on you, I would be asking what the fuck did you do with my son's photo, Sarah?" My words are irate. Loud. And they ring in the air for a few seconds as I glare at her.

I have no idea where that came from.

"What?"

"Toby's photo. It was on my desk, and now it isn't there anymore. What did you do with it? And while we're at it. What made you think that it was okay to go in there and start messing with my stuff?"

I watch her eyes widen. Then her lip trembles before she growls, "I don't know what the fuck you're talking about, but I think we should end this conversation now before I say something we're going to regret."

She moves to walk away from me, but I catch her hand and spin her around. "No, if you've got something to say, say it."

"Let go of me," she says, tugging her hand.

"No. If you've got something to say to me, say it," I repeat and then yell, "SAY IT!"

She yanks her wrist free and proceeds to rub it. There's a moment's pause, then "Why aren't you taking your pills?"

"What?"

"You heard me. Why aren't you taking your pills?"

I'm thrown by the question as a shoal of piranha thoughts start snapping at my brain. I didn't even know she was monitoring that. Why would she? Doesn't she trust me? Does she think I'm starting to lose it again? Did Ethan ask her to?

"I didn't realise you were checking on me."

"It's not rocket science, Marc. I can see that the bottle's still half full."

"Of course you can if you're regularly checking it. Whose idea was that? Yours or Ethan's?" I ask.

She snorts. "Now you're getting paranoid. Ethan?"

"Well, you do like to talk about him, Sarah. Like he's the oracle."

"And you like to avoid, don't you? Can't you see the pattern, Marc? The nightmares, the visions, the paranoia. It's a symptom. You know this better than I do."

I flex my jaw because part of me wants to scream at her, release that hot spring of anger bubbling through me. The other is busy wrestling with the fact that she may have a point. So, instead, I end up seething, "The only thing I see, Sarah, is that I can't trust you."

"Well, then, that makes two of us, doesn't it?" she counters coldly before turning and making her way back up the lawn to the house.

22

WEDNESDAY

3 days until the wedding. 🌹

The view from our spare bedroom is quite stunning, you know. Even if it only overlooks the front lawn and drive out to trees. Not that I saw much of it.

Sarah and I avoided each other last night. Probably for the first time since we've been together. Sure, we've had our disagreements, but nothing like this. This was different. Personal. At least she seemed to get personal. Or maybe Sarah, my Sarah, who generally looks for the positivity in everything, finally reached the end of her rope and decided to *call me out on my shit*. Whatever the fuck that's supposed to mean.

Anyway, I spent the rest of the evening in the study while she set up camp in the lounge. Like the child victim of a broken home, Buddy alternated between the two zones looking suitably depressed.

Daddy. Have you been naughty again? Have you upset mummy? You should buy her a new pair of shoes. She loves shoes.

I woke up to the sound of my son's voice at 06:03 this morning. Yay! A lie-in.

For once, though, I didn't think it was anything supernatural or sinister. It just felt like a dream. A depressingly sad dream where I could feel my little boy's presence, hear the cadence of his voice and feel it dissipate like morning mist the moment I opened my eyes.

Toby.

We didn't discuss my sleeping in the spare room last night; it just felt right; we both needed time to process. At least, that was my intention, but once my head hit the pillow, I barely had time to replay what had been discussed before exhaustion claimed me. And amen to that.

I only have a limited amount of brainpower, and right now, it's diverted to the one singular event that can make or break my friend's happiness. And I will maim and kill anything that threatens that.

Sarah and I, well, we can work through our stuff when I'm able to focus better.

Although that didn't stop me from sending flowers to her at work.

I realised this morning as I was dictating the numbers to my credit card for what felt the hundredth time in the past week that I don't do it that often and probably should. Although Sarah isn't one for grandiose displays of affection. Flowers, chocolates, and dress-up isn't really her bag. She's much happier slouching and cuddling in front of the TV. In fact, now that I think of it, she'd probably be happier if I sent her tickets to the sofa with movies and popcorn.

Still, doesn't hurt to try. Especially since she left for work this morning by telling Buddy to tell *Daddy* that Sarah loves him, *even if he is a dick*. Buddy just looked at me when she left the room…. *Yeah, what she said.*

Shortly after 08:30, Holt told me that he'd detected an intruder on the back lawn. When I looked out of the window, I saw that it was Bernie sporting a pair of unflattering waders and prepping to make those repairs to the jetty.

I barely managed to make the man a cup of tea and ask him, in the nicest possible way, if he could make a start on the meadow instead when a big truck full of planks of wood arrived, and Holt told me that one of the band members from ZZ Top was at the front door. At least that's what the burly guy with dungarees, tattoos, and an unusually long beard looked like. His somewhat weedy, in comparison, sidekick, not as much.

Anyway, they played *chase me chase me* with Bernie, driving the poor old bugger to work up a sweat by laying planks of wood faster than he could empty the barrel of his loud, spluttery petrol mower that belched out more pollution than it did grass. I tried to encourage him to use the electric one in the storeroom under the house, but he wouldn't have any of it.

By lunchtime, the meadow was no more. In its wake was a platform of dark grey wood that gleamed under the autumnal sky.

Exciting. The creation. Something that wasn't less than seven days ago now is.

And this is just the beginning.

23

THURSDAY

2 days until the wedding. ✿

Another uneventful night. How about that? This morning when my eyes sprang open at 06:03, I was ready. No, I was excited to be getting up and on with the day —especially since I spent last night in the comfort of my own bed.

Yes, the flowers did the trick.

Do you believe that? Of course not. Because you, like Sarah, aren't so easily won over. No, I think it was the card that accompanied the flowers that made her come home, put her arms around me and kiss me on the cheek.

If there's one thing I truly love about Sarah is her pragmatism. It's perfect for someone like me who, as you know, does have the occasional tendency to, well, you know, become *overwhelmed*.

That, and the fact that I know she loves the boys.

What happened at Dolce Vita solidified that. We are survivors who have been through a terrifying ordeal together. It has instilled a unique bond in all of us.

This wedding, the boys' happiness, means as much to Sarah as it does to me. So, when I sent her flowers and a card acknowledging that I'm a dick or words to that effect, that what she said made sense, that it had given me a lot to think about, and that I wanted to sit down and talk it through with her in detail, but after the wedding, she understood. Just like I understood that our life was pretty much on pause for over a year while she was studying and taking her exams.

When this is over, I want us to sit down and talk it through with Ethan, she said.

Ugh. Ethan? Really?

With Ethan. As a friend.

I agreed because that's what needed to be done to get back to where we need to be to enable me to get this job done.

I know that sounds selfish, but, again, my brain only has limited processing capacity, and, right now, it's on Saturday.

Bernie was back shortly after 08:00 today to finish transforming the back and front of the house before moving on to shoring up that jetty so that the happy couple and probably me don't end up in the lake mid-ceremony.

At 09:45, Holt announced the arrival of a skinny duo of chatty cockney blokes from the marquee company. And I have no idea why, but their arrival gave me butterflies.

Shit is getting real.

How the hell do I end up saying this stuff? I mean, what does that even mean? I'd like to think that I'm a man of relative intellect, but dude, seriously?

Anyway, *it felt like things were getting real.* The decking is all laid out. Now the marquee. And at eleven- something—because I lost track of time and delivery people—the chairs arrived courtesy of a happy couple.

Chatty husband and wife team, been in the business for years, thought it was sweet I was doing this for my friends, etcetera. Expressed just how glad they were that they could help *at such short notice.* I responded by enthusing gratitude until they eventually set about laying out the chairs. As agreed, 8 rows of 10 on one side of the aisle and eight on the other, making sure that the aisle was perfectly aligned to the jetty, even if this meant the marquee being pushed way off centre.

When I asked if it might be a bit early to put out chairs, they told me, not to worry. *These are top-of-the-range chairs. They won't be going anywhere.*

I was thinking more about them getting dirty, you know, birds, leaves, and stuff.

Oh no. That's no problem. We come back out on the morning of the big day to make sure everything's spick and span.

Oh right. Excellent. Thanks.

By late afternoon, the skeleton of the marquee was finally up, and I breathed a sigh of relief when the thing fit to the side of the lawn as I had measured.

Thank eff for that!

It's all looking a bit snug out there. As well as weird. I'm used to looking out of the window and seeing a green field framed by trees to the jetty and the lake beyond. Now, all the greenery in the foreground is gone, replaced by greys, sparkling glass-like chairs, and patches of white.

But it's looking good!

I don't want to speak too soon, but I may just pull this off.

24

FRIDAY

1 Day until the wedding! 💍

Last night, it was chilli bean wraps for supper and an early night. I barely had time to share the events of the day with Sarah before I was ready for bed, which was odd yet at the same time comfortably familiar because this is precisely how we functioned in London; eat, sleep, and go about our respective commitments.

There's no doubt in my mind that Sarah will be picking up exactly where we left off at the earliest opportunity, but first things first. And I love that about her!

Ellie was the complete opposite. If there was an issue, it had to be dealt with immediately because she wanted instant satisfaction. If she felt something, she reacted to it immediately. And, on those rare occasions where she did bottle things up, say if other people were around, she would explode as soon as we were alone. I suppose, in some warped way, that's why we worked well as a couple because when she was angry, I was passive, and vice versa.

That was our Yin and Yang.

Last night, I dreamt that the wedding was going perfectly well until the lads walked up to the aisle and turned around to find none of the guests were human. They were all birds of every shape and form. Ducks, geese, swans, owls, and so on. They were all there, dressed in their best garb. The boys, of course, looked horrified, but I was smiling throughout. I didn't think there was anything wrong until David grabbed me by the scruff of the neck and started shaking me, calling my name, *Marco! Marc! Marc!*

His face then dissolved into Sarah's, who, most surprisingly, had brought me coffee in bed at a time when she would be busy getting ready for work.

What's wrong? Why are you here? was my morning greeting.

Nothing, she said. I've just taken the day off to look for a dress.

What?! You waited until the day before the wedding to look for a bloody dress?

Well, I've been working.

Sarah, I'm organising this whole thing, and you haven't even sorted your dress!

Relax, will you? I'm getting it today.

Relax? How the hell can I relax when you haven't even got a dress?!

I'm taking your car. See you later!

But I may need it.

Use mine!

So, okay, I'll admit it. I'm just a tad strung out right now, and you would be forgiven for thinking that it's me getting married tomorrow, but come on – a day before the wedding? Really?

Welcome Guests.

It's Irvin and the boys, and not a moment too soon. Their brief is to dive into the Amazon boxes that have been arriving all week to form a disorderly mountain in the dining room and fish out anything to do with lighting and decorations.

When Drew opened his mouth to speak, I told him that if he opened his gob and made a sarcastic comment of any kind *before* getting to work, I would scrap the cappuccino I was already making, and he could drink water for the rest of the day.

Irvin laughed. Drew filed out quickly.

"Thanks for doing this, Irvin. I know it isn't in your remit."

"Don't be daft. It's for the boys."

"How are things going at the house? Sorry I haven't been over."
I scoff, "Sorry, I know you're more than capable."

"You don't need to worry. We've got it in hand. And things are
going well. You don't have to be there every five minutes. The rot
wasn't as bad as we thought; I'm gettin' it treated. And we've actually
finished most of the rooms in the west wing."

"Really?" I say, eyes pinging wide, heart soaring.

"Yeah. And would love for ya to come and take a look as soon
as you get a moment."

"Oh Irvin, mate, that's bloody brilliant! You don't know how
happy that makes me!"

"Yeah, well, I thought it'd cheer ya. Consider it your own
wedding gift."

"You're bloody amazing!" I say enthusiastically.

"Now, where's the furry scoundrel? I feel like I aven't seen him
im ages."

"He scarpered out with the boys."

"Best go join em then. Get on with some work, eh?"

I nod with what must be some kind of inane grin, but I'm fine
with that. Half of the house is nearly finished. At last! It took us a
while to get here, but finally. Some fantastic news!

The rest of the day was its usual blur but in a good way. The
boys rigged all the lights and decorations, then did a fantastic job
with the arbour and other ancillary jobs to realise my vision of
transforming Holt into the go-to wedding venue of the year.

Bernie returned to add the finishing cut and style to everything
flora, and there's no doubt in my mind that if the fauna stayed still
long enough, they'd probably end up with a short back and sides too.
I have to give the man credit; he may be getting on a bit, but he is as
spritely as they come.

Sarah returned just after lunchtime from her successful—thank
God—shopping expedition. She also brought groceries, as well as
ready-made sandwiches for the troops.

The marquee duo returned with two of their friends today. All
sporting brand new light blue polo shirts with *The Wedding Company*
emblazoned on them like they were about to shoot a commercial.
They added white skin to the marquee frame leaving one side open,

while their colleagues set about assembling circular tables, then chairs, before laying the tables with pristine white clothes, glass, and tableware.

It's starting to look *bloody* fantastic! And although I still have palpitations, they're no longer exclusively for my anxiety but excitement for the boys to be married here.

At 15:00, the mobile hairdresser arrived to trim my hair before moving on to Irvin and the lads. She'll be returning tomorrow to take care of Sarah.

My suit was also delivered today. I probably should have taken that very expensive thing out of its packaging and inspected it, but as the awkward memory keeps reminding me, it was tailored exactly to my size, so I'm sure it'll fit just fine. If anything, it might be a little loose now!

But I made up for that tonight by ordering loads of pizza to share with Irvin and the lads, who regaled us with hilarious stories from their building site experiences. And I was grateful for them since I realised as I wiped tears of laughter from my eyes that we haven't been doing much of that lately. It seems to be a regular habit for me. But then I think back to some of my clients, and I realise that it's endemic in many of us. We become so caught up with everyday life that we often forget to appreciate the simple things, like laughter.

Sarah must have felt it, too, because she reached for my hand in the middle of Drew's hilarious soliloquies and squeezed it.

And that is the moment I truly believed that everything is going to be alright.

25

SATURDAY

THE WEDDING

So, I am not a religious person. If I'm perfectly honest, the practices of the catholic and churches of England are beyond me, but, apparently, even today, same-sex marriage *still falls short of God's purpose for human beings.* This means that while these churches purport to welcome all, they still appear incapable of finding a broad consensus that would allow gay marriages to be blessed in church.

This came as a bitter disappointment to Aaron, who was raised as a Christian. For him, marrying in an open church isn't just a fad, or something to look good in Instagram photos, but it's spiritual.

Unknown to me, the event at Porthcove wasn't the only reason the lads postponed their wedding; it was also because they were holding out for a church to stop cogitating and make a universally accepted decision.

Aaron, being ever the obliger, was happy to settle for a Register Office wedding, but David turned his nose up at that because, well, what was the point of getting married in good ole historic blighty if all they were going to do was end up getting married in a grey government building anyway?

Hardly the ceremony of a lifetime.

Still, the venue that let them down had a licence to conduct wedding ceremonies. Holt, obviously, does not.

So, the plan is for the boys to sign papers and be legally married at 09:00 am this morning at Camden Register Office. From there, they'll be picked up by a gorgeous silver *Rolls Royce Phantom* in which they'll make the two-hour journey (traffic permitting) to Holt, where they will be officially married by a celebrant at 11:00 am.

Most of the American contingent, including Aunt Martha and Bertha—the spinster sisters of Aaron's mother—Melda, yeah, their parents obviously had a thing for names ending with an *a*, are already installed at hotels and B&Bs in the area. As are most of the other guests who had initially been booked into the previous venue. This is good because it means no last-minute dramas of people getting stuck in traffic. Just the grooms. Yeah, maybe I didn't entirely think that one through.

It's fine. It's all good. The fact that I had yet another sleepless night last night and was already up and watching the golden haze of dawn grow beyond the trees is absolutely to be expected. As is the fact that I am so nervous that you would have thought it was me walking down that aisle made of ninety-five per cent reclaimed oak, you know—why on earth do I feel like I have to say that every time?

Shit.

It's fine. It's all good.

It's 06:00 am, and I am downing my third espresso of the day.

After all the planning and prepping, I should be ready for this, but I realise that it's the opposite. All that planning has only fed my neurosis and my newly metastasized obsession, doing right by the boys.

A hand on my shoulder startles me, but I'm pleasantly surprised to find that it's Sarah—who else?

"Hey," she says sleepily, running both of her hands over my shoulders.

"Hey."

"Oooh. Lots of knots back here. How are you holding up?"

"Yeah. Good. I'm fine. It's all good. No problem."

"Ooh, that bad, eh?"

I nod. "That, and I think I need to lay off the espressos."

She slides fingers from my shoulders up into my newly shortened hair—despite the number of times I have told her that I don't like people touching my hair—and plants a kiss there. I consider pulling away from her fingers by masking the act in a stretch and a yawn, but she heads me off by saying, "You do realise that you've pulled together a fantastic event for the boys in a really short period of time?" Her words are soft. Kind. "I know it still needs the finishing touches this morning, but from what I've seen, Marc, you're going to make David and Aaron proud."

I smile gratefully then feel my pulse quicken when I notice how much the day has burgeoned beyond the window.

Oh, that's interesting. I've just realised that I'm not actually irritated by Sarah's fingers in my hair. Normally, I'd be squirming by now, but instead, um, I'm starting to feel emotional.

"Th…" I clear my throat, "thank you for saying that. You know, I am aware that we–"

"Shhh," she interrupts, "I know. But let's not talk about any of that stuff today. Okay? Today is about the boys."

I nod. "Okay. Would you like a drink?"

"Latte?"

I turn to face her and see that she's wearing one of my t-shirts. Her hair is down and spilling messily around her shoulders. Eyes squeezed into a sleepy squint, and suddenly, I'm feeling aroused.

Okay. Where did that just come from? What the hell is wrong with me today? Emotions, feelings, and urges, apparently, are all over the place. I know all about these triggers, and yet when it's happening to you, it's weird.

Pull it together!

I kiss Sarah on the lips. "One latte coming up."

By 07:00, I am down by the jetty, dropping giant pods, like props from the set of *Invasion of the Body Snatchers,* into the lake. Then, I watch with incredulous wonder how they slowly unfurl into giant water lilies in a variety of violets, blues, and pinks. Apparently, the meticulously detailed origami flowers are specially treated to last up to 24 hours in the water before naturally biodegrading if not fished out sooner.

I balked at the price of these things, but now I can honestly say that they are more than worth it. They have transformed this part of the lake into an explosion of colour.

At 08:30, Holt announces the first visitors of the day. They are the duo from the Wedding Company. They, too, deserve praise for their dedication to their craft. There's something about them that fills me with confidence. I get the impression that they really do appreciate that weddings are stressful enough without having to worry that everybody is where they should be in enough time.

In this case, the duo set to tie sashes to the chairs and finalise laying the tables under the marquee.

By 09:00, Emily from the Flowerpot arrives with quite literally a van full of flowers, filling the air with a heady concoction of delicious fragrances as she sets about arranging the splashes of colour at strategic points down the aisle, on the jetty, around the arbour, and on dining tables.

Next, the mobile hairdresser from yesterday makes a return visit for Sarah.

At 09:35, the trio of middle-aged multiracial ladies in black evening gowns arrives like a mafia hit squad lugging cases that, for one lady, is almost as big as she is. They are part of the entertainment and one of the few things that survived the original wedding reception. They set up on a specially raised platform at the back of the seating area. Interestingly, their counterpart arrived by my special request around the same time to set up in the marquee with a specially positioned external speaker.

By 10:00, I am freshly showered and dressed in a blue Carrington's original tailored navy-blue suit that hangs off me like a second skin. My beard is neatly trimmed, my hair styled into a sixties-secret-agent side parting which may I add suits me and, despite the paltry two hours of sleep I had last night, I am looking bright hazel-green-eyed and bushy-tailed.

Holt is a hive of activity. Caterers. Waiters. Ushers. Parking attendants and guests. Lots and lots of them. I know it isn't possible, but it looks like we've inherited guests from somebody else's wedding. This can't be one hundred and forty-nine people; it looks like five hundred. Some are milling around the house and taking pictures, others are disappearing into the woods, and more are taking selfies on the back lawn. That is until the chief usher gets involved and starts quite literally herding them all to their seats like sheep.

I glance at my watch. It's 10:35. When I look up, I see Sarah descending the stairs. Correction, I see her slender feet inside strappy heels through the rung of the floating switchback stairs. Then I see her vision appear around the corner in what I was told is a ruffled-trim crepe maxi dress in carnation pink. It's pinched at the waist and hangs beautifully off her slender frame with a series of delicate ruffles down the front that wiggle as she makes her way towards me.

"Are you okay?" she asks with a timid smile because my mouth must be open.

"Um, yeah. I, um, wow Sarah… you look absolutely stunning." I admire her hair that has been side swept into curls and is cascading onto her shoulder. Her make-up which is normally applied as a functional necessity—sometimes in the rear-view mirror of the car, much to my annoyance—is today quite clearly meticulously painted on.

Of course, me being me, the professional way it has been applied does remind me of Amanda, and I hate myself for even having the thought. So, I bat it away.

"You don't scrub up too bad yourself," she says, taking my arm as we make our way down to the study to collect the other member of the family who has also undergone his own makeover for this special event. Sarah managed to get Buddy into his own salon yesterday, and his golden coat is not just fluffy but gleaming.

He makes a fuss when he sees us because not only are we looking different than usual, but he's seen all of the activity at the house today and is just aching to go find out what it's all about.

"Okay. You. Buddy. Remember. I need you to be on your best behaviour today. Don't let me down," I say pointedly as I strap the black saddle to his body. "This is really important."

The dog's only response is to lick my face, which of course, makes me chuckle. "Is that a yes?"

"Ready?" I ask Sarah.

"Ready," she says with a big smile.

***

They say that the best time to plant a tree is ten years ago. I've no idea how long these sycamore trees have stood on either side of this back lawn, but they are as magnificent as the age-old oak tree that laid down its life to save ours that night at Dolce Vita.

It's unknown when the sycamore tree was introduced to Britain, but the theory is, like most things, that the Romans introduced them in the 1500s. These gloriously majestic trees can grow over one hundred feet high and feature a giant dome canopy, ideal for shade, especially on an autumnal sunny day like today. These trees play a significant role in our ecosystem, where, in life, they provide a habitat for animals and insects while in death yield a hard and grainy wood texture which is often used for kitchen utensils such as spoons and ladles.

It's believed that the Welsh fashioned the wood of the sycamore into heart-shaped spoons as a romantic gesture for their loved ones. That's why I have adorned the low hanging branches of the trees with hand-carved wooden heart-shaped spoons suspended by a selection of multicoloured ribbons that, along with an array of lantern lights, are now languidly bouncing up and down, rocking back and forth in the breeze.

All the glass-like chairs have been decorated with a last-minute change of mint-green bowed sashes, which I felt would be in keeping with our surroundings. Each of the chairs has its own wedding program in the shape of a paddle—should it need to be used as a fan, although the chilled breeze sweeping across the crystal surface of the lake will most likely be cooling enough for most—secured to each chair by bulldog grips.

It's 10:51, and a text message from Aaron tells me that they made good progress and should be here on time.

Holy shit! Yet another one of those ridiculous Americanisms but nonetheless appropriate.

So, I know it's going to sound juvenile, but you often hear people—like me—speculating that in this dynamic with two men getting married, who arrives first? I mean, do they take it in turns or something to arrive traditionally late? I'm being flippant, of course, since when I made that joke, David just rolled his eyes as if it were suddenly beneath me. And it's odd because it was at that moment that I truly appreciated how much things have changed between us. Not in a bad way, but just in a different way. As if we're two children who have finally grown up. It's not like we can't still laugh together, but there's something about the events at Dolce Vita that matured and changed us. As ridiculous as that might sound.

That, or my friend, takes everything and anything to do with his marriage seriously. Although Bridezilla—or whatever the equivalent would be in this scenario—he is not. Far from it. I still can't get over that he entrusted this to me, one of the most important days of his life. His old fuck-up of a friend. He must obviously see something in me that I don't.

So, no, they don't flip a coin on who arrives late. They'll both be walking down the aisle together. I know there are traditions and all that, but today, it's merely a case of start as you mean to go on, as equals.

This means that the surprise that Buddy and I have been training for can go ahead as planned. This is why Sarah is waiting with the golden wonder at one end of the aisle—closest to the house—and I am waiting at the other—by the water's edge, where I'm thrilled to see a whole bevy of swans gracefully float over to inspect the giant faux lilies.

It's the picture-perfect scene beautifully lit by pure sunshine, and I note that it's already being captured by the photographer's drone faintly buzzing overhead as well as his two sidekicks on the ground.

I try to focus on the moment and ignore any niggling thoughts of what the sound of that thing up there reminds me of.

Another glance at my watch tells me that it's 10:59. My heart is thumping, and I can feel the beads of sweat on my forehead, but I forgot to push a paper handkerchief into my pocket. I wonder if I can quickly run inside–

Marco! Holt bellows out of his external speaker, "Mr. David Weller and Aaron Sinclair, your best mates who love you and think you are really handsome and witty, very witty, even more than David, the stars of today's show, have arrived. Ladies and gentlemen, would you please give it up for the grooms!"

There's applause, laughter, and cheers from the assembled guests. Primarily because of the way Holt delivered that line with his natural yet nuanced robotic voice.

Yeah, that's what you get when you wake up in the dead of night and can't do much but program your smart home computer to say whatever you want it to. I told the boys to present themselves at the front door so that Holt could announce their arrival.

The happy couple, decked out with wide smiles and matching navy-blue morning suits with brightly coloured bowties, emerge from the house to additional rapturous applause and make their way to the top of the aisle where Buddy and Sarah greet them.

Here we go.

I make a big show of waving at the DJ over by the marquee, who acknowledges me in an obvious flourish. Seconds later, the *Village People* start belting out their disco hit...*it's fun to stay at the YMCA... it's fun to stay at the YMCA A... A... you can have a good meal....*

A wave of laughter rises from the assembled guests as I make an obvious slicing motion across my neck at the DJ.

"Sorry," a timid voice calls out.

"THAT'S FOR LATER!" I yell, eliciting more laughter. "Can we please have the proper music now?"

Seconds later. Macho macho man... I gotta be a macho man... macho macho man–

"Come on, really?" I yell at the DJ with mock frustration. There's more laughter, and I'm delighted to see that both Aaron and David have heard the joke and are doubled over in fits of chuckles.

I clap at everyone and my friends for being great sports. And then turn to the back row where the trio of musicians await their cue. "Ladies, over to you," I say.

Instantly, the mournful strings of a cello leads in a live rendition of *Pachelbel's Canon in D Major*. It is gradually joined by the harp and then the violin. The sublime live performance of the classic floats over us and ascends into nearby branches where helicopter leaves like acrobats abandon their lifelong perches and dive all around in a ballet of twirls and flutters like organic confetti.

I swallow the lump in my throat as I take in the gathering of love embraced in the majesty of nature. It's hard to believe that today, seven days ago, I was dealing with that nutter who invaded my home under false pretences.

Siedem.

I push the ugly thought aside as I find it particularly repugnant at this moment and instead distract myself by looking up the aisle at my beautiful girlfriend and my gorgeous boy, who is sitting expectantly by her side, with one and a half ears standing to attention like he knows what's coming next.

Well, come on then, if we're going to do this.

I watch Sarah unfasten the buckles from the pockets on both sides of his saddle, rub the dog's head, and then point down the aisle at me.

"Come on, Buddy. Come on, boy. Come to daddy," I say.

The dog barks and wags his tail at me, eliciting more laughter from the assembled guests.

"Come on, boy. Showtime. Come on."

Instantly, the dog starts trotting towards me, so I hold up the palm of my hands. "Slowly," I whisper, "slowly." He responds by glancing back at Sarah, who is still holding her arms out towards me. For a second, I think he's going to turn back, but instead, he barks once at the boys, which I interpret as, *are you two following me or what?* Then he resumes his journey. "That's it, that's my boy. Good boy. Come to, daddy. That's it."

There's a collective "Aw," and chorus of emotional gasps and sighs as the bundle of furry cuteness makes his way down the aisle, carrying the ring box on top of his saddle while sowing a trail of crimson rose petals for the boys to follow in his wake.

Phone cameras click. Cameras flash. That *thing* buzzes overhead.

In the front row, the trio of mother and aunties are all sniffing into their hankies and dabbing damp eyes as the happy couple slowly make their way down the aisle, smiling and nodding at guests they haven't yet seen but know have travelled from far and wide just to be here.

Buddy reaches me with an enthusiastic wag of his tail. I crouch down, kiss and rub his head as my eyes moisten. "Good boy, you're such a good boy," I chant, fishing a couple of treats from the pocket of my costly suit and feeding them to him to emotional chuckles and murmurs of nearby guests.

I straighten up to my full size and compose my jacket. "Heel," I say to Buddy, "heel," as we allow the boys to pass us and step onto the jetty that stretches out to the glistening lake and the manor in the distance.

David's open-taxi-door ears are as scarlet as the rose petals he just walked on. My friend has tears in his eyes, too, and it's all I can do not to follow suit when I watch him thump his chest with a fist while holding my gaze and shaking his head.

Thank you. I love you.

I mimic the motion as the two men walk up to the arbour built a couple of metres into the jetty. It is now adorned by strings of ivy, calla lilies, peonies, freesias, and roses. Underneath it, the celebrant receives them with an eager smile while I hold back and feel Sarah squeeze my hand before taking a seat next to Irvin and the lads, who I have to say are looking rather dapper in their suits. I rarely see them out of their work clothes smeared with paint and dust.

The music comes to a natural stop, and nature takes over with the ubiquitous bird chorus, the lapping on the lakeshore, and sploshing, courtesy of the fish and nosy swans that appear to be smitten with those water lilies.

The celebrant begins the ceremony by talking about the importance of respecting the union that the two men are about to enter into—although, legally, they've already done that—and about how such a union should not be entered into lightly. The speech is delivered to the boys and projected out to the sea of faces as an actor would from a stage.

I look up to see that there are quite a few teary eyes in the house. Hankies are fluttering to and from faces like butterflies, and it brings a smile to my face. These people are assembled here not out of duty but out of love for these two men, and that very notion brings another lump to my throat, which I'm just about to swallow down when I spot something through the corner of my eye. Over there. Just beyond the demarcation line. Looks like one of the guests. A female loitering on the periphery of the woods behind a tree.

What's she doing over there?

I squint and blink to get a better look, but she's gone. Vanished into the midday sun.

I take a step forward like that is going to help any. It doesn't because the trunk that she was skulking behind is still vacant.

She.

I know this because of her hair. The way she was dressed. One of the guests is out in the woods. Why?

I look around at the ushers standing behind the seating in readiness for the end of the ceremony. I try to catch the eye of one of them, but like everybody else, they're looking forward, focused on what's being said. So, I consider going over there myself. When more movement catches my attention, it's a red scarf on blonde hair. Sunglasses and a red dress. "No," I utter as lead drops to the pit of my stomach. "It... can't... be."

"Marco?" It's Sarah in a loud whisper. She's obviously noticed that while everybody is looking forward, I am focussed elsewhere. "Marco. What is it?"

She's gone again. The lady with the red scarf has disappeared. She's evaporated into the sunshine.

"Marco!" It's Sarah again. She's up from her seat now and pulling at my arm. "Marco... the rings!" she hisses discreetly.

"What?" I gawk at her.

"The rings," she repeats urgently, glancing at the trio on the jetty behind me.

"Yes. Rings," I say, snatching a glance at the tree. It's still empty. Nobody there.

"Rings," I say, pulling the box from Buddy's saddle and walking up to the men who are watching me curiously.

"Had you all going there, for a second, didn't I?" I say with a grin and a quick spin to the audience. There's an awkward ripple of laughter.

"Everyfin alright?" David asks, eyeing me warily.

"Yeah, mate. Everything's good," I say. When he refuses to turn around, I grin at him and say, "Well, get on with it."

The service resumes.

I force myself to focus on what's in front of me, yet the lure to snatch another glimpse at that tree is strong. So, I angle my head just slightly; there's nothing there.

Oh, God. I'm losing it.

"…with this ring, do you take Aaron Sinclair to be your wedded husband?"

"I do."

"And it is, therefore, that with the power vested in me in front of all of these wonderfully assembled guests that I declare you both, husbands!"

Thank God!

The newlyweds turn to the congregation, hold hands, lift them high and yell, "YES! At last!"

The congregation jumps to its feet in a chorus of cheers, thunderous clapping, and wolf-whistling.

Both men then turn to each other, hug, and, presumably to spare someone's blushes, settle for just a peck on the lips before turning to the congregation once more, bowing and cheering like actors at the end of a play.

Then, they turn to me and pull me into a group hug. "This place looks fucking awesome," David whispers in my ear, "thanks, mate."

"Do you like it?"

"Yeah!"

"Are you happy?"

"Over the moon, mate."

"You have outdone yourself, buddy," Aaron contributes.

"Thanks, mate, and congratulat…." I don't finish the sentence when I realise that the applause has been upstaged by an almighty cacophony of screeching, cawing, and chirping. When we look up, it's to a sky turned black by a massive flock of birds of all shapes and sizes, moving like they're evading a predator. Sailing over us, the lake and beyond, towards the manor.

"What the...."

The spectacle must spook the swans because they start trumpeting and hissing before flapping and splashing away from us.

A loud murmur runs through the guests, some of whom are already holding their phones up to record the seemingly endless spectacle of hundreds, no, must be thousands, of flying birds that have suddenly decided to empty the woods and emigrate.

I'm gawking up at the sight when Sarah asks, "Marco, what's happening?"

"I don't know. It's as if they've been spooked by something," I utter.

"By what?"

"I don't know."

"Marco Battista!"

"I've never seen anything like it," Aaron says as the flock has grown so big now that it has almost covered the lake in a series of jittery reflections.

"BATTI-STA!"

I hear Sarah gasp. "Marco!"

I look across at her. "What is it?"

"MARCO BATTI-STA!"

Buddy starts growling.

"Hey... you, we'll have none of that," I say, following the dog's gaze up the aisle to the house. "Oh shit," is all I can gasp as a wave of dread smashes over me.

It's *her*. Standing on the lounge balcony like a prophet addressing her disciples. Black hair now sporting streaks of silver, dirty and straggly hanging about a filthy and craggy face. She looks even skinnier than I remember. Withered. Dressed in black. Skirt muddy and ripped like she's been brawling in the woods.

"Siedem! Marco Battista! SIEDEM!" the woman literally spits as there are cries from nearby guests who recoil from the last row of seats.

I step off the jetty, run up the aisle towards the woman with the wild hair and crazed expression, and begin loudly because Buddy is already pissed off and barking, "NO! You can't be here. You need to go. Get out! NOW!" I order, "before I call the police."

The woman doesn't react to my words but instead lifts a bony finger to point at me, head bowed, whites of her eyes glaring at me through that wiry hair. *Usłysz mnie! Usłysz mnie!* She chants, then louder, she repeats, *Usłysz mnie! Usłysz!* Louder. *USLYSZ MNIE! USLYSZ MNIE!* she screams.

She's lifted both her hands now as if summoning the powers of darkness and is looking down on me like I'm an insect to be squashed, and I have no fucking clue what to do because I get a distinct impression that however I handle this, it's going to cause a scene and ruin the day.

So, I try to reason with her by taking a step forward as a bitter, cold wind whips up out of nowhere and begins to animate the hair around her face like a knot of wriggling snakes.

I can hear guests crying out behind me, chairs scraping, shoes clicking on wood as I approach.

The woman's lips are moving now, but I can't hear what she's saying. All I can hear is the chatter and sibilance of the people around me and the clicking and hissing of the dry leaves in the trees protesting their eviction before being pushed to their eternal graves.

I move closer. "Maja?" I venture, holding out a steadying hand. "Maja. I'd like to help you. Would you let me help you?" I ask gently.

"MARCO!"

But the woman doesn't acknowledge my presence. She just continues to fix me with an icy glare. Not a blink, barely pausing for breath, as she continues to mumble those bloody words I don't understand over and over. *Usłysz mnie. Usłysz mnie. Ciemne światło. Spełnij moje życzenie. Spełnij moje życzenie.*

I take another step closer.

"Marco!"

There's more screaming behind me, and it's getting hot, so bloody hot.

"Maja, Maja. I think you need help. Let me help you, please."

Eyes forward. Dirty hands clasped together. She's praying, chanting, holding something between those bony fingers of hers. It looks like a piece of paper and something else.

Usłysz mnie. Usłysz mnie.

The birds are gone now, and the sun attempts to restore some warmth to the moment, but it is blindfolded by giant pendulous storm clouds gathering over us like the wrath of God itself. I watch a woman in a summer dress scurry by me and run off towards the woods.

"Marc?" It's David calling to me. "MARCO! What the fuck are you doing?" But I hold up a silencing hand without looking back at him.

Spełnij moje życzenie.

"Maja? I can help you. Let me help you," I say, taking another step forward as the gale grows in speed and intensity, jangling the spoons in the trees and blowing a fresh batch of desiccated leaves and discarded programs across the decking along with the pungent stench of—What is that? Oil. Gas?

To kończy się dla ciebie. To kończy się dla ciebie.

Suddenly, the woman in front of me stops chanting. She is now barely recognisable as the person who visited my study. Her face is gaunt and withered. Eyes dark and small in ocular cavities full of hate. Then her lips part into a thin malevolent smile before she utters, *Palić się*.

She lifts the paper she's holding, and I can see. It's a photo! It's *the* photo from the study of Toby and me!

I barely have time to register this when there's a clicking, snapping, and popping sound before *whoosh!* To my absolute horror, first, the photo and then the intruder burst into flames.

Instinctively, I jump back, away from the wall of heat that smashes into me. I crash backwards onto the decking with a loud smack that sends a shockwave of pain up my spine and into my brain.

Around me, the birdsong is replaced with a dissonance of human screams as the place erupts into complete pandemonium. I can only watch, stunned, as guests climb over chairs and each other to evade the fireball that is now squealing like a demonic manifestation straight from the pits of hell.

I can feel the heat pressing against my skin and the stench of melting flesh invading my nostrils, and yet, to my astonishment, I find myself folding onto all fours and crawling towards the wall of heat with the intention of doing something, of saving the wretched thing that has dissolved into a black char of bloody flesh and bones.

Then I become aware of strong arms sliding under my shoulders and attempting to drag me back down the aisle, away from the heat, as the sun is snuffed out by a giant cloud of black smoke billowing overhead.

"Marco! Come on! We've got to go!" someone yells. I think it's Aaron. I'm not sure.

"WAIT! WAIT! We need to do something! We need to save her!" I yell over the roar of flames.

"SAVE WHO?" Aaron yells.

"MAJA! MAJA!"

"What are you talking about, Marco? There's nobody there!"

"WHAT DO YOU MEAN? SHE'S THERE! SHE'S RIGHT THERE!" Although when I look back up, all I can see is an altogether different horrifying spectacle. One that can't be right… can it?

I'm being dragged backwards now, down the aisle. The decking that was once the gallery of happy faces is deserted. Chairs upended, cheerful fabric bows dissolved and flapping in the wind like rags of plastic from a hedge.

It's uncanny because, in my stupefied gaze, it seems that although I'm being dragged backwards, away from the flames, the heat is intensifying.

Snap. Crackle. Crash. Snap. Crackle. Crash.

I look up again. Glass crashes loudly. Timber creaks. Oh no. It's the same scene. I… I didn't imagine that. It's still there. I can see it, but I can't believe it. I can't. I won't because I know now. This is just another of those horrible dreams. Just another of those bloody shitty, awful dreams, and there's no point going through the ritual. There's no point because any second now, I will wake up and find out that it's wedding day. All this is just my anxiety. It's just my anxiety manifesting itself through my dreams. But I'm going to wake any second now.

Go on.

Wake up.

"COME ON! MARCO! We need to get away from here, NOW!" someone is yelling again.

"Who said that?" I ask, looking up and around me. Sarah is crying. No. She's not crying. She's sobbing. I think she's sobbing. David has an arm around her.

"Sarah? Sarah. Why are you crying? What's wrong? Don't worry. It's just a dream. It's just another horrible dream."

"Marco, come on. Come on, buddy. I've got you. I've got you." It's Aaron. He's the one with his arms around me, pulling me to my feet, but oops. Shit! I can't walk. I can't walk because my feet are like bloody jelly! I start laughing. Oh no...Shit! Have I been drinking? Have I been drinking already?

"Aaron, have I been drinking already? I haven't, have I?"

I must have because of what I'm seeing in front of me. None of it. It can't. None of it can be real.

So, I keep looking back even as I'm being escorted across the lawn and into the trees. All around, people are talking, murmuring, crying, screaming.

I look across to where that *thing* should be smouldering, but I can't see anything but that giant plume of smoke rising high above the house with big orange tongues of fire slithering in and licking at walls.

Snap. Crackle. Crash. Snap. Crackle. Smash.

My stomach is griping. I think I am going to be sick. "Stop. Stop moving... I'm going to be sick," I murmur as the ball of bile rises in my throat, but it's okay. None of this is true. It's all a dream. Just another shitty dream. Another shitty dream in which Holt, my dream home, the home we've barely lived in for over a month now, is on fire. It's on bloody fire! I'm laughing. I think I'm laughing again. Yes, I'm laughing because this can't be true. Can it?

Oh, go on then, I'll play the silly game.

Could this really be happening here and now?

Yes.

Is anybody else affected by it?

Yes.

On balance, how likely is this to be real?

Most likely.

26

EMBERS & TRUTH

Have you ever singed hair on your body? You know, leaning over the gas hob, lighting a match. If you have, then you'll be familiar with that acrid stench that lingers in the air and your nostrils afterwards. Sometimes far longer than any burn.

Well, you only need to channel that stench to have an idea of what the very air around us stank like during Maja's human fireball performance. It was horrific, in the literal sense of the word, to the point where it made the fact that our home was burning so ardently and belching out enough smoke to block out the sun pale into insignificance.

At least it did initially.

I must have lost at least a couple of hours in which my brain did not know which horrifying detail to deal with first. The fact that my best friend's wedding had turned into that scene from the *Carrie* movie or the reality that Holt, my dream home, was burning to the ground.

The hero of the hour was Aaron. Yes, turns out that the man that I had somewhat facetiously dubbed Captain America a couple of years back is, in fact, that very thing. Aaron, you know, my best friend's husband, the nicest and easily mistaken for a pacifist, he of the bulging metaphorical guns, used to be a marine. Fancy that, eh? He served six whole years and has seen active duty worldwide.

I don't know how I know that. I think I overheard him explaining to a police officer or someone who was praising him for his heroic actions.

Well, they kept that one secret. I had no idea. Well, I kind of did. I just didn't retain all the specific details. Who bloody knows? My mind hasn't exactly been the most reliable thing. Even now, I'm still thinking it's playing some kind of sadistic mind trick on me because this, this shit is all a whole different level of mindfuck. Right?

But then, I can still smell smoke in my nostrils, in my hair, as well as the fact that my throat is still sore from the smoke inhalation like I've just chain-smoked a whole packet of cigarettes. And then, I can still hear that woman mumbling those words, screaming … *whoosh!*

So, yeah. It was Aaron who dragged me away from the inferno of his wedding reception. Then, he proceeded to shepherd his husband and the remaining guests to a safe distance at the front of the house. There, in what I can only describe as an incredulous stupor, we all sat on the ground, red embers floating around us like fireflies, and watched Holt disintegrate into a pyre of gargantuan flames like we were watching a fucking show on bonfire night.

Apparently, and I have no recollection of this, I tried to run into those flames. They had to literally wrestle me to the ground. I've no idea why. No clue as to what I thought I could achieve.

Miraculously, the fire did not spread to the surrounding woodland, or so I'm told. I don't know by whom, some person in authority, I think. It had to be. After all, who could possibly be as moronic to think that I give a fuck about what happened to the forest when I'd just seen my home burn to the ground? I mean, I do, but, at that moment, the environmental and ecological impact was the last thing on my mind.

Anyway, I guess that's thanks to the generous firefighter response. Safeguard the park and its inhabitants. Don't worry about my home; that can burn until there's nothing left but a few cinder blocks and a pile of black ash blowing about the place like funereal confetti.

Ironic, though, that not even the fire wanted to enter those woods. See? I told you there was something evil about that place where not even fire dare venture.

Yeah, so... Bet you can't guess where we're all sitting now. Apparently, it was Irvin's idea, especially after all the other guests had been evacuated to their respective hotels. Sarah, Buddy, and I were left in a shivering huddle, despite the Bacofoil cloaks we were wearing.

Frost Lake Manor.

In the drawing-room, to be precise. Someone even had the ridiculous idea to light a fire to transform the beautiful large space and make it feel warm, cosy, and welcoming.

More fire? Really?

Anyway, the lads have done it again. This room had mould on the walls, ripped wallpaper, a broken window, and literally shit on the floor. I have no idea what creature secreted it, and I don't even want to let my imagination stray anywhere near there. All I know is that it reeked as if something had died in here.

Not anymore. Now it smells of wood, silicone paste, paint, and whatever stuff was required to restore the wood floor to its gleaming former self.

Of course, this new wallpaper with this delicate pattern of daisies and grass was selected by your truly. At the time, I wasn't quite sure whether to go with that or the meadow scene. I remember it reminded me a bit of how the back garden used to look at Holt. I wonder if–"

"Mr. Battista?" calls a deep, treacle-like voice.

"What? Oh."

This bloke. I'd forgotten about him. He rocked up here what feels like several hours ago with a meaningful stride and a tight suit dispensing the usual fake sympathy before launching into a barrage of questions I wasn't really in the mood to answer. And then, as if that wasn't bad enough, he decided to ask those same questions all over again, so I got bored and disappeared into my own little world.

"Mr. Battista?" he repeats.

I look up at him and sigh. "I've told you everything I know," I say irritably, reseating myself in one of the pieces of stick furniture that managed to survive Monty's cull. Apparently, this chair made of redwood and no cushion is still in mint condition but isn't worth much, so I have the envious pleasure of parking my arse here while being interrogated about the events that took place earlier today. Still, it could be worse. We could have collected some of those lovely see-through wedding chairs and arranged them in a circle in the middle of the room like we're about to hold a fucking séance.

"I appreciate that it's difficult," the black man is saying. He's a chunky fella. Not fat. Just, you know, one of those blokes that probably lifts a few weights and looks like he can handle himself. He has cropped salt and pepper hair that you just know metamorphoses into wild afro if left unchecked. He must be around my age. Knowing my luck, we went to school together, and he has some deep and dark mysterious secret that I'll eventually discover when I least expect it.

He doesn't sound familiar, though. He introduced himself as Detective Inspector Peck. I was tempted to ask him if his first name was Gregory, but I chickened out because I thought, well, it was inappropriate.

And yes. Of course, I can fucking hear myself droning on here. But, despite recent events, I have the presence of mind to know that I'm still in shock. You know, on the count of the crazy lady who decided to set herself on fire in front of me and a gathering of David and Aaron's closest friends and family.

Oh, God. The boys.

"Do we know if she started the fire at Holt?" I ask suddenly. The words are just scrambling out of my mouth because I want to ask some questions now. I feel like it's my bloody turn!

"Holt?"

"Yes, Holt, Detective. You know, the house that was raised to the ground today. It's called Holt," I say.

"We don't know much yet. The fire service is still investigating the point of origin."

"The point of origin," I scoff, "the point of origin was that crazy bitch," I say, looking through the window even though there's just blackness out there now.

"I'm sorry, which *Crazy Bitch* are you referring to, Mr. Battista?"

Oh shit… did I just call her that? *Crazy bitch.* Really? You're a bloody therapist for crying out loud.

Pull yourself together, man!

"You mean your patient and former live-in help here?" Peck asks with a lift of an eyebrow and a smile. It's a faint smile, though, yet still enough to lift that moustache of his at the edges. He actually has a full beard.

"Detective, we've told you everything we know," Sarah's beautiful soft voice, a welcome relief from the dulcet tones of Barry White over there.

Sarah is sitting on another stick chair next to me, and I feel her squeezing my hand.

"Wait a minute. What did you say?" I ask with a thoughtful squint.

"She was a patient of yours, no?"

"Client, actually. I call them clients. I don't like calling them patients as it implies that I'm a doctor. I'm not a fucking doctor. Besides, she was hardly a patient. She infiltrated my home under false pretences to steal my stuff and write shit with shit on my toilet mirror. Hardly class her as a client."

"There's a difference?" Peck asked, casually, still hung up on my *client* comment and seemingly, like his colleagues before him, disinterested in the detail of my little outburst.

"Yes. But I'm more interested in that last bit. You said *live-in*?"

"That's right."

"Here? In this house?"

He looks at his notepad as if he needs to check his own words. "Yes. Was housekeeper here for almost ten years."

"Jesus Christ," I breathe as reality dawns, running hands through my now unhelpfully short hair. "Of course. She was the former so-called tenant that they evicted from here when I bought the place," I say.

"You didn't know?"

I shake my head. "No. Yes. I mean… kind of. It all makes sense. Some of the things she said in session. I don't know how I didn't put it all together sooner. And then Mary mentioned it. Oh, shit."

"That's right. You treated her, didn't you?"

"You know I did," I throw out as my mind rummages through some of the things we said during our sessions. *Angry? You have no idea how angry I am.*

Siedem! Seven. Bad luck. Seven—days- until the wedding.

And I didn't see any of that.

"How long did you treat this Maja Szymanski for?"

"I told you, Detective. I didn't exactly treat her. We had a chat a couple of times. Long enough for her to steal from me and..." I leave the last bit unfinished because I've no bloody idea why anyone would do this.

Dirty, broken fingernails on walls. Picture of Toby clutched in those talons. Woooosh Fire! Agonised screams!

"And why was she seeing you?"

I look up at him pointedly because something tells me this guy isn't an idiot and knows exactly what my response to that will be. "Seriously? You're gonna ask me that question again after what I've already told you? Everything else you probably already know is privileged. Although, technically, she wasn't a client as no money changed hands. No contract formed."

"Was she struggling with anything in particular?"

"You mean besides being an unhinged sociopath?" I snap, running my hand over my hair. Shit. I know this is bloody unprofessional to be bandying about these names... but fuck! She could have killed people!

"I don't know," he continues, unabated, "was there anything else that she wanted to discuss with you?" The question is rephrased. He seems to have a knack for that, but my only response is to squint at him because it feels like he's trying to wind me up with this. And he must realise because he tacks on a "generally speaking."

"Do you mean, did she give me any indication that she was going to set my fucking house on fire? No. She seemed lucid. Perfectly rational most of the time."

"Most of the time?"

"Don't get excited. Therapy is sometimes chaotic. You're often dealing with complex psychological, emotional triggers, which means that emotions are often volatile."

"Did she," he looks at his pad, "Mrs. Szymanski become volatile?"

"Kind of. No more than anybody else."

"Including you?"

I cock my head since I'm not sure what he means by that.

"You've been in therapy yourself. Isn't that right?"

"Yes, so?"

"For the best part of three months. Correct?"

"Yes, what's your point, Detective?"

"I'm just trying to establish the facts, Mr. Battista."

"Well, it seems you've already looked into that, so you don't need to ask me, do you?" I counter.

He's about to come back at me with something else but must think better of it because he sighs and shuffles on his feet. "Look, Mr. Battista, I appreciate this has been an ordeal–"

"Ordeal?" I echo. "My fucking house has burned to the ground, Detective. Burned to the ground because some crazy bitch set it and herself on fire during my best friend's wedding. *Ordeal* is a fucking understatement, wouldn't you say? And then, here you are asking these stupid questions about me and my past!" I yell.

Sarah squeezes my hand again.

"I'm just trying to understand why–"

"Well, isn't it fucking obvious? I bought the house that she was squatting in. Had her turfed out. She found herself with nowhere else to go and decided to exact her revenge."

I watch him exchange glances with his sidekick, who's remained pretty impassive this whole time. A weedy little thing in that role-reversal of the stereotype; significant role white man with black minor role sidekick. Here we've got this guy, the *Idris Elba* wannabe and his weedy white sidekick with the receding blonde hairline and raincoat. Raincoat? Really?

"What? What is it?" I ask.

The man looks at me but says nothing, presumably weighing up whether or not I can be trusted with whatever he has to say.

"Okay. I think that's all for now. I'm sure you could use the rest. But I will need you to make formal statements, and we may have some follow-up questions, so I'd appreciate you making yourself available. Where will you be staying?"

I stand up. "Detective, what don't I know?"

He looks at me for the longest time before, "Again, I'm going to need to know where you'll be should we have follow-up questions."

"I've no fucking idea!" I explode.

"Well, if you can let me know when you do, I'd appreciate it," he says calmly, handing a card to Sarah. "We'll see ourselves out."

I watch them leave the room. The sound of the front door barely echoes across to us before the lights flicker.

Irvin, who has been sitting in the window the whole time, perks up. "Don't worry about that. We think it's something to do with the main junction box. I've got the sparky coming out to take a good look first thing Monday."

"I thought we were getting that sorted ages ago," I say.

Irvin nods and says calmly, "As I say, he's coming first thing Monday."

I let out a long sigh. "Thanks, Irvin." I feel so tired, dirty, stinky. My stomach is griping. I just want a shower and some sleep.

"Where shall we go then?" I ask Sarah, "I suppose we could check into that B&B we stopped at."

Sarah shakes her head. I squint at her, so she qualifies it, "They're fully booked, as are most of the places around here. You know that because of the wedding."

"Alright, we'll find somewhere else," I say.

"There is nowhere else nearby, Marc."

Irvin perks up again and says, tentatively, "You could stay here."

I let out a short laugh. "Here?"

He nods. "Well, you do own it after all," he adds softly.

"No. I'm not staying here."

"Why not?" Sarah asks.

"Weren't you in that last place?" I demand like she's lost her mind.

"This is nothing like that," she says gently, "and it makes perfect sense. At least for now. Until we're able to sort out something else."

I look into her red-ringed eyes. She looks like she's been through the mill. *Shit.* I've been so wrapped in how all of this affected me that I haven't even considered the impact it must have had on her.

Selfish prick!

I pull her into a firm embrace. "I'm sorry," I say.

"The master bedroom and most of the other rooms on this side are finished," Irvin contributes, "also, entrance hall, this room, the kitchen. Most of the areas on this side. Everywhere else is a work in progress, but at least you have a roof over your head.

I also stopped to pick up a few things for ya. Nothin' fancy. Just some clean sheets, bread, and some essentials for tonight. In case you did decide to stay. I can do a shop for ya tomorrow if you're still not up to it. But you should have everythin' you need until mornin'."

Sarah breaks our embrace and throws her arms around her uncle, who I can see has a sheen in his eyes. He squeezes her tightly, and the sight brings that familiar lump back to my throat.

I place a hand on the man's shoulders while fighting my own tears as I consider the enormity of what has just happened to us.

27

FIRST NIGHT

If I'm perfectly honest, this place isn't as bad as it could be. More specifically, the areas that Irvin and the lads have managed to work on are good. They've completely transformed the spaces— under my guidance, of course. Well, my general direction, you know, *I don't like this, can't we have something a bit brighter here? What if we get rid of this stuff and just leave it plain?*

That kind of thing works perfectly with Irvin because, along with having the patience of a saint, that man seems to be able to read my mind.

The bottom line is that the places that have been refurbished now resemble a high-end country hotel. The bits that haven't. Well, not as much. They still fill me with a sense of... I don't know.... Reality perhaps? A stark reminder of how this place used to be, but as my girlfriend keeps not so subtly pointing out to me, beggars can't be choosers.

So, yes, just in case you're wondering, I have noticed that I'm a tad egocentric right now. I'm sure you've already guessed why, but just in case, I'm going to run through it for my own sanity.

I'm still in shock after what happened. My brain is still unable to process what took place on the now opposite side of the lake. I'm in mourning for the fact that my dream home has burnt to the ground. And I mean burnt down. There's just a shell now. Where the fire burned, it burned hot, incinerating anything it came into contact with.

It will take days to establish what happened exactly, but that hasn't stopped me from running through all kinds of scenarios. Did I leave something on? The cooker? The heater of some sort – though no such thing existed at the house. Maybe the coffee machine ran dry or something stupid. I don't know! I'm considering anything and everything to try and make sense of all of this, yet I keep coming back to the same conclusion.

Nothing.

I can't think of anything. Everything at Holt was automated. Worse, the house boasted a top-of-the-range fire system. That should have kicked in at the moment Holt detected the smoke, so why didn't it? Even with the best imagination in the world, I can't imagine that… that… *woman* had the presence of mind to disable the system. Besides, she couldn't even if she tried. She'd need to be able to access Holt's human programming interface. So, unless she's a hacker as well as a sociopath, I can't see how she could have done anything like that.

None of this makes any fucking sense! None of it. And my futile attempts to try and rationalise it is bloody exhausting.

I can't even allow my mind to venture anywhere near that woman's whole human torch party trick. Who the fuck does that who isn't a bloody suicide bomber? It's just inconceivable that she should allow herself to burn in the very house she set fire to.

Oh, God. Every time I close my eyes, that's all I can see. Each time I breathe in, it's all I can smell. And all I can feel is the black gunk squeezing my lungs and chest like some kind of cancer.

I've even gone to the lengths of wedging cotton buds infused with fresh wild mint—that I noticed was still flourishing in the abandoned herb garden—up my nostrils tonight to banish that smell because it seems like I quite literally inhaled the stench of that woman's cremated body.

Ironically, after all that, and in a rare moment of clarity – where

I stopped thinking about myself for one bloody second – I told Sarah that the psychosomatic smell is a direct result of the trauma we've sustained and that it will fade in a few days.

She just looked at me most curiously. I didn't really know how to take that. I just assumed it was because I've reverted to selfish prick as an automatic self-preservation reflex. Thankfully, I'm still present enough to understand it.

My reluctant exile at Doctor Holmes' pleasure, the very thing that I seem to spend every waking day trying to outrun like some abominable beast, was a direct result of what happened to Toby. I am so terrified of ending up back there that I'm incapable of focusing on anything other than maintaining my grasp of reality.

What if?

The result is more wood for the guilt pyre as I go about attempting to therapize myself, which everybody knows is fucking pointless!

Fuck!

Okay. Breathe. Breathe. You're okay. You're alright, but you've hit the nail on the head. Trying to get through this on your own isn't healthy for you or anybody around you. You know this.

Shut up!

You know this, Marco.

In true Sarah style, I have to say that she appears to be handling all this much better than I think I am. Don't get me wrong, I'm not flipping out, but inside I mean. I know she's made of tough stuff, but, well, I'm a little worried that she might be internalising rather than dealing with this effectively.

Really? You're deflecting! Focus on you.

Fuck off!

David.

Oh… My mind keeps trying to present me with the memory of David's stunned reaction to what happened. I keep recalling the moment I caught a glimpse of him. He was just staring at me with this incredulous look on his face. I couldn't even work it out. Disbelief? Terror? Disappointment?

All I know is that every time I let my brain even sniff the memory of that moment, I am filled with a sense of guilt so crushing that I can barely breathe.

I can't breathe.

You're okay. You're fine.

Apparently, they left while we were sitting on the ground watching Holt burn. Giant orange flames, roaring like a predator standing on its prey, reaching high into the sky.

David. Aaron.

That moment our eyes met across that chaotic scene of emergency services and people roaming and running around on the front lawn, it felt like the world had slipped into slow motion. Aaron, like a bloody cop with a prisoner, helped my best friend into the back seat of that luxury car before they were driven out of there, orange glow chasing them into the distance.

Sweet Jesus.

I am directly responsible for destroying what should have been the happiest day of their lives. He'll never be able to forgive me for this.

Never.

Apparently, Irvin suggested that they also spend the night at the manor. Explaining that there was plenty of room, but they refused. Well, Aaron flat-out refused. He said that they needed to get away. That they were going to go on their honeymoon and work through it all in their own time. Aaron was resolute in that decision.

You know, for a relatively quiet guy, he certainly came out of his shell when it mattered most, and I'm grateful for that. I'm so thankful that David now has someone like that in his life. Even if it means that neither of them will probably talk to me again,

Now, as I lie on the double blow-up bed, courtesy of Irvin, I have to say that this thing is actually quite comfortable despite my initial reservations.

The bedframe from the previous owner is still here. It's a rickety old wood thing that Monty obviously doesn't think will fetch much, but it doesn't have a mattress.

The best part is that because it's so dark in this room and still smells of paint and polish, it doesn't even feel like we're in the manor. In fact, we could be in any new-build house. If it wasn't for the tick and creak of its wooden bones and the sigh of the draft under the door, we wouldn't know any different as we huddle underneath this quilt.

Oh hello… Sarah has just sidled up and put her arm around me.

I pull her close but don't really need to as she's squeezing fairly tight. I chuckle. "Easy, babe, as I can't breathe." But her grip remains tight. Tighter. "Sarah… S… hey… babe? You're… ch…o…king me."

Tighter!

"Sa-arah!"

Tighter.

"Ssss-arah!"

I manage to extricate myself from her vice-like grip and pull away, rubbing at the throbbing around my neck. "What the…." I pant… "what the fuck is wrong with you?" Part of her face is in darkness, but like some maniacal clown character, the other side is grinning at me.

"What's the matter?" she asks innocently.

"You… you… were hurting me."

She chuckles. "Good."

I gawk at her. "What do you mean, good?"

"This is just the beginning!" she laughs. And with that, her eyes grow wider, larger and then sag under their own weight down to her cheek as her skin begins to bubble and blister before she starts wailing, and I–

I jerk awake. Gasping and panting. Hand darting to my throat, but there's no pain. I'm alright. No pain. I'm alright.

"Shhh…it" I swallow.

I take deep breaths. Run a hand over my hair. The raspy sound is loud in the hollow of the room.

Of course. I'm here.

I clutch my chest as I instantly feel the burgeoning heartburn of sadness. *Holt. The Wedding. That look on David's face….*

I look around the room. It's spacious, beautiful, and full of gold morning sunshine.

The once discoloured peeling vaulted diamond ceiling has been restored and painted a brilliant white. The walls were stripped and freshly papered. The stinky old eggshell-coloured carpet has been lifted and the original wood floor exposed.

I sigh and look across at Sarah's side of the bed and am disappointed to see it empty. I slide out from under the covers and brace myself for a freezing cold floor, but it's okay. It isn't Holt, but it'll do.

I pad over to the giant rectangular window overlooking the courtyard, the lawn, the lake, and beyond to the charred mountain of debris formerly known as Holt, which is still smouldering in the distance like the shell of a body that has been violated.

Oh, God. I can just about make out the arbour from here. The aisle. The chairs. Everything looks so much worse in the cold light of the day after. It did really happen. For once, it wasn't another bad dream. Mores the pity.

Movement draws my attention to the dock. Unlike Holt, this place doesn't have a jetty that reaches out far into the lake but a more practical island of decking jutting out into the water. And it is teaming with... rats!

Ugh.

The sight of those things dragging those reptilian tails behind them makes my stomach turn as I am instantly transported back to that night when we nearly lost our lives. I clutch my belly instinctively in the hope that it will help dispel the queasiness.

The brazen way those things are out there sunning themselves fills me with rage. They've obviously got used to the fact that this place has been abandoned. But I'll fucking show them.

I pull on oversized grey jogging bottoms and a white t-shirt hastily yet thoughtfully purchased for me by Irvin.

Shit. I just realised that I no longer own any clothes, but for my expensive suit. Nor shoes, but for the fancy ones I was wearing. All are sitting in a stinking pile on the bathroom floor. I'm sure I can still smell those things from here.

Creak!

A sound. From inside the bathroom. My eyes dart over to the door's threshold.

"Sarah?"

No reply.

I listen. Crows caw beyond the window.

Movement; light shifting inside the bathroom now. Someone *is* in there.

"Sarah?" I speak. Louder this time. From this angle, I can't see anything, just the haze of sunshine.

I want to go over to investigate. I want to march over there and ask Sarah, *why aren't you answering me?* But I can't, because somehow, I know it isn't her. Sarah isn't in there tiptoeing around for fear of waking me. I know this no matter how much I wish it to be true. There's something else inside that room.

Marc. Don't start. Don't do this. You've barely been here a day.

I look at the bedroom door. I consider leaving. I even step in that direction but no. No. No. Annoying me. Bloody exasperating obsessive me needs to know. Needs to be sure.

"Sarah?" I call again, slowly stepping over to the bathroom door, cringing as I approach. Heart thumping, breath rasping.

Closer….

Cautiously, I peek around the doorframe.

Drip. Drip. Drip.

Nothing in here but sunlight and a dripping shower.

Ugh. I release the breath that I'm holding. Run a trembling hand over my face and into my hair. It's okay. This is okay. It's to be expected. You've felt violated after what happened. It's only natural that you feel vulnerable right now.

Vulnerable? Afraid of a dripping shower?

I take a deep breath. Then another and another. It's okay. You're alright. Think about something else. Focus on something else.

Um, so, anyway…. Do you remember what that bathroom was like at Dolce Vita? If you do, then you'll have an idea of what a shit hole (literally) this place used to be because it was worse. Stained toilets, broken chain flushers, grimy bath with assorted creepy crawlies. You get the picture.

Now, we followed a similar Dolce Vita model with a basic claw bath, separate walk-in shower, and his and hers basins.

Ellie.

What?

Ellie. You saw her by the woods. Remember?

I didn't.

The furniture here isn't as basic as the one I selected for Dolce Vita, and that's for the obvious reason that this is supposed to be a country house. So, we opted for premium porcelain with subtle flower shape edges, which is in keeping with the crap that used to be here before.

You did!

I didn't!

Where's Buddy? How's he doing after all of this?

I make my way out of the bedroom, the floor creaking loudly underfoot, and out into the hallway, which is also awash with sunshine that goes a long way to lift my spirits. This place is nothing like the gloomy, creepy dump we first visited.

I descend the flight of stairs to the first landing and pause because it's so bright in here, thanks to that glass canopy. I can even see clouds drifting overhead now.

Odd, but beautiful.

I'm reminded of Dolce Vita. Not how it was when we were last there, but how I imagined it a couple of years ago, which makes me wonder. Am I awake? This isn't a prelude to yet another weird dream, is it?

No. I don't think so... the smoothness of this wood under my fingers feels real. And that smell... what is that? *Wood? Paint? Coffee?* And is that bacon? I'm sure it is.

There used to be a giant canvas hanging over this landing depicting some kind of religious scene, but it's gone—ooh, does that mean Monty thinks it's valuable? I make a mental note to ask.

The ubiquitous patterned carpet running up the stairs has also been lifted, revealing the original bare wood.

The old grandfather clock, which isn't the most handsome of things, is still slumbering here just like a very old man. It isn't ticking nor tocking, but just leaning wearily against a dreary smoke-stained cream-coloured wall. It's flaking in places and warped in others, having succumbed to the cold dampness. Monty thinks that it needs extensive repairs before it'll ever chime again but that it should still fetch a reasonable price when sold at auction.

Voices drift to me as I descend the last set of stairs. It sounds like Sarah has the radio on, but, actually, no, that's Drew's loud voice. I'd recognise that foghorn anywhere.

What are they doing here? It's Sunday.

By the sound of it, they've bounced back pretty quickly. I wonder how Aaron and David are. I should send a message, but I've left my phone upstairs.

I'll do it later.

When I reach the bottom step, I'm just about to turn and head for the kitchen when I sense movement behind me.

I spin around.

It's the library door. It's moving back and forth as if being molested by invisible hands. No. Not *invisible hands;* it's just moving in the draft, Marco.

Even now, in the full glare of daylight, it's with trepidation that I make my way over and peer inside. Yellow-stained net curtains move lazily in the morning breeze. I have no idea why, but they remind me of cigarette-stained wriggling fingers.

Ugh.

"...Irvin! Uncle Irvin!" It's Sarah's voice. I think she's emerging from the kitchen through a door on the other side of the staircase.

"Yes, my love."

"I really don't want Marc knowing about this."

There's a pause in which I picture Irvin furrowing those bushy eyebrows of his. "He's gonna find out anyway, Sarah, and you know I don't like keepin' secrets from im."

"I know, but a lot has happened, and he's really delicate right now. I mean, you heard what he said about that woman being there yesterday, and I'm worried... I'm worried that he might...." She leaves the sentence unfinished, and I imagine them sharing a look.

I hurry around the staircase. "Tell me what?" I ask with a smile despite the needling I'm getting from the thought that my girlfriend is trying to hide stuff from me and that she thinks I'm too delicate to handle whatever calamity they've already discovered that I'm currently not privy to.

Sarah is wiping her hands on a kitchen towel. Irvin, dressed in his usual work garb and flat cap, is standing next to her.

"Morning, boss," he says with a nod, glancing at Sarah, presumably giving her the chance to fess up.

At that moment, Drew comes bursting through the swing doors, closely followed by Dean. "…Did they say how long they're going to be, and I'm assumin' we shouldn't touch nuffin until they get—" He cuts himself off when he spots me and then recovers with a cheerful albeit stilted, "Morning, boss."

"Morning." I nod. Then I look at Sarah, expectantly. She glances at Irvin and then back at me. "What is it?" I prompt.

She hesitates. Crows caw ominously outside. "They've found something," she says, "in the cellar."

28

DEPARTURE

Hell *fucking* no.

"We're leaving," I say. Grabbing my phone and ripping the charger out of the wall. I glance at the clothes in plastic bags—like those of a vagrant—on the floor.

I don't give a shit about that stuff.

Sarah is following me around the bedroom, calling my name, but I'm not listening. I'm not listening because I only care about one thing: getting us out of this place and now.

I grab the car keys from the windowsill and hurry out onto the landing.

"Marc," Sarah keeps calling as we descend the rickety rackety staircase.

"Buddy!"

"Marc!"

"Buddy! Come on. We're leaving!"

"Marc! We need to talk about this."

"There's nothing to talk about, Sarah. We're leaving," I throw over my shoulder. And then, yell, angrily, "Buddy! Come on!" But instantly calm when I see his cute face appear at the open door like *dude, I'm way ahead of you.*

Good.

It takes me but a few strides to be out of the house and sucking in the fresh air that tastes so bloody good after my visit to Spidersville slash whatever the hell else that was down in that place.

Oh, God.

"Marc!" Sarah yells, grabbing hold of my arm, "wait a fucking minute, will you!?"

Okay. That gets my attention. Don't often hear my girlfriend yelling—or swearing, for that matter. Apart from the other day, of course, when she found out about Amanda.

Shit. That's just reminded me. Something else that needs to be addressed at some point.

I stop and look at her curiously. "Did you, did you just raise your voice and say a swear word?" I ask, exaggerating a lift of my eyebrows.

"Well, it seems to be the only language you understand," she says sternly.

I think about this…Harsh, maybe, but fair. "Okay. What?" I ask, leaning against the car.

"Where are we going to go?" she demands.

"I have no idea. I don't actually care as long as we're away from this place. We'll check into a B&B or something."

"Where?"

"I don't know. Anywhere. The wedding party hasn't taken over the whole bloody region, Sarah. And besides, if they have any sense, they'll all probably have run screaming back to normality by now. Based on yesterday's drill, they were all pretty versed at that."

"Jokes. Really?"

I rock my head. "Too soon?"

"Marc. Think about it for a second."

"I already have," I say.

"No. Really think about it."

I make a show of pausing for a few seconds. Then, "Yep. Still leaving." I frisk myself for the keys but realise I'm already holding them, besides keyless entry.

Sarah snatches them out of my hand, and I'm about to snatch

them back when she growls. "For crying out loud, Marc, would you just *grow up* for one second!"

Okay. The young lady, ten or so years my junior, is telling *me* to grow up, and I look at her for the longest time because, well, I don't know what to say until I throw a serious. "I don't want to stay here, Sarah."

"I know, but we can't leave either."

"Of course, we can. Look?" I demonstrate. "I just open this door, and you open that side; we climb in–"

"We can't afford it. You know this. You've ploughed all your money into this place. Since moving into Holt, you haven't seen any paying clients, and I'm still on a trainee's salary. Think about it. Where are we going to go?"

"Sarah, if you know one thing about me, then you know that I've been skint for most of my life. I've got a bloody degree in it," I say gently, holding her arms, "we just need to find a cheap place until–"

"Until when?" she snaps, "until this place sells? And when's that going to be? Tomorrow? The day after? Next week? Next month? When? *Think about it.*"

I do. Jaw muscles clenching as a cold wind blows at my face, bringing the smell of burnt wood.

Oh, God. My stomach churns as my attention is instantly drawn to that charred mound of smouldering blackness on the opposite side of the lake.

Where are you going to go, Marc? Doctor Holmes' voice sounds in my head. Your house has burned down. And bravo, by the way. Bravo to you for managing to manoeuvre yourself back into the very situation you were in not so long ago. It would be easy to conclude that you enjoy placing yourself in these positions of vulnerability. Why do you think that is? Perhaps we should take a few seconds to examine that.

Shut up!

"…and you've already been living off cards. *Think* about it," Sarah says again. And that's starting to grate because that's all I seem to bloody do; think about things! Over and over. Persistent bloody cogitation!

She has her hands on my arms now as I allow my gaze to wander, but I avoid looking at the lake again. Instead, I look everywhere else but there. The grounds. The forecourt. The trees surrounding us like Indians around a bloody wagon and then this country mansion worth literally millions with sprawling lawns to back.

All this property, and yet we are in an even worse situation than when I first arrived at Dolce Vita. Worse because this isn't about being skint and going into my overdraft. No. This time the *shit is bloody real*. I'm in over my head for quite literally millions.

Although, is there much difference when you're bankrupt? One hundred, a few thousand, a few million. When you're bankrupt, destitute, it's all the same, right?

Wealth—The great leveller.

Sarah is right. We could leave this place now and check into a B&B, but how the hell would we survive in there? We've still got to eat, and it's not as if I would be able to take on clients, assuming I even wanted to. And what about Buddy couped up in a tiny bedsit somewhere? That's not good for him either.

"There's nothing wrong with Frost Lake Manor, Marc." I squint at her, so she quickly nods in acknowledgement and adds, "Besides, the creepy cellar shit, that is *really* weird. And of course, the history you've attached to this place that doesn't exist outside of your head." She adds that last bit gently, caressing my face but nonetheless making her point. "After all, you don't believe any of that stuff, do you?" she asks with a wrinkle of her button nose and a curious furrow of the eyebrows.

I think about the question. "I didn't use to. But now…" I sigh, "I don't know what to believe, Sarah," I say as a smattering of orange leaves sail through the air to land and cartwheel across the gravel. "All I know is that I'm worried. And it isn't just about what's happened… shit, I can't even reconcile any of that right now. No, I'm worried about the impact this is all having on me and the danger that I might spiral again because…." I pause here as the words stick in my throat. "…because, if I'm perfectly honest, it feels like I'm barely keeping it together as it is," I say, clenching and unclenching my fists. "I'm sorry. I know how bloody disappointing it must be for you to hear all this, but that's how I feel," I say, showing her my hands that are bloody shaking like the leaves on nearby trees.

Sarah takes my hands in hers, which are surprisingly warm. Comforting.

"You're not a disappointment to me," she says seriously, looking up into my eyes because, well, she is a bit of a short-arse compared to my six-foot-something pathetic frame. And I mean pathetic.

Have I really been reduced to this quivering mound of excrement? Scared of my own shadow? What the hell has happened to me?

I look at the car door again.

"Hey," I feel her hands on my face, "stop it. Stop," she says. "You need to stop running, Marc. Stop running from this and start facing it. It's the only way you're going to find yourself again."

I shrug because I don't know which of my flaws she's referring to. "A lot of things have happened," she continues. "Bad things. Horrible things. Most people don't go through in a lifetime what you've been through in just a couple of years. And you're going to be affected by that. Who wouldn't be?"

"You're not," I counter.

She scoffs. "I'm just better at hiding it. But I'm scared too. Petrified!"

"See? Then why stay?"

"...Of losing you," she qualifies, "I'm scared of losing you *to this*," she adds sincerely. "I mean, you keep complaining about the man you've become. But I love who you are now, Marc. I'm not interested in the impervious tough nut you used to be. Admittedly, I didn't really know him, but I prefer this vulnerable you."

I hesitate here and then allow myself to break into a smile. "Yeah, well, if Ethan were here, he'd say that's because you enjoy exerting control over the vulnerable me."

I expect her to laugh, but she doesn't, and for a second, I think she's offended, but then she says, "Speaking of Ethan. I think now might be a perfect time to–"

"Don't even finish that sentence," I say, dropping her hands and moving away from her to lean back against the car. "Jesus Christ, what is it with the women in my life that keep wanting to send me back to that bloke?"

"Maybe because we're able to be objective. To see that he is good for you."

I widen my eyes. "Are you serious?"

"You know he is. Just because you don't enjoy it doesn't mean it isn't good for you," she says with a cheeky smile.

I chuckle then shake my head.

"Come on, Marco. Now's the time. At least you'll be able to talk about what happened with someone you can trust."

"I trust you."

"Which is sweet, but we both know I'm no good when it comes to affairs of the brain."

"I don't know. You seem to be doing a pretty good job so far. Better than me anyway," I say with a smile. But she doesn't follow suit. In fact, her nose is wrinkling again, which she often does when she's going to say something I'm probably not going to like. "What now?" I ask.

"It doesn't matter," she says.

"Sarah, seriously? You and I both know that it does; otherwise, you wouldn't be pulling that face."

"What face? This is my face," she says.

"And a beautiful one it is too, but Sarah, spill it."

"Well, you keep resisting this like it's a bad thing, but I think it'll be good for you. Just like I think you need to start seeing patients again."

I scoff at that. "What? Here? In the middle of nowhere?"

"Well, why not. Retreats are always out in the middle of nowhere," she says.

"So, you want me to start a retreat?"

"No. Of course not. I just think you need to get back to what you did best. Especially since you worked so hard for it."

"*This* is what I worked hard for," I say, pointing at the house.

"No. I'm not talking about properties."

"Then what?"

"Therapy. Marc. In it and dispensing it. You've just cut yourself off from both, and I don't think it's been good for you."

I laugh. "Therapy. Sarah, what are you talking about? I took that crazy bitch in as a client, and look what happened?" I point towards the lake but lower my gaze to avoid seeing over to the other side.

"You know what I mean."

"No. I don't, actually. You've been bitching about me not taking on clients, but I did, and she turned out to be a fucking nutter. That's a fact, Sarah. Not a figment of my imagination."

"Are you sure about that?" she counters.

I frown at her, "What's that supposed to mean?"

She doesn't respond.

"Sarah?" I prompt. She holds my gaze, and I know there's more she wants to say, but for some reason, she's holding back, which isn't like her. "What?" I demand.

"You know, when we were in the city, you did nothing but talk about opening your own practice, but you haven't mentioned it once since we moved out here," she says.

I pull a face. "Okay. That's random. But I've been busy."

"Busy doing what?"

"You know what, Sarah. Busy with this place."

"But we've been here a while now."

"It's taken a while."

"But you're always talking about how capable Uncle Irvin is and how he doesn't need any supervision."

"He is, but still."

"Still what?"

"It's difficult. Out here."

"To find clients."

"Yeah."

"Then why move?"

I gape at her. A gust of anger blowing through me.

"What the fuck do you want from me, Sarah, eh?" I growl.

"I *want* to know when you're going to start dealing with things, Marc. I want to know when you're going to put what happened in London behind you and stop blaming yourself. I want to know when you're going to stop running. When you're going to start taking your pills again and stop hiding behind the excuse that they make you feel weird, and I want to know when you're going to get back to being you!" she explodes.

I close my eyes as if that's going to stop the sound of her voice and warn her. "Sarah, be quiet. Please be quiet."

"Why don't you want to hear this?"

"Because it has nothing to do with you."

"It has nothing to do with me?" she asks incredulously. "It has *everything* to do with me."

"I don't want to talk about this anymore."

"Well, I do, and I think you should."

"Sarah–"

"Marc, you keep avoiding this stuff."

"Please, Sarah," I hold out a hand and close my eyes as I attempt to reel in another bout of rage that I can feel clawing at my throat, roaring to be let out.

"No, Marc. We need to talk about this. Why won't you talk to me about it?"

"BECAUSE YOU DON'T KNOW WHAT THE FUCK YOU'RE TALKING ABOUT!" I yell so loud I think I'm going to choke.

My girlfriend flinches. Wings flutter from nearby trees. Crows caw.

But Sarah knows me. She isn't easily rattled. Instead, eyes blazing now, she bites her lip and nods. "You're right. I don't know what I'm talking about, and that's precisely why you need to go and speak with someone who does. For Christ's sake, Marc. We all make mistakes, but all this self-flogging, desperation to atone, it isn't the way–"

"Oh, Jesus Christ, you *have* been talking to Ethan again, haven't you?"

"Yes, of course I have because nobody else is capable of an original thought."

"That isn't what I meant."

"No, it's okay. I'm not offended. What does offend me is the way that you insist on avoiding everything in the hope that it'll all just go away when history has taught you that it doesn't. That it just gets worse. And that's exactly what's happening right now, but you are just too blind to see it. And that includes avoiding doing the things that you're good at."

"What? Like sitting on my arse?"

"Yeah. Okay. More jokes. Good."

"It's my coping mechanism. We've established that."

Seconds drift by. Wood pigeons coo. A wintry wind blows as if the autumn has given everything up as a bad job, and we've skipped straight to winter.

I shiver. "So, let me get this right. Your theory is that not only am I avoiding going into therapy but that I've also *marooned* us out here, so I don't have to administer it either. Right?"

She doesn't respond. And she doesn't need to.

"Well, that's just great. That's perfect."

"Oh, come on, Marc. You said it in your own words. You're so terrified of a relapse that you want to run from anything that represents a potential risk. You ran away from the coast to the city, from the city to the countryside, and now you're looking to run again. Only, there's nowhere else to go; this is it. *This* is all we have. It's time to stop running and face things. Start living your, *our* life," she says.

I sigh and watch how the wind keeps playing with her hair which I realise isn't harnessed today but unleashed and playing about her face. In fact, I don't know if it's the speech she just gave me or the fact that her hair is down, but she looks different today. Not as cute. By that, I mean not as young. Still beautiful, yet older. Wiser. Almost as if yesterday's events have already gone about restructuring her character.

"You know, for someone who keeps professing not to be a psychologist, you seem to do a pretty good imitation of one," I said grumpily.

"You think?" she asks with a smile, "do you think I should consider retraining?" she adds thoughtfully, but I know she's making fun as only Sarah can. Then, presumably noticing the sulky look on my face, she moves closer to me and adds softly, "Again, I'm no expert, but I think you've lost your nerve. You seem to have forgotten all of those commendations about *unique empathy* and are somehow thinking you aren't worthy anymore, but babe, *I know* you are."

I take a few seconds to look into those green eyes. The gale whistles loudly through one of the electrical wires as if to underscore my girlfriend's statement.

"Flattery will get you everywhere."

"I know," she agrees with a cheeky smile. Then picking up the pace, she adds, "If not that, then you could always help the boys out. You know, get things done a *little* faster."

I shake my head. "And there she is."

"Or you could collect that advance. Write that book," she says, lifting those neat eyebrows once more. "It's not as if we couldn't use the money right now."

"You know, Sarah. If I didn't know you better, I'd think that you actually want me to rake up all of my trauma just so we can make a quick buck."

She shrugs. "Needs must, mate. Needs must."

And I'm just about to say something when I'm interrupted by the loud sound of Buddy groaning. He's obviously bored waiting because he follows that up with a frustrated bark that has me thinking that he really does understand everything we say.

Although, I soon realise that he isn't looking at me, but around me. Then there's the growl of car engines. Tyres crunching on gravel. And when I turn around, it's to see a black Vauxhall Insignia followed by a police patrol car driving into the courtyard.

Here we go.

29

CURSED

It must take the police a good couple of hours to do whatever they needed to do in the wine cellar, during which we were all asked not so courteously to stay clear of the area.

And so, once I got over the initial sting of being told what to do in my property, Sarah and I decided to take a comprehensive tour of Frost Lake Manor to establish exactly what kind of progress has been made and just how habitable the place is now.

And so, we've made a rudimentary list of the rooms that are accessible, those that remain off-limits. Rooms that are furnished and those that aren't.

Yep. Because we're literally starting from scratch here. Not a pair of underwear nor a laptop computer. In the space of a day, we've gone from a smart home to barely having electricity, which is the very reason why the boys and the sparky were down in the cellar in the first place.

It's the strangest feeling not owning a single possession but the clothes on your back. It's depressing but peculiarly liberating.

Nowhere near as liberating as us getting the eff out of here, but, as much as it pains me to admit it, Sarah is right. The reality didn't even hit me until we were walking around this maze of a place.

Unbeknownst to her, I was collaborating with the tour while simultaneously testing her theory for weaknesses. I spent much of the time trying to find alternate solutions to our current predicament. But kept coming to the same conclusion. There are none. Staying at Frost Lake Manor is the most logical and economical way out. The best thing we can do right now is hunker down, focus on fixing this place up, and getting it sold because once we do, all the problems, all of the stress, they're gone.

Yeah. I know. Sounds frustratingly familiar, but those are the cards we've been dealt—again.

When this is over, the place is sold, and the money in the bank, we're going to bloody emigrate. Forget being enterprising. We're going to bank the bloody money and run!

So, what do we have? Good and bad news.

The good news is that Irvin and the lads have definitely done it again. Despite the obstacles, they have managed to quite literally finish half of the house. That is the whole right-hand side of the building as you enter the front door, dubbed *the west wing*. It's comprised of the *drawing room, the dining room,* and *the kitchen.*

Upstairs, that's the flight of stairs leading right from the grandfather clock landing; four of the bedrooms are finished. And what was known as the washroom, now rechristened the family bathroom.

Yeah. We won't be slumming it after all.

In stark contrast, the *East Wing* remains a shit hole. Okay. That's probably a bit harsh, but the landing and other four rooms that can be reached by turning left at the grandfather clock are like something out of the last century. Well, to be fair, that's exactly what they are. Peeled wallpaper, mould, that same stagnant stench that makes me think that someone was caught short.

Not all the rooms are wallpapered, which only makes them appear more miserable with flaky plaster, broken floorboards, grimy windows, assorted insectoid, and rodent squatters. Generally everything you'd expect from an abandoned home.

Grim.

Irvin suggested that during our tour, we go up and experience *the view* from the rooftop. It is reached through a small door I didn't know existed at the end of the corridor. It leads into one of the turrets and a spiral staircase of about a dozen stone steps. There are slits in the wall, which I assume are for light and not to fend off marauders from another century. The wind that howls and echoes around that place is seriously atmospheric—note my positive choice of word here—until you emerge through a thick exterior door onto the rooftop.

It's a whole new world up there of chimney stacks and arched shingle sections of the roof that form part of the attic. These surround what looks like a rooftop courtyard, and sitting at its centre, like a diamond, is the newly restored lantern roof.

The wind was bitter and fierce while we were up there, but it did little to spoil the stunning views that stretched as far as the eye can see over woodland, rolling fields, and bodies of water neatly sewn together by the thread of the Beaulieu River.

Up there, heavy black clouds of rain hung so low it felt like we could touch them. And we would have stayed longer had we not started to lose the sensation in our fingers.

And so, it would appear that Frost Lake Manor may not be as bad as I first thought, with one major exception. To keep the west wing protected from all the dust and grime generated from the East Wing over the coming weeks, Irvin has seen fit to hang dustsheets at strategic places to try and minimise the distribution of airborne crap. This means that now not only is the East Wing the house that time forgot, but it also resembles a hangout for plastic ghosts that move and rustle in the slightest breeze.

Like I don't already have an overactive imagination. But that's just it. It's all in my head. I told myself this time and time again as we descended the stairs back to the drawing room.

It's all in your head Marc. Even the stuff they found down there. It's just a load of superstitious crap. It means nothing. Don't let it transform this place into something it is not.

It is *not* Dolce Vita.

Of course, it's going to take some time for me to truly believe that, but baby steps, right?

And, to aid me in this endeavour, I concluded that—for what

it's worth—given that the wedding is over and we're now living in a strange place where someone like me is going to be susceptible to the slightest disturbance, in whichever form it may present itself, E.g., fluttering dust sheets, now may well be an excellent time to get back on those pills.

But guess what?

I don't have any. My pills went up in smoke like everything else I owned. I imagine that, right now, there's a family of owls out there getting stoned.

Ugh. So, guess what that means. That's right. A return visit to Doctor Holmes.

Fantastic. And there's me thinking that things couldn't get any worse.

I'm not going to think about that now. I'm going to think positively. Sarah and I have decided that we are going to treat our stay here as a mini holiday. A mini holiday in a luxurious country home –if you don't look left as you go up the stairs – with wonderfully generous-sized rooms featuring spectacular views of those formal gardens and that stunning lake that gives this jewel its imaginative name. Just, um, need to make sure we don't gaze too far onto the opposite shore.

Thankfully, and again, I use that term loosely; we've been summoned to a conflab in the drawing room like suspects at the end of a *Columbo* episode by inspector *Plod*.

Did you hear that? *Drawing room*. Like I'm some lord of the manor. Although technically, as much as I hate the idea, I suppose to some extent, I am.

Sarah and I take up a seat in the bay window this time. Irvin is sitting on one of the stick chairs, and the lads, because they're wearing their dirty work clothes, are now sitting on the lovingly refurbished wood floor.

Monty hasn't left much in here, but for those chairs, an ostentatious gold mirror overlooking the fireplace, which I assume is all show and no value because it's still in here. One occasional antique table, still worth some money but not enough to auction. Oh, and there's a *Feurich* grand piano in the corner. Apparently, it needs to be tuned so Sarah and I won't be warbling *knees-up-mother-*

brown any time soon. More's the pity. I'm reliably informed it's worth three to four thousand, but like everything around here, with work, could fetch up to twelve to thirteen grand.

That's what I'm talking about! Anyway, nobody is sitting on that because, well, that would just be weird.

"Thanks for your time," the *plod* begins. "I won't keep you long. I just wanted to bring you up to speed with what we know so far, and I also have some additional questions I'd like to ask you," he adds, looking around the room. His voice is loud, and the authority he likes to exude reverberates around the empty space.

"Before you start," I interrupt because this is my property, after all, "do you have any news regarding Holt and the fire?"

The Detective gives me a look. "Nothing yet," is the flat reply.

I squint at him. "They don't have any idea?"

"That's what I said. The fire department's still trying to determine if the cause is natural, electrical, or chemical."

"Natural, electrical, or chemical? Well, it's obvious it wasn't natural," I say.

"Mr. Battista, as soon as we know more–"

"Now, hang on. Why are you deliberately avoiding the obvious?"

"Marc–" Sarah begins, touching my arm.

"No. It was arson, right? That much is obvious. Right?"

"As I say, we're still looking into it."

"I just don't get the big secret. I mean, they were out there *investigating* today, weren't they?"

"Mr. Battista, as I said, as soon as I know more, you'll know more," the man says with a levelled tone I recognise as suppressed frustration. Then, flipping back to his usual relaxed demeanour, "In fact, Mr. Battista, I'd like to start with you. Could you tell me how well you knew Maja Szymanski?"

I rock my head. "Well, Detective. I've already told you what I know. She posed as a client to gain access to my home–"

"Yes. So you said. I'm more interested in what you actually know about her."

"I told you. She was from Poland, lived with her parents. Married an Englishman and told me she worked for some lady she referred to as Mrs. Faversham as a housekeeper. She made a point of not telling me her employer's real name. Said it was unprofessional. Turns out, she didn't want me to know that the woman she worked for used to live here."

The Detective studies my face for a while. "Had you ever met her before she became a client?"

I think about this and then shake my head. "No."

"Never?" he repeats, which, given current circumstances, instantly annoys me.

"No, Detective, never," I respond firmly, and I'm just about to ask him to get to the point when it occurs to me. "Does this have something to do with the fact that she worked here? Whatshername, Emmy, Emmer, Emmerson."

"Lady Emmerson," Peck contributes.

"Szymanski worked for her."

"For the best part of ten years, yes."

"Did she do something to her?" I ask, heart already throbbing at the prospect.

"It's unknown for sure."

"But something did happen to her, right?" I ask.

Peck looks around the room as if he's carefully considering what he's about to say.

"We haven't been able to establish much with any degree of certainty other than Lady Emmerson wasn't well. Pretty much an argor.... arga... agro"

"Agoraphobic," I help out.

"She didn't leave the house much. Her husband, along with the hired help, did everything for her. Word is that they were close. But one day, he went out and never came back. The Emmersons had serious financial problems that it's believed he kept from her. And she was close to losing everything before she sold part of the estate."

"Holt," I say.

The Detective nods.

"Emmerson was able to stay on with one aid, but the house fell into disrepair."

"That's why she was bitter and difficult. She felt abandoned," I contribute, thoughtfully.

"There was a high turnover of staff until–"

"Szymanski."

Peck nods. "She was here quite a while. For whatever reason, her employment lasted longer than any of the others, right up until Emmerson's death."

"How did she die?" I prompt.

The Detective hesitates, then, "The official verdict is that she fell down the stairs and broke her neck."

Sarah gasps and throws a hand over her mouth to stifle the scream I want to make.

SHIT!

The image of some woman I've never met before in a crumpled heap at the foot of the stairs with her head twisted in the opposite direction, eyes bulging and full of incredulous terror, unhelpfully presents itself to my mind.

I squeeze Sarah's arm. The worst bit is that I'm not surprised.

Eager to move on from that mental image and the horrifying reality of what happened just outside the door in the main hallway, I steer the conversation forward by asking, "What happened then?"

"Well, there were no surviving heirs, so eventually, ownership of this property passed to the Crown under *Bona Vacantia* until a claim was made by English Heritage to facilitate, buy, and restore. It then remained empty for some time before your company bought it. It was then that the estate agent discovered that someone was still living here. They had to serve an eviction notice, but Szymanski fought it, citing *squatters' rights*. And her case had to be heard because she'd occupied this place for some time. That, and she believed that she deserved to live here after all the years she'd spent serving her mistress. But the court didn't agree. She lost her case and then had to be served with yet another eviction notice, and that's when things turned ugly."

"Ugly how?" It's Sarah.

"She wouldn't leave. It took three officers to subdue her, cuff her, and physically carry her out of the property."

Drew whistles incredulously.

"That's why the sale was delayed," I contribute.

The Detective nods.

"What happened to her after that?" Sarah asks.

Peck shrugs and shakes his head. "She was taken down to the station referred to social services and a shelter."

"Why didn't she just go back to Poland?" It's Sarah again.

"No point. She doesn't have any family there," the Detective responds.

"Hang on. I thought she had parents?"

Peck taps his notepad with his pen and shakes his head. "Nope. Her parents died years ago. She was still a teenager. She was raised by her uncle."

"Uncle?" I ask.

"Yeah. He died just before she came to England."

"Huh." I think about this. "Why would she lie about that?"

Another of what is fast becoming the Detective's trademark shrugs. "You tell me. You treated her," he says, observing me.

And there's a pause. It's an awkward one because now we're locked in some kind of stare-off, which is actually starting to piss me off because he seems to be behaving like I'm bloody holding out on him or something when I'm starting to feel like it's the opposite.

"I'm sorry, Detective. I'm confused." It's Sarah breaking the stare-off. "You said that she was evicted from the house, so how was that stuff in the cellar?"

Unfortunately, I know the answer to this one, but I stop short of throwing my hand up and squealing *me! Me! Me!* Because I'm too busy being repulsed by the thought of what's coming.

"As far as we can tell, she was living down there."

"Living down there?"

Peck nods. Hesitates and then says, "We think she came back."

There's a murmur from the others as I rage, "Are you fucking kidding me?" I look at Irvin and then back at the Detective. "How's that even possible? We've been working here nearly every day. Someone would have noticed her, no?"

"Not with that front door," Irvin pipes up, "the key hasn't been changed or anythin' anybody could've wandered in. This place is so big we wouldn't even have noticed. Remember, it's only because we're having problems with the electrics that we went down there."

My heart is thumping. I don't even know why. And even the

weather's shocked because it is starting to make itself known by blowing eerily through the gap in the window, and I bet you can't guess where I'm reminded of, instantly.

"We don't think she stayed here the whole time. There's some evidence that someone has been sleeping rough in the woods," Peck says.

"Here?" I ask.

He shakes his head. "No. Not here."

I squint at him, and he responds by nodding at the window. I follow his gaze.

"You mean she was camped outside of Holt?"

"We don't know for sure if it was her, but as I say, we found some suggestion that–"

"Suggestion?" I echo. "What, like little love notes? What do you mean by suggestion?"

"As I said–"

"You mean those things, don't you? Hanging from the trees? Those twig things!"

Sarah looks at me. "What twig things?"

"I didn't want to tell you because it's creepy as–"

"Excuse me!" Peck asserts himself.

We look back at him. My breath is coming thick and fast, and I'm already regretting our decision to stay.

"What's this got to do with what we found in the cellar?" Drew pipes up.

"I was getting to that," the Detective says, holding his notepad and pointing at Drew with his pen. "As you've already guessed. We believe that the thing you found is some kind of cardboard effigy of a house."

"This house?" Sarah asks.

Peck shakes his head. "We don't think so."

"Holt?" I ask.

The Detective nods.

I scoff. "You think *she* built that thing?"

"Why?" Drew asks.

The Detective shrugs, but I don't think it's because he doesn't know, but more because he doesn't want to be the one to say it out loud.

Sarah, who generally speaking is more into the subject, helps him out. Her tone is ominous as it is reticent. "What, like some kind of voodoo doll, witchcraft thing?"

Another shrug from the cop.

Drew whistles air over his teeth again. I've noticed that he isn't cracking a joke, though, which is more in character for him, and I bet I know why. For the same reason that I'm not openly making jokes and why Irvin and Dean are just listening but hardly blinking.

We were all at Dolce Vita. No matter what kind of slant each of us has allowed our memories to spin on what happened that night, this is all a little too bloody creepy for comfort.

I chuckle. It's a nervous one, but I'm hoping nobody notices. "Are you suggesting that woman set fire to Holt via that thing in the cellar with some kind of...what, spell?" I ask sceptically.

"No. That isn't what I'm saying," Peck says with obvious restrain.

"But that's what you're implying. Right?" I demand without holding back because I am sick of this shit. "You've already said you can't find a point of origin when it's bloody obvious. IT WAS HER!" I rage. "What? You think that it's a coincidence that she showed up at my best friend's wedding and my house just happened to spontaneously combust? *She* did it! *She* did this, Detective! And it wasn't via some bloody voodoo cardboard box trick but with her two bare bloody hands. I suggest you start with that!" I say, pointing at him.

Silence reigns as my angry words hang heavily in the air. It appears that the turbulence storming around the building agrees with me because it buffets the front door, causing it to tap, knock, and rattle in its frame.

"Have you finished?" Peck asks flatly.

"Detective..." Sarah begins, but he ignores her.

"Because since you've brought it up, I'd like to discuss your statement in more detail."

I shift in my seat because I'm ready for this bloke.

"You say that Szymanski showed up uninvited at your friend's wedding, is that correct?"

"You know it is. I've already told you."

"And that she ended up being burned by the very fire *you* believe she started, is that right?"

"That's the logical conclusion, yeah."

"Logical? Logical according to who. You?"

"Logical according to anybody who was there," I say, looking around the room. "Everybody saw her."

"Everybody?"

I squint at him. "Yes, everybody."

"Did you, Miss Collins?" he asks. Sarah doesn't answer.

"You, Mr. Smith?" Irvin hangs his head.

"How about you two, did you see—"

"Alright, Detective, you've made your point," Irvin chimes in.

I screw my face up because I'm confused. Why are they all reacting to his questions like this? Why aren't they speaking up? Oh shit. I've been in this situation before. There's more to this, and I don't think I'm going to like it.

Then, as if he's been reading my thoughts, Peck declares, "Nobody saw this woman at your friend's wedding, Mr Battista. Nobody in this room and none of the hundred or so other guests."

I shake my head. "No. You're wrong. She was there. She was there. I saw her," I insist, "*We* all saw her standing on the balcony," I say, looking around the room.

"Not everybody, Mr Battista. Just you."

Oh, what the fuck is going on? "But that isn't possible." I utter. "She was there. She was there! I saw her holding that picture of Toby and me." I look at Sarah and then back at the Detective. "I saw her. I watched her burn!"

"So far, no bodies have been recovered from the property formally known as Holt," the Detective says flatly. "How do you explain that?"

I shake my head. It doesn't make any sense. "I, um…" the words dry in my mouth.

"Anyway, the investigation is ongoing," the man says dismissively. Like we're in court, he's made his point and is now bored with this witness.

I become aware of Sarah squeezing my hand. I think it's been there the whole time; I just didn't notice it until now. "Would that be all, Detective?" she asks curtly.

"I do have a few more questions, yeah–"

"Well, can we do it some other time?" I hear her say. "You may have noticed that we don't have anywhere to live, and we need to try and make this place habitable." Her tone is blunt. Cold. Unlike her. And although I can't see her face because I'm too busy gawping into empty space, I somehow sense her having a stare-off with Peck before I hear him say, "Sure. I can come back tomorrow. Or you could come visit us at the station if you remember anything further," he says.

"Come on, boys," I hear Irvin say as they rise from their seats, breaking the moment. Then he walks up to me, puts a hand on my shoulder, and says, "We'll prioritise getting rid of that stuff tomorra. Unless the Detective has any objection," he adds, looking at the man.

Peck shakes his head. "Nah, we have everything we need, for now."

30

THE DUST & THE DARKNESS

You won't be surprised to hear that I was happy to see the back of Peck and his band of unmerry men. It isn't that the man has done anything wrong; if you ignore the whole, *I'm going to make you think you're losing your mind* bit, but I think it's more because I need time to process everything.

I messaged David for the fourth or fifth time now without a response. And his silence is worse than him telling me to fuck off and never darken his door again. It feels like part of my life support has been severed.

Sarah says that he'll *come round* when he's ready, that like the rest of us, he needs time to deal with what's happened. And I want to believe that, but I can't shake this horrible feeling that this may well be it. That my friend won't want to have anything to do with me. And I realise now that I would be devastated by that. David, and by association, Aaron, are the only true friends I have now. All my other so-called mates gave up on me a long time ago. I like to think it's because they couldn't handle the fact that one of their comrades had checked into the loony bin, but I think that things started to fray long before that, when Ellie and I first got together as friendships often do when priories change. Back then, it was her and me, and then, after that, it was Toby. Nothing else mattered to me.

And yes, as a therapist, I'd be the first to say that that isn't a particularly healthy relationship dynamic, but I didn't know any better back then.

I do now, I think, as I watch Sarah pluck a set of sheets from the shelf and put them in our trolley.

As much as I wanted everybody to leave the manor, I instantly regretted it when my wish was granted. That place is enormous and particularly vacuous when empty.

So, I decided that it made sense for us to get out for some retail therapy. My motivation was more practical than indulgent. If we're thinking of making that place our home for the next month or so, then we're going to need some creature comforts. Decent bed linen is right up there with chocolate biscuits as far as I'm concerned.

"No. We need these ones," I say to Sarah, replacing the pack in the trolley. "Those have polyester in them; it's barely 200-count. We need a more luxurious cotton count if we're going to live in a mansion. 500-count should just about do it," I say with a wink.

Sarah lifts her eyebrows at me.

"Trust me. They feel much better," I say, putting an arm around her shoulder.

"If you say so." Yeah, unlike Ellie, shopping for homeware isn't this girl's idea of fun.

"So, how are you doing?" I ask.

She cocks her head. "I'm okay. Why?" she asks warily.

I give her a broad smile. "No reason. I'm just asking," I say. "How about we pick something up to take home with us? Sod grocery shopping. I'll do it tomorrow."

"Oooh… Takeaway. Chinese?" she asks excitedly.

"Your wish is my delight," I say with a flourish of my hand and a bow which makes her giggle.

After the homeware store, we stop off at Sainsbury's for some essentials. I'll come back out for the rest tomorrow. Normally, I'd drive out to the village store as I've been making a point of supporting it, but Mary will have no doubt heard about what's happened, and I just don't have it in me to field any more questions today. So, we grab just what we need, which these days includes cookies and chocolates for Sarah. She seems to be into that lately. And, wow, that sounds like I'm being judgemental. I'm not. On the contrary, Sarah's eating habit tells me a lot about her state of mind.

I wonder if she's much more anxious than she's letting on. I dare say I can't be helping much. I need to work on that.

I need to work on many things, but that would mean setting my mind free and allowing it to scurry back and forth, like a squirrel, from thoughts that I've been actively burying this whole time because they can only mean one of two things. Either all that weird shit has followed me here from Porthcove, or I *am* losing my mind again. Neither of which is good. Obviously.

It's become clear to me now that I need to see Ethan as much as I've been avoiding that too. Sarah is right. I need his cold analytical—sadistic—mind to look at all of this and help me make some sense of it. That, and I desperately need a new prescription because what I learnt this afternoon has made me realise just how susceptible I am to anything remotely stressful.

Maja Szymanski does exist.

Or, more specifically, she sought me out, infiltrated my home under false pretences, then wrote that creepy prophetic shit *with shit* on my bathroom mirror.

Siedem.

Seven days from her visit until the fire. Coincidence?

Maybe.

The important part is that her visit was real. The police can corroborate this. At least, they can confirm that I filed a police report with them. And I checked my phone, I still have those disgusting pictures.

This much is true.

What came next. That's the bit I'm struggling with because I *saw her* on that balcony. *I saw her* clutching that photo and – God help me – watched her go up in flames. I can still smell the acridity of it all! And yet, if nobody else witnessed it, there can only be one explanation.

Yet still, on the drive home, I almost opened my trap to ask Sarah if what she told the Detective was true. What the hell? I've only just finished telling myself to be more aware of her state of mind, and yet I was ready to drag us back to this subject just so I could satisfy my inability to accept the facts.

Luckily, I had the presence of mind to resist the urge. I spoke her name, but in that lame Hollywood movie way, I swapped out my serious expression to a display of affection. I said I loved her, which made her smile, take my hand, and kiss it.

This is why, like it or not, I need to see Ethan because I can't keep burdening my girlfriend with my neurosis but come on. Did that shit really happen? I'm talking about the police at the house and all that witchcraft voodoo shit in the cellar.

I mean... what the.... "Did we leave the lights on?" I ask, piloting the BMW onto the forecourt.

Sarah thinks about this and wrinkles her nose. "I don't think so. It was still light when we left, wasn't it?"

She's right. It was. But then, we were so wrapped up in everything that happened, we probably just didn't notice that the lights were on. At least they're working. Power cuts have been plaguing this place for some time now.

We step out into a bitter, cold wind that's herding leaves across the courtyard and into an untidy heap against the stone wall. Wow, it definitely feels much colder perched up on this hill compared to the shelter of the woods.

I glance across the lake but can see nothing but darkness. Just as well; I'd only be making myself miserable. I know this must be our home now, but the loss of Holt makes me feel surprisingly empty inside. And I'm not just talking about the house, but the AI. Yes, I know that's ridiculous because he was just code and a series of predetermined responses and routines, but still, it feels like we've just lost a friend.

David.

Great. Don't you just love how the mind works? You're already wading for one quagmire of shit, so it instantly dumps a whole new truckload of –

"Bloody hell!"

I've barely made it through the front door with the shopping bags before the thing slams noisily behind me.

Yeah. Holt, this place is not. It's big, cold, and I want to say unfriendly, but I think that would be unfair. It is, after all, the product of its creation. Like a child with a strict upbringing, this place only knows about formality, etiquette, decorum. It was built to impress while being functional, and it does this very well. I mean, just standing here – if you ignore how the old lamps affixed to the staircase and wall flicker from time to time like something out of a theme park haunted ride – you can't help but be in awe of the space. I imagine many aristocrats will have paused in this very spot and thought the same thing.

Movement draws my attention to one of the balconies on the east wing, where those dust sheets have already started their ghost impersonation.

I shake my head. It was only a matter of time. We've barely changed the bed with our new sheets, and we're already back to drafts and creaky unidentifiable sounds.

That said, why is that sheet moving? The door's closed.

"Oh, shit!" I drop the bags and rush back and pull the front door open.

"What happened?" Sarah complains. Hair flying about her face in the gale.

I take the bags off her. "Sorry. The door slammed shut behind me."

"Does it lock automatically then?"

"No. I don't think so."

"Well, it slammed in my face. Then, I couldn't get in. It's freezing out here."

"I know. Sorry."

She rushes by me.

"Come on, you," I say, dancing on the spot as the meteorological bluster spits in my face and starts biting my ears. It's Buddy, and he's decided to retake a seat outside the door.

"Buddy, come on. In!" I order, jerking my head towards the hall, but the dog isn't moving. He just keeps looking at me and the open doorway.

"Buddy! Come on," I say, dancing from foot to foot, but he isn't budging. He's just sitting there with his head bowed like an obstinate child.

"Marco! Come on," Sarah calls, "it's freezing in here. How do we warm this place anyway, and please don't tell me it's just the fireplace?"

"Buddy? You alright, mate?" I'm reminded of the first day we came here. He wasn't keen then either. "I know, mate. Me neither. But this is our home now, and we're just going to have to make the most of it. Come on," I say, pushing the dog's butt until he reluctantly makes a move, and I can finally lock the wind out.

The relief is instant.

I turn to Sarah, but she's already disappeared through the door to the kitchen, where I hear her say, "Holt... oh shit!" And it brings a smile to my face. I wonder just how many times we're going to be speaking to the walls here only to realise that there's no AI built into them. Just history.

That ghostly flutter from the balcony captures my attention once more, and I would like to say that it doesn't have any effect on me, but it does.

It's creepy. It looks like someone is up there, peeking around that thing at the new hapless victims down here.

But there isn't anybody up there.

No? What did happen to Maja? She just came and went as she pleased.

Oh, fuck! I slowly look around the entrance hall. It's empty. Quiet but for the howling of the wind and the rustling of those bloody sheets.

And so, responding to the flare of irritation, I march back to the front door and throw the oversized metal bolt across it. Then, I go over to the cellar door and make sure it's still locked. It is. And then, I make my way up the first flight of the rickety stairs. At the grandfather clock landing, I pause and look back down. Buddy has taken a seat in the middle of the entrance hall and is watching, although clearly not tempted to join me.

"Thanks, wingman. Appreciate it." I roll my eyes at the hound and climb the rest of the stairs to the *ugly* zone.

The bluster seems much louder up here as if the wind is systematically testing each window and door for weakness.

Rustle. In. Rustle. Out.

It seems the house has been resurrected, breathing once more through doors and windows like a fish through its gills. Pulling and pushing those dustsheets with every breath.

It's darker up here. Most of the bulbs on this side of the house are on strike, presumably in protest that the opposite side of the building has received all of the care and attention.

"Hello?" I say softly as I make my way towards one of the dust sheets, then promptly shake my head. Now, why would I say that? I have no idea.

It smells up here. Musty. Dank. Dirty. And it feels so strange. Like I've just stepped into a different building.

I glance back at the sanctuary of lights opposite, then down at Buddy, who's still watching with his head cocked to one side - *Are you really going up there on your own?*

Apparently. No thanks to you.

I turn back to the sheet and... shit! What's that? I stare at the thing. Is that a bloody shadow loitering behind it?

Oh, God. I run my hand over my face as my heart obviously thinks we should turn back by punching some sense into me. And I consider it. I consider running back down the stairs but almost instantly have a reaction to that. A sudden flare of inexplicable anger.

"NO!" I yell, sweeping back the plastic curtain that protests with a loud hiss and rustle.

"Sssshiiit...." See? There's nothing behind here. No ghoul or ghost, or shadow for that matter. It's just the light passing through the plastic and refracting with every movement.

The gale has called in reinforcements and is now driving rain like bullets against the glass of bedroom windows and the sky lantern overhead. While, on the other side of the sheet, I can hear the turbulence whistling wildly as it flees from the darkness of the bedroom opposite.

Someone must have left the window open in here. Who? I don't think the lads even venture over this side of the house. Monty, maybe?

Whoever it was. It's cold up here. So cold that I can feel it prodding at my skin, nipping at my nose, and I think it's even fogging my ragged breaths, but it's too dark up here to tell.

I step across the hallway, the wood floor creaking and groaning loudly underfoot, and peek into the bedroom.

The room is filled with blackness which makes it hard to tell, but the loud drum, whistle, and snap tell me all I need to know.

I feel the wall for a light switch and flick it, but nothing happens.

Of course.

A shiver runs through me, and for once, it's because of the breeze blowing at me and not something altogether different.

I turn back to look at the distilled light coming from the other side of the building and consider leaving and closing the door behind me until daylight, but then the image of Irvin and the boys finding us in bed, lips curled up, teeth-baring, frozen into spooning human popsicles pushes itself into my head.

I'm done being the fodder for their amusement and, of course, being afraid of my bloody shadow.

So, I pull my phone out of my pocket and tap it a few times until the LED light springs to life. It's bright, and I enjoy how it scares back the shadows as I wipe it around the room. I think this is some kind of sowing room as there's a rail to one corner with what looks like dusty rags hanging from it. Everything is covered in dirt, grime, and cobwebs. Ugh. I just got an image of the eight-legged freaks that would have weaved those things. All I need now is a bloody dress mannequin in the corn–

"JEEEEESUS CHRIST!" I juggle the phone a few times, narrowly saving it from clattering to the floor. "SHIT! SHIT!" I hiss.

Okay, I'll admit it. I nearly wet myself just then because I'd barely had the thought, and one of those things jumped out from the corner of the gloom. The mannequin is crudely made of wood with two holes for eyes, a clutch of pins sticking out of its forehead, and an awful wig.

Yep. I can confidently say that the sight of that thing is enough to scare the crap out of anyone, not just me. I really wasn't expecting to find Norman bloody Bates standing in the corner of the room like he's in detention.

Okay. Alright. Okay. I take a deep breath… then another, and then another before rubbing my hand over my face and head in an attempt to dislodge the creepy, crawly feeling settling on me like the dust particles in here.

OK. Alright. So, this place is going to take some getting used to. It's okay. And tonight, the wind, the rain, the bloody freeze. All significant contributors to autosuggestion. I'm fine. I'm okay.

I move forward. Fast now because I'm done with the whole haunted house thing and pause in front of the dirty, ripped net curtains billowing towards me like outstretched bony arms spitting freezing rain like spittle into my face.

I consider how exactly I'm going to slide the window down shut. It will take both hands, which means I won't be able to hold the light.

Why did they even open the bloody window in here? It's irritating. I don't see the bloody point. And if you do decide to aerate the place, then bloody remember to close the window behind you.

Stop whining, you big girl's blouse.

The ragged curtain is fluttering and hissing now, reaching for my face like the wild outstretched claws of a shackled creature, but I pull back to avoid it. God knows what these things have seen.

Creak!

I spin around, but as I do, the net curtain tickles my hand and panics me into dropping my phone. It falls to the floor with a loud clatter slashing the darkness with light and my gut with terror because OH FUCK! I think I just got a snapshot of something! I can't be absolutely sure, but I think there's someone standing on the other side of the room, watching me. It's her! Wild hair flying about her, eyes glinting in the light. "SHE'S HERE! SHE'S HERE!" She's been bloody hiding inside the house the whole time!

I feel something reach and wrap itself around my body and then yank me backwards towards the window. I yelp as something screeches at me, dribbling into my eyes.

"AAAARGH! AAAARGH! HELP! HELP! GET IT OFF ME! GET IT OFF! ME!" I struggle to free myself from the material shackles as the stench of dust and decay fills my lungs.

Then a dingy light flickers a few times before revealing the jaundice shapes of the room, and Sarah's perplexed voice asks. "Um, what are you doing?"

I've been here before. There's no time to waste, and while I'm being pinned by the window, drenched with freezing rainwater, I yell through ragged breaths, "SHE'S IN THE HOUSE! SHE'S OVER THERE, IN THE CORNER OF THE ROOM! RUN! SARAH! RUN!"

But to my dismay, she doesn't. Instead, I watch her turn the light of her own phone around.

"THERE! The–" I cut myself off here, panting and shivering when Sarah's light beam clearly reveals that the shape in the corner isn't Maja, a mass murderer or anybody else for that matter, but just a piece of a rolled-up carpet. One of the lads must have left it there today.

Sarah turns back to me, and I cringe under the glare of her light. "New wardrobe?" she asks with a lift of her eyebrows.

She's referring to the dusty, now sludgy, ragged net curtain that's wrapped around my body like a bloody toga!

She walks over and helps untangle me from the cocoon while we sputter at the dry dust still floating in and around in the light like a miniature constellation.

Eventually, standing on my feet once more, I catch my girlfriend looking at me, face still mildly amused.

"What?" I say. She cocks her head. "I thought I saw something," I add dismissively. "And instead of poking fun, why don't you shine a light here, so I can finally close this bloody thing!"

There's a giggle as I watch the light beam slide over to the open window.

"Yeah, yeah. Laugh it up."

"You were squealing like a little girl," she teases.

"I wasn't squealing."

"You were squealing," she adds with a chuckle. "*Sarah, get out of the house!*" she says, mimicking my yelling in a loud whisper and then giggling some more.

"I was *not* squealing," I insist through clenched teeth as I struggle to pull the window down.

"Need a hand with that?"

"No. I'm fine. Thank you."

"You sure?"

I throw her a look before pulling down the window with all the strength I can muster. It yields with a loud scrape, spitting flakes of paint at me.

I cringe and sputter but don't let go until the thing closes with a thump, shutting out the meteorological onslaught and leaving the rain to drum on the glass in frustration.

"Aw, are you alright?" Sarah asks with mock sympathy.

"Yeah… I really appreciate the help, thanks," I say, brushing my arm, but it's futile. I'm half soaked, half caked in God knows what, and bloody dusty.

"Come on," Sarah says with another giggle before linking my arm and escorting me to the door.

"Let's make a deal to steer clear of this part of the house, eh?" I say as we leave the room, pulling the scrappy door shut behind us.

31

THE WRESTLERS

I'm spinning like a ragdoll in a washing machine of salty water. The freeze, wrapped around my chest like a vice, is squeezing, pushing, and forcing every bubble of life support from my body until there's nothing left but paralysis.

Daddy! Over here.

Toby! My flesh. My blood. My pride. My joy. I can hear you, buddy, through the water. I can feel you all over me. And it's no longer cold. No longer freezing. That smile of yours is as warm and as bright as the sun itself.

This is where you end.

This is where I end.

No. Daddy. Look closely.

Toby? Is that you?

Daddy. Look closely. I'm... alone.

Toby, is that you, buddy? I can hear you, but I can't see you. It's so dark down here. So dark.

I am alone, Daddy.

Toby!

Alone.

"Toby!"

I wake with a start to a sunshine-filling bedroom and birds chattering outside the window.

Staring up at the ceiling, I breathe in and then release a long sigh. How I would love to just wake naturally, for my eyes to just flutter open to a brand-new day.

I look across to Sarah's side of the bed. It's empty again, but for the golden wonder who's still out by the looks of it. He's obviously, not affected by my bad dreams, although I just realised that there's a warm paw on the back of my hand like he's been holding it while I was asleep.

The thought brings a smile to my face.

"Hey, sleepyhead," I say, rubbing his paw between my fingers, "it's time to get up."

The dog opens one eye and feebly wags his tail before letting his eyelid flutter shut once more.

"Really? Get up, lazy bones," I say, sliding out of bed then snatching my feet up from the cold wood floor. And it is as cold as a bloody sheet of ice. I never thought I'd miss underfloor heating so much.

I fight the urge to look out of the window and across the lake. You know, just to check that this isn't all a dream and that the house somehow supernaturally restored itself to its former glory. Instead, I pad over to the bathroom.

So, okay, I'll admit it. Apart from the usual dream of drowning in the ocean, albeit with some heart-wrenching variation, our second night at Frost Lake Manor was uneventful. I'll even go as far as saying that I slept well. This is a real surprise since I would have put money on me dreaming about Lady Emmerson's crumpled body at the bottom of the stairs, filmy white eyes gaping beseechingly at the demonic manifestation of her aid at the top of the stairs.

Even the shower was good. Despite all expectations to the contrary, the water didn't start sputtering halfway through and stayed powerful and hot throughout.

I find Sarah in the newly installed kitchen making coffee and toast.

"Good morning," she says brightly.

"Good morning," I respond, giving her a quick kiss.

"Did you sleep okay?" she asks, pouring coffee into a mug.

"Do you know what? I did. How about you?"

"Yeah. It was a bit cold but otherwise good. I miss Holt, though," she says, placing the mug in front of me.

"Yeah? Me too. What did you miss?"

"Oh, you know, climate control for a start. Lights. Temperature check. And, as much as this is going to sound odd, just missing the fact that he's there, you know? Would you like some toast?"

"Yes, please. Yeah. I know what you mean. It's strange to think how attached we'd become in a short period. You're up early," I add, sipping from the mug.

"Yeah. We're going out on site today. To a dairy farm for more hands-on stuff."

"Oh no. Not more arms up cow's arses again?"

"Something like that," she smiles, pushing toast into the toaster and then turning and leaning against the sink. "This place looks great," she says enthusiastically.

"I know. It's an amazing transformation. The last time I was in this room, it was dark and dingy, but now...." I shake my head as I take in the space.

It's a generously sized room. Like the one at Holt, but much darker since it doesn't have the skylight. But still, it has a similar country rustic theme with lightly distressed wood units and *Farrow and Ball* Pigeon-coloured doors and fasciae.

Yeah. I'm into this stuff now, you know. Farrow & Ball isn't a cheap paint by any stretch of the imagination, but this matt bluish-slash-greyish-but-leaning-on-the-green colour looks bloody good in here, as evidenced by Sarah's comment.

"You've obviously got taste," Sarah says as if she read my mind.

I shrug bashfully. "Of course, I have. I've got you, haven't I?"

She's about to respond, but the toaster makes a loud clang, ejecting the bread.

"So, what are you up to today?" she asks.

I think about this. "Where do I start?"

"Are you going to help out with the house?"

I'm about to reply but pause when I notice her gaze. It's intense.

"What?"

She rocks her head. "Oh, you know."

I squint at her. "No. I don't."

"Well, you know that Irvin and the boys tend to work best when you aren't around."

"Wow. Don't hold back."

She laughs. "Oh, come on. It's no secret. It's one thing you supervising the general design of this place and another with you, you know, breathing down their necks, chipping in every five seconds."

"Have they been moaning about me?"

"No. But I've seen you in action. You can be a bit of a pain."

"Wow. Easy. I'm tearing up here." I take another sip from my mug. "You know, it's a good job you're a vet because your bedside manner leaves a lot to be desired," I say as she spreads butter on the toast. I can't see her face, but from the jiggle of her shoulders, I can tell she's giggling again, at my expense. "Actually, I have a busy day ahead of me," I say.

"Yeah?"

"Yeah. I need to go shopping for a start since we've hardly got anything in. We're going to have to start feeding Buddy cereal soon. Then, there's a whole load of stuff we need for this place, including new laptops."

"That's a brilliant idea," she says, placing the plate of toast in front of me. We can only live on this stuff for so long."

"Okay then. Househusband for the day it is. Yay."

"You could always ring that publisher."

I stop mid toast chomp. "Are you serious? I thought you just said that as part of your speech to get me to stay."

"Why not?"

"Because."

"Because?"

"Because I'm no bloody writer."

"Well, you won't know until you try," she says with a shrug.

I cock my head. "Why is it you always think you know what's best for me?"

"Because I'm arrogant," she says.

I nod.

"And you're an avoider," she adds.

"And there she is."

"Just a suggestion," she throws out as she goes back to making her toast.

A couple of hours later, the house is alive with activity. Irvin and the lads are here with a full crew. Monty has made an appearance, and even Bernie has returned and is outside sculpting the landscape into something that doesn't resemble an overgrown field.

Everybody skilfully avoids the wedding subject as if it never happened. I don't know how I feel about this. On the one hand, I'm grateful, but on the other, it makes me feel shitty as if I'm in some way trying to forget how I managed to royally stuff up my best friend's wedding—especially when the thought prompts me to check my phone yet again, only to find that my messages remain unanswered.

So, I busy myself. I use a credit card I didn't realise I owned to go online with my mobile phone and shop for some of the stuff we need around here. Not least are a couple of new laptops for Sarah and me. We both use those things for work. The ones I've ordered are nothing special, but they're good enough to enable us to get on.

If there's one good thing to come out of what happened at Dolce Vita, it's that I've become a stickler for ensuring all my stuff is backed up to the cloud. This means that by the end of the day, I should be able to simply log back in and find all my stuff there. Sarah, on the other hand, well, she's a bit like Ellie in that respect. Although where Ellie didn't like being told what to do, Sarah just can't be bothered and–

Bloody hell! It just occurred to me. All that weird stuff that happened at Holt. *Shutters coming down. Appearances at the front door.*

I asked Holt to replay the video logs from those days, but he kept telling me none existed. Which was odd, but I just wrote it off as data corruption—of my own. But I distinctly remember the estate agent telling me that all of Holt's data was backed up to my account in the cloud. That should include all the video surveillance.

I'm in no hurry to revisit that shit, but it would make sense to check just in case. There could be evidence in there that the crazy Polish woman had been stalking us for some time, and, who knows, there might be helpful footage about what really happened that day.

So, now, as I pull into a parking space at the superstore, my mind keeps wandering back to Sarah's comment.

You could ring that publisher.

It does sound like a ridiculous idea but is it really? That advance would come in handy right now, and since I'm not generating any other income, then this would be the perfect opportunity—

No. It's a rubbish idea.

Is it?

It can't be that bad because I'm still thinking about it as I wander down the fruit and veg aisle, absentmindedly pushing and filling my trolley.

I hate how comfortably familiar it feels to be living off credit cards again. It seems that I'm happiest when I'm in debt yet fostering the illusion of having money. And I know why that is. It's because when you're poor, you feel like you have less to lose.

What a shitty outlook to have on life. Almost as shitty as the muzak that's pumping through the public address system. Why is it that supermarkets think we're incapable of going through life without a bloody soundtrack?

Ugh.

I pass the Butcher's counter that's doing a great job exhibiting all its dead flesh, and I consider buying myself a nice juicy steak.

Since Sarah's a vegetarian, it's often easier for us both to eat the same thing rather than prepare two meals, and I've just realised that I haven't eaten anything like this since we were back in the city. Oh, and just the idea of that big… fat, juicy sirloin sizzling on a grill with

—

"Usłysz mnie! Usłysz mnie!"

The whoosh of igniting flames. The acrid stench of burning flesh. The piercing sound of agonised screams.

"Oh, God," I rasp. My throat dry as if seared by the mental image of that *thing* on the balcony.

It wasn't real, Marc. It wasn't real.

Then why does it bloody feel like it was? I lean on the butcher's counter for support. Heart throbbing. Breath fast and shallow. Palms sweaty.

"Sir, is everything alright?" the burly butcher asks from the other side of the counter.

I look up… "Wh… what? Yeah, yes. I'm fine."

I hurry away, pushing the trolley in front of me as giant signs seemingly jump out in front of me like would-be roadkill in front of a car. *BUY ONE GET ONE FREE! HALF PRICE TODAY ONLY!*

I just need somewhere where I can catch my breath. Somewhere quiet, but every aisle is crowded. Every aisle is barricaded by other trolleys.

Calm down, Marc. Calm down.

I can't calm down. I need air… air. I… I… need some fresh air. I rush past the *Bakery—EVERYTHING FRESHLY BAKED RIGHT HERE!* The smell of baking yeast makes me want to vomit right now. I need to go. I need to get out–

"What the eff…."

Over there. At the other end of the aisle, about thirty feet from me. It can't be. Blonde hair. Side profile… it isn't possible. Oh my God. IT IS! IT'S HER! It's bloody her! She looked right at me!

"Ellie?"

"Ellie!"

But she's moved away now, out of this and into the next aisle.

I abandon my cart and mirror her.

"Hey! Excuse me, you can't leave that there, I can't get through," somebody whines behind me, but I don't care.

Household goods. Side profile still. Moving fast. Green coat flapping behind her into the next aisle.

Confectionery. "ELLIE!" I yell. "ELLIE!" Faces look at me. One woman cries out as I nearly crash into her. "Sorry!"

Tinned Foods/Pasta - A flash of green

Tea/Coffee—Nothing

Frozen / Fish/ Pizza—a flash of green. "ELLIE! WAIT!"

Fruit & Vegetables—Nothing!

DVD/Electronics/Toys on one side of the aisle and *Household* on the other. Up ahead, I can just about see the back of the green coat making for the exit.

"NO! ELLIE! WAIT! WAIT!" I yell, racing up the aisle. People stopping. Faces watching. Murmuring. Gasping.

"ELLIE! ELLIE!"

A boy, about Toby's age, with short black hair and round glasses, steps out in front of me. I crash into him, knocking him sideways and to the floor in a sprawling heap. His spectacles skitter to a halt nearby.

Shit! There's a shooting pain in my wrist, but it's not going to stop me. I crawl onto my knees and then over to see if the boy is okay.

He isn't. He's crying.

"Are you alright?" I ask, holding him by his arms and helping him to his feet.

"OI! You! GET YOUR HANDS OFF MY SON!" a woman screams, emerging from a nearby aisle.

"I… I was just helping him–"

"SECURITY! SECURITY!" she starts screaming.

Security to DVD electronics immediately. Security to DVD electronics immediately. Thank you, comes the sing-song announcement over the public address system.

"No. Wait. You misunderstand…."

A group of curious faces has already converged on us. The woman with a bobbed haircut and spectacles that seemingly match her son's glares at me as the murmuring of voices grows louder.

I don't have time for this. I get to my feet, ignoring the pain in my knees, and turn to start back up the aisle.

"STOP HIM! STOP THAT MAN! He was touching my son!" I hear the woman yell behind me.

I've barely reached the top of the aisle when an overweight rent-a-cop squeezed into some semblance of a black uniform appears out of nowhere to intercept. Holding out the palm of his hand to me, he says, "Sir, I'm gonna have to ask you to stop where you are."

"Get out of my way!" I yell.

"STOP THAT MAN! Stop him!"

The guard glances over my shoulder and then back at me. I try to make a run for it, but he grabs my arm. I slap him away. "Get your fucking hands off me!" I growl.

"Sir. You need to calm down," the man says seriously, taking a step back from me and spreading his legs like his next move will be a rugby tackle.

I'm considering running at him when a tall black man in a matching uniform rushes, breathless, towards us.

"SIR!" he says, also showing me his palm. "I'm afraid I'm going to have to ask you to stay where you are."

I look past him at the exit. "No. I need to get out there. I need to stop her!"

"Stop who? Who do you need to stop?"

"My wife! My wife!"

"He doesn't have a wife. He was just molesting my son," Four-eyes screeches, clutching her child to her duffel coat.

I see the guard glance at her and then back at me, and I know it. So, I make a move to leave, but *chubby* reaches for my arm again. "Touch me one more time, and I'll break that fucking arm," I growl.

"Is that so?" the sumo-wrestler wannabe asks, eyes narrowing.

"Yeah," I say, and then attempt to launch myself past him, but he was ready for me, and I've barely made it a few feet before I feel his hands anchor onto me and then all of his weight dragging me down like a bloody lion—or in this case elephant—would its quarry. Then another pair of hands and then another. There's swearing, yelling, spit flying everywhere, and then the whole thing descends into a humiliating wrestling match.

Shit.

32

ALONE

LATE AFTERNOON.

The sun is obviously disappointed with my behaviour because it's gone from shining brightly to averting its gaze behind some angry black clouds by the time I get back to the manor and pull up behind Irvin's truck.

I was so busy processing the latest instalment of the Marco Battista freak show that I drove on autopilot straight past the manor, and before I knew it, was crunching down the gravel path to the charred remains of my dream home.

The birds seem to have returned to the area despite the mangled black mess that doesn't in any way resemble Holt as it was. Instead, it looked more like one of those ancient ruins that has been left to dilapidate. Only blacker and smellier.

Oh, God. Even with the windows and vents firmly shut, the stench of charcoaled wood still managed to permeate the cabin of the car, instantly taking me back to that bloody moment!

Usłysz mnie. Usłysz mnie. Ciemne światło. Spełnij moje

życzenie. Spełnij moje życzenie.

Woosh! Flames! Screaming!

So, here's the thing. If I imagined all of it, then how the hell do I remember those words? I don't know a word of bloody Polish. And yet, I keep hearing her mumble those words. Now, how the eff is that possible? Worse, they are so far etched in my psyche that I remember them well enough to translate them via the web.

Hear me. Hear me. Dark light. Fulfil my wish. Fulfil my wish.

Dark Light? What the fuck?!

So, okay, putting aside the whole *Pendle Witches* mind trip for one second. You tell me, could I have imagined that?

Part of me wants to talk it through with Sarah, but I don't know if I can after our latest *heart to heart*. Besides, what if I somehow subliminally picked it up somewhere? It's possible. God knows I've watched enough horror films.

I just don't know anymore!

One thing's for sure. These flashbacks are undoubtedly some form of PTSD, which I know should not be underestimated, but I have bigger fish to fry right now. The fabric of the new world I'd managed to weave for myself is fraying around the seams. Alright. Maybe not fraying, more like ripping into giant holes like the legs on those ridiculously overpriced designer jeans.

You're seeing your dead wife, Marc. Not just in the shadows or the mist, but in the middle of the bloody day in the frozen foods aisle.

I really don't have a clue where to go from here. I know what I should do, but I can't. I've conceived and am fostering such a negative association with Ethan and his office that no matter how hard I try, I just can't talk myself into going back there.

Shit.

Putting my hands on another child like that. What the hell was I thinking? But that's just it. I wasn't.

I hold my head in my hands as flashbacks of me, face down on that cold floor with the security guard equivalent of *Shamu's* arse sitting on my back while people milled about, doing their shopping.

Oh, God.

I was in that position for what felt like the best part of ten minutes before the police arrived. Then I was frogmarched to a very untidy back office for questioning. By that time, I'd calmed down somewhat and told the officers what they wanted to hear. I *thought* I saw my wife, but *I was mistaken.* And that I was *wrongly* running in the store and *regretted* losing my temper with the security man *who was only doing his job,* and *of course, I am very sorry for any distress I may have caused to that little boy and his mother. And if there's anything I can do, they need only ask.*

I think my words carried some weight, but it was only after the police thoroughly reviewed the security footage that they contemplated letting me go with a warning.

The thought of it is making me cringe all over again, but I wanted out of there so badly I would have confessed to anything.

In all, my fruitless shopping trip must have lasted at least five hours, and I sat outside my former home for at another. Part of which was spent trying to slap the images out of my head. Oddly, I didn't feel any pain, just sinking misery laced with horror each time those flashbacks regurgitated in my mind like yesterday's dinner.

I'm unravelling. I need help, and I need pills because I'm worried about what I'll be capable of next.

If I can't bring myself round to seeing Ethan, then I need to see someone else. But then, Ethan knows his stuff, and he knows me. He also has a unique appreciation of what happened that night at Dolce Vita. I'd be cutting my nose off to spite my face starting anew somewhere else. This means I just need to get over myself, even though that's easier said than done.

Thanks to those miserable clouds, dusk is making yet another early appearance. The nights are definitely drawing in. Winter is well and truly on its way. At this rate, we may just get that early snow that Irvin's radio keeps talking about.

I step out of the car into the windchill that seems to have moved in with us and is now busy reanimating leaves that have long left this mortal world.

I'm half expecting a reception committee as I imagine the supermarket telling on me like a bloody teenager caught shoplifting.

Thank God the police decided not to drive me home.

"Oh, Marco. I was hoping to catch ya before we clock off for the day." It's Irvin carrying what looks like a broken wooden chair. "This is the last of it," he says, throwing the piece of furniture onto the back of his truck and then walking back to me.

"Everything okay?" he says with an observing squint of those astute eyes of his.

"Yes. Fine, everything's absolutely fine," I say, forcing a smile.

I'm not sure he believes me because he gives a brief cock of the head and then asks, "So, do you need us to give ya a hand with the shoppin'?"

"I, um." I scratch my head because I've been so busy thinking about nothing that I haven't even prepared my excuse. "Um, well… it was rammed, so I couldn't bring myself to go inside. I think I'm just going to see if they deliver."

"Out here? Unlikely."

"Yeah. Well, I thought I'd check. Otherwise, I'll try and brave it again tomorrow." I chase that with another smile, but I'm not sure he's buying what I'm selling.

And yet, after a few seconds, he says, "Okay. Well, as I say, we've cleared the rubbish out of the cellar. Nothing down there now but some crates, wine bottles, and stuff that I'm still waiting for valuation. Oh, and you received a load of boxes today too. I've put them in the drawing room for ya."

"Okay. Great. Thanks," I say with a nod. "Could you also make sure the door to the cellar stays locked from now on? Someone left it open, and it was blowing back and forth during the night. This place's already drafty and noisy enough."

"Yep. No bother."

"How's Buddy been?"

"He's been as good as gold. We've agreed that next time we're gonna give im a paintbrush of his own."

I force a chuckle, but I'm not feeling it. "Thanks," I say, turning to go inside, but pause for a second to take in the mammoth building towering over me like it's a giant I need to slay. For all intents and purposes, I suppose it is. I need to make this into our new home for the next month or so. And I have a choice; embrace it and stay focussed on the ultimate objective or indulge every single one of my neuroses and ask Irvin to throw me on the back of his truck like that chair and have done with it.

"Marco?"

"Yeah?"

"Are you sure everything's okay?"

"Everything's fine, Irvin," I say decisively, "just, you and the lads, if you can focus on getting us out of this place as soon as you can, please. *As soon as you can*," I repeat, underscoring the importance of the fact that I don't want us to be here any longer than we need to.

He nods. "Aye, we're doing our best."

"I know. Thanks."

Inside isn't as dark as I expected, but I suppose, as always, that's thanks to the giant glass ceiling in the entrance hall, which would be extraordinary under any other circumstance.

Just snap of it, will you?

Drew and Dean pass me, each carrying their own chair.

"Evenin' guv."

"Evening, Marco."

"Alright, lads. Oh, Drew."

"Yes, guv," the man says, pausing next to me.

"I best not see one selfie, one family memento of this place anywhere online, on your phone or in your wallet," I say, giving him a serious sideways glance. "You get that?"

"Loud and clear, Gov," he says. I pretend I don't see Dean's grin as they resume their journey.

"See you tomorrow," Dean calls back.

"Yeah. See ya," I say as I feel the emptiness of this place wrap its cold arms around me.

"Holt!" I begin… but then remember. "Shit" When did I become so reliant on a bloody machine anyway?

Cold wetness touches my hand, and I snatch it away before sighing. "Buddy. You made me jump. You alright?" The dog sits and looks at me expectantly while giving a few swishes of his tail.

"Do you want din-dins? Eh? Din-dins?"

He barks just once, and I'm not sure if that's a *yes* or a complaint about why it's taking so long. If I didn't know better, I'd say it's the latter.

As Irvin's truck starts then makes its way out of the courtyard, I push the door closed, shutting the approaching darkness out.

It's still a bit early for lights, so I don't know why I have an urge to switch them on, but I do. Then I pause to take in the stairs for a few seconds before my attention is drawn to the movement of the dust sheets hanging over the staircase like bloody Nazi flags on a building. This side of the house is now occupied by the 21st century; ye 18th century can stay the fuck out.

Don't worry about the movement. It's perfectly normal. This place is drafty. That has already been established. Creaky floorboards and achy timber limbs are also perfectly normal for a house settling at the end of the day. Everything is fine.

"Why don't you like going up there?" I ask the dog who's observing the stairs as if he's sharing my thoughts.

He doesn't respond. Obviously, but, as always, I do wish he would. Then we could dispense with all the creepy intrigue and get straight down to what his super canine senses can see that my woefully inferior human ones can't.

"Come on," I say, "let's get you some food."

I try not to hurry through the entrance hall to the kitchen because, well, that's silly, but I do turn on more lights as I go. After all, it is a new house, and I need to get used to it. Makes no sense stumbling around in the twilight.

In the kitchen, I check my phone again for messages. Nothing. I think about sending another casual not too desperate, *just checking in* message to David with maybe a CC to Aaron but decide against it for fear of *trying too hard*. I've done my bit. Now I just need to give them time.

Ugh. There's that sinking feeling again. Every bloody time. Oh, shit! A wave of rage just washed over me. That woman has scarred all of us for life. And why? Because I decided to buy this place which was for bloody sale anyway. If not me, it would have been somebody else.

Yeah, but it was you.

Maybe we should get away too.

Stop running away.

I don't know how I feel about Sarah's little lecture. Besides, I haven't been running away... have I? *First to Dolce Vita and then here.*

No. I wasn't running away; it. It was the circumstance that put me there, London and now here. Right? Fate or whatever else you want to call the thing responsible for kicking you back into the cesspit of shit the moment you manage to drag yourself out.

I look at my phone again. No messages from anybody. Something I used to cherish but now detest, and I know why, I'm feeling needy.

I should respond to Ethan. He checked in a couple of times after what happened. I'm assuming somebody told him. I can't imagine who.

Sarah.

I'll do that in a bit. I need to get my head straight first and think about something non-committal like, *Hi. All good, Ethan.* No. Don't start with that. He'll see right through it. *Thanks, a bit of a shock, but business as usual.*

Business as usual? Seriously? What kind of a cold bastard are you anyway?

I walk over to the fridge that, to be fair, is looking a bit sad, which is the very reason I was at the supermarket today. I need to see if they deliver.

Ellie.

No. That was just a figment of your imagination, idiot.

Was it, though? Security cameras. I wonder if they'll let me see the footage?

Dude? Really?

The security footage from Holt. Don't forget to log on.

Need a laptop for that.

I retrieve the last can of dog food from the empty cupboard and spoon it into Buddy's bowl.

Yeah, can't say that the symbology of this empty place with empty cupboards is doing anything to improve my mood. As always, elements outside are just as grumpy because the gale rarely featured on the other side of the lake is definitely stalking this part of the land, shaking tree limbs and casting shadows like gnarled claws in the rapidly fading light.

Ivy leaves, like bat wings, flap and tap against the kitchen window as they tumble and slide to a dramatic death, and when a bramble or whatever starts scratching against the glass, I'm done with the kitchen.

The pile of boxes in the drawing room is substantial. It didn't feel like much when I was tapping on my phone, and yet… there's probably a box for each item. So much for saving the planet.

I sort through them, trying to guess what is in where without having to open each one. The laptops are easy, and I'm eager to fire mine up and reconnect to the world through a window that's several more inches wider than that of my phone.

There's one large box I can't identify, so I pull at the tape and open it. *Bait stations for the rats.*

Excellent. Just what the doctor ordered. When you've had a shitty day, there's nothing better than going on a murderous killing spree.

A figure of speech, by the way. I wouldn't know what it's like to go on such a spree, but I imagine it must feel immensely satisfying.

Okay. Now I'm starting to scare myself.

I glance up at the skylight. It's still light enough out there. I could set these things down in about half an hour if that, and then they'll be performing their dastardly deed overnight.

Sounds good to me.

I consider leaving the hound because this isn't stuff I particularly want him exposed to, but on the other hand, I don't know if he's been out. Besides, he's already sitting expectantly like there are treats in this box.

"No treats," I say seriously, "no treats in here."

He cocks his head. Do you think I'm stupid? I know that.

"Yeah, but do you?" I observe him for the longest time and am reassured only by the fact that bait stations, by their very nature and marketing spiel, are safe for most birds and animals.

"Come on then," I say, lifting the box and jerking my head at the door.

It's cold outside. The air is damp and still tainted with the smell of burning wood. To think that this is a smell that I used to love. Now, all I can wonder is if it's emanating from across the water, my mind or somewhere else.

The skies seem to be clearing, which would explain the chill and the dampness. I think there's a good chance that we might get to see how *Frost Lake* got its name.

Buddy bounds across the lawn towards the lake, and the sight of him frolicking brings a smile to my face. At last! Just being out of the house is already making me feel better, although I'm very much aware that this is all in my head and has absolutely nothing to do with the building.

I glance back to prove my point and see nothing but amber lights glowing innocently behind large windows.

Setting the box down, I do a quick survey to determine where exactly to set the stations to maximum effect, which is apparently on popular *rat runs* and places with the *most activity.* Well, that would be all over this place then. I only have three of these things, so I want to choose wisely.

Ignoring the urge to look across the water, I focus on the job at hand.

It takes less than half an hour to fill the bait stations and set them. Now I can only hope they do their job because the thought of looking out of the window and gazing at those wriggling things every day makes me want to spew.

After Porthcove, I took a break from dreaming about my dead wife's hands wrapped around my throat and instead dreamt about being dead yet conscious of the flies buzzing over my corpse, the maggots eating my rotting flesh, and the rats crawling over me, gnawing at my bones.

Yeah. Can't say I enjoyed it that much either.

Darkness has almost devoured the land by the time we return to the house. And I don't know what it is about this place, but I just can't seem capable of walking in and going about my business. Instead, I always feel compelled to pause in the entrance hall and listen for anything untoward. I have no idea what I'm expecting to hear, but as long as it isn't the sound of ghosts roaming the halls, weeping while rattling those obligatory chains, then I'm okay with that.

I roll my eyes at myself and smile at the hound who almost had to be dragged over the door's threshold when we first arrived, but now happily trots over to the kitchen no doubt to finish the rest of his food without a care in the world.

Maybe I should take a leaf from his book.

I try. But it's the hollowness of this place that gets me. There's no space or anything about it that makes me feel cosy. I can only assume this grates because it reminds me so much of that feeling I'm already carrying with me ever since that day on the pier. I'm like the insomniac that can't find a comfortable sleeping position.

I turn right at the entrance hall into the drawing room, where I unbox one of the laptops, plug it in, and start interacting with the tedious setup wizard in Windows. Every time the AI says something, I laugh because she's not a patch on Holt, and I don't think she'll ever—

What the hell is that?

I look down at the machine because, at first, I think the sound is part of the setup procedure. It isn't. This is…

Music. Vintage. Echoing to me from the hallway outside.

"…sleep talk…. Because I miss you, sleep talk."

What the hell?

I get up from my seat on the floor and move over to the doorway, where the singing is much louder.

It's a song that I don't know but recognise. It's one of those 50s songs with a piano and strings. *Sleepwalk*.

At first, because of the hollowness of this place, it sounds like it's coming from upstairs, but then I realise that it's closer than that. It's coming from the *east wing,* the occupied side of the hallway, beyond the plastic curtain to the study.

Slowly, I make my way over there but stop when a creaking sound catches my attention. It's coming from the other side of the staircase, and when I round the steps to see what it is, I freeze….

The door to the cellar is open and moving back and forth in some invisible breeze. I was specific. I asked Irvin to make sure this bloody thing was closed, locked shut, and yet….

Just like that, I'm angry. But I know this is less about the lads ignoring me and more about the creepy way that thing is moving, unaided.

It's okay. You know what this is. Your anger born out of your inability to control the situation. Breathe. Stay in control of your emotions. Start out wrongly, and you won't last the week.

I stomp over and shove the door shut. The catch clicks reassuringly loudly, and I don't hesitate to turn the key which I consider removing but decide against it because, well, that's just being silly.

Satisfied with the deed, I turn back towards the music as the lamp lights on the stairs begin to flicker.

It's just the lights. You know this. You know there's a problem with the lights.

Yes, but you're also choosing to ignore the research you did about entities absorbing energy from objects.

Be quiet!

I turn back towards the study but pause when I see Buddy pad towards the centre of the entrance hall, sit on his hind legs, and stare in that inimitably creepy way of his at the front door.

I walk over to him. "Hey, Buddy."

He turns to look at me and then back at the door, almost as if he's afraid of missing something.

"What, mate? What is it?"

But I needn't have asked the question because I can hear it now. It's faint yet clear. The large, thick front door is shaking. I can't even describe it as it doesn't make sense. *It* is quite literally trembling as if afraid of something. But obviously, that can't because, well, it's a door. I can only assume it's that bloody gale that appears to have transformed each and every crevice into a mouthpiece for its deep guttural moan.

Sleepwalk… the night fills my lonely place. I see your face.

Betsy Brye. It's Betsy Brye. I have no idea how I know that, but what I do know is that I don't like the sound of her joining the creepy acapella of this place. And I'm just about to stomp over to the study when I hear something else.

Growling.

"Buddy?"

I'm not sure. I approach the dog as lights flicker again, and I realise that we have no contingency in this place should these things decide to pack up entirely besides our phones and those oil lanterns. I should really buy a couple of flashlights.

Buddy looks at me and then up the stairs where–

"What the…" I whisper because I can't believe what I'm seeing. Am I seeing it? A couple of the bulbs have already surrendered to the dark, so I can't be sure, but it looks like… oh, what the hell is that?

A shadow, like a cloud in front of the sun, with no distinguishing features, slowly crawls over the wall, down the stairs and across the hallway floor to the study. Then, there's a buzzing sound; the lights flicker and die, plunging the place into blackness.

"OH SHIT!" This isn't happening. This isn't happening. My heart obviously disagrees because it's already tapping a warning against my chest. I listen carefully in an attempt to hear any sounds besides the meteorological onslaught outside.

Nothing.

There's nothing–

"SHIT!"

The sudden flick and rustle of the dust sheet make me jump backwards, tripping over my own feet.

WHAT THE HELL IS THAT? I squint into the gloom ignoring the shockwaves of travelling up my back.

The wind is howling much louder now. Knocking at the door and tearing down the stairs, tugging at my hair.

Mercifully, one of the stair lamps flickers halfheartedly back to life.

I turn to Buddy, more for validation than anything else, and, sure enough, he's staring at the sheet that's now peculiarly still.

Sleepwalk…cos I miss you.

The music restarts.

I rub my face and my hair, and that's when I feel the sting of another injection. Anger. Rage. I want this stuff to stop. I want these visions or whatever they are to leave me alone. I want, I *need* some fucking normality!

So, I jump to my feet, march over to the study door, and sweep back the plastic with a deliberately loud *Swoosh,* half expecting to see a creature crouched on the floor glaring back at me with demon eyes.

But the reality is, I can't see shit. It's dark in here. Empty. This would explain why the music coming from the workman's bloody radio is so loud.

I step inside. Feel the wall for the light switch and flick it, but nothing happens.

"Of course it doesn't." But it's nothing sinister. They will have switched off the power to this room while they work on the fittings.

So why is the radio playing?

Maybe the bulb is out. I move cautiously towards the music. *"Sleepwalk. Every night I just sleepwalk...."* It's getting louder now, and all I want to do is yank the cable from the wall, but as I near it, the thing just cuts out, leaving nothing but ringing in my ears.

I sigh and turn around but jolt backwards when I see the blurry outline of something right there, through the plastic curtain. I can't work it out because it seems too short to be a person.

"Buddy?"

No response. No movement.

"Buddy? Come to Daddy. Come on." Nothing. Not a twitch nor flick of the tail. Nothing.

Click. Click. Click. Pop. Pop. Pop.

No. Nope. No. It's not real. And yet, the sound of limbs extending and cracking is unmistakable as the dark blur begins to change, ebb and grow.

Sleep talk... cos I miss you. I sleep talk.

The radio sparks back to life. I swear and spin around groping for the power cord. Sweat beads on my forehead as I slide my hands down the wall while keeping my eyes on the dark shape on the other side of the curtain. Then, that's it; I can feel the cable between my fingers. I yank it! That's when the claw of terror rakes down my spine; the thing isn't plugged into a socket! I look down, seeking visual confirmation, and can just about make out the shape of the plug.

Oh, God is the raspy whisper that barely leaves my mouth.

My stomach lurches as that familiar rustling sound grabs my attention. I look up to see the outline of a distorted face up against the plastic. Nose flat. Features distended.

"OH MY GOD! LEAVE ME ALONE! LEAVE ME ALONE!" I yell, stumbling backwards over the radio before I hear a giggle.

"What the fuck?"

"SARAH?!"

The plastic sheet is swiped back, and I can just about make out her face in the overspill from the hallway.

"Sarah, what the hell is wrong with you?"

"I'm sorry. I couldn't resist exacting my revenge. I'm sorry," she says. "That'll teach you not to try and sneak up on me."

"What do you mean?"

"Well, why else are you loitering in dark rooms? We both know you were going to try and jump out at me."

"I wasn't," I say grumpily, making my way towards her. "I heard music."

"Music?"

"You didn't hear that?" I ask, stepping out into the glorious light of the hallway.

"Hear what?" she repeats.

I'm about to answer, but I think better of it. I'm not in the mood to perpetuate the game. "Never mind. I just thought I heard the radio. That's all."

"I didn't hear anything, but then I just walked through the door, which by the way, you need to make sure you close because the leaves and rainwater keep coming in, and they make such a mess. Exhibit a…" she says, stepping backwards and pointing at a clutch of rain-sodden leaves scattered over the floor along with muddy wet footprints.

Were they there before?

"What's for dinner? I'm starving!" my girlfriend asks, reaching up to kiss me on the cheek. "Ooh, I hope you bought goodies today; I'm in the mood for chocolate. No, I *need* chocolate."

"Well, actually–"

Woof! Woof! Woof!

"Why have you locked him in there?" Sarah asks, but I don't answer. I'm still staring at those prints. "Marc?"

"What?" I look up. Sarah is walking over to the cellar door. "Why did you lock him in here?"

"I didn't," I say.

I watch my girlfriend unlock the door and pull it open. Buddy falls out and makes a big fuss of her.

"There he is! There's my boy!" she says excitedly, folding her legs and collapsing onto the floor so that she can make a fuss of the dog.

I run both my hands through my hair as I watch the dog shower Sarah with kisses, such is his excitement at being liberated.

Oh, what the hell is happening? I didn't do that. I wouldn't. I couldn't. Could I?

33

COLLECTABLES

New week. New month. November has barely started, and we're already getting a taster of what's to come and, if I'm perfectly honest with myself, if this were any other circumstance, I'd be in awe of the spectacle that awaited us this morning.

Last night, Jack Frost was out and busy transforming the landscape into a breath-taking winter wonderland of contrasting greens and sparkling white hues. Freezing water in buckets and puddles and transforming leaves and webs into miniature ice sculptures. The lake hasn't frozen over yet, but it has adopted a peculiarly dark stillness reminding all who care to gaze upon it that it's only a matter of time.

I slept relatively well last night. Hardly any bad dreams. At least none that I can remember. Maybe I should terrify small children in supermarkets more often.

Yes. I heard that, and yes, it sounds terrible. But I was really expecting some kind of unconscious expression of what happened, and to not get one, well, it's put a bit of a spring in my step. Especially since the sun is out and the land is gleaming.

I made a frittata for dinner last night. We ate at the kitchen counter and talked about Sarah's day, so I could avoid talking about mine until she asked for chocolate biscuits later in the evening, and I had to break the bad news.

When she gave me an equivocal look, I gave her the same excuse as Irvin; the supermarket was busy, and I couldn't face it but that I planned to go back. I really need to see if there is even a slim chance that they will deliver out here, but if they don't, then I'm going to have to find another supermarket.

Why didn't I tell her what happened, including the fact that I received a ban for life from that supermarket?

Why do you think?

I tried. I definitely tried. But each time, just the idea of telling her that I believed I had seen my dead wife in the supermarket, ran after her, knocked a little boy over, made him cry, was accused of being a child molester, and then sumo wrestled a couple of rent-a-cops until the real ones arrived... Well, I just couldn't bring myself to do it. Sarah already thinks I'm still obsessing over Ellie, which is why she thinks I need to go and see Ethan.

Instead, I busied myself setting up my laptop and then offered to configure hers too.

I have moved us into an old house that doesn't have TV or much else in the form of modern gadgetry, so you won't be surprised to hear that there's no Wi-Fi either. Something I'm planning to change later this week. In the meantime, we're just going to keep using the mobile data on our phones a little longer.

By 10:30, the manor is its usual hive of activity. And it contributes to my cheery disposition. Activity equals progress, in theory. Progress equals getting this place finished, sold, and us out of here.

Don't get me wrong. Now that I've been here a few days, I've truly been able to appreciate the beauty of this place. The architecture, the grounds, and gardens—which by the way, are starting to resemble the set of a period movie, thanks to Bernie. Especially this morning with all the multicolours of greens, reds, and oranges dusted in frost and the glassy mirror of the lake to reflect it all. I couldn't help but snap some pictures on my phone.

It *is* beautiful here.

But I've lived through the whole dilapidated house thing, and I'm done with it. I can't say I'm a fan of living on a building site, either. But needs must.

… "And so, I have managed to evaluate all of these items on the first and second floors," Monty is saying, pointing at his notebook, which is definitely a bit of a brick compared to the streamlined things we received yesterday. "There are still many items in the east wing, but given that I'm over halfway through, I thought it would make sense to give you an update."

I nod. "Thanks. I appreciate it," I say, admiring the fashion statement of the day, which is a mauve number with a white cravat that reminds me a bit of something *Austin Powers* would wear.

Now, I also have some appreciation for how those saps on the Antiques Roadshow must feel, sitting on a chair, the camera zoomed into their face as they await the words that may or may not change their fortunes.

My heart is jumping with anticipation. If Monty has found enough decent stuff here that he thinks he can offload, that will solve our initial monetary woes, and the pressure to sell won't be anywhere near as immense as it feels right now.

"…most of the paintings of former tenants are original as you can tell from these signatures, here and here," the antique's expert says, pointing at the foot of the giant canvas in front of him. Although, I have to say I'm distracted by the dour face of the man in the painting who appears to be glaring at us as if outraged by our insolent act of removing him from his perch.

"…I would say early sixties, perhaps seventies," he continues. "But I haven't really come across much from before then. You see, earlier prints were made using a raised wood surface that could be inked. What we commonly refer to as *woodblock inks*. Some earlier woodcuts are extremely valuable because of their rarity, you see–"

"But we don't have any of those here?" I ask eagerly.

I watch the man's lips curl up at the sides. "No. sadly, I've found no such paintings here thus far."

I force a laugh. "More's the pity, eh?" I follow that up with a big sigh in the hope that it might hurry the man along.

"Quite…" he says. Then adds, "But I did find several articles of value that might excite you. Sadly, I cannot say the same about the item you left for me as it's not quite what we would call a *collector's dream*. These things are widely available from most department stores, even now."

I squint at him because I have no idea what he's talking about.

"Item?" I ask.

I watch him reach behind one of the canvases and pick something up that he presents to me with a rare grin I had assumed he was incapable of. My gut twists when I look down to see what he's holding.

I take the green figurine and turn it in my hand. The green dinosaur's white-painted roar looks up at me as I gawp at it.

I can hear the workman laughing in the distance, even over the tinny sound of that obligatory radio which has been annoyingly echoing throughout the house with incessant golden oldies and inane speculation about the early onset of winter no matter the hour.

My heart has also noticed what I'm holding in my hands because it's already changed gears, pumping a spike of adrenaline through my veins so immense, I'm feeling giddy.

There's no mistaking it. It's the same one.

"Mr. Battista?"

"H… H… How… how did you get this?" I stutter.

I watch the man's face crease into a pensive frown that ends with a shrug. "I found it here on the chair when I came in this morning."

I stare at him for what must be the longest time, truth scanning which is ridiculous because it's obvious that practical jokes aren't in his programming. Besides, he doesn't know anything about this toy dinosaur, but I know someone who does.

"Mr. Battista, is everything alright?"

Oh no…the room's getting misty, slowly colourising into a blood-red blur that is powering my legs forward guided by the radar of my ears, across the hall to the east wing and the study.

The music is much louder in here. There are now fabric dustsheets like body bags over the few sticks of furniture in here. Drew is up a ladder on one side of the room, spotted by Dean. Two other strange blokes mirror what they're doing on the opposite side of the room while Irvin scribbles notes on a clipboard. All must be sharing some kind of a joke because they're laughing when I explode through the dust curtain.

"Oh, Marco," Irvin begins with the dregs of a smile, but I cut him off.

"I suppose you think it's funny!" I yell, competing with the radio.

The boys stop what they're doing and look at me.

"What's up?" Irvin asks.

"*This!* This is what's up!" I yell, holding up the figurine to the chorus of Bobby McFerrin's *Don't Worry. Be Happy.*

Of course.

"You think this is funny. Do ya?" I repeat.

"Marco, mate. Probably best we–" Irvin begins calmly.

"Who brought this here?" I yell. "*WHO? WHO* brought this here?" I yell.

All smiles vanish, and that fucking song, which I hate at the best of times, is really getting into full swing now. So, I don't even think about it. The radio, an old, dirty, and tattered thing plugged into a socket on the floor, receives the brunt of my rage in the form of a kick so powerful that it yanks the device from its electrical shackle—instantly silencing that shitty song—and sends its sailing through the air. It misses Irvin's face by inches—so close that he throws his clipboard up as a shield—before smashing against the opposite wall, spitting fragments to the four corners of the room.

All wide eyes are now fixed on me in bewilderment as I wrestle back tears and snarl, "WHO? *Who* of you thought it would be okay to bring this here? TELL ME! TELL ME!"

"For God's sake, Marco!" Irvin snaps, puffy cheeks now glowing red. "Nobody! Nobody even knows about that," he yells, shaking his head hopelessly.

I gape at him for several seconds and then look around the room. Everybody is frozen into a stupefied trance. Nobody looks guilty. The only person probably feeling that way right now is me.

34

THE INTENT

MID-MORNING.

Okay. Alright. Not my finest hour.

Yesterday I was mowing down a child, and today, I'm losing my shit in front of the entire workforce.

What can I say? I'm obviously trying for a hat-trick.

If you were here last time, you'd remember that toy dinosaurs are a favourite in the Battista family and that I happened to discover this by chance when first showing Irvin the job at Dolce Vita. Several days later, I found one of those same toys drowned in my water glass in the kitchen. Again, this was witnessed by Irvin. I concluded that Ellie had put it there as part of her not so elaborate scheme to have me committed.

But now, over a year later, I find that very same toy in some strange dusty old mansion. What are the chances of that?

But then, Irvin's right. He and I were the only two people who knew what that dinosaur looked like, which, of course, makes him the only suspect. That, or I put it there. Did I? I don't remember. It's unlikely. I'm off the meds, am not drinking. If I had anything to do with putting that thing there, then I'd remember.

Wouldn't I?

Monty definitely didn't put it there. He has no motive and no clue about it.

Oh, God… what's happening to me? Is this it? Have I strayed beyond the boundaries of sanity without even realising it? Because, like it or not, I must face it; I haven't been doing too well lately.

I was considering this when Irvin joined me outside fifteen or so minutes after my episode. We were both silent for a while before I just came out with, *I'm sorry, Irvin. I really don't know what got into me.* I followed that up with the promise to replace his radio. And Irvin, being the top bloke he is, told me not to stress because it needed replacing anyway.

I could have cried. I don't deserve these people in my life. I know that.

That said, he didn't let me off that lightly, just in case you're wondering. He did go on to add that while he could deal with the fact that I had destroyed his property, what he couldn't have was me *upsetting*—yes, that's the word he used—the harmony of his worksite. In the future, if I had anything I wanted to *get off my chest,* I should do it in private.

The last words were serious. Reproachful. Like a father's final warning to his son. *Don't embarrass me like that again, mate, or I'm done.*

And who can blame him? My reaction was somewhat unhinged, especially after Monty said that those toys are widely available. The fact that it happened to be there is *circumstantial* at best. It could have been there the whole time. In fact, now that I think about it, it probably was. I just overreacted.

Did you?

I'm considering this still when my phone rings.

"Hey, Kal," I answer flatly.

"Good morning, Marco. How are you?" he asks with his usual enthusiasm.

"I'm okay," I lie, taking a deep breath and allowing nature to blow the dregs of my outburst from me and carry it away on a cold breeze. Wood pigeons coo. Crows caw and ducks natter loudly in the distance as if amused by the latest spectacle I've made of myself.

"Marco?"

"I'm here."

"Oh, I thought I'd lost you. How did the wedding go? Did Buddy play his part as you'd hoped?"

Oh, God. Small talk. I'm not in the mood for…. Oh, he doesn't know. "Um, yeah, it all went as planned," I lie because I just can't get into that right now.

"Oh, Good. That's wonderful. Do you have footage? I would love to see it. I know the girls would too."

"I, um. Yeah. I'm sure that can be arranged," I say with all the cheer I can muster while repelling the moving images in my head of Holt on fire.

I close my eyes. Pinch the bridge of my nose.

"Excellent. Just excellent. Well, I thought I'd give you a call, you know. Just to go over our meeting today. Make sure we're on the same page."

I watch trees sway in the wind. Leaves laying themselves to permanent rest. Tree branches shaking off clouds of ice. This usually is my favourite time of the year.

Sarah's right. The side effect of all this running away, all this avoidance, is that I'm not actually living my life. I'm just focused on getting through it the best I can while avoiding a litany of emotional land mines.

What was the point in surviving if you weren't going to live?

"Marco?"

"Um, our meeting?" I ask, finally tuning back into the conversation.

"Yes, with the hotel chain. I sent you a meeting request."

"Kal. You've lost me."

"The meeting with Karlson Group about Frost Lake Manor."

"Meeting? Sorry Kal, We've had some computer problems. I've been doing everything through my phone and must have somehow missed it. Can you just bring me up to speed?"

"Oh, right, well, that makes sense now. I thought it was strange that you hadn't responded or accepted the M.R. Yes, so I've got us a potential buyer! The Karlson Hotel Group no less."

It takes me a few seconds to absorb what I just heard. "Sorry, did you say that the Karlson Group is interested in Frost Lake Manor?"

"That's right. Do we have a bad signal or something?"

"No. I, heard. I just... I can't believe it! That's brilliant. When do they want to come over?"

I hear the estate agent laugh. "Marco, come on now, you're pulling my leg, aren't you? You know that nobody meets in person anymore. It's a video conference."

"Oh, right. When? I'll need to get to somewhere with decent Wi-Fi. Although I have to say Kal, this week isn't turning out too well."

"Marco. It's important that these people meet with you, remember? A commitment from them now could mean that the property is sold before you've even finished the refurbishments. That's what you wanted, right?"

"Yes, of course," I say, my brain finally cranking up and focussing on what the man is saying to me. *A potential buyer for the house. NOW!*

"So, you can at least *dial* into the conference call. Right? Since we're successfully managing to talk on the phone right now, no?"

"Yes, but that's because I'm outside."

"Well, there you have it. Problem solved. From memory, I'm sure that area has 5G. You know, it's part of that whole rural development program, which is more than I can say for me right now. Anyway, look, we're due to connect in a minute or so–"

"In a minute?!"

"So just let me do all the talking. OK? You just find a nice place with a decent signal, please. Ideally, I'd like you to give them a quick tour with the phone camera. You know, I think the kids call it *going live*."

"Wait.... What? Kal–"

"Just show them a few rooms. Let them see how things are coming along."

"Kal, wait!"

"I'll talk to you soon... find a nice signal."

"Kal! Wait!"

But my pushy estate agent is gone.

I look at my phone's display. Sure enough. I can see the 5G symbol. That's more than enough speed for a video conference.

Shit. I'm not ready for something like this right now.

Okay... alright... breathe.

An angle grinder fires up and starts buzzing loudly in the distance. Shit! And the boys always insist on trying to have a conversation over the sound of that bloody thing. Why can't they just wait until they've finished what they're doing?

Shh.... Focus, Marco. Focus.

I turn my phone screen off and look at myself in the display. Hair's still relatively short enough for it not to look like I just got out of bed, and I actually look better than I feel.

Okay. This is good. This is good. I take deep breaths, roll, straighten my shoulders, and then shake off all the negativity.

This is good for us. This is good for us. This is really good for us! It's what you want. It's what you need. Come on! Get in the game. Get in the game!

My phone rings.

Incoming video call from Khalil Khan. ANSWER? YES. NO.

I take a step away from the racket inside the house, and then after one more deep breath, I shrug out the dull ache in my shoulders and then press YES. The call is connected.

"Good morning, Marco," Kal says as if we hadn't just been talking.

"Good morning, Kal," I say with an equally joyous grin.

"Marco, please allow me to introduce Kevin Johnson. Kevin is Senior Executive of Property Acquisitions for the Karlson Hotel Group."

I look at the head and shoulder image on my phone screen of a young bloke, probably Sarah's age, with slicked-back hair, open shirt, and jacket sitting at a desk with a sunlit window in the background. Kal is his usual immaculate self, with a black suit and tie neatly pinned to his shirt.

"Morning, Marco," the *Senior Executive of Property Acquisitions for the Karlson hotel group* says. You wouldn't want to say that when you're drunk, would you? It's just a few words, but from that slicked casual look, the overbleached teeth, I reckon the guy is either American or from Essex. I'm going with the former.

"Morning, Kevin. A pleasure to meet you," I say.

"How are things in the glorious New Forest, Marco?" Kal asks like a news anchor talking to a reporter on location.

I suppress the urge to assume that role and launch into a full-blown overexcited journalist ready to interview some hapless pigeon on its morning run but retain my smile. "It's all good here, Kal. You know it's a typical day in the countryside if you can ignore the sound of the buzz saw in the background," I say.

"Give us a quick look at that, would you please, Marco, since, as you can see, I'm stuck in my stuffy office here in Southampton."

"Of course," I say enthusiastically. Turning my phone and slowly panning it across the courtyard, trees, garden, lake over the front of the building and then, eventually, back to me.

"Wow. That's glorious. Simply glorious," Kal says. "Isn't that marvellous, Kevin?"

"Sure beats New York," the man agrees as I suppress my cringe reflex and will them to get on with it.

"So, look, Marco," the American begins, and I can hear his accent now. "I know you're busy, so I don't wanna take up too much of your time, so I'll just get straight to it. The Karlson group is going through a major expansion. My remit at the beginning of this year was to scout and secure various properties in strategic parts of the UK. One of those properties was Frost Lake Manor. Unfortunately, for whatever reason at the time, the property became unavailable. We then had to close out our financial year and had to withdraw our interest."

We had to cuff her and physically carry her out of the property.

"Since then, Kal informs me that your company has acquired the property and is undertaking a *sympathetic restoration*. I think those are the words you used, right, Kal?"

The two men chuckle, amiably. And the fact that Kevin is on a charm offensive tells me that he's keen. Emboldened by this, I nod and squint at the screen casually in the early morning sun, "That's right," I say with a big grin. Then, there's a pause filled in by the chorus of birds upstaged by the noisy operatic of blackbirds perched on the building somewhere above me.

"I understand the restoration is cosmetic, though, and that you're not planning any further developments. That you're looking to sell once the remodelling is complete. Is that right?"

"That's right, yes," I say calmly, casually, heart thumping, palms sweating so bad I expect the phone to slip through my fingers at any moment.

"Well, without putting too finer a point on it, we want first refusal, Marco. If that's something you'd be interested in," Kevin says.

I put a smile on my face as I think about this, pausing as if there's a delay in the transmission, which is actually surprisingly good.

We want first refusal.

Holy effing shit!

I take a deep breath masked as a sigh. "Well, of course, as a seller, Kevin, I'd be very much interested," I say plainly and watch both men grin as if they were expecting me to say something else. Then, I add, "but that's only if *you* are interested in drafting a formal letter of intent."

Nope, I don't know where that came from either, but I can see that it momentarily wiped the perpetual grin from Kal's face.

"You see, Kevin. We've already had a lot of interest in the property post-completion. And if the Karlson Group is serious, then I need some indication of that. I mean, you've seen the property, right?"

"Only in pictures."

"Only in pictures?" I say with mock surprise. "Well, I can tell you now. They do not do this place any justice. Am I right, Kal?" I say enthusiastically.

There's a pause then, "Oh yes... yes... absolutely."

"Let me give you a very quick tour of this baby," I say. "You've already seen the outside. Let me give you a sneak peek of some of the rooms inside," I add.

Without waiting for an answer, I walk the phone through the front door, turning the camera and keeping it low and steady so that my American friend gets the full cinematic impact of the entrance hall. Then, I give him a quick peek into the finished rooms and even venture over to the noisy side of the house, where I encourage the lads who are covered in dust from sanding the walls to wave at the camera.

They do, and it's all smiles and marketing spiel as I walk my meeting delegates back out into the hallway, passed the cellar door–

Which is bloody open again! I casually shove it shut without losing my smile and make my way to the library.

I haven't been in this place much as there's something about it that I don't like.

It's exactly what you expect. Average size room. Shelves from floor to ceiling bowing under the weight of books of all shapes, sizes, and colours. There's a giant reddish-pink rug on the floor that has seen better days adorned by twin upholstered armchairs that are sunken and stained. There are no dust sheets here, which means everything is covered in a thick layer of natural and recently displaced dust.

The room is lit by one large bay window that tries its best to bring light to this cave but is fighting a losing battle due to the overgrown shrubbery outside. I need to talk to Bernie and ask him to deal with that sooner rather than later.

It's weird; by stepping in here, it feels like I've stepped into a soundproofed room. The buzz of the sander seems so far away now. An insect in the distance. There's no sense of hollowness in here either. It's calm. Quiet.

The air is thick and tastes bad. Cold, musty and tainted with the stench of decomposition.

I make my way over to the sun-filled window where giant webs hang instead of curtains and shiver at the thought of the size creature it would have taken to weave these things.

Ugh. I look out of the grimy glass and pan the camera there too, but I don't linger. Instead, I turn the lens back to me.

The thought of taking a window seat in the thin rays of sunlight does occur to me, but the dusty red cushions and desiccated insect corpses aren't selling it, so I remain standing–

"….and you say this room hasn't even been touched yet?" comes the tinny voice of the American.

"That's right. We're evaluating all the fixtures and fittings. We're only keeping those things that are deemed to be in mint condition. You know, anything that adds value to the property. I've actually hired an antique's expert to make sure that anything left behind is of top quality."

Okay, so this isn't entirely accurate, but what can I say? I'm on a roll with this sales patter.

"It all looks quite impressive, Marco. Aint' gonna lie to ya. It's just what we're looking for in that area, you know. Hotel slash country club. Golf and whatnot because I can see here," he looks off-screen for several seconds, "that the property comes with some decent acreage."

"That's right. As well as the partial ownership of the lake, there's the formal gardens, lawns, and even woods."

"Perfect, just perfect," the American is saying with a nod, then he glances over the camera and says, "I'm sorry, can you guys excuse me for just one second, please. Just a second." Then the muted microphone icon appears, and his window goes black.

I can tell by the look on his face and the way he's squinting in the camera that Kal is desperate to talk to me, no doubt about my going off-script and taking over the meeting, but I couldn't help myself. I saw the opportunity, and I had to take it. Besides, I doubt he will–

"Oh, is someone else joining the meeting?" Kal asks, suddenly, peering into the screen.

"I'm sorry."

"Somebody else joining us?" he repeats with a friendly smile.

"I can't see anyone," I say, peering at my phone. All I can see is us and Kevin's blank screen.

"No," Kal says, "the person standing behind you."

I whip around. Sunshine. Dust moats. Shadows. Then I look back at my phone and behind me once more. There's nobody here. I scan the room, scrutinize the shadows.

I'm alone.

I turn back to the phone screen and laugh, "Yeah, yeah. You got me," I say.

I watch the agent's face crease into a frown. "Oh, well, that's strange."

"Yeah? You do realise that around here, I'm called the *king of pranks*."

"No, I swear… I thought I could see someone standing right behind you, but they're gone."

I turn to look once more. There's nobody in here but me.

"Huh," Kal pulls a face, "you must be haunted," he says casually.

"Hey, guys… sorry about that. Minor emergency with my next meeting."

"We were just saying that we think Frost Lake Manor might be haunted," Kal offers.

"Really? How cool," Kevin says, "Hey, you're not thinking of charging us extra for that, are ya?"

The two men laugh, so I laugh with them, although I'm not feeling it. I casually turn in profile, so I still have the light on my face but can watch the rest of the room through the corner of my eye.

"Well, I think I've seen all I need to for now," the American says, "I really appreciate your time, guys."

"Oh, no problem," I say.

"If it works with you guys, I'd love to have a follow-up call in a couple of weeks, you know, just to see how things are progressing and then, subject to that, we can talk about an actual visit maybe, and then that letter of intent. If that works for you both?"

"Oh, absolutely," Kal says, filling the screen with that grin of his.

Me, I'm not too sure. And I don't know if it's because I can still feel the hairs prickling at the back of my neck or what, but I want more. I want progress because I want out of here."

"Actually, Kevin." *Oh shit. Don't do it.* "I was thinking…" *no, don't think it!* "That I'd prefer it if we did it the other way around if that's good with you."

I watch the man focus on the screen once more. I'm committed now. "How about you send that letter of intent and make it *subject* to your visit and site survey?"

Several seconds drift by. I watch Kal lose his smile once more, feel the tide of saliva go out in my mouth and resist the urge to put a hand on my chest where my heart is trying to pickaxe its way out to throttle me. I've blown it! I've bloody blown it by coming on too strong and desperate!

"Okay," Kevin says suddenly with a nod of the head. "*LOI now, subject to the site visit.*"

I let the breath I was holding escape as casually as I can.

"Kal. I'd love to talk offline with you if that's okay about some of the detail. Marco, I'll ask Kal to arrange our next conference."

"Fantastic," I say with a smile.

And that's it. Both delegates leave the meeting and me with a mixture of WTF and absolute elation!

I take in the room once more. There's nobody in this place of light and shadows. It's just me in here.

I hurry across the room and out into the hallway just in time to see Drew push the dust sheet to the study aside.

"Drew?"

He stops in his tracks and turns to me. "Yes, boss?"

I scrutinize his face. "Were you just in here?" I ask, pointing to the library door.

He looks behind me and then back at me. "No. Why?"

I observe him for several more seconds before saying, "Just wondering."

He nods dubiously, then disappears through the plastic sheet.

That's when I feel cold, stagnant air drifting over me, and when I turn around, I can't believe what I'm seeing.

The cellar door is wide open once more.

35

THE REVENANT

& THE RAGE

So, I don't know what's going on with the cellar door. What I do know is that I won't be venturing down there like one of those hapless heroes with a flashlight and without a brain to investigate some creepy shit that's only going to feed my neurosis.

No. I'm not.

Instead, I shoved that bloody door shut, tested it a few times to ensure nothing was wrong with the catch, locked it, and removed the key.

I am done with that negativity because, finally, I can see the light at the end of a dark and miserable tunnel.

I, we need this, badly.

In the meantime, it's bloody exciting! I mean, it's still early days, but this is bloody fantastic news! Wooo-hoo!

Okay, Marco. Breathe. That's it, breathe. It's okay. It's alright. Don't worry. I know it all means nothing until I have that piece of paper in my hands or in my inbox. And even then, nothing's guaranteed, but still, this is more than enough for me to allow myself the luxury of being cautiously optimistic.

The lads must have thought I was on something when I burst into the study and started offering bacon butties and drinks all around. They observed me warily, no doubt wondering if I was going to lose it again.

Of course, it was only when I got to the fridge that I realised that we don't have any bacon in the house. In fact, we don't have much of anything for reasons we already know. I got so wrapped up in everything else that I forgot I still needed to go grocery shopping.

So now, I'm at the village store. The plan is to pick up some essentials, fulfil my promise to feed the lads, then I'll get back in the car and go track down a supermarket where I haven't been designated *persona non grata*. And yes, the less I dwell on the reason for that, the better.

Mary, immaculately turned out as if she's planning to attend an interview later, is behind the counter as always, gossiping. I mean, talking to two other women who I assume are from the village, but I haven't met before.

She interrupts her conflab to greet me with a smile.

"Morning, Marco."

"Good morning, Mary," I say cheerfully. Then, when I notice that the other two ladies are eying me with interest, I give them a gentlemanly nod of the head and add, "Good morning, ladies. It's a lovely day for it."

They respond with churlish smiles. Wow. The Battista charm is still in top form. I can still pull. These spring chickens are still in their prime. Seventies, eighties, maybe?

Back of the net!

I make my way over to the bread shelf, grab a couple of loaves, and am just about to retrieve milk from the refrigerator when Mary speaks up from across the room, "Oh Marco, did you see her?"

"See who?"

"That attractive lady. She was just in here looking for you."

"Ah, Mary. You know I only have eyes for you," I say, scanning the glass window of the fridge for semi-skimmed milk.

I hear a titter from the trio across the room, but then Mary continues. "Oh, you smoothy. But this girl is much more your age."

"Come on, Mary, you know age is just a number," I say with a big grin as I close the refrigerator door and make my way over to the counter.

"You really didn't see her on your way in?" The shopkeeper asks. "She was just here."

"No. I didn't see anyone out there." I turn towards the door as if whoever it is might still be loitering.

"Oh," the shopkeeper says with a frown.

"Okay, Mary, you've got me," I say, placing my purchases on the counter. "What did she look like, this lady?"

She thinks about this for a few seconds. "Well, she was very attractive. Short blonde hair, gorgeous blue eyes. Said she'd lost touch with you since that place, uh, what's the name now. I've already forgotten…."

A shiver ripples through me as I suggest… "Porthcove?"

"Yes, that's it. That's the one."

The mere mention of that place is enough to wipe the smile from my face, but it's Mary's description of the young woman that orders the hairs on the back of my neck to attention.

I allow the milk bottle I'm carrying to slide through my fingers and smash to the flagstone floor, eliciting anguished squeals from the trio, and race back out into the sunshine.

Birds tweet innocently. A truck trundles by, but there's nothing out here but my car and a chilly breeze seemingly gliding around me like a director's camera.

Ellie.

I did just hear her correctly, didn't I? I didn't just imagine what she just said. You heard her, right? You heard her too.

When I walk back in a couple of minutes later, I'm half expecting the shop to be empty, quiet like I hadn't just been in there; instead, there's a noisy commotion among the trio of women that I absorb is because the vintage glass bottle of milk that I dropped has shattered, spraying the bystanders, and smothering the floor with a white slick.

Shit.

Mary has abandoned her position behind the counter and is

upfront gingerly applying a grey mop to the spillage while attempting to isolate the shards of glass.

Upon hearing the cowbell on the door, the two other women pause from dabbing the invisible splodges of milk from their coats, lookup, mumble something, then hastily make their way towards me and the exit.

The thought of apologising to them does present itself before it's trampled on by a herd of other thoughts all vying for my attention which means that I don't even turn around when the bell sounds angrily as the door is pulled shut with a loud scrape.

"Mary?"

The shopkeeper glances up from her impromptu housekeeping activity but doesn't give me her attention. "I'm sorry, Mary, I'm sorry," I say quickly, "but I need to know if what you saw was real," I say.

She doesn't answer; instead, she continues to corral the shards of glass through the river of milk with the tendrils of the mop, making them scrape and tinkle.

"Mary? Please. I need to know."

"I told you everything I know, Marco," she says, still avoiding my gaze.

"Mary, please," I repeat, desperately catching her arm.

She looks at me and then my hand, so I let go. "I'm sorry. Please."

"I've already told you."

"Yes, I know. But can you tell me *exactly* what she said? Please. Word for word."

The shopkeeper sighs, straightens her body, and then sweeps a renegade lock of hair from her eyes. "She was nice enough. All smiles. Came in and said she was looking for you. Asked all sorts of questions."

"What kind of questions?"

"I can't remember exactly, but all sorts of questions. How you were settling in. How things were going with your new family. Were you happy? Had I met your girlfriend? What was she like? And so on."

"What did you say?"

"Well, I answered them the best I could. I told her that as far as I knew, you were happy and that things were going well."

"And what else?"

"That was it."

"That was it? Nothing else?"

"No. Nothing else. She just thanked me and asked me to let you know that she'd been looking for you but that she'd get in touch when the time was right."

My stomach is in knots as I reach for the phone in my pocket. I tap and swipe several times until Ellie's profile picture—which, along with my other contacts, had synced to the cloud before the tragedy of Porthcove—fills the screen.

"Is this the woman that was in here?"

I watch Mary bite her lip and eventually nod her head. "Yes. I think so."

"You think so? Mary, are you sure?" I ask forcefully. The shopkeeper looks up at me and scowls, but I'm undeterred. "Mary, please... are you sure?"

"Yes. I'm sure." A wave of relief floods through me like an instant sedative. It's so powerful that it turns my legs to jelly. "Why is this so important that you decided to throw milk all over my floor?" Mary continues unhappily.

"She's my wife," I state, stupefied. Somebody else has seen this woman. Somebody else has seen Ellie here. Alive and well.

"Don't be silly," Mary says, "everybody knows that your wife is..." she trails off here when she realises. Then with wide eyes, she glances at the image again and quickly adds, "Oh, well, now that I look at her. I'm not so sure it's her. I think it is, but the hair is different and–"

"No! No. Mary, don't do that. You know it's her."

She shakes her head. "I can't be sure. Her hair is different."

"Mary, don't lie to me."

"I'm not lying. I'm just telling you that–"

"Don't lie!"

"I'm just telling you that I can't be sure–"

"Don't fucking lie to me now!" I yell, grabbing the shopkeeper's arm and thrusting my phone at her once more. "This is the woman you saw, isn't it? Answer me, Mary! She's the one, isn't she? Isn't she?"

The shopkeeper, eyes now wide with fear, is shrinking away from me in an attempt to free her arm when the cowbell jangles and Neil, the local policeman, walks in with a smile which he loses the moment he takes in the scene before him.

"Everything alright here, Mary?" he asks seriously.

Mary turns to him and then looks back at me before snatching her arm away and rubbing it. She hesitates and then, "Yes…. Yes. Neil. Everything's fine," she says confidently, "Mr. Battista was just leaving."

I glance at the copper, then at the shopkeeper. "I'm sorry," I mumble before hurrying towards the exit.

***

By lunchtime, the sun is hard at work, melting winter's prelude.

I barely bring the BMW to stop outside of Frost Lake Manor before pulling on the door handle to get out.

Trees tremble in the wind as once-crisp frosted leaves slowly fall to earth in loud clumps.

Buddy, whom the boys have obviously left to his own devices, comes bounding across the lawn from the lake like a shampoo model, wind fanning the fur around his eager face.

I pause briefly to make a fuss of him. "What have you been up to, eh? Been terrorising the poor ducks again?" I ask with a smile which I allow to disappear the moment I enter the house in a scene that I must admit is reminiscent of *Sigourney Weaver* in *Alien 3.* My face must look pale like I've quite literally seen a ghost, I'm sweating, and I'm somewhat distressed when I swipe the plastic sheet to the study aside and announce, ominously, "SHE'S HERE! SHE'S HERE!"

Both Dean and Drew pause their usual banter and look over. Irvin, who is up a ladder, must sense something is up because he descends immediately and steps over to me. "Who's here?" he asks.

"Ellie," I say, "Ellie is here!"

Irvin glances at the boys, who are already exchanging *that* look, then places an arm on my shoulder and escorts me back out into the entrance hall.

"What, what are you doing?" I ask, shrugging the man's hand off my shoulder. "Don't do that. Don't manhandle me. I know it's crazy, Irvin, but she is. Ellie's here. She's been looking for me."

I watch him glance back at the study and then around the rest of the building—presumably to make sure he isn't overheard—before coming back to me. "Marco. Ellie's dead, mate. You know this."

I laugh. Admittedly, it does sound a little hysterical, but what do you expect? "I know what this sounds like, but Mary at the shop just told me that Ellie has been looking for me, for us. She's been asking questions about how we're doing and everything," I say.

"Marco—"

"She's not dead, Irvin," I say sharply. Then add, because the bloody cat is out of the bag, "I've been seeing her."

I watch my foreman's nose wrinkle, closely followed by a furrowing of those bushy brows.

Oh shit.

"Seein' er?" he echoes, lowering his voice. "What do you mean you've been seein' her, Marc?"

I run a hand through my hair. "I, um, I've been seeing her, at Holt, and the wedding. She was there that day. I saw her next to a tree. I mean, at the time, I wasn't sure, but now I'm confident it was her. Then I saw her in the supermarket too, and now this. She's been watching us all along. Sarah and me," I say. My voice is obviously a tad louder than he likes because, ignoring my previous warning, my foreman puts his hand on my shoulder and guides me closer to the front door when a pair of lads wearing masks and white overalls emerge from the billiard room, carrying stick chairs.

I still don't think I even know who they are.

Irvin nods and then waits for them to disappear into the dining room before repeating, "Ellie's dead, Marc."

I shake my head. "No. You don't know that. How do you know that? I mean, think about it. How do we truly know she's dead? Her body was never recovered."

"Which isn't unusual with those lost at sea," he says like he's an expert. "You know that mate. They told you."

"I also know what Mary told me. I showed her a bloody picture, Irvin, and she agreed it was her. She agreed it was Ellie." I run both hands over my head. "Oh shit. I need a drink. Do you want a drink?" I ask, looking around the place as if a waiter will come sailing by at any time.

There is no booze in Frost Lake Manor. I know that, but it doesn't stop me from craving it right now. Maybe I should go and get some.

When I turn back to Irvin, I see that he's now removed his cap and is scratching his head the way he does when presented with a complex problem.

"Don't do that, Irvin."

"Do what?"

"Scratch your head like that."

"You don't like me scratching my head?"

"You can. Just not like that," I say.

He pulls a face then asks, "Does Sarah know?"

"About Ellie. No."

"Why not?"

"What do you mean, why not?"

"Why didn't you tell her?"

I shrug, grappling for words. "I don't know. I didn't want to scare her."

"You didn't want to scare her?"

"No."

"Then, what's changed, Marc?" he asks seriously, astutely—like he's some bloody therapist or something.

"What's changed is that she's been asking about us. She knows where we live."

"So?"

"So," I echo. "She's dangerous!"

"Dangerous? Dangerous how?"

I hesitate but, oh well, "I think she's the one that pushed me that night."

"You said you don't know who pushed you."

"I don't, but I've got good reason to think it was her."

"And what is that good reason?" my foreman asks. Again, like he's bloody Doctor Holmes.

I make a show of thinking about this and then say, sarcastically, "I, um… well, she tried to have me committed. Don't you think that's a good enough reason?"

He's about to answer, but the duo in white overalls return from their excursion into the dining room.

So then, like he's trying to completely wind me up, the man grabs my arm and pulls me out of the front door and into a cold wind laden with the scent of rain.

Thunder rumbles.

"Why have you brought us out here?" I ask as multicoloured ivy leaves fall around us.

"Because, Marco, mate. I ave to tell ya somethin' now that you may not want to hear."

I'm just about to ask him what he means by that when we're both interrupted by the sound of tyres on gravel. I turn to see the headlamps of a blue mini scrunching up the drive and come to a halt behind the BMW.

I hear Irvin mutter something under his breath before he steps in front of me and says, "Marco, mate. Why don't you go inside and let me deal with this? We can pick this up again in a bit," he says without turning around.

"Deal with what?" I ask.

"DEAN!" the man yells, suddenly glancing back at the house. "DEAN! DREW!"

Thunder groans, closely followed by lightning. Leaves scamper and click around and in front of us like eager chicks to the feeding trough.

Two people are in the car, but only the driver exits, buttons up his jacket, and then makes his way towards us. He's a weedy thing with thinning mousy blond hair that ends in a widow's peak and a grey suit that flaps wildly against his spindly frame.

Buddy, who obviously followed us outside and is now slumped at my feet, starts barking but doesn't bother getting up.

"Oi, didn't I tell ya to get out of ere?" Irvin says, adopting that serious fatherly tone of his and stepping in front of me once more.

The visitor looks around him, eyes focussed on me instead. "Mr. Battista?" he asks.

I cock my head. "Who wants to know?" I retort.

"James Bailey, Count-y News. You must be devastated by what happened at your friend's wedding, right?" the man says in a nasal estuary tone.

I squint at him. "What? Get away from me."

"You heard the man. Sling ya ook," Irvin contributes.

"Tragedy seems to follow you, don't it, Mr. Battista? First, losing your son, then your wife, and now this. Can you tell me a little about how you're feeling right now?" he says, thrusting a digital voice recorder in my direction.

"How do I feel?" I repeat with a nod of my head. Then stall for time by looking around at the gathering gloom because I can quite literally feel the pulse throbbing in my neck. Just looking at this little shit's ferret eyes makes me want to gouge them out with my fingers.

Thunder rumbles again. "Well, um, my heartbeat's elevated, adrenaline's pumping, you know. And this feels like a pretty dangerous place for you to be right now. So, I suggest you get off my property."

"DEAN!" Irvin yells.

Ferret's grey eyes rove over the building, and then he whistles over his teeth, "Yeah, nice gaff you've got here, mate. Is it true you evicted the old lady who used to live here so you can pay to defend yourself against the suit your fathers-in-law's brought against ya'?"

I glare at the weed. "Yeah. Fuck off," I say, pacing on the spot, part of me thinking that I should just go inside while the other, well, he is having different thoughts. Feelings, impulses that have been repressed for a very long time.

My heart is pounding so hard it may as well be ape fists on my chest for the urge I have to pummel this arsehole into the ground.

Dead son. Wife. Lawsuit. Evicted old lady to pay for it.

Then, there's a clunk of the Mini's passenger door as a heavy-set Latino wearing a back-to-front baseball cap leaves the car and makes his way towards us.

"I told you to wait," the weedy reporter says quickly.

"I did!" And with that, he lifts his hand and, well, I guess lightning must have flashed because I'm momentarily blinded!

Shit. Blue spots float in front of my eyes, and it takes several seconds for me to realise what just happened. The Latino is clutching a camera like a weapon and is training it in my direction. I throw up the palm of my hand to stop him—

Click/Flash!

Another searing blast of light burns my eyes.

"STOP THAT!" I order.

Click/Flash! Click/Flash!

Lightning flashes. Thunder groans.

"STOP!"

I can hear the boys running up behind us now, yelling something I don't understand because although I can sense that they are close, they still sound far away.

It's starting to rain now only it isn't the usual colour of grey, but it's red. Deep red. No, crimson. And it's bathing the whole world in that same colour.

Lightning *flashes*. Thunder *moans,* yet all I can hear is the furious rhythmic thump of my heart. *Thump! Thump! Thump!* Like an angry war drum. *Thump! Thump! Thump!* And then, through the red mist, I hear raised voices and see weedy reporter bloke trying to push Irvin, but he stands firm until weedy reporter barges my foreman out of the way with such force, the man loses his footing and falls backwards onto the gravel, iconic flat cap peeling off his bald head and running off with the wind.

Then, the world shifts into slow motion. I see the reporter thrust the voice recorder in my direction once more, and without thinking, I kick the device out of his hand. Then, I barely give him a chance to react before I shove another booted foot into his sternum. The impact is so powerful; it launches him back to land in a crumpled heap against the Mini, setting off the car's alarm.

Then, I swipe my left hand at the photographer's camera, sending it smashing into the passenger door of the BMW. The impact leaves a giant crater in the metalwork, which only enrages me further. So, I bring my left hand around once more to grab the

Latino by the scruff of his polo shirt and jab him in the face with my right fist. His head snaps backwards from the shock, and I let go, allowing him to crash onto the gravel just like the grey rain that's falling all around us now.

Using one hand to nurse his nose and the other to ease himself up from the ground, fat-boy attempts to get to his feet, but I stomp over to him, shove my boot into his face and then collapse onto my knees to straddle him. Then, momentarily pausing to enjoy the terror in his eyes, I raise my right fist and bring this down into his face. Then left and then right. Left and right once more. Then, screaming like a beast that's just scratched and clawed its way out of his psychological prison, I unleash months of my pent-up aggression.

This is followed by yelling, strong arms pulling at me, dragging me backwards, and pinning me to the wet gravel as the weather sets about having its turn.

36

THE INTERROGATION

FAWNHAM· EARLY EVENING·

There are some very fortuitous moments in life. You know, a stranger happens to be standing on the pavement next to you and grabs you just as you're about to step out in front of a bus, or missing your flight and having to catch the next one then learning that your original flight crashed moments after take-off, killing everybody on board. Well, right now, I think I might be better off on that first flight.

It turns out that *PC Plod,* otherwise known as Neil, the policeman who *walked in* on Mary and me from the store, must have cogitated—because let's face it, he can't have much else to do around here—on what he saw and then decided to drive out to Frost Lake Manor with one of his colleagues *rather fortuitously* just moments after I finished, um, rearranging that photographer's face.

I was cuffed, bundled into the back of a police car, and transported to an airless interrogation room, quicker than I could say, *take care of Buddy* to the lads.

Shit.

I think I've really done it this time. There's no coming back from this. I mean, I'm no expert, but the law doesn't take kindly to citizens like me punching the shit out estuary whiny journalists who've got the cheek to talk about my boy, not to mention having the temerity to shove *Uncle Irvin* out of the way and knocking him to the ground, why the man is a bloody national treasure, for Christ's sake!

Do you think I can use that as a defence strategy? Maybe. I need to think about it when I'm a bit calmer.

I mean, I had calmed down on the ride over here, but then they started asking questions about who I was, where I was from. Did I understand why I had been arrested, to which I was like, *well, hello, yeah, I've still got blood all over my t-shirt and over my battle-scarred knuckles!* Although I think some of that might be mine.

Of course, then I had that famous moment like I was on *Who Wants to Be a Millionaire?* I mean, I do, for fuck's sake; that's what's got me into this mess in the first place. That, and impressing my dead father. Yes, of course, I know I have *daddy issues.* I mean, seriously, you'd have to be blind not to see my relentless compulsion to succeed, to make something of myself, to emulate my father's financial success story.

Yeah, the financial bit is important because Italians generally only measure success by the amount of money it brings in at the end of the month.

Anyway, I digress.

So, it's, do you want to phone a friend time, and I'm like, who the fuck do I call to tell them that I have just been arrested for beating the shit out of those two pieces of shit?

The answer, of course, was logical.

In the meantime, even though it has fuck-all to do with him. Inspector, *not Gregory,* Peck, felt compelled to stop by and say hello by asking me a barrage of tedious questions, to which I mostly said *no comment.*

Well, it works on those documentary shows all the time, so I thought I would give it a go and see where it got me.

Now, I am on my own. Sitting in this windowless shithole of a grey room that smells of sweat, or is that arse? I don't know.

Whatever it is, they really should give this room an airing. It's oppressive, stifling. But then, maybe that's his plan, to sweat the truth out of me. That's why he's left me here with my thoughts and the small plastic cup of cold, dirty water. When I first arrived here, it was tea, but that was weak as piss, and I couldn't drink it. But then, I don't know if it really was that bad, or I just wasn't feeling it because the Detective was getting on my tits.

You know, I can hear the neon light buzzing, and it's driving my misophonia fucking nuts! Do you think they'll put some music on if I ask nicely?

Uh oh. He's back. Peck and his mute friend. Why does he even bother with that bloke? He doesn't do anything but stand, or in this case, sit around in his cheap suit and look like he's a fucking extra in The Sweeney or something.

Peck goes through the same preamble advising me that the interview is being recorded and reading out the names of those present like there aren't cameras in the room that can see that for themselves.

"So, Marco," the Detective says, sitting down in a cloud of, what is that? Calvin Klein? The black Detective is no gorgeous bird on the underground, but I'll take Calvin Klein over the scent of arse any time. "Let's go over this one more time."

I run my fingers through my hair and glare at him. "One more time? Are you fucking kidding me?" I snap. "We've been at this for what feels like hours. How many times do you want me to answer the same bloody questions?"

"Until they start to make sense," he retorts, "you'll understand that. You're a therapist. Don't you have to ask a lot of questions to get to the truth? And this, mate," he says, thumbing through pages in his manila folder like they've spent weeks collating information on me, "it's full of a lot of stuff that doesn't make any sense to me." He holds his palms out on the table. "So, what do you say? You gonna help me out or what? You gonna start giving me some proper answers so that we can let you out of here and home for a good night's kip?"

Oh, God… the thought of that sounds so bloody good right now. I feel drained. My energy, like a sand sculpture at high tide, has been washed away, leaving behind nothing but exhaustion and the thousand or so thoughts I've locked out of the processing plant of my brain simply because I don't have the capacity to deal with them right now.

I just want to go home. Hug Buddy. Talk to Sarah.

"What exactly do you want to know?" I say with a sigh. I watch the man shift in his seat like a ravenous person readying himself for a big meal.

"Well, why don't we start with—"

There's a knock on the door, and a uniformed policeman appears.

"What?" Peck snaps.

"His phone call's here," the copper says.

Peck rolls his eyes and throws his pen on the desk in front of us. Then I watch the copper step aside, and Amanda rushes in a cloud of deliciousness. Perfume. Shampoo. I don't know, but it greets me before she does like a warm embrace, and it instantly brings a smile to my face. My heart and my energy levels soar.

"Good evening, gentlemen," she says, taking a seat next to me.

She looks fantastic, by the way. No, better than that. She looks positively dazzling, radiant. Like this is the start of her day and not the end.

She gives me a reassuring smile, and she may as well have kissed me on the lips for the effect it has on me.

"I hope you haven't been questioning my client without legal counsel, Detective." The question is directed at Peck like she knows him of old, but I don't think she does. I imagine it's because she can sniff out authority, and the fact the fart-in-a-trance in the second seat can barely command that pen and notebook sitting in front of him is most likely obvious to her.

"Nothing your client hasn't volunteered, counsellor."

She looks at me. I shake my head and shrug. I haven't said anything much beyond confirming my name as instructed by my lawyer. *Do not say anything until I get there.* I did as I was instructed.

"Okay. We're ready when you are, Detective," I hear Amanda say enthusiastically, like we're here just for a chat. And I look at her. Raindrops clinging to that beautiful hair gathered loosely at the back of her head, flawless makeup, luscious lips, and I'm in awe.

Okay. Easy Battista.

It's okay. I recognise it. It's because I'm in a position of vulnerability, and she is quite literally my protector. That, and, um, I've never really seen her in action before, and I have to say, it's a sight to behold.

"So, Marco. I want to ask you about this woman, Maja Szymanski."

"Are you bloody joking?"

"Who's this?" Amanda asks.

"She was a client," I say, frustrated.

"You know that stuff is privileged, Detective. I know you don't need me to explain that to you," Amanda says.

"The fact that your client thinks she set herself on fire at a wedding organised by your client at his home is a matter of, for want of a better expression, public record," Peck says, retrieving photos from the manila folder and sliding them across the desk.

I shrink away from them like they might physically burn me too. Interestingly, Amanda doesn't. She looks at the charred, mangled mess that was once my home like it's a family portrait. On the other hand, I can't take my eyes off the dishevelled, dirty fabric that was once a bow carelessly discarded in the background, along with several wedding programs.

"Why do you think she did this, Mr. Battista? Why would a woman who—he reads from the notes in front of him—who was in your own words *lucid* and *perfectly rational for most of the time* set that building, and according to you, herself on fire?"

I glance at Amanda. Still no visible reaction.

"I don't know," I say.

"No?"

"No."

"So, she didn't threaten you seven days before?"

"Well, it wasn't a threat per se?"

"No?"

"No."

"Well, if it wasn't a threat, Mr. Battista, why did you report it as such? He slides another piece of paper across the desk, which I assume is my original complaint to the police.

Amanda picks it up and studies it.

I shake my head. "I don't know."

"You don't know."

"No."

"Isn't seven the total number of days between the day that the threat was scrawled on your bathroom mirror and the day of your friend's wedding?"

I nod. "Yes."

"But you don't know."

"I didn't know she was going to do that!" I whine.

"No? What do you think that message meant? Did you think it was a curse?"

I look at him. "What?"

"Didn't you tell me that you thought it was some kind of curse, oh, um, what was it again? It sounded so ominous," he searches through the papers in front of him, "ah yes, that's it. See... si... *siedem... means seven in Polish. It's also an unlucky number.* According to you, this woman scrawled seven on your mirror and then showed up exactly seven days later, clutching a picture of you and your son, and then set herself on fire in front of a hundred or so witnesses, none of whom actually saw her. Don't you think it's a curse anymore, Mr Battista? Don't you?"

To kończy się dla ciebie. To kończy się dla ciebie.

Woosh! Flames. Screaming. The sound of sizzling flesh. Screaming! Screaming!

"Detective," I hear Amanda jump in, although I'm busy running fingers through my hair and hiding my closed eyes senselessly, trying to banish the image of that *thing* from my brain. "As fascinating as all of this hocus pocus is, perhaps you'd be so kind as to explain the relevance of this whole line of questioning to the events that took place earlier today and the reason for which my client was cautioned."

"Oh, don't you worry, I'm getting to that," Peck says dismissively.

"I'd rather you get to it sooner than later," Amanda retorts, "because this sounds very much like a fishing expedition in a separate pond, neither my client nor I have even heard of."

"Oh, your client has heard of it, alright. He knows it very well," Pecks says with a smile.

"Be that as it may, Detective. Please get to the reason we're here, or if you have something else that you're thinking of arresting my client for then, I would like to know about it so that I may advise him accordingly."

"I'm just gathering relevant background information."

"Well, I look forward to hearing how that relates to the reason why we're here. Because from where I'm sitting, you arrested my client for evicting a pair of trespassers, neither of whom are interested in pressing charges. So why exactly are we here?"

"Mr. Battista, do you know a Lucy Wells?"

My stomach lurches. I can see Amanda glance at me through the corner of my eye, but I don't engage. I keep my gaze on Peck.

"Detective?"

"Mr. Battista? What happened to Lucy Wells?"

"Don't answer that. Detective, I thought I'd made myself clear."

"Who is Lucy Wells, Marc? Is she the reason why you ended up here? Why you left London?"

"Right. That's it. We're leaving. Come on, Marc," Amanda stands.

"Sit down. We haven't finished," Peck orders.

"Charge my client, or we're leaving because I'm done with you throwing out names that bear no relevance to why we're here."

"Sit down, Miss Stapleton. Your client wants to talk about Lucy, don't you, Marc?"

I clench my jaw as I feel the pressure building in my head because I don't want to talk about her. I don't, but I do.

"She's the reason why you left London. Isn't she? She's the reason you stopped taking on new patients until this Maja Szymanski. Why is that, Marc? What went wrong?"

"Detective!"

"What did you leave London, Marco?"

"Detective, that's enough!"

Tears prick my eyes, but I can't speak for the lump in my throat, and I'm scared that if I move just a muscle, this prick is going to see how he's affected me. So, we just continue our stare-off until I feel Amanda tug at my arm.

"She was a patient," I whimper, "A teenager. One of my first real patients."

"Marc…"

"She'd been in and out of foster care," I say, tears welling in my eyes. "I'd been struggling to get to a breakthrough. And, um, she was part of my thesis, and um…" my voice cracks here. My hands are shaking. And part of me is ready to run screaming from the room, but the other part is tired. It's so bloody tired. It just wants to unburden itself.

"What happened?" Peck prompts.

"Marc," it's Amanda.

"It's alright, Miss Stapleton. It isn't anything the public doesn't already know," Peck says.

I swallow the sawdust in my throat. Pick up the plastic cup and down what's left. "I, um, she was struggling with elements of her past; we. We weren't getting anywhere. We weren't making any progress, so I suggested we try hypnosis as a *useful and fully acceptable psychoanalytical tool*," I recite the official line drummed into me at the time. "And she… she agreed." I pause here because I can still see the look on her face afterwards. It's how I imagine I looked when I found out about Toby.

"She, um, the repression… the hypnosis, it unlocked part of this. And we discovered things about her past. Things that shouldn't happen in a foster home where children, teenagers are supposed to feel safe and secure."

"But she couldn't handle that truth, could she?"

I shake my head. Swipe a runaway tear. "No."

"She committed suicide," Peck offers softly.

I close my eyes and nod.

There's a long pause. Loud voices in the corridor. A door slams.

"Did you hypnotise Maja Szymanski, Mr Battista?"

I look up and squint at him, incredulously, "What? No."

"Are you sure about that?"

"Am I sure whether or not I hypnotised a patient? Of course, I'm fucking sure!" I explode.

Did I hypnotise Maja? I don't remember that. Did I cause her to do what she did like I did Lucy before her? Oh my God.

"Wait, are you suggesting that I'm responsible–"

"Marc. Detective. That's it."

"It wouldn't be such a leap, would it, Marc? She came to you for help. You weren't making any progress with her, so just like Lucy, you decided to go straight for the so-called *fully acceptable psychoanalytical tool*–"

"No. No. It wasn't like that. I barely knew this woman."

"That's right. You barely knew her. You hadn't done the work. You didn't lay the foundation, and then it went wrong; it. It all went wrong!"

"No. No. That isn't true," I protest.

"Marc… Detective!"

"There was, and there is no curse, is there, Marc? There were no seven days. You wrote that on your mirror yourself, didn't you? Just like you fantasized that it was Szymanski that started the fire!"

"What? No! That isn't true! She was there! She was there! I saw her!"

"Detective!"

"…but nobody saw her. Nobody. Not your girlfriend, your friends, or any of the one hundred so guests there. Did you start that fire, Marc?"

"What? No!"

"Did you start that fire?"

"Detective!"

"You're sick! You're fucking sick! I didn't do that. I could never do that!"

"Oh, no? Sorry. You're right. The woman you didn't hypnotise did it for reasons you don't know."

"I told you. She was evicted because of me–"

"And then decides to leave love notes on your mirror, gifts in your cellar, and then set your house on fire. I mean, can you hear what that sounds like?"

"Yes, I can. It sounds like the fucking truth!"

"Okay. That's it. We're done here. Marc, come on, we're leaving," Amanda declares, standing up once more and placing a hand on my arm. "They're just wasting our time. You haven't even heard from the CPS, have you?" she says, squaring off with Peck. "You don't even know if they want to prosecute without witnesses, do you?" she asks with a swish of the head and a flash of those eyes.

"Oh, don't you worry, Miss Stapleton. We'll be hearing soon enough."

"Well, when you do. Then and only then do we want to hear from you. In fact, I'll go one further." She leans down on the table so that she is at eye level with him and adds with a growl, "You detained my client under false pretences. Now I am going to petition for a copy of this tape, and I am going to lodge a formal complaint against you. And, if by some miracle you manage to keep this case, Detective, I suggest you think very carefully before you ask us back here for one of your chats. Have I made myself clear?"

Peck doesn't respond; instead. Instead, he hesitates and then, *for the tape,* declares that the interview is terminated.

37

THE STAG & OWL

LATE EVENING.

The tires hiss and slosh as the SUV makes its way through the night. The beam of its headlamps spotlighting the shimmering wall of cascading water in front of us.

We travel for at least a couple of minutes in silence, during which I deny entry to the crowds of thoughts knocking on my brain, demanding processing.

All I can think about right now is the woman sitting in the driver's seat next to me, expertly piloting the vehicle through the downpour as she did me through that interrogation.

For the first time, it felt good to have her sitting beside me. Safe. Secure. Like I was in capable hands, instead of the usual contradictive anxiety I usually experience in her presence. Good. Bad. Pleasure. Anguish. Wrong. Right. Faithful. Disloyal. Tonight, she was on my side, defending against a wrong instead of encouraging me to perpetuate it.

"Marco. What was all that back there?" she asks in the gloom of the cabin. "I thought I was there to represent you on a charge for GBH, but instead, he kept going on about this woman I've never heard of before. Who is she? How does she have anything to do with what happened today?"

I look across, but her face is barely discernible in the glow of the dashboard. "She doesn't," I say, "at least I don't think she does. Not directly."

"Not directly? What's that supposed to mean?"

I sigh, and for the next five minutes, I give Amanda, my ex, my lawyer, a synopsised version of everything that has led us here. She listens without interruption or reaction. Eyes fixed on the road ahead. Windscreen wipers at full speed.

When I've finished, I relax back into my seat, and it feels as if the confession sapped the last of my energy, yet I feel better for it. Unburdened. Partly because the act is familiar. Like most cheaters, I spent a good part of my time with this woman unburdening myself about my imperfect existence. The same existence that I would later have laid down my life to have back.

"Wow. You do seem to attract drama, Marc. Anybody would think you'd been cursed," she says wryly.

I take my eyes off the windscreen wipers that are busy performing their own hypnotism and look across at her. "I know it all sounds ridiculous," I say flatly.

She rocks her head. "Well, it did happen. At least parts of it did," she says casually.

"Do you really think that?" I ask, oddly encouraged.

She glances across at me, no doubt searching for my facial expression for a smile or other indication that I'm making a joke, but I'm not.

"That she cursed you?"

"Is it really that hard to believe?"

"Marc–"

"Think about it."

"I don't need to, Marc. Come on."

"That chanting, the picture of Toby and me, that effigy thing in the cellar. It isn't exactly a leap, Amanda."

"No. It isn't. To think that she went through those rituals

believing that it could negatively influence your life. Yes. That's believable, but to think that it *actually* can have an impact on your life, that's something else."

I cock my head. "I don't know. Seems to be doing pretty well so far," I say flippantly.

The only answer is the patter of rain on the roof. The whir of the wipers.

"Marc, I really need you to focus on the facts here. This is very important because back there at the station, it may have appeared that we won that battle, but we were just put on notice. That Detective has hard facts. Hard evidence that you assaulted those two men today. That's no supposition or mysticism. Those are hard facts. Serious charges have been levied against you. And whether or not those two idiots come forward as witnesses, it's the CPS, the Crown Prosecution Service, that ultimately decides whether or not to prosecute you. That's a maximum of five years in prison, Marc. Can you hear what I'm saying to you?" I nod, but that obviously isn't good enough for her. "Marc?"

"I hear you," I say.

"This is serious. Now, the editor is known to our firm, we've defended the paper on a couple of libel cases. I was able to speak with him on my way over, which is one of the reasons why you're here with me and not spending the night in lock-up."

I look at her. "You did that?"

"Yes. Of course."

"Thank you," I say, stupefied, "I had no idea."

"You don't have to thank me. It's my job to serve your best interest, but you need to know that this may well end up costing you. And if it isn't time spent at her Majesty's pleasure, then it'll at least be to give these people an exclusive."

"What?"

"Beggars can't be choosers, Marc. We need all the help we can get right now because this does not look good for the other case your in-law is bringing against you."

"Thanks for reminding me."

"Well, you need to be reminded because you seem to think that you can act with impunity. Like your actions don't have consequences. They do. This doesn't help our case. It just reinforces the fact that you have a predisposition to violence."

"Are you joking? I've been living like a fucking monk for the past year!" I explode. She doesn't react. She's seen it before.

Then, she asks, suddenly, "Did you hypnotise that woman?"

"What?"

"Did you hypnotise that woman?" she repeats more forcefully.

"No, I did not!" I yell. Then, seconds later, "So that's what this about? That's why you dismissed the whole cursed thing because you believe what that arsehole said about me?"

"It doesn't matter what I believe, Marc, only what I can prove."

"It matters to me for fuck's sake!" I yell again, my voice resonating in the cabin.

Seconds wash by. Wipers beat loudly at the rain.

"Why?" my lawyer asks suddenly. "Why is it so important to you that I believe. I'm your lawyer, not your wife or girlfriend, for that matter."

I shake my head. I can't speak for the lump in my throat because suddenly, like the darkness surrounding us, I feel a sudden and overwhelming sense of loneliness. It's always going to be like this. Because of my history, it won't matter what I say or do, or even what the so-called evidence might prove; people will always wonder about me. I am, after all, defective, *an unreliable witness*. I don't trust myself, so how can I expect anybody else to?

"You've missed the turning, by the way," I say flatly.

"We're going for a drink," she says.

I look across at her, "Um, well, really, I should be getting back. I've been gone for hours," I say.

"You could use it," she says softly, "and you can always ring ahead if it makes you feel better."

"I don't have my phone. I can't remember where I left it."

"You can use mine if you want to," she takes it out of its dashboard cradle and hands it to me in the gloom.

I look at the illuminated display and then back at her. "So now *you* think you know what's best for me?" I ask with a half-smile.

"Of course. I'm your lawyer."

I watch her return the phone to its cradle. Truth be told. I could do with a drink, some food and a shower, and some sleep, but not necessarily in that order.

So, my instinct is to say yes, but Amanda and I have been here before. Many times. I know how our drinks have ended up in the past, and given the quagmire of shit I'm already in, I could really do without piling on some more.

"I want to. I really do," I say, and I do. "But–"

I cut myself off here because I can see that she's already pulling over to the rain-drenched pavement where, through each wipe of the windscreen, I can see the illuminated reflection of that familiar sign, *The Stag & Owl.*

Shit. There goes that stomach churn again. This is the place Sarah and I stayed in.

"Amanda–" I begin.

"Come on!" she interrupts, bending down to her feet and pulling off her shoes.

Then, she pulls on the door handle. The open-door alarm rushes out, and the sound of the rain rushes in.

Hiss. Slosh. Gurgle.

The precipitation is cold. Heavy. More like sleet than rain. And yet, I watch her walk in front of the headlights like a model in front of a beauty dish, shoes in hand and feet immersed in the river of water, rushing down the road and into nearby drains.

"Come on!" she repeats, flinching into the precipitation as she comes around the vehicle. "We're going to have to make a run for it!"

I've barely opened my door before she catches my hand, and we're running up the path, giggling and panting before imploding into the building.

"Good evening," Amanda says through smiles as we shake rainwater from our bodies.

"Evenin'," the landlord says, pausing from his chat with a couple of his other guests in what is the lounge slash mini bar area.

The skinny middle-aged man with a sleeve tattoo whom I remember goes by the name of Danny, glances at Amanda, and then gives me a knowing smile. I instantly feel like I should explain that this isn't what it looks like, but I don't get the chance because I feel myself being tugged by the arm up the stairs just as I was that night with Sarah.

And I'm confused. I thought we were having a drink in the bar area, but that doesn't appear to be the case which sends my tapping heart into a thump of a different kind.

The small room is, of course, the same one we were in that night, and I have to check myself because I think I've just stepped into some kind of strange timeslip and that this is another of those weird dreams.

From the intoxicating scent I'm picking up in Amanda's wake, I'd say that I'm not and that this is real. This is happening right here, right now, and unless I do something about it, there's a good chance history will repeat itself.

A hand tugs me into the room. The door closes behind us. Panting. More nervous—at least on my part—Giggling. And yet, it feels good. Familiar. Safe. As always. As if my life inside this room has nothing to do with the one out there.

I reach for the light switch but feel her hand on mine again. It's cool. Rain damp. "Don't. I like to sit with just the overspill of the streetlights," she whispers.

"Amanda, the... this the... I... this isn't–"

"What? We're just having a drink," she says quietly. "Jack still your favourite?"

"Actually, I don't drink anymore."

"Oh, why not?"

"It's just. I don't think it's good for me. Amanda, I can't do this," I say softly yet seriously.

"Do what?"

"Come on... you know what."

She doesn't respond, but I see her silhouette move away from me. I hear the rustle of fabric as she shrugs out of her wet coat and lets it slide to the floor. Then I hear the chink of glass on glass.

Rain drums on the skylight overhead. Reminding me of the last time I was here. And for a second, one split second, I'm back to that night. Happy. Excited. Tired. Content. I want to feel that way again.

That cool hand is on mine once more, leading me across the room, around furniture, to the window seat overlooking the wet courtyard and country road softly illuminated by the overspill of lights from the building and sign.

Rain taps at the window. Rivulets of water wriggle patterns over the walls as we collapse onto the lusciously padded window seat. Hands tug at my shoes and, before I know it, my legs are being lifted, and I am being spun so that we are facing each other. Then, I feel her long legs slide in between and around mine.

Damp hair. Sweet renewal of shampoo in the air and heat. A lot of heat burning off the two of us as it was from the fireplace last time, which is now dead. Cold.

There's a chink of the glass, a glug of liquid, and then that familiar woody aroma of nuts and honey fills the air between us.

I watch Amanda's lips slide over the glass and drink generously before she offers the glass to me. I catch her wrist.

"Amanda, no, I… can't. I don't think I can do this."

"It's just a drink, Marc. Just a sip."

I look at her. Water glistens off her skin. Damp hair now hanging around her shoulders, and I remember what it was like between us. Fresh. Furtive. Exciting. Every time felt like the first time because it was illicit. Forbidden. Erotic.

She feeds me the glass. Reluctantly, I take a dainty sip, but she keeps the glass in front of me, and I oblige with a more generous gulp. I feel the warmth of the alcohol burn its way down my throat and into my belly. And *oh God*, it feels so good. Tastes like nectar. The act alone is already melting the knots from my shoulders, releasing the tension in my extremities.

"I love the rain," she says, gazing out onto the courtyard.

On the other hand, I am reminded, as always, of that night by the ocean. But I shake away the memory like the rain droplets still clinging to my hair, take another sip from the glass and bask in the deep massage it's administering to my muscles.

"I never stopped believing," Amanda says suddenly; then she gulps the nectar before adding, "in you." Her hand finds mine. It's warm now. The alcohol is obviously working the same magic on her as it is on me. I watch her take the bottle from its resting place between her thighs and lift it to refill the glass. The bottle is large, thick, heavy, and nearly slips out of her small hands, but I catch it by placing my hands over hers, supporting the refill to the point where some of it slops over the side and onto our fingers.

I watch her as she allows the bottle to slide between her thighs once more. The act deliberate. Erotic. Then she takes my hand and licks the remnants of the alcohol slowly, delicately, before offering her hand to my mouth and encouraging the same. I comply, keeping my eyes on hers the whole time, talking the language that we haven't talked in so long yet is as familiar to both of us now as it was then. I'm finally starting to relax for the first time in a long time. I don't have to keep up the charade. I can just be me.

And it's at this moment, as she leans closer to me and we proceed to share the glass like it's an oxygen mask, that I realise that I have a choice to make. One of the toughest yet.

38

THE UNTHINKABLE

"Okay… Lucy… I want you to stop looking at the screen now. Stop looking at the screen. It's time for you to wake up. Time for you to come back. I'm going to count to three. One…"

…screaming. Eyeballs swivelling behind closed lids.

"Two…"

Back pressed into the couch. Belly thrust into the air.

"and…"

Everything stops. She sits up in her chair, eyes tightly shut, and faces me.

"Lucy?" I attempt.

Nothing.

"Lucy? Can you hear me?"

I'm about to lean forward but stop when her eyelids spring open, revealing nothing but black ocular cavities that fix on me before her mouth opens and a voice that shoves a dagger of ice into my stomach. "Daddy? Is that you? I'm alone, Daddy. I'm alone."

"Toby!" I yell and bolt upright in bed in my odious early-morning Dracula pose.

Oh shit. My head is bloody killing me. I groan and run fingers through my hair, then to my temple, where they perform an impromptu massage that does absolutely nothing to stop the elephant tap dancing on my skull.

"Ugh." The sky beyond the rain-spattered window is still in a dark mood, which would account for the opaque light in here. I look on the side table for my phone, but the charge station is vacant. I have no concept of time.

The other side of the bed is empty, which means Sarah must be feeling better and has gone to work. So, it's got to be after eight. Unless she left earli–

Oh no. Sarah! Oh, shit, my head's suddenly feeling worse, as if that's even possible.

It was late and still raining when I got home last night. How did I get home? Cab? I think it was a cab... Sarah was still awake. She was in the drawing room enjoying a hot beverage with some strange bloke I'd never seen before.

Apparently, she'd felt unwell during the day yesterday, and this bloke, this colleague of hers, had been so kind as to give her a lift home because they didn't trust her driving herself.

Didn't trust you driving? What do you mean? How unwell were you exactly? I demanded.

To which she explained that she had felt faint. I asked why she didn't call me. I would have picked her up. She said she did but that I didn't answer my phone. After a while, she got worried and called Uncle Irvin, who reluctantly told her what had happened, and that was it.

We started talking about me, about my time at the station. Then it was twenty questions. Why didn't I call? Why did they keep me there so long? How could I do something like that? What was I thinking? She topped that and more off with the fact that she had been worried sick. She called the station. They informed her I had been released and that I had left hours ago with my lawyer.

To which the inebriated me retorted, Well, you don't look too worried. Meaning that they were both giggling like school kids when I walked through the door. She was looking pretty cosy with good ole... whatever his bloody name is. I can't remember. I think he introduced himself, but all I can remember are those blue eyes and the fact that he seemed at least ten years my junior. Much closer to Sarah's age than mine.

Anyway, there was an awkward silence, probably prompted in part by the way I was pointedly looking at the young whippersnapper that forced him to offer his apologies and leave to which I said, yes, that's probably a good idea. It's a bit late for you to still be out.

Sarah—for reasons I still can't fathom—took offence at that and, after accompanying the little boy out to his Passat, like he was afraid of the dark or something, stormed back in and asked me the most ridiculous question of all, have you been drinking?

To which I scoffed and said—I think it was probably more a slur actually—what do you think?

She took offence at that too. Gave me that look that females give men when they are deeply disappointed, to which I told her—again, I think it might have been more of a slur—to fuck off. I already had one wife like that. I didn't need another.

Oh… bloody… hell… how bloody pissed was I?

Rain. Wipers. Amanda. Rain. Hotel room. Alcohol.

Oh shit! Oh, fuck! What did I do?

I slide out of bed, and for once, the freeze in this room feels good, easing me back into the present, into the now.

"Okay. Magic paws, you're up. I could do with some sympathy even though I probably don't deserve it," I say, and then wait.

No bark. No tap of claws on the wood floor. No rush of displaced air as the giant golden wonder comes bounding over. Nothing.

I look around the room. Wood pigeons coo, something drums. I think it's a woodpecker, but it could just be my sore head. I'm not sure.

"Buddy!"

Nothing.

Did Sarah take him to work? I can't imagine why. He's already had his check-up.

I go over to the window and look out to a miserable grey-slate day. Even the drizzle is drifting about in the breeze as if reluctant to landfall on such grimness.

No sign of the dog, though. He's probably off exploring one of the rooms and has got himself locked in again. I consider hunting for him, but I really need pills, rehydration, and, ugh, a shower. All of which are readily available in the room next door.

I pad over. Okay. I hobble over the cold floor like it's hot sand—or is that just wishful thinking?—and make my way to the bathroom where I open the cabinet and pop two aspirins from their blister pack, swallow and rinse them down by using the tap like it's a water fountain.

I straighten up, gulping and willing both to work their magic as I glance at the door's threshold.

Still no hound.

Should I go look for him now?

No. I'll shower, wash some life back into me first because I still reek of booze, for Christ's sake. What was I bloody thinking?

Police station. Peck. Lucy. Therapy. Amanda. Skin. Perfume.

Oh, God.

I step out of my clothes and run the water as hot as I can stand it as if that might in some way evaporate the fumes that are still hanging around me like a swarm of flies.

Oh. That feels good. The hot water is quite literally massaging my head, and it feels good.

Amanda, barefoot in the water. Her hands on my chest. Unbuttoning my shirt.

What was that?

I shut the water off. Wipe droplets from my eyes. Birds chirp. Water gurgles.

I'm sure I heard something. It sounded like Buddy.

Seconds drift by.

"Buddy?"

Dripping water is the only response.

I listen and wait....

Ducks natter in the distance. Leaves drift and thud miserably against the window.

Then it comes, slicing through the muffled birdsong, echoing around the bathroom, and yanking at my heartstrings.

Buddy. Wailing pitifully as he was in the woods that day.

I'd recognise that sound anywhere! He's hurt!

"Buddy!" I yell, jumping out of the shower and racing into the bedroom, bare feet slapping and squeaking loudly as they slip and slide on the wood floor.

I skid to a halt. Look at the bed. It's still empty.

There's nothing in here but me. That isn't possible.

It is. You know it is. Phantom Auditory Phenomena. Most likely brought on by guilt just as it was that day at Holt when you were agonising about your financial commitments.

Or it's a premonition, maybe?

What the hell are you thinking? You clairvoyant now?

Yeah. I know. Sounds ludicrous, but it also sounded so real. I definitely heard him wailing as he did that morning in the forest. Only this time, it was different; not like a puppy but like a dog. A dog that was being hurt, tortured. A dog in excruciating pain.

And yet….

What was that? A shadow? Beyond the doorway. Like a cloud in front of the sun, only faster.

"Buddy?" It's an instinctive reaction. I don't even know why I'm calling him, but I think it may have something to do with the fact that I'm feeling particularly vulnerable right now, standing here, naked, water wriggling down my skin like crawling insects and dripping to the floor.

Tapping on the window startles me, and I whip around to see that it's just rain spitting at the glass.

Ironically, it's the quiet of this house that has me more unnerved than – no. I'm not going to finish that thought.

I reverse into the bathroom, eyes fixed on the open bedroom door. I've been in this situation before too, and no matter how much I try not to think about it, I can't help it.

I like your dog.

That hideous voice at Dolce Vita. Or you imagined that too.

I'm shivering by the time I reach the towel and proceed to dry myself as fast as I can. Eyes darting everywhere. Head pounding, only marginally happier since taking those pills.

I hurry back into the bedroom and into boxers, jeans, and a jumper before gingerly stepping out onto the landing, fingers running through damp hair.

Amanda. Damp hair hanging around her shoulders. Lips on glass. Lips on mine.

There's nothing out here but distilled murky daylight. No shadows. No ghosts, and most disturbingly, no hound.

"Buddy?"

I need to call Sarah. She might have taken him, and I'm making a complete tit of myself reacting to the silence in this place and somehow amplifying it with separation anxiety.

I realise that ever since I rescued that puppy in the woods that morning, Buddy and I have barely been apart. I mean, he does spend the odd day with Sarah, but otherwise, it's always just the two of us.

Is that you, daddy? I'm alone. Come find me.

I am.

"Buddy?"

I continue calling his name as I descend the stairs ignoring the sheets opposite, billowing in and out like plastic over a breathing mouth.

I listen for the sound of the radio or any other sound of work. Aren't the boys here either?

"Hello?" I call out to the empty space, but the only response is my echo.

I pointlessly look at the grandfather clock that, according to Monty, stopped performing its primary purpose many years ago.

I'm not enjoying the silence in this place. Even during the day, nothing but the moaning of that bloody wind through gaps in seemingly everywhere.

"Buddy? Come on, boy. Time for breakfast." But there's no reply. "Buddy?" I yell. "Come on! It's time for breakfast!"

I listen carefully for some scratching, wailing, which has been the hound's reaction a couple of times now when he dared venture into other rooms and managed to trap himself inside like that night in the cellar.

But I hear nothing.

Click… click…. Pop! Click! Pop! Drag…. Drag….

I freeze. The sound is loud and seems to come from all around me. I squint up into the skylight, down the stairs. Nothing obvious beyond the quivering plastic ghosts.

I hate those things.

I look east and then west side. Nothing. Just that obligatory moan of the disgruntled gale.

"Buddy?"

Click... click... pop... click... click... drag.

I move to the side of the stairs and peer over the westside.

Nothing.

I move over to the east side and look over.

What was that?!

I just saw something. A shadow of something snatched a leg out of my line of sight.

No. No. I slap my aching head a couple of times. No. You're supposed to be hungover.

I run down the rest of the steps and turn right. There's nothing there. Did I just imagine that too? It happened so fast. I'm not sure.

Slowly, I walk over to the cellar door. Heart thumping and with a shaky hand, I reach for the door handle and give it a reluctant twist and pull.

It doesn't budge.

I let out the breath I'm holding and slowly survey the space around me. There's nothing here but shadows.

I check the study. Maybe Buddy drifted beyond the sheet. But he didn't. Instead, I find the room empty. Immaculate. Another room finished. But I'm too preoccupied to appreciate it.

Maybe Sarah did take him after all.

The bloody irony. Holt had a house phone that I thought was pointless. Now that I need it, I'm in a place that doesn't even have internet.

Where's my bloody phone? Oh. The car. I think I may have left it in the car! I'll put the kettle on first and then look. Sarah knew the condition I was in and probably thought Buddy was better off with her. It's got to be that. She probably didn't leave a note because she's still annoyed after my behaviour.

Can you blame her?

Shut up, you.

I hurry into the kitchen, fill the kettle, switch it on, and am just about to leave when; who should I notice sprawled out on the kitchen floor as if I hadn't just been going through a mental crisis?

That's right.

"Buddy!" I shake my head irritably. "Hey you, sleepyhead. Why didn't you answer me? You had me worried. What are you doing down here?" I say reproachfully.

The dog doesn't respond. He doesn't even bother to get up. Lazy git. "Oh, no, Buddy, I'm not falling for anymore of the weird stuff."

The kettle starts squealing,

OK. I roll my eyes. "Are you not even going to bother to say good mor–" The words dry in my mouth because I realise that the dog isn't reacting to my proximity at all. And I know he can be lazy sometimes, but even at his most lethargic, he twitches, lifts an ear, swishes a tail when called.

But right now... He's lying on the floor without even making eye contact. This jump-starts my heart into a sickly thump.

"Hey, Buddy. What's up?" I ask, falling to my knees and petting his head. Now, his big doe eyes flick over to me, but still, he doesn't move.

Terror grips me in its icy claw, sending a shiver through my body so powerful, it freezes my thoughts.

Okay. Alright. Okay. Alright.

"Um, Buddy," is all I can utter, running my fingers through the fur on his body. But again, to my dismay, he doesn't react. When I pick up his paw, it falls to the floor once more. He's breathing rapidly. Eyes dark. Unresponsive.

"Do something, you idiot! Do something!"

Fuck! Get in the car or call the vet? Call the vet or get him in the fucking car and drive.

I glance at the door. I know that Buddy weighs around sixty pounds from his last check-up, so it's a bit of a struggle to manoeuvre him into my arms. Still, I half drag and half lift him into a cradle, invoking a series of whimpers that stab at my heart as they resurrect memories of how I felt the day I found him. The terror of him dying in my arms that day was so palpable, but it's nothing compared to the way I'm feeling right now because, well, I can't even explain it, but it may as well be my son that I'm struggling to manoeuvre to the kitchen door for the difference it would make.

I stagger through and into the hallway, Buddy's lifeless body spilling out over my arms. Each step, another rung on the ladder of my anxiety. Oh, Jesus. Please let him be alright. Please let him be okay!

Realisation and cold rain slap me across the face the moment I open the door.

"FUCK!" The car keys. I look at the car and back into the house, then at the car again. Heart pounding. Sweat beading on my forehead.

I decide to move as fast as I can without dropping the giant bundle of fur to the car where, heart hammering, breath catching, I lay Buddy half on my boots and half on the gravel, eliciting another whimper as I wrestle with the door, "I'm sorry, mate. So sorry."

To my immense relief, the door opens. That doesn't make sense unless–

I look back down, and Buddy's chocolate eyes gaze up at me helplessly, and I want to cry.

It's because I'm cute and I say cute things.

"No," I growl, lifting the dog into my arms once more. "I'm sorry, Buddy. I know it hurts. But we need to get you to the hospital to make you better. Make you feel better," I chant, struggling with the backdoor of the vehicle and half heaving, half pushing the dog onto the back seat, slamming the door shut.

Then, I glance down at the key fob in the drink well and my phone in the cradle of the car and feel a momentary sense of relief before clicking into the seatbelt, pressing the ignition button, shoving the car into drive, and speeding forward in a shower of gravel and leaves.

I look up, adjust the rear-view mirror, and am engulfed in another wave of anxiety when I discover that from this angle, I can't see Buddy's face. I can only see the patch of white fur on his belly. And I don't know; I think I'm imagining it, but I think he's still breathing. "Buddy, are you okay? Are you alright, boy?"

The blast of an angry car horn yanks me back to the main road in front of me, and I realise that I was about to pull out in front of another car.

"Oh, shit!"

The driver holds up an angry middle finger, but I'm too stunned to react, so I just sit here clutching the steering wheel as if our lives depend on it, momentarily hypnotised by the way the windscreen wipers are savagely swiping at the rainwater sluicing over the glass.

Another car swerves around us with an angry blast of its horn before I finally wake up and complete the manoeuvre.

"Shit. Oh shit, shit…." I chant while breathing deeply to calm the tornado of thoughts whizzing around in my head. I can't seem to make sense of anything. I'm thinking yet not processing. Driving yet no idea where I'm going. I think I have an idea, but I've only been to Sarah's work once. From memory, I think it's about twenty or so minutes from here. I can't remember, and twenty minutes seems like too long.

I put my foot down, and the car growls forward.

I press a button on the steering wheel. "Call Sarah!" I yell at the cabin.

Home or Mobile?

"Mobile, fucking mobile!"

I glance up at the rear-view mirror and that patch of white. "We're on our way, Buddy. On our way, mate," I coo, wiping my sleeve across my forehead.

There's ringing on the line and then, "Hello."

"Oh Sarah, thank God! Sarah, listen, something's wrong with Buddy. I don't–"

"Ha! Caught you out, you thought it was me, but it isn't. I can't come to the phone right now, but if you leave a message, I'll get back to you. Have a wonderful day."

"Fuck!"

I dial again.

"Hello… Ha! Caught you out–"

Again.

"Hello… Ha!–"

"FUCK!"

I don't even know how I drive the rest of the way. No doubt it's like a maniac. I think I was on autopilot, ignoring angry car horn blasts and generally doing the opposite of driving with due care and attention because my focus wasn't on everything happening around me. It was on one thing.

Toby.

My son. The anguish I felt when I saw that drone plummet downward and my son's careful yet urgent steps as he climbed onto the railing and reached out to it.

"Oh!" I clutch my chest as if the thought is reopening the gash left in my heart. And now, all my sadistic mind will play for me is the image of Buddy crumpled over the rocks, tongue lolling from his mouth as the tide slowly envelops him.

"NOOOOOOO!"

Ten or so minutes later, I'm abandoning the car, half running, half staggering through the creaky barn-like door of the vets in that scene I've always joked about and yet bizarrely find myself reconstructing today. "HELP! I need some help here! SARAH! SARAH!"

This branch of The Forest Veterinary Association isn't a small place as they don't provide exclusive care for domestic animals, but they are, in conjunction with other branches in the region, the go-to place for much of the wildlife around here. This means that there are at least half a dozen people in the box waiting room. All of them look up when I crash through the door with a dog in my arms, frantically yelling at the top of my lungs.

"Sir! Excuse me. Sir!" the receptionist is saying as I yell at the door behind her like a mad person. Dogs bark. People mumble, but I'm oblivious.

"SARAH!"

"Sir, please," the receptionist continues coming out from behind her barrier. She's a diminutive middle-aged pixie of a woman with short white hair. "If you tell me what's wrong, I can try to he—"

The sound of the door opening cuts her off, and tears spring to my eyes when I see Sarah's curious face switch to immediate alarm. "Marc? What's wrong? What happened?"

"It's Buddy, Sarah. Something's wrong with him," I say,

turning my body towards her so she can see his face as if she can perform an on-the-spot diagnosis.

"What happened?"

"I don't know!" I wail, losing all decorum because I can't even look at my beautiful dog anymore. I can't look because all I can see is the limp ragdoll body of my dead son.

Oh, Jesus. Toby. Oh, Jesus. Help me.

"Okay, Marc," Sarah says, switching to professional mode and touching my arms, "I need you to tell me what happened exactly. Can you tell me what happened?" she says, putting her hand on the small of my back and guiding me through the swing doors into what looks like a barn decked out with cages on one side and a series of medium-sized examination rooms on the other.

"I don't know," I wail, feeling the dead weight in my arms and the now cold fur on my fingers. I dare to glance down, and when I do, I see sandy-gold hair and the lifeless body of my son gazing up at me with filmy white eyes.

"Marc!" Sarah yells, snapping me out of my spell.

"I don't know what happened! I just called for him, and he didn't respond, then I found him on the floor in the kitchen."

"Did you feed him anything today? Anything out of the ordinary?"

"No."

"When you let him out. Did he go anywhere unusual? In the woods. Down by the lake?"

"That's just it. I didn't let him out. I found him like this."

"When did he last eat something? Can you remember?"

"No. No. I don't know!"

"Sarah, what's going on?" I don't recognise him at first in his green scrubs, but then I see those blue eyes. It's the bloke from last night.

"Oh, Craig," she says, holding her chest like her knight in shining armour has just arrived. Then, she crouches down out of my line of sight, and I assume she's examining Buddy's face, but I can't look. "Not sure," she says pensively. Calmly. But I can hear that she's repressing her own emotions. "Suspected poisoning." Then she adds with a quiver of her voice, "He's my dog."

"Poisoning?" I echo.

I note that young Craig feels compelled to touch her bare arm before saying, "Bring him into my room. Let's take a look."

He glances at me and says, "Marc, right?" And there's something about his gesture that annoys me. A certain familiarity. Like he knows everything he needs to know about me from just that one meeting last night, but I know nothing about him. Sarah's never mentioned good ole blue eyes to me. She talks about most people at this place, but not Craigy boy.

"Marc!" It's Sarah again. "Let go of him," she's saying, wrestling the dog from my arms and manoeuvring him onto the examination table.

It smells in here. Disinfectant. Stale. Just like that other place. That tiny room at the vets in the back arse of nowhere. And I'm instantly transported back there, back to that brand of anxiety. The frantic drive through narrow roads, tree reflections on the windscreen, and a sun-flared morning where all seemed well, but for the lifeless body of Buddy—then just a puppy—swaddled in my fleece on the passenger seat.

Toby.

I step backwards, running my face and hands through my hair as I seek to dispel the images of my dead son strapped into the passenger seat, lifeless eyes gazing forward as his head rocks from side to side with the motion of the car.

There's a loud crashing sound, and I look down to see that I've knocked a metal pan to the floor. There's the sound of footsteps, voices at the door and then hands touching my arms.

"Marc! Marco!"

Sarah's face comes into focus. "Marc. I know you're upset, but I need you to focus. I need you to listen to me right now. Do you understand? Right now, we need your help so that we can help Buddy. We need information, Marc."

The mention of his name forces me to look up, and I see my son's body, leg dangling over the side of the examination table. I instantly cover my eyes and shrink away from Sarah's hand, stomping on the metal pan on the floor, renewing that clanging sound.

"What's going on?" An older man is at the door, gawking at me curiously. "What are you staring at?" I hear myself say like a fucking drunk. "Clear off! There's nothing to see here. Go on!" I rage.

"Marco." It's Sarah again. "Marc."

"Get off. Get off me!" I slap her away.

"MARCO!"

Sarah's angry voice and then a searing pain burns my face. And the room comes back into focus. A beeping sound. I think it's a heart monitor.

Sarah's green now brown eyes are looking at me. "Are you here? Are you with me?" she's asking.

I nod gormlessly as I glance across at the furry mound on the table, and my stomach turns over. "Buddy?" I wail.

"Yes. Marco. Buddy needs us right now. I need you to think. Was Buddy exposed to anything? Anything. Did you bring anything into the house that I'm not aware of?"

"I um…" I can't think. I'm trying, but I can't. After the jump start of what I believe was a slap from Sarah, my mind is stuck in first gear, and I can't seem to move on from there.

I glance at the fur on the examination table. Two people are fussing around Buddy now. The Craig bloke and the older guy.

"Marc!"

"I um…" …second gear, "I can't think of anything recently. We've just been doing the usual stuff. You know, I let him out, the garden, the woods, the lake. Usual stuff. Although… I haven't been there all the time. He's been there with the lads. Yesterday, he was with them."

"Okay… did they take him somewhere? Could they have left any of the paint out or something? Think. What else has been brought into the house lately?"

"I don't fucking know! They could have brought anything in there. They're rebuilding the place, for Christ's sake. But they know. They know to be careful."

"What about you? You've been buying stuff for the house. Anything toxic? Anything you may have left out? When he's with the boys, do they let him wander alone outside?"

…Grating gears. "Left out? No nothing. I can't think of

anything."

Lawn. Lake. Trees.

Buddy!

…Third gear.

What have you been up to, eh? Been terrorising those poor ducks again?

Fourth gear.

"Oh fuck," I breathe.

"What?"

"But it can't be because I made sure–"

"What, Marc, what?"

"I um…."

Fifth gear.

"I came back yesterday. I think it was yesterday or the day before. He was down by the lake."

"Right. What?"

"Well, it can't be because they're sealed. They're locked away.

"What, Marc, what?"

"I bought rat poison for the rats."

"What kind?"

"What?"

"What kind, Marc. What kind?!"

"I, I don't know."

"But it can't be that. It's illegal. It's in bait stations."

"We need to know what kind, Marc. What kind?"

"I don't know."

"Look at your fucking phone!" she yells.

Sixth gear.

Hands shaking, I pull my phone out of my pocket and clumsily open my email. A task that seems to take forever.

Meanwhile, Sarah is already consulting with her colleagues across the room, but all I can hear are a few words. Ingestion. Rodenticide. Poisoning. 1st and 2nd generation.

Oh my God. This isn't possible, though. Is it? I didn't leave the bait out. Did I? I didn't! And the bait stations are locked. Aren't they?

Focus!

Oh my God. Buddy.

Tears prick my eyes. Oh, God. Did I do this to him?

Sarah's back again. "Have you found it?"

"I'm looking! I'm looking," I say, swiping and scrolling through. "Yeah. Here. This… um. It's Big Cheese; it's. It's called Big Cheese," I say aloud for all to hear.

Sarah looks over at her colleagues, who both nod, consult a chart, and then exclaim—like weirdos at a science fiction convention—"Difenacoum!" before busying themselves with opening cupboards and rigging equipment.

"What's that? What does that mean?" I ask Sarah, confused.

"It's a poison used in rat killer. An anticoagulant."

"Right. Okay. But what does that mean?"

"It means that, well, depending on how much he's eaten, Buddy's very sick."

"Sarah. I need the dog's chart. Weight please," it's blue eyes.

I have no idea why because the man is trying to treat my dog, yet I still fucking dislike him. "It's Buddy! His name's Buddy," I yell uselessly.

"I have to go. Wait outside. I'll come find you as soon as I know more," Sarah says.

"No. I'm not waiting outside. He's my dog," I retort angrily.

"Then stay, but please let us do our job," she warns, no longer my girlfriend but the professional once more.

She doesn't wait for a response but instead busies herself at the computer, presumably pulling up Buddy's medical chart.

Slowly. Gingerly. I make my way over to the examination table. Half averting my gaze as I'm afraid that the furry mound in front of me is going to metamorphose back into the lifeless body of my son. Sandy blonde hair. Sandy blonde fur. Chocolate eyes. Brown eyes.

Mercifully, he doesn't.

But it doesn't mean the ache in my chest is any more tolerable, the breath in my lungs less constricted. I'm almost hyperventilating by the time I approach my dog's body that, not unlike my son, usually is so full of life and yet is now still. Motionless.

I don't even recognise this. For a split second, I wonder if it's even him. Maybe, somehow, I lost time on my way over here and have stumbled into the wrong examination room. That's it. That must be it. Right?

What if?

No. This is my reality as much as I want to disassociate myself from it.

What if, though? What if none of this is real? What if those two men at the examination table aren't really fixing an IV drip to my dog's paw? What if I am imagining all of this based on that previous traumatic event? It would be easy to do. So easy to recall and recycle those memories and replay them now.

I throw my hands to my mouth to stifle an agonising cry when I see Buddy's eyelids flutter open and my reflection in those dull, sad eyes.

"Toby. Hey. Hello, mate. You can't leave me. You know that, right? You can't leave me because I love you. Daddy loves you. He loves you so much," I say through ragged breaths as I reach a shaky hand for his face, but the dog doesn't react to me; instead, his eyelids slowly blink until they flutter closed once more.

"NO! BUDDY! WAIT! BUDDY, NO!"

39

CAN YOU SEE IT?

The sun has passed the baton to a premature moon that is already sprinkling twilight instead of water on the rain-washed land. Bats flutter, jerkily overhead. Groups of birds rush back and forth to the woods for a quick supper before bedtime while I sit here, clinging onto the steering wheel, listening to the car tick over as my flock of thoughts aimlessly flutter around my brain. They're exhausted with nowhere to nest, for I appear incapable of processing anything meaningful.

I am numb.

Tears prick at my eyes once more as I contemplate exactly what I need to do next.

What I should be doing is getting out of this car and making my way down to the lake to examine those bait stations. But I'm paralysed. I know why. I'm scared. I am absolutely terrified of what I might discover. A truth so hideous, I'll never recover from it. A truth that will no doubt become my tipping point back to insanity.

Ethan believes it's *unhelpful* when I think like this. Branding myself insane since it's technically inaccurate, pointless, and counterproductive to all the work we've done together.

Yeah? Well, he wasn't the one running through that waiting room today with an animal that had morphed into the body of his dead son.

I feel for the doorhandle and tug it without even looking. Biting cold air rushes in to remind me that I need to pull on a coat. I drag my puffer jacket from the backseat, slide into it and am instantly reminded of Buddy. He was lying on here. I can smell his fur. Now the jacket is not only warm but comforting.

I take a deep breath and then slam the door shut.

This is the part where I miss Holt because he'd be switching on the floodlights about now, but here, there's no such thing, but it's fine. I reckon there's still enough natural light for me to complete my reluctant mission.

I look over at the mansion, and it glares back at me with its dead windows and austere, angular features. Expressionless. Just like the portraits it harbours.

I turn away and spot the pathway into the woods. I hadn't noticed it until now, but it looks like the opposite equivalent of the archway into the forest from Holt. This must be the scenic route to the other side of the lake.

A shudder runs through me, for no matter how picturesque this pathway might be, there's still a point at which it disappears into a canopy of trees that now, as darkness slowly devours the light, makes me think it might just be the gateway to hell itself.

There's nothing in the darkness but the sum of all my projected fears. Yes, I know, it's irrational. But it still gives me the creeps.

So, I quicken my pace, out of the courtyard and across the lawn where the rays of the fading sun have turned the lake into a strawberry swirl of marble. The effect momentarily lifts my spirits as it has done ever since we arrived here, only this time it's immediately suffocated by the dark thoughts of Buddy lying on that table.

I'm here for a reason.

I make my way through wet grass towards the wood deck, where I set two of the bait stations as it's where there was the most rat activity.

The first is on the left, inside a nook of the stone column

supporting the structure. I carefully climb down to the water's edge, which is sloshing loudly despite the calmness of the surface.

Air. Water. Air. Water. Air. Water.

This is where you end.

I shake my head.

Air. Water. Air. Water. Air. Water.

"NO!" I growl through gritted teeth as flashbacks of that Christmas Eve night replay unhelpfully in my addled brain. That's over now. History. I survived. I'm alive! And yet, like a phantom limb, I can still feel the freeze of that water squeezing the air out of my body.

Crouching down, I look under the wooden struts to find that the black cylindrical plastic box is exactly as I left it. So, I climb over to the other side to check the second box. It, too, appears undisturbed.

Shit. Maybe they were wrong. Maybe it's something else.

I scramble back up from the shore as loud honking overhead startles me. I look up to see a large V formation of geese sail over the lake and trees on their way to warmer climates. They've obviously got the right idea. And for a moment, I imagine what it would feel like to be able to fly, to be able to rise above all this and leave it behind.

You can't keep running.

They're wrong. They assumed it was poisoning, but it isn't. It's obviously something else. What though? If it isn't poisoning, then what else could it—

I don't finish the thought when I realise… How could I be so bloody stupid? I bought a set of four bait stations, not two. I considered just two but thought they might not be enough, so I purchased two more, and just to be sure, I placed them topside of the wood decking, opposite their counterparts on the bottom, flush against one of the rotting struts of the wooden guardrail.

A boulder drops to the pit of my gut. If I forgot something like that, how hard would it be for me to forget something else equally important, like closing and locking one of those things?

So, it's with deep trepidation that I go back. Boots clunk loudly against the wood. Water laps gently against the shore.

Air. Water. Air. Water. Air. Water.

I clutch my chest. It's getting harder to breathe, but I don't know if that's triggered by the memory of the cold or the fact that I can feel it gnawing like those rats at my face and ears.

I reach the bait box on the left side. Test it. It's undisturbed. Suddenly, I can feel the tension in my head pressing against my skull as I make my way over to the right and...

Oh... What the fuck is going on?

The bait box is still here, seemingly undisturbed, but the large blue bait cubes that should be sitting inside the box are instead sitting on top. Like innocent gems, they're glistening with rainwater. Unlike precious stones though, these things are partially chewed in sections with pieces of the poison strewn across the wood decking like blobs of paint.

Oh no... this must be where Buddy and or whatever other creature has gnawed at them.

Oh, sweet Jesus. How is this possible? I run both my hands through my hair and hold them there as I struggle to remember exactly what I did. I'm sure I put them inside and locked the box just as I did with the others. Didn't I? Or did I lay them out but forget to place them inside the box? Did I become distracted by something else?

Oh fuck... What is happening to me?

I rush to recheck all the other bait stations. They're locked. They're locked! So, what happened to this one?

Suddenly, the trapdoor to my throat closes, and I'm unable to breathe! I can't breathe!

I stagger backwards, boots scuffling loudly. Nearby wings flap in a startled frenzy as I'm instantly transported back to that day on the pier.

Sunshine. Summer breeze. The smell of hotdogs. The carousel is in the distance. Toby climbing up onto that railing.

"No! Toby No!"

I collapse onto all fours as I attempt to swallow back the ball of bile in my throat. My body spasms, convulsing, retching as I try to eject everything I haven't eaten.

I must remain like this for several minutes. Stomach clenching, body taut, eyes bulging as I seek to comprehend, *what I have done?*

More wings flutter. This time it's a pair of blackbirds competing to sound the alarm with a loud, repetitive, *chink, chink, chink,* and… oh, that's interesting. Although I feel like death right now, my misophonia is still able to lodge a complaint about the repetitive sound.

Groaning, I roll into a sitting position and breathe in the fresh air. The photographer's *golden hour* has passed. The sun is no longer a portrait-flattering light strobe in the sky, but a fiery glow beyond the treeline as a band of dark clouds drift into and then occupy the horizon. All of the technicolour majesty of the world around soon reduced to the result of a filter on a lens.

I suck in the gelid air as my heart slowly returns to a resting state.

I think about Buddy, my boy lying lifeless on that table, and tears suddenly spring to my eyes. I don't know what I'll do if he doesn't make it through this. I'm lucid enough to understand that it's perfectly natural for a human to become attached to a pet. They are, after all, members of the family, but with Buddy, I don't know… I can't explain this even to myself. With him, there's no distinction. For all intents and purposes, he is my boy.

My son.

I don't think I truly appreciated until this very moment just how much of a crutch he has been for me despite his creepy ways.

When Sarah told me that it was now a waiting game and that I should go home to get some rest, I only needed to give her a look for her to know that bloody wild horses were not going to drag me away from that place. But my girlfriend, in her usual astute way, immediately switched tack and told me that they needed to be sure that Buddy was, in fact, poisoned by the bait I put out.

She asked me if there was *any* chance that he could have got into one of the bait stations, to which I replied that I had no clue. *We need to know for sure, Marc. We could be treating him for the wrong thing.*

There's no doubt my girlfriend wanted me out of that place. I'm assuming it was for my sanity and that it had nothing to do with my constant pacing back and forth and the fact that it must have been driving staff and customers alike crazy.

Of course, what she doesn't realise is that, as much as I didn't want to leave my boy, I wanted, no, I *needed* to know if I was in any way responsible for his condition. And, sadly, it would appear that despite my meticulous research as to the safety of these things both for pets and the indigenous wildlife, I am ultimately responsible for–

Movement catches my attention, and I look over towards the manor's equivalent of that ominous demarcation line between house and trees.

The boundary between light and darkness has grown exponentially, and yet, once again, even though I can feel eyes on me, I cannot see–

"Oh shit," I gasp. "Oh shit."

There! Something in the shadows. I can't make it out exactly, but it's a shape. A dark humanoid shape of… someone… something? It's now staying perfectly still. Probably thinks I can't see it, but I can. I bloody can! I can see the displacement of light from tall vertical tree trunks to softer outlines of *something* else.

What do I do? What do I bloody do?!

"Who's that? Who's there?" I yell. Fight or flight mode engaged. Adrenaline pumping. Heart engine, revving.

There's no response. No movement, but it's still there. Watching. Biding its time.

Run for the car!

I'd barely make it halfway there. It's too far!

Without taking my eyes off the distortion between what's left of the light and dark, I casually reach into my pocket, pull out my phone, feel for the side button, and whisper, "Turn on the flashlight." My words are careful. Clear. The LED light springs to life, and I'm just about to shine it at the anomaly when it moves!

"HEY! STOP! STOP!"

I give chase. First stumbling and then slipping over the grass until I reach the demarcation line, where I pause to acclimatise to the light fluctuation for a few seconds.

"Oh, fuck it," I grumble angrily before sprinting forward, light bobbing ahead of me, dissolving shadows.

"I can see you, you fucker!" I scream through breaths as the shape merges and emerges from the surrounding gloom.

A fox cries in the distance, wings flap and flutter noisily overhead as I race along the muddy path, my body rapidly falling into its usual rhythm, albeit at a faster pace.

Branches reach for me, but I twist and duck to evade them, all the time being sure to illuminate the trail ahead of me, carefully choosing my foot placement because I have no intention of stumbling. I'm on a mission now. I'm going to catch this bastard, and I am going to… I've no idea what I'm going to do, but that isn't going to stop me trying.

I can see it, clearly now, as the humanoid thing keeps falling in and out of the light's beam. It's about ten feet ahead of me.

"STOP! Y… YOU… B… BASTARD!" I yell angrily. Mostly for show. I want them to know that I'm not messing around. For all I know, whoever this is could have tampered with the bait station. Maybe it wasn't me after all. Maybe it was them, and like a fucking sicko, they hung around to witness the deed.

Oh, shit, if that's even remotely true, I have no idea what I'll be capable of.

I can see now; it's definitely a person—not sure what else I was expecting—and this person is tall. Lanky. Probably around my height. Wearing a hoodie and… what the…?

"D… DREW?! DREW, IS THAT YOU? DREW!" my voice rings out, and he must hear me because the person hesitates, slows to a jog and then a reluctant stop before turning into the beam of my phone.

"What… w… what the… hell?" I yell between breaths. It *is* Drew!

He puts his hands on his hips. Panting. Squinting into the light.

"Drew…. What… what the fuck are you doing out here?" I ask.

"I'm… I'm sorry, Marco. I didn't mean to… I didn't mean to pry."

"What?"

"I didn't mean to pry. I just… I… I was just already out here when you arrived…."

"Doing what?" Why were you watching me?" I demand, jabbing the light beam in his direction and watching his breath fog out in front of him.

"I um…... I…" he rubs his forehead with his sleeve. "I um… I… I heard something…."

"Heard something?"

"Yeah. I think I heard… heard something… I think I saw something. I… I came out to investigate… and then you came b… back."

"On your own? Where are the others?"

"They're dropping stuff off at… M… Monty's. He has an auction tomorrow."

"And you… you decided to stay back and watch me like a… like a fuckin' weirdo?"

I watch him scowl and then hold a hand up to fend off the glare of the light beam. "What? No!"

"Why were you watching me just now without saying anything? Why didn't you answer when I called out and why… the fuck did you start running?"

I watch him screw up his face. "I wasn't watching you."

"What were you doing then?"

"I… told you. I came out because I thought I saw something. Then, on my way back, I saw a light coming towards me, shoutin'. It scared the shit out of me, so I about-faced and started runnin."

"You started running?"

"Yeah."

"Why did you stop then?"

"Because I recognised your voice."

"But you didn't before?"

"Not at first, no," he says irritably, squinting into the light. "Then I thought you were having one of your…" he leaves the sentence unfinished.

"What?"

"You know… moments."

"For fucks sakes, Drew," I grumble.

"Do ya think you can get that thing outta my face?" he says, holding his hand up and turning away from the glare of the LED light.

I turn the phone downwards.

"I thought I was doing a good thing," he offers.

I sigh and take in a deep breath as my body slowly recovers from the exertion. I scan around us with the light. The blackness inside the woods has thickened. And now that the initial adrenaline rush is dissipating, the place is starting to take on a whole different vibe as the trees shrink and grow, branches like limbs reach for and pull away from us under the phone light.

If Drew wasn't watching me, then who or what was?

"What do you think you saw?" I ask quickly.

"I… I don't know. I'd just finished packin' away the tools for the day when I saw something through the window."

"Like what?"

"I don't know."

"Well, was it a person, an animal, what?"

He thinks about this and shrugs. "I think it was a person, but it was too dark to see. It happened really fast, and when they spotted me, they legged it."

"You think? If it wasn't a person, then what else could it have been?" I pose my question carefully, secretly willing the man to tell me something that might go some way to making me feel like I'm not completely losing it.

A loud snap of a twig gets our attention. And I whirl the light beam in that direction.

Trees. Branches. Giants. Talons.

"Did you hear that?" I ask.

"Yeah," Drew says, and by the tone of his voice, he's not enjoying the darkness either.

Another snap. This time in the opposite direction.

"Who's there?" I yell angrily.

The only response is the hoot of an owl in the distance. Shortly followed by something equally ominous in the opposite direction.

We're both frozen now. Squinting into the night. Ears on full scanning mode for telltale sounds.

I notice, rather interestingly, that Drew has taken a step towards me.

"I think we should leave now," I say.

"Agreed," he replies.

And I'm just about to start back towards the house when my phone rings. The ringtone is as loud as a fire bell in the still of the night.

"Fuck!" Drew breathes.

I look at the screen, but it's the strangest thing. Although the display is illuminated, there's no incoming call notification, and yet my phone is still ringing.

"What the…" I lift the phone to get a closer look, and when I do, the ringing stops and is instantly replaced by loud static blasts through the speaker eerily reminiscent of that day in the lounge.

Something screams somewhere in the distance. I spin in that direction, stabbing at the blackness with light, but there's nothing out there but the rustle of dead leaves and now the return of that most unwelcome of creepy mists.

Shit.

A shudder ripples through me as I watch how it repels the light as if it's wearing a shield protecting what may well be lurking within.

"Can we go now?" Drew asks anxiously as he watches the wall of whiteness ebb and flow towards us.

"Yeah," I say warily because I'm getting that feeling again. That skin-crawling feeling of being watched.

Static. Loud. Squealing.

It's the phone again, startling both of us, although the sound is different this time. No ringing phone, but more a call. Already connected with the ear-cringing feedback of two microphones in close proximity.

I shine the light at Drew, who instantly snaps his head back. "Hey!" he complains. But I check him over to make sure he isn't pranking me, but he's busy just now retrieving his own phone from his pocket as if realising that he has one of these things too.

"Why did you do that?"

"I'm making sure this isn't you pissing about," I say.

"Why would I do that?" he asks, affronted as if he hasn't been enjoying the title of *resident pranker* now that I've retired.

I don't think it's him anyway. He looks pretty shaken and is now wildly swiping the beam of his phone around as if it's a lightsaber.

"We… we need to go," he says. There's a clear note of alarm in his voice.

"Why are you saying that? What did you see?"

"I… I don't know," he whines.

"Tell me!" I order.

"I don't know, but… but… I think that tree just moved," he breathes, but when I follow the shard of light from his phone, all I can see is that fog, slowly, eerily drifting closer.

That's more than enough for me. I turn away and am just about to start back when my phone starts ringing again.

Unknown Number.

I spin around to look at Drew. He's aiming his phone behind us. I can see his screen. It isn't him!

I press the answer button. There's a burst of static, and then…. what's that? Voices? Faint at first…. No. Not voices, whispering, drifting, like smoke out of the speaker and filling the air around us.

Drew is affected too because he stops training his light on the surrounding trees and slowly turns it towards me, over my boots, and then up at my hand as if illumination might somehow help us hear better.

The incoherent whispers continue, rising and falling in volume for several seconds with both of us instinctively leaning in closer before it stops suddenly, and a voice I don't recognise rasps, THIS IS WHERE *SHE* ENDS. Then there's an ear-splitting metal scraping sound before the screen flickers out.

We run.

As fast as our legs will carry us, back towards the house. Lights bobbing up and down, juddering from side to side as the leaf-strewn path reveals itself before us. We dodge the claws of branches, ignore the sounds in the distance until finally, mercifully, we explode out of the woods at such speed that I stumble over myself multiple times. But I don't stop until I reach the forecourt and the car against which I allow myself to crash into an exhausted heap.

And it's as we're recovering from our exertion, breaths coming thick and fast, that we hear it. Loud. Unmistakable. Alien. Guttural. Haunting. The roar of a demon reaching out to us deep from within the bowels of darkness.

"What… the… fuck is that?" Drew gasps through breaths. He's clearly as alarmed as I was the first time.

"It's… it's okay. I think… I think… it's just a deer," I pant.

"A deer?"

"Yes. A muntjac. I freaked out the first time I heard it too."

Drew is staring at the path into the woods, no doubt dreading, like me, the possibility that something else might emerge from there, and when he snatches a look back at me, I can clearly see that he's terrified, especially when he starts reversing further inland without taking his eyes off the forest.

"I told Irvin this would happen," he says suddenly.

"What?" We're facing each other now, shining our respective lights just off each other's faces, highlighting clouds of our breaths as we recover from our ordeal.

"You know, you and all this creepy shit. I told him I didn't want to come."

"Dude, relax; it's. It's just a deer."

"That creepy phone call was no deer. I fucking hate this shit, but I picked the wrong bloody straw, didn't I?"

"Thanks. Wait, what? You drew straws?"

"We wanted to leave one of the newbies here." When I squint at him, he adds, "Sarah rang her uncle. Told him you were on your way back and, you know, to keep an eye on ya, so I said to leave one of the newbies, but Irvin wanted to make sure it was someone you knew, so me and Dean, we drew straws and…."

I tune out here because I've been distracted ever since we emerged from the woods. It felt like something had changed, but I couldn't work out what it was until now.

It's light. Out here on the forecourt. Light. Which doesn't make sense because it's dark out now, drizzling freezing rain.

Shit.

The lights are on in the house. Those black cavities that were scrutinizing me when I first arrived are now glowing amber. Both floors.

But there are no other cars on the forecourt.

"Did you turn the lights on?" I ask suddenly.

"What?"

"The lights, inside. Did you turn them on?"

I watch Drew look up and then shake his head. "No. It was still light when I left. I thought you did."

I shake my head as my heart that was just about to return to its resting state, starts to pick up the pace once more.

Maybe someone came home.

Who?

Movement draws my attention to somewhere on the roof. I can't work out where or see because the light spilling out from the downstairs windows blurs my peripheral vision. So, I'm squinting now, scanning the building. I saw something I'm sure I–

"Wait... did you hear that?" I ask suddenly, without turning.

"What?"

"I don't know. Like a scuffling sound."

We wait and listen. A fox cries out, another responds. Drew scrunches closer.

Something is moving around up there on our bedroom terrace. And it's...clicking like the sound Buddy's nails make on the hard floor. It's definitely an animal of some kind.

I squint upward but can't see anything. Nothing on the wall. Nothing on the balustrade, nothing in the shadows where the overspill of light can't reach, but there....

OH SHIT!

For a second, I think my eyes are playing tricks on me.

Oh, no. Oh, no, no, no. This isn't possible.

This can't be right. It can't be right. I close my eyes, open them again, and then slowly choke down that dreaded wave of anxiety scratching at my throat.

I'm not imagining it. It is there. I can see it! Looking right at us. Oval, unblinking eyes like glass glistening in the partial light. Oversized head. Small ears and... horns! No, not horns, but branches sprouting out of its head. Camouflage? Oh my God... it's a tree! A bloody living tree. No, a demon. A tree demon! Hiding behind our balcony wall.

Oh... I'm incapacitated by snakes of cold shivers slithering all over me. I want to call Drew. I want him to see this, but he's talking, he's still bloody jabbering, and I don't want to take my eyes off this thing for fear of losing sight of it.

"...so anyway, I then drew the straw, and they're like well you're gonna have to stay now–"

"Drew?" My voice is nothing but a whisper which means that gobby doesn't hear me and keeps prattling on.

"Drew!" I say a bit louder. Sharper.

"What?"

"Can you see it?" I whisper without even blinking away from those cold, expressionless eyes.

"What?"

"Up there," I say, through my teeth because I don't want to break the spell.

"What?"

"On the fucking balcony," I seethe, glancing over at him for barely a second, but when I look back, it's gone.

"No!"

"What are you on about?"

"The balcony! Look at the fucking balcony!" I yell as there's a thumping and scuffling sound, but I can't see anything but then–

"There!" Movement. "It's scrambling up the shadow of the building towards the roof!"

"Can you see it?"

"I can't see shit!"

"There! In the shadow. The right-hand side of the building! Towards the roof."

More scuffling and then nothing before there's a crash, rustle, and snap as something large lands and then moves about in a nearby tree.

"Oh shit!" I exclaim, holding my hands on my head. "It jumped from the house to that tree! Oh shit! That's like twenty-something feet!"

"Marc!"

"It's getting away!"

"Marc!"

But I'm not listening. I'm running over to the tree and then back to the demarcation line.

"Marco!"

Scrunching. Snapping. Scuffling of leaves, and then the sound fades as fast as it appeared.

I consider whether to give chase, but a dazzling light grabs my attention, and when I turn around, I see headlamps approach and roll to a stop behind the BMW.

I watch Irvin and Dean jump out of the truck absentmindedly before Irvin catches sight of Drew, who is standing expectantly with his hands on his hips.

"What now?" Irvin demands, looking at the man and then at me. Drew says nothing. Probably because he doesn't need to. The look on his face says it all; *Marco's been on one again.*

"What happened?" Irvin repeats.

Don't do it. I tell myself because I'm very much aware of the fact that I must be on the man's very last nerve. "Something's been in the house," I say, "and on it."

"What?"

"There was something on the roof just now. It was watching us, and then it ran back into the woods," I add, looking at Drew, but when he doesn't offer anything to the conversation, I prompt, "you saw it too, didn't you?"

Oh no. He's got that look, facing you but avoiding eye contact. I watch Irvin look at him expectantly, then I prompt, "Drew?"

"I'm sorry, Marc, mate," he says, shaking his head. "I didn't see anyfin."

"What? But you saw it in the tree, though, didn't you? You heard the rustling and everything, right?" I counter.

He shrugs. "Yeah, but that could have been anyfin," he says, looking at Irvin.

"What about in the woods. Didn't you see anything in there either?" I demand.

He hangs his head and shakes it.

"What? You didn't hear the phone call?" I ask, at this point probably a tad desperately because, well, that's what I am. It isn't that I particularly need him to validate me in the eyes of Irvin, but more that I need him to confirm that I didn't imagine this shit.

"I heard the call, yeah," he agrees, and I allow myself a subtle sigh of relief, but it's short-lived when he adds, "but I couldn't really hear much because of all the static."

"You didn't hear the voice?" I ask with a scowl.

He shrugs again. And, yeah, I want to punch him.

Irvin jumps in, "Marco, mate."

"Don't start, Irvin," I say, walking away from them towards the house because I know what's coming next. Irvin, with his compassionate brown eyes and gnome-like magical qualities where he says everything and nothing all at once, and I'm not sure I can hear that right now. I'm so pent up. Confused, over bloody wrought that I can imagine myself blubbering in front of this lot, and that incident in the bathroom at Porthcove is more than enough emasculation than I'm prepared to bear. No pun intended. If you weren't there to witness that, just as bloody well.

When I reach the front door, I pause because it would appear that tonight's weirdness isn't over. The door is wide open. Like someone just walked through it.

"Marco, mate–"

"The front door is open," I say without turning, "did you leave it open?"

"We left Drew here," Irvin says.

I don't need to ask because Drew pipes up, "No. I closed it behind me. I'm sure I did."

"Did you open it when you came back?" Irvin asks.

"I haven't been in the house yet," I add, peeking into the entrance hall. Lamps burn brightly on walls and the stairs, which is odd because it's usually the bloody reverse with this place. They're either dead or flickering like special lighting effects.

Welcome home, Marco. I imagine Holt greeting us and so wish he was here now so I could ask him *who's home?* On second thoughts, he'd probably say, *No other household members detected,* which would just scare the crap out of me—if that's even possible at this stage.

Cautiously, I enter the house. The place feels its usual empty, and yet something's off.

"Marco–" Irvin begins, but I shush him.

"What's wrong?" the man asks, lowering his tone.

"I think there's someone in the house," I say. Eyes wide, pulse racing, gingerly stepping forward with my hands out in front of me as if I'm having trouble walking in a straight line.

"But he just—"

"Shhhh!"

On cue, the theme park haunted ride lamps revert to type, flickering on the stairs and randomly in the downstairs rooms.

"They shouldn't do that," Irvin narrates, "we've replaced the whole panel down—"

"Shh!" I silence him.

I take in the space. The *breathing* ghost sheets on the second floor, the balconies, the stairs, the entrance to the drawing room, the study. Everything's in order but for that bloody buzzing and flickering of the lightbulbs.

POP!

One of the lamps on the handrail is snuffed out, startling all of us. It's closely followed by the other, and even the chandelier overhead threatens to follow suit.

"*JESUS!*" someone cries.

"SHHH!" I hiss. "What *is* that?" I add in a whisper.

"What?"

I freeze suddenly to the point where my foreman almost crashes into me. "Can you hear that?"

Voices drift out of the shadows in front of us, and I take a cautious step to my left. There, beside the stairs.

It takes Irvin a few seconds before he finally whispers, "What is it?"

I shake my head and start forward. As I do, the voices become progressively louder. "Sounds like…" I strain to listen… "sounds like laughing," we say in unison.

We've reached the foot of the stairs now. The chandelier gives up the fight, plunging the entrance hall into darkness.

There's a murmur from the lads behind me, and yet I, despite the thumping in my chest, seem to be keeping it together.

That's until I see it. Then, those familiar chills start tap-dancing on my spine.

Oh, no.

The cellar door is open again. The sounds are coming from down there.

And it's odd because I'm not getting a negative vibe, which I suppose is because there is something about these voices that's upbeat, jovial. It's nothing discernible yet, but they have a certain tone, rhythm, and pitch.

However, as we single file it closer to the open doorway, the sound's effect on me starts to change, bringing with it that dreaded tightness in my chest, dampness to my palms, and that choking sense of foreboding.

Oh no. Please no.

I clench my fists, willing myself forward, fighting the compulsion to run screaming from this place, never to return.

I can see it now. Faint yet distinct. That familiar bluish hue spilling out of the cellar door and puppeteering shadows on the opposite wall.

I pause, resting a fist on the thumping in my chest to listen, even though I don't need to. I already know, and the realisation has already chopped my breaths in half and is dragging on the tension in my shoulders.

"No," I gasp, "this isn't possible. This isn't possible."

"…now might be a good time to finally lay this question to rest. Who is your favourite parent?"

"Da-ad!"

"Marc! Stop asking him that."

"Well, he keeps abstaining from answering. He's got the diplomacy of a bloody politician. Is that what you're going to be when you grow up?"

"I love this, and I love you both so much for exactly the same amount."

"Okay, and how much is that?"

"Um, more than all the stars in the galaxy… no, more than all the grains of sand!"

There's no mistaking it. That Christmas home footage that I found at Dolce Vita, the one that somehow survived what happened there and was brought to Holt by Sarah, has somehow made its way here now.

"That's impossible," I whisper. Shaking my head.

The hand on my shoulder is like a cattle prod to the system, and

I yelp. It's Irvin. He's obviously realised, presumably from the look on my face and the fact that I'm now leaning heavily against the staircase wall, that I'm in no condition to continue, so he takes the lead.

I can't do this. I can't go through it again. I can't see that. It isn't possible. This is not possible. It's not. I'm dreaming this. It's a bad dream. And I'm going to wait here for their return or until I wake up. I don't. I can't see what's down there. *I can't!*

Buoyed from Irvin's lead, the boys overtake me too. And it's with a peculiar sense of abandonment that I watch all three men slowly disappear through the cellar door like moths to a flame.

I wait for several seconds that feel like minutes. The house is tomblike but for those voices. Almost like it's settled down for the show.

I need to know.

You don't!

I do. I need to be sure.

And against all my instincts, I bloody follow.

The steps down into the cellar aren't as steep as I remember, but I take each one slowly. Flicking the wall switch as I go, eager to break the spell of the flickering blue light, but it doesn't respond, which only accentuates the roll and swell of the shadows generated and projected over the walls by something at the foot of the stairs. Something that is still out of my line of sight but already in my mind's vision.

It smells down here. Dank. Earthy. Sweet.

I have to descend several more steps before I can see the three men standing with their backs to me facing the opposite wall like it's some kind of mystical energy source.

"Jesus Christ," one of them utters.

I watch the light and shadows dance over and all around them as the hauntingly familiar voices appear to suck all the oxygen from the room.

I can't breathe.

You're fine, but you will induce a panic attack if you don't keep it together.

No. No. I can't breathe. I can't breathe! There's no air.

There's plenty of air. You just need to keep it together.

I grab onto the railing as my legs threaten to buckle right here on these steps when I feel something displace the air next to my ear.

I freak-out! Swatting at the space around me, but there's nothing here! There's nothing here! But I felt it. I felt a clicking sound, and the air moved and–

Oh, dear God. I can see it now. Its jittery silhouette looks so big in the blue light that for a second, I think it's a bat, that we have bats down here, but then, slowly, I realise to my horror that it isn't a bat at all, but a moth. One of those moths from Dolce Vita. The ones with the skull on its back.

I close my eyes as I seek to push back the mental image of that thing and everything that came after.

Breathe. You're okay. You're fine. Just breathe.

When I reopen my eyes, it's just in time to see the insect flutter towards and then around the men who seem oblivious to it, but that's because they're already surrounded by at least a dozen of them, wings beating around the room until eventually gravitating to the one light source; my laptop. I can just about see it through the profiles of the trio standing in front of me.

I will myself to move forward by pretty much staggering down the rest of the steps, holding onto the stone columns for support.

"Toby," I croak as the men step aside, and I watch the image of my son and wife fill the screen. Toby, just as I remember—gold hair radiant in the sunshine streaming in from the nearby window— is emerging from a hug with Ellie, who looks at the camera, at me, and grins. *We did good.*

"Good job, mum."

Toby, my glorious little boy in his superhero pyjamas, walks up to the camera and throws his arms around it, making the image wobble.

I throw my hand up to my mouth to stifle the agonised cry that's trying to leave my lips as I watch the camera's frame tilt down and fill the screen with the image of a drone shaped like a ship.

"I love you, daddy."

"You do?"

"Yep. But not more than mummy. I love you both the same

amount."

"I love you, too, little man. Merry Christmas. Just remember the number-one rule."

"Yes, I know. No flying that thing over people...."

"Over people, that's right...."

"Ever."

"That's my boy."

The camera tilts up again, and Ellie comes into view. Her face is beaming. Her grin is wide and beautiful as she looks at the camera and blows it a kiss.

All three men are looking at me now, and although I can't see their faces clearly in the gloom, I assume that they're watching me with posthumous sympathy, and I can feel myself becoming overwhelmed–

What's that? I didn't notice it at first because of the limited light, but now that I've moved closer... oh... what is this?

It's everywhere; on the columns, the ceiling, and all over the only bare wall down here, transforming it into an altogether different kind of feature wall. Large, small, neat, jagged. There's a whole rash of them, daubed in what looks like paint, a hundred maybe even thousands of times on every available surface.

Words. Or from what I can tell, one word intermingled countless times with hundreds of hieroglyphics like a bizarre wall edition of *find-the-word.*

a l o n e a l o n e a l o n e a l o n e a l o n e

"Alone? Wh... what... is this?" I gasp, holding onto one of the columns. I feel nauseous. The flashing blue hue is making me want to puke right here. Right now.

"Answer me!" I yell.

Nobody responds. The trio just keeps looking at me with those inane impassive expressions. Pity. Sorrow. Like there's something wrong with *me.* There's nothing wrong with me! This is not my doing. This is you. One of you!

"WHO did this?" I demand as the screen flickers to a snow blizzard of static before switching to the overhead shot of my son and me on the beach.

"NO," I wail, clawing at my chest like I can somehow excise the ache in there. There's no air in here. No air, just a stagnant vacuum of dampness.

"WHO DID THIS?! ANSWER ME!"

"You did, Marco," Irvin says calmly.

I glare at him. "What?"

"You did, mate," he responds calmly.

"No, I didn't. Why would I do this? Why are you lying?" I don't even recognise the shrillness in my voice. *Oh, God. I'm having a panic attack. I'm becoming hysterical.*

"I'm not lying, Marc. You're the only one with the key," the man persists.

I shake my head while avoiding the images playing on the computer screen as I allow the tears to bubble and spill from my eyes.

I squint at Irvin, incredulously, crushed by an overwhelming sense of betrayal. Of all people, why is he doing this? Why would *he* be doing this to me? "Why Irvin? Why are you lying?" is my incredulous whine.

"He isn't lying, Marc," Drew pipes up. "You said you were going to keep the key from now on. You said we couldn't be trusted to keep the door locked, so you were going to keep it. We don't even know where it is."

And that's when it occurs to me. "*You*," I gasp, "you were outside the library the other day. *You* have been opening doors, calling journalists, pretending to see things in the woods. *You* did this."

"Marco. Calm down," the man says warily because he's seen this before.

"YOU did this. YOU! And I'm going to kill you," I growl. "I'M GOING TO FUCKING KILL YOU!"

I lunge for the man, hands outstretched, ready to clamp them around his throat, ready to choke the life from him once and for all. But the other two men were seemingly expecting the attack because they moved immediately to intercept.

"NO! NO!" I struggle. "I'm going to kill him! I'm going to fucking kill him!" I scream, thrashing wildly at the arms that bind me.

But it's futile, for it isn't long before the three men overwhelm and wrestle me to the cold stone slabs where I dissolve into a hysterical snivelling wreck.

40

UNEXPECTED

Daddy! Over here.

Toby? Oh, buddy, I've missed you. I've missed you. Daddy's missed you.

I know, but you need to go now. You need to let me go.

What? No. I can't. What about you? What about mummy?

She's with me now. We're together.

Toby, I don't think I can. I don't think I can go without you, buddy. Not anymore.

It's alright. I'm with you. But you'll need to choose.

Toby. I don't understand.

Please, daddy... you need to listen to me. I'm alone now. Alone.

I wake up to the sound of barking. And isn't Buddy's usual acapella but a whole cacophony of dog orchestration that I can't say I'm a total fan of first thing in the morning.

I try to move, but there's quite literally a pain in my neck, and my arse feels cold, numb.

I suppose that's to be expected when you spend the night sitting on what is effectively a concrete barn floor with nothing but a cushion under your backside, a coat and dog blanket over you.

Wait. Was that blanket here last night? I must have dozed off or something. Ugh. It must have been Sarah since I was pretty adamant, alright, a little hysterical, that I was staying and that I wouldn't be going anywhere not unless they carried me out.

What can I say? I'm going all out to piss absolutely everybody off while single-handedly proving what a bloody nutter I am. I think I'm doing a pretty good job. What say you?

Oh, shit, some of the memories of last night are filtering in, and I can only react to it all with another groan. I'm doing a lot of that lately. Have you noticed?

Meanwhile, Buddy is going all out with the slobbery kisses today. If I didn't know better, I'd say that David has been training him to–

"Buddy!"

My eyes spring open, but I'm forced to close them again because it's so bright in here today. Dazzling even. Hey… did someone leave all the lights on or something? It's hard to tell.

I allow my lids to open to slits, and the first thing I see is a golden blur in front of my face. So, I open them a little more and pull my head back so I can refocus; inky velvet snout, black eyes.

"Buddy!" I breathe.

My dog. My boy is sitting up in his cage, looking at me, one and a half ears almost at full, eyes faintly gleaming in the usual way.

"OH MY GOD! bud!" I throw my arms around the dog's head, and he switches to licking my ear, which tickles and makes me chuckle like the pathetic big kid I am.

"Oh, Bud." I hug the dog like the proverbial long-lost child because that's what it feels like. Oh, and it feels so bloody good to feel something positive for a change!

If I hadn't already made enough of a tit of myself this year, I would probably allow these moist eyes to blubber some more, but I swallow that way too familiar lump as I pull the fluffy hound to me. Close but delicately. His fur is its characteristic musky aroma, although tinged with a chemical undertone.

I love you, mate.

It's because I'm cute and I say cute things. Toby's voice fills my head.

No Buddy. It's because I love you.

When I've eventually squished what little energy the poor dog must have recovered, I release him from the hug that I, I mean he so desperately needed. Then I examine where I am by carefully moving my head as it feels like it's frozen to my shoulders. Stiff as a bloody board. And it's so cold in here. Really cold. How the hell are these animals supposed to heal in these sub-zero temperatures?

I'm at the other end of that backroom barn thing with the cages and the examination rooms. I am sitting on the floor next to Buddy's open cage. My back feels warm, and a glance over my shoulder tells me that's thanks to the large radiator nearby. High above me, small rectangular windows dotted at intervals are like movie spotlights, flooding this family drama set with dazzling white daylight.

The back barn doors are to my right. Made of wood. They must be the original doors. Closed, but there's a gap in them. That would explain the freeze. A peek through to the outside world. Oh… wow…. I think that's white rolling fields!

Smell's quite funky in here, like rabbit hutches and disinfectant.

Oh… movement to my left. I turn towards it to see a pair of wellington boots and legs clad in blue scrubs.

It's Sarah.

"Good morning," she says brightly, "I hate to break up the reunion but thought you might be needing some of this." She hands me a mug of steaming black coffee and a paper bag with a savoury pastry in it. If I'm perfectly honest, I don't know which one to start with first. I opt for the coffee.

"Thanks!" I say, sitting up straight. I take a sip from the cup and then wrap both my hands around it, enjoying the little heat that it has to offer. Then, I seek out the pastry and fall on it like I haven't eaten in days. Yeah, probably not the most hygienic of breakfasts, but I don't seem to care, which is a bit of a revelation even to me.

"It's freezing in here," I say.

"Yeah. The snow came during the night."

"Really?"

"Yeah. Quite a lot too. Now they're worried about black ice before we get more of the same later."

"Blimey," I say, suddenly feeling colder—if that's even possible.

"I came back last night, but you were out of it," Sarah says as I break off some of the food to feed to the hound, but he sniffs it and turns away from me.

"He's already eaten a little and won't have much of an appetite for a while," Sarah says, crouching down and gently rubbing the dog's snout. "He was lucky. Normally it takes repeated consumption over a sustained period for the poison to take effect, but it appears that he didn't ingest much yet became symptomatic early."

I look at my girlfriend's profile. Her hair is pinned up at the back in the usual way but with strands hanging around her face like she's half ready for a night at the opera. "Sarah," I begin.

"It's fine," she says with a smile. "Just enjoy this moment with him because it was touch and go there for a second."

"I'm um, I'm so grateful," I say with a swallow. The butterflies in my stomach are flapping out the reality of what could have happened, instantly killing my appetite.

"He's my dog too," she says quickly.

"Of course. But I'm not just referring to that. I mean everything." I shake my head because words fail me. "Just the whole way you've handled this. And pulling strings to let me stay here. I know it wasn't easy and that your boss wasn't keen, but it means so much to me."

"It's fine," she says dismissively.

I touch her leg. "No, I mean it. I know things have…." I pause here and lift my eyebrows as I consider the enormity of the statement I was about to make. It's so encompassing that I don't think I have words to describe it… think brain, think! What's the matter with you? "I, um, I know I've been a complete tool with everything, and you… you were right, are right. I should have seen it sooner, but I was an idiot. But I promise, as soon as Buddy is back on his feet and we get back to some semblance of normality, I'll be calling Ethan and working through all of this with him."

She looks at me with a wry smile, stretches back up to her full size, and slides her hands into her pockets. "What? Just like that? And would that be because I pretty much begged you to, or because of what happened yesterday?"

Shit.

"I was hoping I dreamt all that," I say with a groan.

"No. Marc. You didn't. Do you have any idea what it's like to have to stand back and watch you do this to yourself… to others?"

I frown up at her. "Do what?"

"Torture yourself like this."

"Torture myself? What are you talking about?"

"Ellie, Marc. You started dreaming about her. And at first, I thought that was natural. That it was your way of dealing with her death, but now you've started seeing her, at the house, at the wedding, even at the bloody supermarket, for crying out loud."

I sigh… right. We're doing this now. "So, Irvin told you then."

"Of course, he bloody told me. He's my uncle."

"And a big mouth, apparently," I say flippantly, looking at my beautiful boy, who has his head resting on his paws now. Eyes flicking back and forth with the volley of dialogue.

"Do you know which part of what you just said scares me the most? The bit where you seem totally fine with seeing dead people but are pissed off Uncle Irvin actually told me about it."

"Fine with it? I'm not bloody fine with it. I just didn't want to tell you because I knew you'd freak out."

"Freak out? Of course, I'm going to bloody freak out, Marc! It isn't normal."

I scoff. "Normal. What's bloody normal?"

"Exactly. I don't know if you're even capable of telling the difference anymore."

I widen my eyes. "Wow. Easy there with the support."

"Don't give me that shit, don't you dare say that to me. I've been nothing but supportive of you, and in return, all you've done is sneak around and lie."

"What?"

"What else have you been hiding?"

"Hiding? What are you talking about? Where's this coming from?"

"Where were you the other night?"

I widen my eyes in surprise. "Sorry, Sarah. You're going to need to be a little bit more specific."

"It's a simple question, Marc. Why can't you answer it?"

"I can't answer it because I don't know what you're talking about."

"The night before last."

I nod. "You know where I was. I was at the police station."

"That's right. After beating some bloke to a bloody pulp and sending him to the hospital, you were at the police station. And who were you with?"

"You know who I was with."

"I want to hear you say it," she says through gritted teeth.

"I was with my lawyer."

"Who happens to be your ex."

"Are you fucking serious? With everything that's been happening, and you're jealous of her?"

"No. Not of her, but of the secrets you keep. I don't even recognise you anymore."

"What's does that even mean? Sarah, look–"

"Why were you home so late the other night?"

"That place isn't my home. And it wasn't that late."

"It was late, Marc."

"Well, you didn't seem too fussed. From what I could tell, you and Mr. blue eyes seemed to be doing just fine without me."

"We're not talking about me."

"No? This inquisition reserved just for me? How come?"

"Because you're the one that's losing his bloody…."

She trails off here, but I know exactly where she was going with that, and it's okay. "Go on. Finish the sentence," I say.

"What did you do in all that time, Marc?" she asks casually, controlling the narrative. Calmly, methodically. No doubt drawing on that rudimentary media training we received after Dolce Vita sunk into the bloody ocean. But she's upset. Angry. I can tell by the way she's pursed those lips, narrowed those beautiful eyes. Although, there's something else here too. Something I can't quite identify. I want to say Fear… but of what?

"I've already told you," I say.

"But you haven't told me everything, though, have you? What are you hiding, Marc?"

"I'm not hiding anything. What's wrong with you?"

"Why won't you tell me?"

"Because I can't."

"Why not?"

"Because I don't remember!" I yell. Buddy whimpers. I stroke his head, which prompts him to move it and rest it on my thigh.

What have you done to upset mummy? You should buy her shoes, she likes shoes.

"Not this time, Buddy… it's okay… it's okay." I look up again to see my girlfriend nodding her head while chewing on her lip. "You don't remember?"

"No. I've been trying to, but for some reason, all I remember is being in the car then going up to her room." I stop myself here. Shit. I said that out loud.

She nods again. "So, you do admit to going up to her room?"

"No. That isn't what I meant. It wasn't like that."

"No?" she asks. "You just started drinking again for the fun of it, right? What were you doing? Going over your legal strategy or hers?"

"Sarah. Come on. What's the matter with you? You're not normally like this. You know me. Hey Sarah… come on." I reach out to her, but she pulls away.

I watch her run both hands through her hair as if she's contemplating the fate of the world, and if I could move, I would be hugging her right now, but I get the distinct impression that if I tried, my movements wouldn't be rapid since I think my limbs have all gone to sleep.

"I'm sorry, Marc. I'm really sorry… I love you, but I just can't do this anymore. Not now. I just can't. Everything's different, and I just can't take the risk," she says, looking around the place as if looking for inspiration in one of the cages, then she turns back to me. "You haven't taken your meds in weeks. You've been hallucinating your dead wife. You; you let that crazy woman into our home–"

"Now hold on–"

"No. You hold on." Dogs bark in synchronisation as if egging her on. "You need to hear it. I need to hear it out loud because, in my head, it just sounds so… so bloody unbelievable…. You've been hiding behind a curse that quite obviously doesn't exist outside of your head. You've assaulted two people. You nearly killed our dog, whom you're supposed to love. You see demons on rooftops. You've redecorated the cellar and have obviously transformed it into a shrine for your dead son and wife... not to mention all the subtext in that."

"Subtext?"

"Alone. Really? What's that supposed to mean anyway?"

She's with me now. I'm alone. I'm... alone!

I shake my head. Unable to find the words because hearing all that stuff summarised like that. "Fuck," is all I can say before taking a sip from my cup.

"What? Not even going to attempt to theorise?" she prompts.

I shrug. "I've no clue. I really couldn't tell you."

"No? Well, I have a theory. I mean, I'm no expert or anything, but for you to write that word over and over, I can't help but wonder if that's how you're feeling in this relationship. If your subconscious might be in some way expressing how you truly feel about us."

"Now, wait a minute," I say, "you're assuming that it was me who wrote that stuff?"

I'm... alone!

"Oh my God, after everything I've just listed, are you seriously going to try to argue that somebody else did? You were the only person with the key, Marc!"

"So? Doesn't prove anything. Just means somebody else could easily have a copy. Look at that crazy bitch. Work was going on at that place every day, and she was still managing to slip in and out undetected. And what about the hieroglyphics, Sarah? We've both seen them before, or have you forgotten that too?"

"Don't try and turn this on me. So that's your answer? You're telling me that what you found down there was the work of ghosts?"

"No. I'm just telling you I didn't do it."

"Yeah, but you also said you can't remember things."

I sigh. "Look. I don't have all the answers. I wish I did, but we both know that something isn't right. Something is going on here, and it does have something to do with Ellie–"

"Stop it...."

"...Something to do with Toby. This alone. I'm alone.

Remember how he tried to warn me before? And the dream I've been having. I think he's trying to warn us about Ellie…."

"Marco, stop it…."

"…And yes, I do think that crazy witch person did something to us, I mean look at us. We're not normally like this…."

"Stop it"

"…and if you stop repressing what happened that night and allow yourself to…."

"…I don't want to hear anymore!"

"…No. Sarah, listen, I'm telling you something isn't right. It isn't all in my head. You've got to–"

"SHUT UP! SHUT UP! SHUT UP!" my normally mild-mannered girlfriend screams, her voice so loud one of the dogs in a nearby cage starts howling.

"Sarah!" Sarah's boss, who must have been in one of the examination rooms, appears at the door and then makes his way over to us where he takes in the scene; me, six-foot-something huddled on the floor. Animal blanket on top of me with the dog now resting his head on my thigh.

I'll admit, it's awkward. I mean, how do you greet someone in such a situation?

With mutual nods, apparently. Because that's what he does before turning to Sarah, who heads him off. "I know, Martin. I'm sorry," she says with a shake of the head and a pained expression.

"It isn't just the fact that you're here, but you know as well as I do that in your condition–"

"Yes, Martin. You're right. I'm sorry. Marc will be leaving shortly. Thanks very much. Thank you."

The man observes her for several seconds before nodding, then with a glance in my direction, he disappears once more back into the examination room.

I watch my girlfriend curiously as I wait for her to turn my way, but she's avoiding my gaze, so I feel compelled to prompt her. "What did he mean?"

"He thinks it's time for you to leave," she says with a glance.

So now I put the coffee and the bag down, gently lift Buddy's head off my lap and slowly unfurl myself. It takes a while for me to get to my feet again because my right leg is locked into some kind of spasm, my left foot has gone to sleep, and I generally ache all over.

Finally, back to my full height once more, I move in close to my girlfriend and repeat. "What was he talking about?"

She finally gives me her eyes and says, "He's worried about you. We're all worried about you."

"I'm fine–"

"About your mental condition, that is."

I squint at her. In all the time Sarah and I have been together, I don't think she's ever said something like this to me. I mean, there's no doubt in my mind that she's thought about it—and who could blame her?—but she's never verbalised it. And oddly—although I've never mentioned it—I've always been grateful to her for it. Presumably, because it expressed an unconditional acceptance of me, of who I am, despite my flaws.

"I see," is all I can say because I'm taken aback, "you think I've lost it again."

She doesn't respond. And this second knifing hurts even more than I expected.

Much worse, because there are now tears welling in her eyes. "I didn't know what to do, Marc. After Uncle Irvin told me what had happened, I asked them to bring you back here so you could be with Buddy, but I didn't know what else to do."

"It's okay. It's alright–"

"It isn't alright because you left me no choice. You're out of control. You have hurt people! And if something isn't done about it, there's a good chance you'll hurt someone else." Oh, shit. That familiar and unwelcome boulder of dread drops to the pit of my gut again. "I had no choice," she continues with an exasperated wail. "You need help, and I don't know how else to help you. I've tried to be understanding, supportive, but I don't think that's what you need, Marc. You need something more," she says, lifting hands and cupping them to my face. "Something I'm not," she adds decisively. "I've just been enabling you, and it has to stop. Now more than ever."

It takes me a few seconds to process that because, well, I'm hearing it for the first time. Eventually, I ask, "What do you mean?"

Her only response is to burst into tears.

Buddy starts whimpering, and I turn to see something that melts through my initial shock and has me pulling my sobbing girlfriend to me. "It's okay," I whisper, "it's alright," I say as I watch Buddy collapse back onto his haunches.

Upon seeing Sarah's distress, my dog had attempted to scramble to his feet—IV drip and all—presumably intending to limp over here to administer his magic paws trick on her.

I am overwhelmed with emotion.

What have I done?

My world as I knew it has been imploding around me for some time now. And not because of some evil supernatural force or life event but by my own hand. I have been systematically dismantling my new world from within. Refusing to see what was right in front of my face. I've been so busy looking for ghosts that I was incapable of seeing that they were all inside my head. And they started the moment I stopped taking those pills. I can see it now, but I'm terrified that it might be too late.

I hold Sarah's shuddering body close to mine for several minutes before I think I hear her say something. The words are whispered so quietly, I think I imagined them. "What did you say?"

"I said… I'm pregnant."

I take a beat to absorb what that means before I gently break the embrace so that I can look into her tear-stained eyes.

I open my mouth to speak, but she heads me off with a sniff and a shake of her head. "I know how confusing this must be right now."

"I'm not confused… I–"

"I am too. The timing is lousy. And I need to think about it."

"What? Sarah–"

She pulls away from me, drying her eyes on her sleeve. "I need time, Marc. We both do."

"Sarah, wait–"

"So–"

"Sarah, no, hold on a–"

"Listen–"

"Sarah–"

"Listen to me, Marc," she says forcefully. "I need to go get some air right now. I need to think, but you should go home. Get a shower. Get some sleep. We can talk tonight when I get back, but you should know that I'm leaving tomorrow. Buddy should be feeling much better then. I'll be picking him up and then driving on to Porthcove."

"What? No. What do you mean?"

"We're going to spend some time with mum. I need time to think about all of this. And so do you."

"I don't need to think about it. I told you. I realise now what needs to be done. I was an idiot. Sarah, come on, please, let's talk about it," I reach for her, but she twists away from my outstretched arms.

Buddy starts barking slowly.

"No. Marc. Not now. Not like this. You need to talk to Ethan first."

"What do you mean? I don't need to talk to Ethan. I need to talk to you," I say. My voice loud, desperate.

"I'm sorry, but it's too late," she says before turning away from me and rushing through the double doors to the reception area. I half race, half limp after her but skid to a halt when I find my own reception of an altogether different kind.

Doctor Ethan Holmes, Detective Peck, and two other cops have packed out the square room and are waiting for me. There's nobody else in here. No customers. No staff. Which tells me that this was planned.

"Hello, Marco," Holmes says like he's just made the two-hour drive for a social visit.

I look at the door out of the building now closed and barricaded by a hefty, bearded cop with a shirt-wrapped paunch spilling over his belt.

"Sorry, Ethan. Can't chat," I say, moving forward. Instantly, the two cops converge to block my path. The bear of a colleague now towering over them and giving me some serious stink-eye.

I consider barging my way through and imagine the men tumbling backwards like bowling pins. But that's just in my head. The reality, no doubt, would be altogether different.

I scan the room for other exits. There are none. So, I think about retreating and looking for a back exit, but they'll have thought about that, no doubt.

"Looks like this autumn's fashion trend is men in black, not white, eh, Ethan?"

"Please don't make this any harder than it needs to be, Marco," Doctor Holmes says quickly. "I just want to talk."

"You just want to talk? Ethan, come on. We both know that's the understatement of the century."

"Mr. Battista," Peck begins, taking a step forward, but he's shut down by a raised hand from Holmes.

"Wow. You already have him trained. That's impressive, Ethan."

"Marco—" Holmes begins but cuts himself off when he sees me look up at the sound of a car's engine starting outside.

Sarah.

She's leaving. I need to talk to her. "I need to talk to Sarah, Ethan."

"I know," he says.

"So, let me go do that."

He cocks his head. "It isn't that easy, Marco. I'm afraid."

"Why not?"

"It just isn't. Why don't we go have a chat, just you and me, first, eh? I just want to talk through what's been happening with you lately."

I run my hands through my hair as I ponder once again the odds of ramming those cops. They aren't good. So, I take a step backwards towards the barn, which is in an uproar. Buddy seems to have roped in all his new mates at protesting the injustice that's going down in here.

"Marco…" Ethan begins.

I look behind me, and before I even have the chance to contemplate my next move, I'm smacked in the face by the double doors that suddenly explode inward. Then I feel the wind knocked out of me as someone tackles me to the cold tiled floor, unceremoniously bending my arms behind my back before chinking and clicking my wrists into tight cuffs.

"Ethan, please, don't do this! Please!" I beg. "I need to talk to Sarah. Please, Ethan. Please. Please! I think she's in danger! She's in danger! SARAH! SARAH!"

Woof! Woof! Woof!

Buddy is leading the angry charge behind the double doors by growling and barking, inciting the rest of the convalescing patients to the point where my wailing is lost in the din.

"I want my lawyer," I say through garbled breaths. "I want my fucking lawyer. NOW! Ethan, I want my lawyer, Amanda Stapleton. Get me Amanda Stapleton!"

Detective Peck responds to my demand by raising his voice over the din of the menagerie behind us and yells, "Marco Battista, I am detaining you in accordance with section 136 of the mental health act...."

"NO! Ethan. Please. Don't do this! Don't do this, Ethan!"

"...so that you may be taken to a place of safety for a full evaluation...."

"ETHAN!"

41

CUSTODY

It's gone lunchtime by the time we get back to Fawnham police station. Traffic was almost at a standstill thanks to a series of accidents in the region. According to the car radio, last night's snowfall has compacted and frozen over, creating treacherous road conditions.

This, of course, did nothing for my state of mind since I know Sarah is planning to travel down to the Southwest coast despite the forecast for more snow with my dog and unborn child. This meant that when I was unceremoniously deposited back in that shitty interview box room, I was in no mood to talk. I was so fucking angry; I could have ripped Ethan's head off. It was his fault I was in there. His fault that everything that mattered to me in the world was at risk.

So, as you'd expect, when Doctor Holmes attempted to engage me in conversation for the best part of an hour, I ignored him. I was in no mood to exchange words with that prick that didn't start with *F* and ended in *you*. *My girlfriend is in danger, Ethan! Sarah is in danger, and you're keeping me locked up in here!* To which he'd respond, *I'm not keeping you in here, Marco. You are. I just want to talk to you. I need to talk to you to understand your state of mind. You know this. Help me. Help you.*

Well, you can imagine how I reacted to that. Help me, help you? Help me help you?! I raged. I've just told you that Sarah's in danger, and all you can do is spout this Jerry Maguire shit?! I ought to rip your fucking head off!

And round and round we went until Doctor Holmes, obviously bored with my shit, called in an officer and asked if I could be escorted to one of the cells *to cool down, after which I'll be more than happy to resume our conversation.*

Resume our conversation? I echoed promptly, followed by a series of expletives as I was being physically dragged out of the room to a cell and had the door clang shut behind me.

Shit.

That was at least three or four hours ago. I have no bloody idea because, in this windowless cheerless body-odour-infused place, it's easy to lose all track of time.

But the doctor's right. I feel much calmer now. Stupid, too, for making such a spectacle of myself. He's right. And I should know better. The fastest route out of this place is through discourse. I need to convince him, and he needs to feel satisfied that I am, in fact, not a danger to myself and or others. He's not going to do that if I keep threatening to rip his head off in between a sandwich of swearwords.

Luckily, the coppers from earlier are making a comeback. The chunky bear one is jangling keys in the lock as I think this.

"Ere, Battista. You gonna be a pain in my arse again? I just need to know whether or not I need to cuff ya."

"No. I'm fine."

"What's that?"

"I said I'm fine."

"You best be because I ain't in any mood for more of your crap. Do you hear what I'm sayin?"

"I hear," I mumble.

"What's that?"

"I said I hear," I say loudly, like a sulky child.

And yet, things take a turn for the worse when I'm escorted past that shitty interrogation room and am asked to put my jacket back on.

"Where are we going?"

"*You* are on your way back to London, mate."

"What?"

"The Doc thinks he isn't making any progress with ya ere and wants to get back before the worse of the snow hits."

"No. I can't go back to London," I protest, pulling away from them."

"Na, didn't I tell ya we weren't aving none of that?"

"I don't want to go back to London. ETHAN? ETHAN?!"

Ten minutes later, I'm back in cuffs and being escorted out into a somewhat apocalyptic evening, or is it late afternoon? It's bloody hard to tell because the sky is a bubbling cauldron of dark grey clouds seemingly prepping to annihilate the land with God knows what.

"What the ell is that?" says one of the cops.

"It looks like one of those supercells you get before a tornado."

"A tornado? In the New Forest?" The *bear* cop asks with a smirk.

"I didn't say it was going to be a tornado," the other grumbles. "I said it looks like those clouds you get before a tornado—"

"Are we ready, gentleman?" It's Ethan; I watch him fasten the buttons of his coat and walk up to *Tweedle Dee* and *Tweedle Dum,* who are both gawking up at the sky. "I'll be following you at a safe distance. You both have my number if you need to pull over or anything."

I bang on the window with my forehead because I am bloody cuffed in the backseat!

"Why is he handcuffed?" Ethan demands.

"It's standard procedure," the *bear* cop responds.

"For criminals maybe but not my patient. Please uncuff him. He can't possibly make the journey like that."

I watch the cop roll his eyes, "Will you be responsible for im kickin' off again?" he asks before opening my door.

"I'll take full responsibility."

"Ethan, please," I say before the door's barely open. "You can't take me back to London. You can't take me back. I need to be here for Sarah."

"Marco, the officer is going to take your cuffs off so that you'll be more comfortable. Can you give me your word that you're not going to make things difficult again?"

"Ethan–"

The bears sigh visibly.

"Marco. One thing at a time. Do I have your word?"

I look at him. I know I'm not going to get anywhere if I don't start doing this by his rules. I nod.

Ethan looks at the cop. The cop pulls a face. *It's on your head, mate.*

Hands-free, and I have to admit, it does feel more comfortable. "Ethan. I know I need to earn your trust. I get it. But please, can we at least go check on her?"

The doctor furrows his brow, making a show of thinking about it. Bear protests. "Now, hang on a minute. We're here to do a job. To get him back to London not do house visits."

"Funny, officer. I thought your job was to preserve and prevent all offences against people and property. Despite his current predicament, Mr. Battista is still one of Her Majesty's subjects, is he not?" The cops look at each other with confusion. Ethan doesn't wait for them. "As such, he has a legitimate concern.; I believe it's your duty as police officers to investigate this. We have to drive past there anyway."

I clasp my hands together and bow at the Doctor. He doesn't acknowledge me, and I don't know if that's because he's had enough of me for the day, or he just doesn't want to be seen *fraternizing* with the *detainee*. Instead, he turns and walks over to his car, leaving the cops to squabble over who will drive and who will sit with me before we finally get underway.

For once, the news reports weren't an exaggeration. We pass cars abandoned on the side of the road. Some sporting severe collision damage, others seemingly abandoned by their owners for whatever reason. And yet, despite this, we must be travelling at least sixty miles per hour once we're on the main road, tyres hissing and crunching over the freeze with ice and snow strafing the side of the car like bullets. For me, we're travelling a little too fast given the carnage out there, but not fast enough to get to Frost Lake Manor.

This is where SHE ends.

That phrase has been playing on my mind ever since we heard it in the woods. The last time I dreamt a similar phrase, I was in a house that ended up collapsing into the ocean, which is probably why I can't shake this feeling that something awful is going to happen.

"Wow!" The sound of both cops chatting anxiously gets my attention. The car just fishtailed a couple of times on what they're saying must be *black ice*. Nothing dramatic but enough to tense up the atmosphere in the car. This isn't helped by the driver insisting we listen to doomsday news reports on the radio.

A car whooshes by us in the opposite lane.

"…he's going way too fast for these conditions," the driver complains.

"Well, maybe you should stop to give him a caution while we're at it," the disgruntled bear sitting next to me grumbles.

"Your missus gonna give you a hard time for being back late?" the driver asks, looking in the rear-view mirror.

"What do you think?" the bear grunts.

Bloody hell, I'm starting to feel like I should be apologising for the inconvenience, but what these two morons don't seem to appreciate is that I want to be in this car even less than they–

"What the fuck is he doing?" the driver yells.

"Lay off the brakes, lay off the brakes!" Bear responds.

"I have! It's im! He's all over the place!"

"LOOK OUT!" bear yells.

Then we're gliding in a series of judders, swerving from one side that has my face slammed against the passenger window and then the other where I'm up close and personal with bear's prickly beard and coffee breath in a medley of shouting, metal bending, engine revving, wheels hissing, and car horns before I'm being tipped steeply onto bear once more and we crash to a halt.

Now, my first thought is, thank God this bloke is a ton of lard because he makes for one hell of a soft landing. On the other hand, he has his blubber face pressed up against the car's passenger window, and there's blood grossly trickling from it.

Oh shit!

The same fate has befallen the driver apparently as the car is lying on its right side at an awkward 120-degree angle. Only his window is smashed, and I can hear him groaning. Looking out of the windscreen, I can see a snow tunnel on either side of the ice, and I can hear running water.

I think we've ended up down an embankment and in a bloody ditch.

"Fuck!" And there's water running into the car!

Air. Water. Air. Water. Air. Water.

"NO! Focus!" But my heart is pounding at the memory of that night at Porthcove.

This isn't the ocean. You're fine. You're okay. You just need to get out of this.

Oh shit… that water is rising, but slowly, the car being only a partial and not complete damn. Still, it's enough to freeze my right leg, which is now submerged in it.

I need to get out of here, but there are no handles on the door, so I can't open it from the inside, assuming I even have the strength to push it open at this angle, and I can't wind down the window as that's controlled electronically from the front, I assume.

On the bright side, the bear is still out of it, but I don't want to be here when he wakes up quite literally with a sore head.

Movement catches my attention outside.

"Hello! Are you alright in there?"

"Ethan!" Thank God. I forgot about him. "Ethan, there's water coming in!"

I watch him carefully scramble around the car, but he's most likely going to struggle to open one of the doors.

"Marco! Protect your face!"

"What?"

"Turn your face away; I'm going to break the glass!"

Or maybe not.

I awkwardly twist my body sideways and spread my arms so that I'm covering the bear's head and face. "Okay!"

There's a loud thwack! Another and then another before there's a splitting sound, one more blow and the glass cracks showering me with several pieces, but the bulk of it remains as one chunk that

Ethan carefully pries apart by using the sleeve of his coat as gloves.

Before long, I'm half climbing, half being hauled out of the car and into the freezing air.

"Are you alright?" Ethan asks. "I saw what happened. That car skidded right at you," Ethan says, in his rare high-pitched, panicked voice.

"Yeah. I'm fine. I had a soft landing. I don't think they fared as well," I say, looking around, trying to get my bearings. It's getting dark now. Headlamps and taillights of passing vehicles burn brightly in the twilight, highlighting the fact that it's started snowing once more.

We're on the dual carriageway. The only main artery out of the New Forest from this side. Frost Lake Manor is several miles from here.

"I've called for help," Ethan says, "but they're obviously stretched."

I look back down towards the stricken patrol car in the ditch. "Well, those two can't wait. That thing's taking on water."

"We best get back down there to help them," Ethan says.

"You got your phone on you?"

"Yes, why?"

"Can I borrow it?"

"I told you. I already called for help."

I give him a look. He sighs and pulls his phone out of his pocket, and hands it to me. I find Sarah's number and dial it but get voicemail. "We can't stay here," I say. It's dangerous with these passing cars. I dial it again. Still voicemail. "Shit."

"Agreed," Ethan says warily as he watches the cars scrunch and hiss by.

"Keys in the car?" I ask.

The doctor squints at me. "Yes, why?"

"Good," I toss the phone back at him, "help them out of there. The water's rising slowly, but they'll freeze to death if you leave them too long," I say, looking at the Merc parked on the side of the road.

"Where are you going?"

"The same place I've been trying to go all bloody day," I grumble, walking past him.

"Marco, I can't let you–"

I stop, turn back to him and glower. "You're lucky I don't throw you down that ditch to join those two," I growl.

"I was doing my job. You know that."

"At the risk of Sarah's life?"

"No. You don't understand."

"Oh, I understand perfectly," I say, and then I walk away.

"You don't understand, Marco! Sarah is the one who called me. She's the one who thinks you should be taken into care!" The doctor throws after me. The bite of his words is worse than the cold out here. Still, I don't turn because I have somewhere else I need to be.

42

FACE YOUR FEARS

FROST LAKE MANOR· EARLY EVENING·

When the car can no longer gains transaction and starts fishtailing left and right, threatening to throw me off the driveway and down into one of the fields, I know it's time to kill the engine and continue the rest of the journey on foot. I've already been on one of these rides today. Not in the mood for another.

I step out into the night and wince. I'm aching. Neck and back mostly. I think I may have taken more of a knock than I thought.

The snow is still falling, but it's just flurries now that it's topped up the winter wonderland of sparkling cotton wool. Surreally, the full moon—an iconic reminder of that night back in Porthcove—makes the occasional churlish appearance behind giant grey clouds, periodically transforming night into day.

The sound of my boots crunching in the snow, which is no more than a few inches deep in places, is supernaturally loud in the quiet of the freeze, where it feels like I'm the only person left in the world. The thought of that is now as scary to me as the prospect of what awaits inside that mansion. I would like to believe that it's just a disgruntled Sarah—the second woman in my life that thinks I'm a menace to society—rushing back and forth throwing clothes into a makeshift suitcase while I cling onto her leg and beg her not to leave, but I don't know, I feel like–

Wings flutter to my left, and I turn to hear the ominous deep hoot of an owl perched high on a tree branch, staring at me as if it's deeply disturbed to see me here.

You and me both, mate.

Like one of those Halloween portraits, Frost Lake Manor looms high on the hill ahead, partially draped in shadow like a proverbial giant waiting for battle. That's okay. I'm not afraid. I'm done running. It's time to face my fears.

The house, seemingly aware of my bolshy demeanour and eager to scare it out of me, beckons by shining one solitary light on the second floor.

Our bedroom.

Sarah's car is parked out front, which is reassuring on so many levels. She isn't out driving, and I get the chance to talk to her.

By the time I reach the front door, my nose and hands are numb from windchill, so I'm eager to get inside but….

What the hell are these?

Footprints. From the woods to the house. Partially covered over. It's hard to tell if they're male or female, but their mere presence is unnerving.

Maja?

I turn to the door. Only one way to find out.

With a shaky hand, I grip the handle and push. It opens with an echoey creak that I don't think I even noticed before. Or maybe it was there, but it just sounds so much worse right now as I stand here on my own in what feels like the dead of winter.

I try the light switch, but nothing happens. Of course.

"Sarah!" I call, my voice ringing out in the vast space. I wait. But there is no reply.

It's slowly becoming brighter in the entrance lobby now that my eyes are adjusting to the gloom and the moonlight flooding in through the glass canopy overhead.

The house is deathly still. Not a creak or a sigh. Just that obligatory rustling from the dust sheets on the first floor. One of the windows must be open again.

"Sarah!" I yell once more," but there's still no response.

I make my way over to the small table next to the stairs. I light one of the lanterns placed here precisely for such an eventuality. *Yeah. I'm ahead of you, house.*

So, now. Part of me thinks I should just rush up there, like ripping off a plaster, check out the bedroom, explore why exactly there's one solitary light burning in our bedroom. The other part of me thinks I should just take it slowly. One step at a time, holding the lantern out in front of me like a crucifix and readily available weapon should… anything emerge from the dark.

Really?

Come on. I've been in this situation enough times to know that there's always something lurking in the dark.

"BLOODY HELL!"

The grandfather clock, you know, that old dead thing sitting on the landing between the east and west stairs has suddenly sprung to life by chiming a hauntingly warbled rendition of Big Ben's *Westminster Quarters.*

The fog of my breath instantly turns ragged as I hold the lamp up at the ordinarily ineffectual thing, and…there's nothing different about it. It hasn't magically transformed back to its gleaming former self or into some kind of hybrid time monster but remains aged, discoloured, and blistered. And yet, it's suddenly decided to chime again after all these years.

Yeah. That's lovely. Not creepy at all.

Um, and I don't know if I'm imagining this, which, at this point, we know is entirely possible, but I'm sure it's getting darker in here. Before I could see shapes and outlines of the furniture, stairs, and doorways, but now they've mostly merged into the shadows. My sight is now limited to the amber glow cast by the lamplight, which can't be more than five or six feet in front of me.

A glance up at the canopy says it all. The snow clouds are back, and they've smothered the moon to death, leaving nothing but blackness.

On the second floor, the dust sheets now stretch over the railing and stairs on the wind like the tongue of an abominable arctic creature with frigid breath and spittle made of snow that floats, twirls, and eventually settles on all over the staircase. Bringing the outside in. That northerly gale is back, too, scaring doors in their frames and howling through every available crevice.

"SARAH!" I yell out again to nowhere in particular. But there's still no response. *Why isn't she answering me?* It's a rhetorical question that I don't think I want an answer to. I'm worried now, and I don't even bloody know why!

I want to turn left at the grandfather clock to the unfinished *east wing*. Just some weird compulsion. But if Sarah is here—*if?*—I would expect her to be in our bedroom where that light is. In the *west wing*.

So, I take a step up.

Click.

What was that?!

Sounds like it's coming from upstairs. A click *of a limb*. A rustle *of clothing*. As if somebody has just moved. As if somebody is loitering with intent at the top of those stairs just waiting for –

Click. Pop! Click. Pop. Click. Click. Click.

Oh, what the bloody hell is that?

I brandish the lantern high above me and to the right staircase… and recoil in horror when I see two cat-like eyes glinting back at me in the darkness.

"Oh fuck!"

I barely have time to process that when there's a heavy scuttling sound akin to one Buddy makes when he's bounding towards me, only this is different, it's—*Click! Click! Click! Pop! Click! Pop!*

Shivers flush over me as I see something scurry down the stairs. It's an animal of some kind because it's moving on all fours, but then—*Oh sweet Jesus!*

As the thing crawls—*limbs clicking and popping with each movement*—down the stairs and into the light, I can see that it isn't an animal at all but something else. Something much more horrifying with long wiry white hair hanging in ragged curtains in front of what should be a face but is instead a mishmash of puckered leathery skin.

It pauses on the landing in front of the clock, and that's when I see it. Oh no. No. No. No! I think it's supposed to be a woman... or at least, oh God. I think it is. But it can't be. It can't be because... because its head is twisted upside down—eyes and scalp trailing off the floor, mouth where her forehead should be—and it's fixing me with a lifeless stare.

Startled, I move backwards, forgetting that I'd already climbed a step... and lose my balance. I flail in the air for what feels like seconds before crash-landing onto my back, pain shooting up my coccyx, the lantern clanging loudly somewhere behind my head.

I barely have time to recover when those grotesque sounds stretch out to me again, plucking at my eardrums—*Click pop! Click pop!* The nerve-jangling sound of cartilage and bones rubbing against each other as the *thing,* with the dexterity of an arachnid, crawls down the rest of the stairs. Hair dragging. White eyes watching. Face contorted into an agony inflicted on it erstwhile.

I drag myself backwards in my own crab-like way as it scuttles towards me, but I crash into the lantern, somehow smothering the flame and plunging the room into darkness.

I freeze as I hear nails click and tap off the stairs and onto the floor towards me.

Oh no. Please no.

Click. Tap! Pop! Click. Tap! Pop!

Closer.

Click. Tap! Pop!

Closer.

Click. Tap! Pop!

"Aaaaaaaaaaaargh!" I yell and throw my hands over my face when I sense the thing touch my boot.

...seconds tick by. The wind howls. The dust sheets crinkle and flap...

...nothing happens.

I remain motionless. Barely breathing for my body is numb, incapacitated with terror. I cannot see in front of me. I can barely make out the outline of the steps or anything else in the gloom.

You're okay. You're alright. You imagined that. It wasn't real.

I'm not okay. I'm not alright, and it did feel fucking real!

Okay. Calm down. Focus. Relight the lantern. The matches are on the table next to the stairs, in front of you. Just feel your way.

Oh, God. All I can hear are various horror film scores filling in the gaps between the howling wind and fluttering curtains.

Stop it! Stop!

Mercifully, there must be a break in the clouds because the moon makes a fleeting reappearance redrawing the outlines of the doors, stairs, and balconies once more.

There's nothing here. I'm alone. I'm okay. I just need to get the lantern relit, so I turn… and find myself staring straight in the face of my darkest nightmare; *ragged hair like straw, decomposed skin, wriggling termites, and glassy white eyes.* I open my mouth to scream, but the thing unleashes an ungodly sound of its own through the gash up where its forehead should be.

The screech is so loud and powerful it blows my hair and me backwards, but I roll with the motion onto my knees, screaming, only to realise that I am alone once more.

Wind howls. Sheets crinkle.

I can't breathe! These short, ragged breaths aren't enough. The pressure is building in my skull, squeezing the tightness in my chest.

Calm down. You're alright. You're okay. That isn't real. It wasn't real. Calm down. Pull yourself together. Just breathe, Marco. Breathe. That's it. Breathe slowly. Slowly.

I choke a few times, feeling like I'm going to pass out. I'm going to pass out!

You're not. Pull yourself together. Your mind is projecting this stuff. Take control. Breathe. Take control. Breathe.

I do this for several seconds. And then, without thinking, I push myself up onto my feet, ignoring the pain in my back, all the while scanning the shadows.

I return to the table near the stairs, relight the lamp, and instantly feel better when I see that I am, in fact, alone. There's no upside-down head creature in here. *It* is long gone, Marco.

Slam!

A door. Upstairs somewhere.

Soft footsteps. Creaking floorboards.

"SARAH?" I yell, my head thumping with a sudden tension

headache.

There's no reply, of course. Leave now, Marco. Sarah isn't here.

Of course, she's here. Her car is here. If she isn't, then who's that up there?

Do you really want to find out?

No, but I feel like I should. There's no easy way out of this. This is where I'm supposed to be.

Daddy. Come find me.

I move closer to the steps and hold the lantern high towards the west wing balcony. I can't see anything up there, just the faint glow of the lamp still burning in our room.

I perform a 360 turn all around. There's nothing here but me.

You know that. It's just an old creepy house. That thing was just a hideous psychosis brought on by the reality of what happened here before.

The image of some faceless woman crumpled at the foot of the steps just where I'm standing presents itself to me.

I'm here for one reason and one reason alone.

"MARCO!"

Did I imagine that too? Sarah or *someone* calling my name from somewhere upstairs.

"SARAH? SARAH!" I call urgently. Desperately.

No reply.

I gingerly place one foot on the first step and then the next while all the time keeping my eyes on the railing above, scanning for any signs of any*thing*.

Surreally, snow is falling all around me from one of the billowing dustsheets, reminding me that the moon has disappeared once more and that I'm back to relying solely on the lamp in my hand for light.

The sheet rustles again like the red rag to a bull as if tempting me to turn left at the clock, but I ignore the ghostly fluttering and turn right at the thing that is now surreally still *ticking,* and *tocking* in that miserable way clocks do in a quiet house. I have no idea how this is even possible. Monty insisted that it needed major repairs.

I climb the second flight of steps. The glow of the lamplight is like an amber forcefield around me, repelling the darkness.

"SARAH!" I call again. My nerves pulled taut because as much as I'm trying to keep it together, my body is nonetheless physically shaking with the tension. That or it's the bitter cold gale wailing up here like a godforsaken ice demon.

At the top of the stairs, I tell myself to focus on the bedroom light and not look down the rest of the corridor.

Don't look down the rest of the bloody corridor.

And yet… I can't help but brandish the lantern, like my weapon, to the dark, enjoying the power it wields.

There's nothing down there. Just closed bedroom doors and–

What the hell is that? At the end of the corridor—*EYES* glinting back at me! It's that thing! It's waiting for me!

I move to turn and run back down the stairs when I hear the loud screeching sound echoing up the hallway, the bloodcurdling sound momentarily paralysing me as I watch the eyes grow larger and larger as the thing speeds towards me.

"AAAAAAAAAAAAAAARGH!" I scream as the barn owl glides over my head, circles around the entrance hall, and then perches itself on the opposite railing.

Oh… I can't even express myself anymore. All I can produce is a series of babbling sounds as I run hands over my face and fingers through my hair.

The owl screeches one more time as if mocking me. Oh, God. What is it with these animals sounding like bloody monsters anyway? You're supposed to sound like a bird. Sound like a bloody bird!

How the hell did that thing even get in here? *Window on the opposite side?*

Oh, I am so done with this place. I move forward, eager to get to that room to confirm that Sarah isn't here, and then leave never to bloody return.

Creak!

I spin around. That odious inimitable sound of someone or some*thing* stepping on a wood floor.

What is that? Did I just see something move down there? That shadow at the end of the corridor. I'm sure it just moved. *Stop it!* It's hard to tell. There's a window there, but without any moonlight, it's just a black hole of–

Creak!

Against my better judgement, I hold up the lantern in that direction. But it's too weak to penetrate that far.

"Sarah?" The word pushes its way out of my lips, and I wait as the wind makes its presence felt by thumping on doors like beasts in their cages and rattling terrified keys in their homes.

What is that, in the dark? I can't be sure. You don't need to be. This is all in your head, remember? Autosuggestion. You're in the perfect place for it. You know this. You've been here before. Focus.

"*B o y,*" a voice, barely a whisper, reaches out from the dark and punches my heart, knocking it up a gear.

I squint into the gloom, wishing the light from this lantern to travel further, but it can't.

"*B o y!*" It's a loud whisper now. Sharper. Closer. But I still can't see anything. I can't–

…there! Barely noticeable, something shifting, living on the edges of the light, bending, and shaping the flickering peaks of the l beam into an outline of some kind.

Oh… what is that?

Stop it. Stop. This doesn't exist. It doesn't exist. It's in your head!

I squeeze my eyes shut. Wait a few seconds and then reopen them. The *thing* has gone. There's nothing there now but blackness.

"*BOY!*" a voice screams in my left ear so loud, I jolt sideways, smack my face against the doorframe, trip and stumble into the bedroom, the impact knocking the lantern out of my hand and snuffing it out once more.

"Fuck!"

I shuffle backwards, hands, butt, and feet into the room in a sideway slide until the cold wall touches my back, startling me.

I gawp at the open door, at the blackness beyond the threshold, and wait for it to shift and for something to step through into the light cast by the lantern on the bedside table. This is the light I've been seeing.

"SARAH!" I yell. Hoping with every fibre of my being that she's going to emerge from the bathroom.

She doesn't. She isn't in here. My heart sinks.

I look around the room and catch sight of something that gives me both hope and dismay in equal measure. Her bag is on the bed. Her car keys are beside it. There's even a closed medium-sized box nearby, which means she must have started packing. So, she's got to be here.

My cheek is burning from its impact with the doorframe. I gingerly feel it and wince. It hurts, but I don't think it's bleeding. Probably just grazed.

Flickering catches my attention, and I look over. One of those moths has appeared out of nowhere. It flutters around the box on the bed several times before landing on it. I watch its cylindrical abdomen tattooed with a human skull as it crawls, antennae twitching, testing for clues.

I don't know if it's my imagination, but it sounds like there's very faint tapping coming from inside that box. I can't be sure because it's barely audible.

Tick! Tick! Tap!

I snap my head upward to the window and then slowly release the breath I'm holding. I thought it was more of those things, but it's actually a swarm of a different kind; snow pelting the glass, mimicking the sound of beating wings.

Flickering again, and turn back to the box. The moth takes flight to run a jittery sortie above and around the lantern on the bedside table, moving across the room over to the open door where–

"OH…SHIT!"

A pair of round unblinking eyes and a ghostly white face is wearing the dark like a shroud. Watching me!

With that door wide open, I'm totally exposed. Maybe I should make a run for it, shove the door shut, but the thing is too close. It'll be in the room before I even make it over there.

We stare off. Neither of us blinks as I slowly slide my way back up the wall. I've got to try.

Screeeetch!

"OH! FUCKING THING!"

The eyes fall backwards. There's a beat and whooshing sound, and I run shaky hands over my face and hair.

That bloody owl!

Creak!

The sound is coming from outside. Out of sight. Down the corridor.

I take a deep breath. Rub my temple. My head is pounding, but I can't tell if that's due to the impact with the doorframe or the fact that my nerves are pulled so tight, I feel they're quite literally going to snap at any moment.

"Sarah?" I utter, hopefully, even though I know it isn't her. *Oh, Sarah, where are you? What's happened to you, baby?*

"B O Y!"

I don't think about it. I launch myself at the door. As I do, I hear footsteps running up the corridor to intercept me; I scream. A whole animalistic roar reverberates around the room as I grab the door and shove it closed, but the thing barely connects with the lock before an almighty blow from the other side propels it open once more, smacking me in the face, launching me backwards, crashing to the floor once more.

I remain where I am for several seconds. Stunned by the pain burning through my nervous system. I'm bleeding from my nose. The blood dribbling over my lip. I dab it with the back of my sleeve and look up to see what hit me....

There's nothing there, just the door swinging eerily back and forth. I wait, listening for telltale sounds, but there's nothing but the disgruntled wind buffeting the building.

I touch my nose with the back of my hand and look at it. It's smeared with a dark sticky substance that can only be blood. I am *not* imagining this.

I groan as my left wrist pulses with pain. I think I've sprained it or something, and putting weight on it is not helping. So, I turn to inspect it to see if there's any visible damage and yelp when two small pale hands reach out from the shadow under the bed and grab it.

I snatch my hand away and shuffle backwards. *Oh, god...* There's something under the bed. I can see the outline now, but I somehow know it isn't that *thing*.

So, cautiously, I peek under the bedframe. It's dark underneath here but light enough for me to see two small dark eyes glistening with tears in the flickering lamplight.

Oh hell… what kind of mind trip is this?

I open my mouth to say something but stop when the eyes turn to become the facial profile of a little boy! He's about Toby's age, in his pyjamas. Even in the dim light, I can see that he's shivering and scrutinizing the open doorway as if expecting somebody to walk through it at any moment.

Shivers wash up and down my spine. I don't know what the eff is going on. I'm so confused. This has got to be a nightmare, another of those shitty dreams. "Wake up, Battista… wake the fuck up!"

When I refocus, the boy is looking at me once more. Small Roman nose. A mop of black hair. There's something vaguely familiar about him, but I can't quite work out what until I notice the pattern on his pyjama sleeve.

No. I chuckle to myself. *No.* Now I know I'm bloody dreaming because… *No. Dinosaurs? Really?*

My chuckling must be out loud because the terror etched on the boy's face increases as if he's afraid that someone might hear me to the point where he places a small chubby finger over his lips.

"Shhhhhhh," he says and then, slowly, turns and points towards the door. I follow the action back to the doorway and to the blackness beyond the threshold. But I see nothing.

Seconds drift by. The wind whistles and howls. Nothing happens.

When I look back at the boy, I see the vapour of his breath drift out into the lamplight as it becomes faster and shallower as he waves at me rapidly, desperately.

He wants me to join him under the bed. *Hell no!* This isn't happening.

Come on, Marc! Wake up. This isn't happening. It isn't real. Just wake up and–

B O Y!

The angry shriek is coming from the black corridor that has seemingly taken on a sinister force of its own. A living, breathing thing hellbent on dispensing terror.

I feel a cold hand touch mine and yelp again.

"Fuck!"

It's him. Pyjama boy has crawled out from under the bed to take my hand and urge me to follow him back to his makeshift sanctuary. To hide under there.

I glance at the door.

Creak. Clunk. Creak. Clunk.

Footsteps. Moving fast now. Drawing nearer.

I glance back at those supplicating eyes before reluctantly obliging. I wedge my six-foot-something-frame under the bed as the lantern flickers and sputters, begging to be released from its metal enclosure so that it too can abscond with us as the footsteps… no, not footsteps, more like a series of creaky floorboard protestations, draw near.

B O Y! The voice calls with a reptilian hiss. It's closer now. So close, it almost feels like whoever it is has entered the room.

My heart is hammering so loudly I'm sure it can be heard tapping on the floor. Seconds ago, I was ready to confront this bully, but now I'm not so sure.

And I can hear my little companion's breaths coming thick and fast now. Those tiny plumes of vapour chugging out in front of me. And I reach out to put a comforting hand on his arm when he starts screaming.

At first, I think I've done something to hurt him, but then I realise as I watch those small eyes glint with tear-streaked terror that it isn't me at all, but something else. Something that, to my incredulous horror, I cannot see! And it's tugging at him. Tugging at him as a wild predator would its prey, each horrifying jerk dragging him backwards from under the bed.

Tug! Scream!

Tug! Screaming! Eyes wide. Beseeching!

I reach out, grab the boy's outstretched hand, pull him close to me, and feel his sobbing body tremble against mine. "It's okay. It's alright," I whisper.

The tugging has stopped. The room has fallen silent but for the meteorological elements and the hiccup-riddled sobs of my ward.

"Shhhh…" I comfort holding the boy's body tight. "It's okay, buddy, you're okay."

The room seems empty again. No air displacement. No negative energy. No creak of floorboards.

I think of Sarah and wonder… is she okay? Did this happen to her too? *Sarah!*

More screaming! When I refocus, it's to see long bony talons with ragged black nails crawl, like spider legs, down the side of the bed.…

Click… click… click… scratch.

…they linger there, unmoving for several agonising seconds before bony hands, shaped like claws, reach out of the dark, just inches from my face, to snap at the boy's hair.

I snatch my head back.

He wails in horror.

Then again! Reaching. Snapping. I slap them away! Reach! Snap! Slap! Reach Snap! Slap!

Again…. Swipe! Scrape! Swipe Scrap!

"No! Stop it! Stop! Leave him alone!" I yell angrily. "Leave him alone!"

But the withered claws relentlessly persist no matter what I do, until eventually, the hideous tendril fingers slither into the boy's mop of hair and start tugging. I watch him jolt forward.

Once!

Twice! In an ear-splitting series of traumatised wails. I wrap my arm around the boy's tiny body and hold on with every fibre of my being until I hear the gruesome sound of hair being wrenched from its roots.

"NOOOOOO!" I scream. "NOOOOO! LEAVE HIM ALONE! LEAVE HIM ALONE!"

Drag. Tear. Rip! Drag. Tear! Rip!

But it does not cease, and with an agonised wail of my own, I reluctantly let go. I let bloody go and watch the boy being dragged away from me and out from under the bed until the dinosaur-patterned pyjamas are swallowed up by the gloom once more.

"NOOO!" I shriek. "NOOO!"

I told you what would happen if you wet the bed again.

No, mummy, please. Please don't put me in there again. Please! MUMMY! MUMMY!

Dragging. Splinters in my fingers. Grazes on my body. Pain in my scalp.

"MUMMY! MUMMY!" I am still screaming this when my eyes refocus, and the amber-coloured room comes into view once more.

Oh, shit.

I'm lying on the corridor floor. My extremities are numb from the cold, and my head is killing me. I groan as I sit up. Then wince at the pain on the side of my face. I think I've grazed it.

"Shit," I hiss.

It's the usual spooksville up here. Wind moaning. The eerie silence and flapping sheets of plastic that I've come to loathe almost as much as the real thing.

Did I just dream that? Doesn't feel like a dream. I must have bumped my head even harder than I thought.

Shit. I move to stand up.

What's that? Tickling my hand. *A spider!* Relatively small, but I can already feel the disgust when I flick it away, and it immediately rights itself and scampers off. Gigantic shadow companion trailing after it. Ugh!

Oh, God. I crawl to my feet because the idea of spending another second at eye level with that thing is already making my skin crawl.

You know why you hate spiders, right?

Shut up.

That dream says it all.

Shut up.

She used to lock you in that dark cupboard after dragging you there by your hair and–

"I said shut up!" I snap, although there's nobody here to hear me.

I sigh. "Fuck! Now I'm talking to myself."

I shouldn't have come back here. Yes, you should. You need to find Sarah.

I straighten up. Ignoring the stab of pain in my back and the sting on my cheek, I half walk, half stagger across the bedroom to the window where I cup my eyes with my hands and look out of the glass. I can't see much out there. The moon's back again, but I can still see gigantic dark shapes scurrying across the sky. It definitely snowed again. The walls seem whiter where snow is being blown across the courtyard.

I won't be leaving this place any time soon, assuming I can even get back to the main road and a car.

My heart sinks. How have I managed to get myself in this mess again? I mean, I know it's been my life's work to see how I can royally stuff up anything good about it, but this time, I think I may just have outdone mys–

What's that? No. I wasn't dreaming it after all. Sarah's bag and keys; they're still on the bloody bed! She's still here! And… that carton is still on the bed too. I can see its reflection and… I don't think I'm imagining it; that box is shaking. It's bloody shaking!

I turn around. It's stopped. Or has it?

I stare at the thing for several seconds. Snow collapses against the glass. Timber creaks.

I walk over to the bed and stand in front of it. That box is shaking. It's definitely shaking. Why is that? And why am I loathed to bloody find out?

I close my eyes. Wrestle with the ridiculous anxiety that's pulling at my last nerve, bringing a twitch to my face that does its level best to aggravate the thumping in my head.

Reluctantly, because my life is nothing but a series of perpetual shocks to the system, I reach out, pick up the box and shake it.

It seems empty.

So, I carefully unfold the flaps, yelp, and throw the thing back towards the bed, only it misses by a few centimetres, and instead of landing back on top of the bed, it rebounds off it, spins in the air, and dumps its contents at my feet.

I react instinctively and leap backwards so far that I end up crashing against the dresser and sliding down to land on my backside on the floor, wincing at the flare of pain in my back.

Now, I am in pole position to experience the one thing I have declared to be my worst possible fear. Somehow, and I don't know how, but it is being realised before my very eyes. The result is that I now find myself literally incapacitated with terror and can only watch as the wave of horror spreads out in an arc of scampering limbs heading straight for me.

Spiders!

Hundreds. Maybe even thousands for the difference it makes of black, shiny, bulbous compound eyes scurrying their way to the four corners of the room.

Head paralysed, I swivel my eyeballs to look right, to the exit, and imagine myself being there. When that doesn't work, I do it again. I imagine myself getting to my feet and running screaming from here, but my limbs have no intention of obeying.

I am so scared of these eight-legged freaks of all shapes and sizes that I can't even bring myself to wipe my face, which is now itching with the wriggling beads of cold sweat. I'm shaking. Nerves tight. Teeth chattering as I watch the tsunami of horror inch closer.

They're at my feet now. Some of the thick black ones hesitate at my boots, while the smaller ones relentlessly crawl up and over my legs towards my crotch. Others, soft and hairy, crawl over my hands and then my arms, triggering a wail of an inhuman scream that I can't even believe is being produced by me. Still, I'm instantly silenced by the one big black bastard I see through my peripheral vision crawling up my chest in a jittery, jerky motion. I picture its angular legs prodding at my lips and tongue as it makes its way into my open mouth, causing an involuntary reaction to bite down, crunching on its limbs and tasting the pâté squishiness.

Oh…. I can feel that bile slithering up my throat now. I'm hyperventilating. Tiny, short gasping breaths through my nose as I clench my jaw together in an instinctive reaction to avoid realising my premonition.

I swallow down the bile, but it regurgitates, bringing with it waves of shivers that wash up and down my extremities.

The lack of oxygen is making me feel giddy.

Breathe! You're not getting enough air! You're going to pass out, you idiot! Breathe! Breathe properly!

I can't. I can't!

The giant *thing* is closer now and is being joined by a posse of its mates; only it has changed direction, crawling sideways like a crab as if offended by my thoughts.

Oh God, help me! I think I can smell them. Oh no. I'm not imagining this. It's real. I can smell their disgusting vinegary stench.

I swivel my eyes around the room. They are everywhere, enlarged and multiplied by their shadows.

I'm going to be sick! I'm going to be sick! There's no stopping it now. "UGH!" The vomit explodes out of my mouth and over my chest in a disgusting burning porridge-like spatter.

Tears burn my eyes as the acidic stench fills my nostrils. I gag, willing my hands to move, my body to do something, but it won't. I can't fucking move!

MOVE! YOU BASTARD! MOVE!

Tears slide out of my eyes, making a pair of the insectoid marauders hesitate. I'm going to pass out, or I'm going to have a coronary right here, right now.

The big bastard is moving again. He was temporarily deterred by the spatter of puke but now seems hell-bent on revenge as it prods my neck with its chunky black legs. Testing the area before it brings the rest of its limbs forward.

I'm just a trembling wreck now. Frozen to the spot. Head and eyes gazing forward. Throat closing. Open mouth squelching as I try to suck in air. Try to absorb oxygen.

Move, Marco! Move!

I can't. All of my motor functions have been disabled. The only thing I can do is stare forward and watch as the shadow under the bed stirs in the lamplight.

No, wait. I'm not imagining this. That shadow *is* actually moving, morphing into a humanoid shape of some kind, but that can't be. It can't be. Can it?

But it is… crawling out from under the bed, slowly, methodically. It appears in no hurry to evade the arachnid invasion.

Oh no. It's one of them. That's it. No! NO! NO! That's not possible. Spiders aren't that big, and, um, shadows don't move like either! SHADOWS DON'T MOVE!

And yet, this one is. That's it. It's happened. The straw that broke the camel's back. I have finally skidded back down the snake into crazy land.

The big bastard is crawling up my neck now, spindly legs prodding and then walking over my beard as its comrades party in my hair. My only response is to tremble, to shiver like some mentally afflicted wretch, eyeballs swivelling everywhere but focussing on nothing but the shadow that is slowly unfurling, rising, standing.

But this can't be right, can it? A person in a long coat with a furry hood for a face is slowly walking over to me.

"No… n… n… ot… re… al…. n… not… n… n… ot pos… possible," I jabber. All of this is just an illusion brought on by immense trauma.

And yet, the figure is getting closer, casually squelching and scrunching arachnoids with each step.

The shadow is lowering its hood now, and I can see. I can see, but I don't believe it. I don't. I can't believe it.

"Y…. You're… n… not her!" I wail. "You're… n… n… not real! You're not real!" I whine as my eyeballs swivel upward to the figure towering over me. And… and. What's that? What's that in your gloved hand? What are you going to do with that? I say. No. I didn't say that. I think I thought it.

They're lifting it now. Lifting that thing with both hands.

I squeeze my eyes shut. This isn't real. This isn't real. Go on. Run through it. Check through it now.

Could this really be happening here and now?
"No."
Is anybody else affected by it?
"No."
On balance, how likely is this to be real?
"Ow, that hurt!" Then my world turns black.

43

THE LETTER

Dearest Doctor,

Yes. I know you don't exist anymore, but I still like addressing this stuff to you anyway. After all, you were the one who started all of this. The one who encouraged me to *explore* my feelings. Well, I did, and look where that got me.

Anyway, surprise!

I know, you probably thought you'd got rid of me, but I did say that there was only one reason why I watched those black and white movies, and that was to remind myself never to be as pathetic as some of those simpering bitches.

I am a fighter. A survivor. In this case, literally.

Now, I know you'd love nothing more than for me to repeat the same mistakes of old, but I'm much cleverer than that. That's why I've changed my passwords to something much more suitable to how I'm feeling right now. However, without mentioning names, I can tell you that there's one person who, for all his grandstanding, has not.

Wow. What a night, eh? Talk about *a night to remember.* Did you know that there's a black and white film by that name? It's about the sinking of the Titanic. Rather apt, don't you think?

Yes. My husband has put me through a lot over the years. And yet, despite everything, all of the lies, the cheating, the humiliation, the imminent *death*, it wasn't until the very moment when he spoke six of the last words we'd ever share that I truly appreciated just how much he has damaged me.

Picture it… it's biblical stuff. The house had half sunk into the ocean, and we were quite literally standing on the brink of oblivion. There's the cacophony of wind turbulence, the roar of the waves, and this fucking mist whizzing around the room playing havoc with my hair, and…you know, I'll admit it, I was scared. Actually, I was petrified. So, like one of those damsels in distress, I grabbed his arm, I clung onto it and said – well, it was more of a scream actually – I screamed, *STAY! I am your wife!*

And do you know what he did? He just looked at me, at my hand on his arm like I was some bloody stranger, and told me to let go. Well, I think his words were more like, *get your fucking hands off me.*

I couldn't believe it. Because, as you know, it isn't always about the things people say. It's how they make you feel. And he spoke those words with such venom, such coldness, that I just felt cheap, discarded, worthless.

Again.

And why? Because of the bumpkin bitch.

And *that was* the moment I knew. *That* was the moment when I truly understood I was never going to recover from this as well as the agony of losing my boy, again, by his hand.

It was all too much to bear. I just didn't see the point in surviving that place. I was ready to give up. Prepared to walk over that cliff of my own free will.

But then, an opportunity presented itself. You know, one of those spur of the moment things where you quite literally have seconds to choose the course of your destiny.

What do you do?

Well, if you're a cardboard cut-out, you let yourself get shafted, *again*. But if you're Elisabeth Stevenson, you take action.

So, when I saw that man, my husband, turn his back on me, the mother of his child, to save that bitch, you can imagine how I felt. The sense of betrayal was so overwhelming I could barely breathe. I mean, seriously…even as we're facing imminent fucking death, that bastard was putting yet another of his whores before what was left of his own family.

Well, I just started trembling. And it had nothing to do with the cold up there and everything to do with the rage that I could quite literally feel bubbling beneath my skin like hot tar. Clogging my veins, oozing through the hole in my heart.

I was like, hang on a minute, after everything that's happened, everything you've done, *this* is how you treat me, this is how you try to make amends?

Oh no. Oh no, no, no. I can't have that. I just can't. You need to pay. You need to fucking suffer for what you've done, for what you've turned me into.

I HATE YOU! I FUCKING HATE YOU!

I didn't even think about it. As he was gawping into the abyss, I saw my chance, and I took it. I really don't know what came over me. It was weird. Just this surge of energy. Of power, you know. Like I could do anything, I was afraid of nothing. So, I yelled, I yelled at the top of my voice, *MARCO, THERE'S SOMEONE BEHIND YOU!*

That someone being me, of course. And dear doctor, I can tell you, in my whole life, I don't think anything has ever felt as sublime or as satisfying as shoving that cheating traitor of a bastard over the edge.

My only regret was that it was over too soon. One second, he was standing there, and the next….

So, my first thought was to step over...You know, take a look, make sure, but I thought no way. No bloody way, knowing my luck so far, the floor will break away, and I end up down there with him.

No, thank you.

So, instead, I heeded the very last suggestion my husband ever made to me, and that was to make my way down the corridor to the kitchen.

Luckily, I'd left my bag with my phone, purse, and some cash I had already withdrawn for eventualities.

I grabbed them, then climbed out of the window as fast I could, just as other sections of that shitty place collapsed into the ocean.

And I'll be honest. It did take me a while to pull myself together. Sitting there in what was the driveway now turned into a rushing river complete with assorted bloody rodents.

Ugh!

It was odd because just minutes before, the thought of those disgusting furry things anywhere near me repulsed me, but there, in that moment, it all felt different. I assumed it was because I was in shock. You know, after losing my husband and everything.

So, it took a few minutes of me gormlessly gawping at the remains of that place and trying to keep my balance in the freezing torrent of water for me to absorb some of the enormity of what had just taken place. And I kind of braced myself, you know, because I expected to feel bad. Start sobbing or something, but it was so weird. I even pulled one of my ugly cry faces, expecting the tears to come, but they didn't. Instead, do you know what I did?

I started smiling.

Can you picture that? Me, sitting in the middle of a river like one of those cheap water features, just staring at that place with this whole strange warm sensation flowing through me like an electric current. You know, I felt more alive in that moment than I ever did in all the years of living with that prick!

It was a sign. A signal. A rebirth.

So, I finally dragged myself to my feet, kicked a few of those furry things from me, and, slowly, through my cold-numbed mind, started processing what should happen next.

The logical thing was to get to a payphone. I knew I couldn't use my mobile phone because, well, it had been soaking in the water all that time. But it wasn't just that. I knew the signal was crap there, and, most importantly, I wasn't sure I wanted a record of my making the phone call. Not yet anyway. Not before I was sure about how I wanted to play this.

So, I took the soggy notes from my bag and ditched everything else.

It made sense to wait. This was the one thing that was clear to me. You know, reflect on how I was going to deal with the aftermath.

For a start, I needed to know if there were going to be any survivors. Not likely but, I knew I needed to be sure. After all, it would only take one survivor, one witness, to cause me to lose control of the narrative.

So, I took the blanket from our car, wrapped it around me, and made my way through the woods and out to the only phone box. I told myself that if one of those weirdos happened to see me, I would just have to play victim, but luckily it was the middle of the night. Not a soul in sight.

I asked the operator for a cab and waited for him to finally show. And, do you know, we'd barely climbed the hill out of that place, and I could already see the flashing blue lights of the emergency services.

Someone had already called it in. I could only hope it wasn't soon enough to make a difference.

I asked the driver to stop at a 24-hour supermarket, bought some cheap clothes and other essentials with cash, and changed in the women's toilets. Then I asked him to take me to the nearest place where I could spend the night. Lucky for me, the driver knew a dump run by one of his mates. Not somewhere I would usually choose, but hey, beggars can't be choosers. Besides, I was cold, tired, and a bit shaky.

So, I camped out in front of the TV, duvet wrapped around me, snacks I'd bought from the supermarket to hand, and waited. Slept.

Waited and slept some more with the TV tuned into the news channel the whole time until eventually:

BREAKING NEWS. *Landslide in the sleepy village of Porthcove kills three.*

I stopped mid-chomp on one of those cheap, no-flavour-mass-produced croissants. Suddenly, I'd lost all appetite, and, in fact, I was quite ready to puke.

Three people, *only*? Out of all of them. Fuck! Not quite what I expected. And what about me? No mention of me being missing, presumed dead. Nothing.

It took them a whole fucking day to finally announce the names of those *who perished in the freak accident.* Well, you can imagine my surprise when one of those names was mine! *Missing, presumed dead,* along with those two idiots from the institute.

So okay. Not exactly how I expected this thing to go down.

Crap.

I would just like to take a moment to say that I am *not* one of those psycho killer bitches from hell. *I'm not*. At least, I didn't think I was. That whole thing with Marc at the end was just me acting on the spur of the moment. This is why *take your time* and *don't do anything rash* have become a bit of a motto. I had already been caught once for not thinking everything through. I wasn't going to let it happen again.

It wasn't easy. Oh no, because the urge to go over there and smother him once and for all with a fucking pillow or even with my bare hands for added satisfaction was strong, but I resisted it.

I had a choice to make – yes, another bloody one – make myself known by becoming one of the *survivors,* or take a little longer to think things through. After all, I was *missing, presumed dead* now.

So, I emigrated to Scotland. I don't know why for the difference it made, but it was furthest away from the scene of the crime, and it made me feel better. Then, I did the obvious spy movie rubbish; I bought a cap, sunglasses, grew and dyed my hair.

As it turns out, nobody was really looking for me. Certainly not on land.

As you already know, my parents are and always have been overbearing. Nothing was personal for me. Especially that whole awful time where, thanks to my arsehole of a husband, I was forced to move back in with them. So, they knew all about my current accounts, but nothing of the cash I squirrelled away in a safety deposit box for my love nest with Cristian.

And yes, of course, I told myself that everything would be easier if I just appeared on their doorstep and feigned amnesia or something, played the whole *Gone Girl* routine. But days turned into weeks,

weeks turned into months, and I just loved hearing all about what a wonderful person I was from people I hadn't spoken to in years, including that two-faced, cheating bastard of a husband of mine.

Yes. At first, he obviously resisted but eventually jumped on that bandwagon of shitty daytime talk shows, instantly killing interest in the story. I mean, really, how amateur can you fucking be? Everybody knows that once you give it up to the media, they lose interest in you.

And so that was it. The world forgot about me. Oh, alright, England forgot. I became a punchline like those two twats from the mental home. Rest in peace and all that crap.

So, now what?

The idea came to me during a bad dream in which I was standing on one side of a busy road and Marc on the other. I kept calling to him, but no matter what I did, how loudly I screamed, how much I waved, he couldn't see or hear me. It was like I was a ghost to him.

A ghost. Suddenly, I was grinning again.

By this time, my hair was getting quite long, which was good when I was *off duty*, but there were times when I needed my hair to be exactly as it was that night. So, I bought a wig and a few other accessories.

And then I started researching in meticulous detail all things Marco Battista. He'd already spilt his guts about the stuff happening in his life. Him; completing his qualification as a therapist. Her; becoming a vet. Both; playing happy family in London with that shitty dog.

I watched endless YouTube videos on a variety of subjects and learned a lot of new handy skills. I had no idea that there were so many *how-to* videos out there! There is a tutorial for literally everything, including a whole collection on CBT (*Cognitive Behavioural Therapy)*. It's something I've heard my husband drone on about countless times. CBT helps retrain the mind to overcome certain obstacles. It included elements such as *systematic desensitisation,* which helps the mind overcome phobias and fears. For example, I hate spiders, but I know that my husband hates them even more. That's why I've enrolled in a course and am confident I'll be ready by showtime.

And so, for this to work, I can't be seen. So, I'm careful to avoid places with security cameras. I wear hats and glasses, except when I want him to see me. That's when I pull on the wig, follow him at a good distance, and occasionally let him catch fleeting glimpses of his dead wife. It's fucking priceless! Even at a distance, I can literally see the blood drain from his face.

Of course, there have already been a few close calls. One time in

London, the other in a supermarket where, luckily for me, he knocked a little boy over while trying to give chase. The police were called. Brilliant. If I could, I'd have asked them for a copy of the security footage. Although, there was a moment I thought he might. Not that they could see much. I'm always careful.

Anyway, so they moved from London to some fancy house in the New Forest. Can you believe this fucker? I had to carry him for years while he was *studying,* and that amounted to nothing. Now, he's a bloody property developer with a gorgeous country house and brand new BMW parked in the driveway.

Oh, I just realised that I hate him even more now. Is that even possible? I don't know. I just know that now more than ever, I'm determined to make him suffer.

So, I stalked the estate agent's website and found out all about HOLT. Then, I scoured the web for all information about Carson's super modern smart home; it's the first of its kind, it controls everything - Lighting, heating, security. Etc.

Perfect.

I visited the support website, downloaded a PDF of the manual. There's a smart display in every room, an app and a web portal through which all of this stuff can be controlled remotely.

All I needed to do was guess my husband's password. Well, not quite. You see, after all the preaching that prick did about password security, he still hasn't changed the one we shared. I suppose he must have thought that with me gone, there was no reason to.

That, and he still uses the same email address. Duh.

So I was in. That was bloody easy! *Insert eye-roll here – idiot!*

Now, I can change, update anything I like and then delete all traces of it.

That's when the fun truly began.

Lights on. Lights off. Security system activated and deactivated. One day, I waited in the woods—at a healthy distance because that fucking dog keeps detecting me—and after they left, I went in and created my own biometric profile for some extra fun. The best part, with admin privileges, I could literally make any change I want, and then—because it's such poorly designed software—I could erase the audit trail to make it look like it never happened.

Beautiful.

So, while all this was going on, I kept a close eye on his email. Learned all about the wedding and how those two must have been desperate to entrust it to him. That bloke couldn't organise a piss-up in a bloody brewery!

Anyway, I decided that Halloween—which by the way, is a shitty day for a wedding—is going to be particularly gruesome for my husband this year.

I bought myself a new dress for the special occasion. I deactivated the security system and the super all-bells-and-whistles fire management system and made my way over there.

I used my usual route through the woods, careful not to reveal myself to anybody other than the old hubby. Yes, I had a little fun playing peekaboo with him from behind a giant tree. Then, when they were all busy watching the rest of the ceremony, I snuck around to the front door and saw the strangest thing.

Smoke.

Odd. It's almost as if I thought it, and then it happened. And for one second there, I was really freaked out. But then I saw someone standing in the hallway. I've no clue who she was, some scruffy urchin with wild silver hair. She was just standing there, staring at me as the smoke thickened around her until she was wholly absorbed by it.

I was monetarily transfixed until I heard someone scream. Then, I snapped out of my daze and ran back into the woods only to find a whole crowd of people running towards me.

Luckily, I didn't recognise any of them, so I assumed they didn't recognise me, but I kept my head down and hurried off but not before snatching a glance of the back garden. And there he was, my husband, screaming and ranting at the house like it was a person, but there was nobody there. And all I could think was…. *yes, finally.*

I know that sounds awful, but that bastard was setting up home with that new trog just months after my death! What does that say about him, eh?

So, they've moved into *Frost Lake Manor*. Things are so much easier there. And creepier. I bet he's hating it. The place isn't even finished. There's no security. Nothing.

One thing's for sure; it's worth millions. A quick search confirmed that. *Millions!* He's come a long way from the peasant I married. I think it's only fair that I should get a share of that. Oh, alright, that I should get all of it. You know, when he's carted off, and there's nobody left to inherit any of that money, but his long-suffering wife who has spent the last year or so as an amnesiac trying to find her way home.

The plan still needs a little fine-tuning but based on today's performance that I witnessed from the safety of the forest, I'd say that it's well on its way. I mean, he's already reverted to type, punching the shit out of the reporter I anonymously tipped off. I've seen that man at his worst, but even I haven't seen him like that. This is a stark reminder that if the situation calls for it, I need to be extra careful, you know, make sure he's kept under control.

So, this is it. The plan is finally reaching its climax. It's been a long time coming, but this was definitely worth the wait. I have had more fun in the past year than I have in all the years I was married to that man.

And the best part is yet to come. God willing, everything will go to plan this time, but if it doesn't, then so be it. I have nothing left to lose.

44

THIS IS WHERE

I LEAVE YOU

…I'm being dragged down the corridor by my hair. My scalp ablaze with pain. Tears are streaming down my hot and blotchy face in sharp contrast to the cold, wet patch at the crotch of my pyjamas.

"Mummy please! PLEASE! I promise I won't do it again! MUMMY! PLEASE! PLEASE!"

Stop wailing, or I'll cut it off! A voice behind and above me hisses. Do you want me to cut it off? DO YOU?

"NO!"

If it acts like an animal, it gets treated like an animal.

"I'm sorry. I promise I won't do it again. I p… p… promise, mummy, please! Mummy. I don't want to go in there… please! There's a sp… sp… spiders down there."

Scraping. Furniture moving. Metallic clang. A squeal of a wooden trapdoor.

Get in!

"Mummy, no!" I cry. Cowering on the cold floor, small hands

trembling protectively above my head.

It gets in, or it gets punished!

"MUMMY, NO!" I scream with terror as I look down at the gaping square mouth of blackness. "MUM–"

But the word is cut short, my breath taken away by the sudden tug of strong hands on my arms. I look up into the maniacal face of a woman with long black hair that looks like my mother but whose face seems much different. Wild. Angrier. It's the demonic twin sister, the one that hurts me when my mother disappears into herself.

She is glaring down at me. Screaming into my face, with narrowed eyes and a snarling mouth, demanding that I let go of the table leg, but I can't. I'm scared. I'm so scared.

"PLEASE, MUMMY. PLEASE!" I beg, clinging on for my life.

But my supplication goes unheard, and one by one, my mother's long bony fingers pry open my small chubby ones, and my hold is slowly but surely relinquished.

Now, my legs are dangling over the black hole. The howling monster of the dark is already calling to me, beckoning me inside as the cold, dampness encircles my toes and tugs, willing me to yield to the gloom. And eventually, tears streaming, heart-pounding, my achy wrist tires, and I'm falling, falling, falling….

I jerk awake with a yelp!

And relief floods through me when I discover that I've landed on the relatively warm wood floor and not the cold stone slabs of the cellar.

But the feeling is momentary as I slowly become aware of the ringing in my ears and the throbbing pain at the side of my head.

"Ow fuck…" I touch the area gingerly. It's crusty with dried blood. I've been bleeding. Bleeding?

What happened?

I look around the room. It's nighttime. Lantern burning on the side unit. And it's hazy in here. Not sure how. Is that the room or me?

Oh shit. I think that might be me?

What happened?

I rummage around in the fog of my mind for an answer, but there's nothing there. Just blankness.

A tickling sensation draws my attention to my hand, so through a somewhat blurry vision, I look down to see a spider on it. "Ugh!" I shake it off, but then I see another on my leg, chest, and others on the floor around me.

I yelp and jump to my feet, but the room starts swaying, and I crash against the doorframe as a sickly, giddy merry-go-round sensation grips me and threatens to knock me off my feet more.

"Oh shit."

Oh…. All the lights are out, yet it's still quite bright in the hallway, which doesn't make sense. But then I look up through the glass canopy. A supernaturally large moon is shining like a lighting rig on a movie set, highlighting the outlines of doors to bedrooms, the bannister, and stairs out of here.

The dust sheets are still flapping in a breeze, but there's no snow now. No snow! That's it. It was snowing, and I was in the bedroom. No lights.

I flick the switch on the door next to me a couple of times, but nothing happens. So, I move forward, gingerly, tentatively because every movement, every turn of my head makes me feel queasy and like I want to spew. Ugh… I can already smell the acrid stench of vomit. How's that possible? No. Wait. It happened already.

Ugh… tickling in my hair. What's that? Ugh! I flick at it. Something drops heavily to the floor and scampers off.

Oh, God. My head is killing me. Have I been drinking, had an accident? I need my phone. Need help.

I frisk myself, but there's nothing in my pockets. No phone. No keys.

Sarah.

Yes. Sarah! Where are you? You left. Didn't you? Went back to Porthcove.

Oh, God. Now I feel worse. The throbbing in my head seems thicker, the pain more acute —if that's even possible.

What happened? Feels bad, like a hangover. Tighter though, skin stretched over my skull. Is that it? Did I drink too much? That makes sense, right? Yeah, but the injury? This stuff on my head feels like dried blood.

Buddy.

Buddy. What about Buddy? Where's he? I was in a cage with him. No, not in the cage. Next to it. The vet. Oh no. He was; he *is* still at the vets. I was in trouble. Trouble? Why? What happened?

Shit. This gets worse by the second. Not sure I even want to remember any more if it's all going to be this grim. It can't get any worse than a room full of spiders.

Oh God… yes… that's it! *The room was full of spiders.* What? No. *Full* of spiders? Fuck. That's like something straight out of my worst nightmares. Nightmare! I'm dreaming again. This is one of those dreams. Wait… um, no, I don't think so. The pain in my head, the numbness in my extremities. Doesn't feel like a dream.

I rub my face with the back of my sleeve, then look back through the door's threshold. *Oh, God…* that's not a nightmare. That shit's real. Oh, what! Real? Spiders and shadows decorate the room's walls and ceiling, dialling up the squirm factor, but it doesn't feel as bad as I expect it to. I think it might be because they're crawling slowly and not scuttling.

It's cold.

YES! I'm fucking cold! I'm so cold. Shivering. So, they must be too. Oh, fancy that… their crawl is nowhere near as disgusting as their scuttle.

I turn away from the sight.

Focus. You need to get help. I think you have a concussion.

Why would I have a concussion?

I can't remember. But the fog in your brain. The pain. The memory recall. The blood. There's a good chance you bumped your head.

I'm in front of the stairs now, but I hesitate. I can't. I can't let go of the wall. If I do, I'll fall over. I'll fall over! I'll fall down the stairs.

I need a car. I need to see Sarah. I need to talk to her, although I'm not sure why. Where are my keys?

I launch myself across the hallway to the railing, where I find myself staring into the precipice of the stairs. I gag and wretch as I watch them extend away from me then snap back like something out of dramatic movie zoom.

"I need to get down there. I need to get down–"

Slam!

What was that? It's coming from down the hallway, somewhere beyond in the dark.

Ignore it. Get out of here. Get to Sarah.

Sarah was here.

No. She isn't here. She left.

Car keys.

Yes. She left. Come on. Let's go.

Slam!

What is that? Ignore it. Get out of here. You don't know what's down there at the *end of the corridor.* That's where that banging is coming from.

I should be afraid. Big mansion lit only by moonlight, can barely see a few feet in front of me. My head is killing me. Yeah. All that. But I'm not. I'm actually in too much pain to care anymore. Is that in my head, though? The pain?

I prod at the ache on the side of my head.

"Ow fuck! That bloody hurts! That's real. That's got to be real! Ow… shit!"

Okay. Get out. Get to a hospital.

Run! You can't keep running.

Sarah?

Slam!

The exit is here, yawning in front of me. That noise is just a door slamming. Moving in a draft. It's of no interest to me.

None at all.

So why the fuck are you moving crablike across the balustrade in that direction?

I have no idea.

The banging is getting louder now, but the moonlight diminishes as I reach the end of the hallway, blocked out by the arch design of the alcove balcony overlooking the entrance hall.

Oh, bloody hell… I'm not feeling good. I think I want to be sick.

You've got a concussion. Turn back.

Slam!

Oh, yes. I can just about work out what it is now. The door to the roof. It's open.

Why?

I don't know.

I shuffle over to it… feeling my way across the wall as I can barely make it out in the dark.

Yep. Door open.

I open it and peer inside. I can't see much because of its circular shape, but I can hear that bloody ominous whistling of the gale through those slits. Oh, and look… moonbeams shining in like lasers. Yeah. Cute. As if the place isn't supernatural enough already.

Okay. I'm done. I need to go and get help as I really don't feel good.

I let the door go and feel my way back up the corridor but cower in place when a scream echoes down the stairwell and pierces the night.

"Sarah?"

I don't think… I stumble, feel my way back to the door, pull it open again. Oh shit! It's so much colder in here. Is that even possible?

Okay… I feel the wall, but my head just wants to lie down, so I kind of crawl up the rest of the way as the wind screams at me as if I have no place being here.

I agree.

The stone steps and walls are abrasive, freezing under my fingers. Maybe I should go back. I don't think that was Sarah. What would she be doing here? She left. *Oh shit! She did. She left me. Oh, no.*

I shake my head as I reach the top of the stairwell where I hear and see the thick wooden door is off the latch, swinging and banging back and forth in a bitterly cold wind that intermittently blows in my face with each open of the door.

Wow. Okay. Alright. That's quite refreshing. Good. It's clearing some of the fog from my mind, but I can still barely keep my eyes open. I could do with a nap, just a little one, right here.

Stop it! Wake up!

I shake the grogginess away and feel my way for the door by keeping my eyes closed because somehow that feels easier, not as nauseating.

I emerge from the well and am slapped across the face by a freezing wind screaming across the snow and whistling through cables with all of the boisterousness of a bully in a school playground.

The shock literally takes my breath away as I take in the winter landscape of sloping arches and chimneys that sparkle under the moonlight.

Porthcove. Dolce Vita. This is how it was that night. The only difference is that tonight the ice queen is already at work solidifying the snow. I can taste the frost in the air, and it's both invigorating and nausea-inducing.

I glance down. There are footprints in the snow, leading away from the stairwell, past the chimney stacks and sloped arches towards the centre of the roof.

"I can see your footprints," I hear someone say in a taunting, sing-song voice.

Did I just say that?

No. It was a female voice, but I don't think it was Sarah.

Movement catches my attention. Someone has just emerged from behind one of the arches. Short. Wearing a coat with a furry hood and, um, I squint into gloom… are they carrying an axe?

Someone was hiding under the bed. Oh, shit! Yes! That's it. They were hiding under the bed. Hit me across the head. With that thing?!

The door slams and I realise I let it go in my bewilderment.

Shit.

The figure turns to me. The face is now partially illuminated. No. It can't be.

I take a step forward almost lose my footing. I slip and slide a couple of times, arms failing back and forth. Head spinning. Stomach and balls-churning.

"Ellie?" I utter, incredulously. But it can't be. We've established this. It's in my mind. It can't be her. She's dead. And yet, glancing at the axe in her hand, I ask, "What are you doing?"

Ellie, my wife, pulls her hood down, releasing long blonde hair. Then she wipes her face with the back of her sleeve, cocks her head, and asks, "What does it look like?"

I close my eyes to dispel the vision in front of me, but when I open them again, she's still here.

"Seriously? You're bleeding from the head, and you still think this is one of your delusions?" my wife asks with one of her familiar irritated tones. "Maybe I should have hit you harder after all."

I squint at her and rock my head, "You hit me? Why?" I gasp incredulously.

"Why? Because it looked like you were about to have a heart attack, and that wasn't part of my plan."

"You planned... this?"

I watch her rock her head. "With a few deviations along the way. Yeah. Not as crazy as last time, eh?"

I squeeze my eyes and then open them again. No. Still here. "I don't know, El. You're standing on the rooftop of a creepy mansion with an axe in your hand."

"Oh, I see you're becoming your usual witty self. Maybe you need another swing."

I see the glint of the axe as she lifts it slightly, and somehow, it telepathically amplifies the ache to the side of my head. "You hit me with that?"

"The blunt side, obviously. Had to pull the *chop* a little as I didn't want you to snuff it. Not without witnessing the grand finale."

"Why would you do this?" I gasp in confusion.

She rolls her eyes. "Oh no. I'm not doing this last-minute villain reveals their motivation shit. If you haven't worked it out on your own then, you deserve everything that's coming to you. I'm fucking freezing!" She turns away from me and screams out into the night, "BITCH! Where are you?" Then she adds, "Just kidding... you know I can see your footprints, right?"

I step forward. "E...llie!" I call, but my voice is so feeble, it's stolen by the wind chill and carried off into the night. I try to increase the speed of my advance, but I don't have any energy reserves left. My mind feels like an old warehouse shutting down at the end of a long day. I've lost the sensation in my right hand, and I don't know if that's related to my head injury or the fact that I keep plunging it into the snowclad structures in front of me so I can use them as support.

Step, scuffle, step after step, scuffle step. Breath coming short and fast, in gasps rather than lung-filling usefulness like I've scaled a mountain.

I can see Ellie now. She's down by the sky lantern, about twenty feet in front of me, and I'm sure I can still see that maniacal grin on her face.

I wriggle my cold fingers.

What if, eh? What if this is all a dream? What if this pain, this dizziness, this cold that I'm feeling isn't real? That would be much better than this weird reality, right? Dead wife chasing current girlfriend with an axe on the rooftop. Come on, that's got to be a delusion, right? Help me out here. Help me because I really don't know how to recover from this. Made worse by the fact that I seem incapable of thinking straight. It's like my brain has been enveloped in this fog and, I, um, I think I might pass out right here in this patch of snow and just have a sleep. Just a little one.

"Oh Marco, quite the hero, eh? Not going to give up on his little family. Shame you didn't feel as strongly about the previous one." The last part of that sentence is spoken with disdain so ardent I expect it to melt the snow.

I've just realised that I've followed Ellie down to the centre of the roof. Oh shit. I'm sure that fog's getting thicker.

"Ellie... p... please stop this," I say seriously. Or at least I think I did.

My wife scoffs. "Or what? Are you going to stop me?"

"If I have to."

Her bitter, empty laugh bounces off the snow structures around us. "Have you seen the state of you lately? Not quite the handsome stud all those bitches, including this one, flocked to," she sneers at me. "When push comes to shove, Marc, you can't even stand up," she says. "Make no mistake. This time, I have full control of the situation. You're only here because I want you to be. You're only alive because it suits me. It suits *my* purpose. Do you understand?" she seethes.

She's about ten feet away now, axe twinkling from time to time like the rest of the glittery world around. "This is exactly as I want it. I want you to suffer in the same way you made me suffer. I want you to experience loss the same way I did. Raw, up-close, and personal."

I scowl at her. "What are you talking about? You think… you think that you're the only person who grieves for our son?" I shake my head. It's starting to feel really heavy.

I hear my wife scoff. "Yeah. You're heartbroken. New house. New girl. New life."

"You have no fucking idea," I spit.

"Of course I have!" she screams. "I have every fucking idea! I was there, remember? I just didn't have the luxury of retreating into a fucking fantasy to avoid the truth."

"Ellie… I know you're in pain. I know you suffered, and I know you blame me… but this isn't you," I say, shuffling forward.

My wife rolls her eyes, "*This* is your strategy? Try and *shrink* me to death? I'm more likely to die from terminal boredom."

"Ellie–"

"Look. Can we not do this? I'm just not interested in going through the whole *why* thing. All you need to know is that I did it because I hate you. I loathe you. I fucking despise you. And I want you to pay. No. Sorry. That's incorrect. I want you to suffer. Like I did. That's why I tampered with those rat poison thingies. I knew that would not only take care of the dog but that you would never forgive yourself. Genius. Right? Well, it was until *she stepped in*!" she speaks that last bit in a high tone and out to one of the slanting roofs.

"It…it…was you?" I breathe.

"Of course it was, you idiot."

"Oh, El, what happened to you?"

"Oh my God, you still don't get it, do you? *You! You* happened to me, Marc. *You!* And now you're gonna pay."

I take a step forward, and the world starts spinning again. Shit, I think I'm going to throw up.

"Ooh. You alright? Looking a bit green around the gills, there, my love. Yeah. I think you're definitely concussed. You need to be careful. Left untreated, you might have a stroke. Or worse," she says, then turning back to nowhere in particular, shouts, "Bitch! Come on, let's wrap this up."

"L… Leave… her… alone," I say through breaths.

"Or w…w…what you gonna do, hubby dearest?"

"Just leave her alone."

"Yeah. Okay," she says before stepping away from me. "Come on, bitch. Time to take a run and jump."

I take another step forward and grab my wife's arm, but she must see that I can barely stand because she casually looks at my hand like it's an alien object and casually says, "Get off me."

"No," I slur, "leave her alone."

I watch my wife smile that reptilian smile of hers that usually precedes her thinking or doing something naughty. "Aww," she says, puckering her lips, "how sweet. Even though you must be feeling like shit right now, you still want to defend her. Maybe you need something else to focus on. What do you say, eh?"

With that, she twists away from my grasp and, in one single motion, lifts the axe above her head, spins it on its butt, and then brings it sharply down on my arm. I hear, or maybe I feel a sudden crack. And when I look down, my right arm is dangling and swinging like a pendulum from my elbow. I scream at the sight of it and then at the savage ache that shoots up my shoulder and into my brain.

"See? I told you. You just need something else to focus on. That's when you're at your best. When you're just ignoring everything that's happening around you. Now that I think of it, I should probably do your leg too."

I watch her eye my left leg, and I take a terrifying step back, but my movements are sluggish.

"Yeah. if I just swing at your kneecap here, I reckon that should get you to finally sit still."

"Ellie, please…" I start begging, "for God's sake!"

"Don't worry, it won't kill you, but you should be conscious long enough to watch your little bird fly."

"Ellie, NO!" I hold up my left arm in a futile defensive gesture as I watch my wife step around me as if inspecting a tree that she's about to fell.

To my horror, I watch her pull the axe backwards. "ELLIE! NO! NO!" I howl as I brace myself for the inevitable. I know that they'll be no evading this in my condition.

Then, a scream pierces the night. It's loud, animalistic, primordial. It's followed by beating and scrunching sounds before there's a sudden flash, and Ellie disappears from in front of me, careened sideways. Seconds later, the ear-splintering sound of shattering and smashing glass fills the night. And this part is definitely a dream because when I look over, through the haze in my brain, I see that Sarah, my girlfriend, is straddling my wife in the middle of the glass roof, part of which has been smashed away.

The duo then proceeds to wrestle. Ellie's blonde hair fanned out beneath her. Sarah's sailing in the breeze. There are screams and loud grunts as I shuffle closer through the snow.

"S… s… Sarah!" I yell at the blurry spectacle, which is pretty much all I can do because I can barely stand now. My energy levels have just flatlined. I don't know how much help I can be. But nonetheless, stagger over there as fast as I can.

At the edge, I watch my girlfriend lift a fist and plunge it into my wife's face. This seems to subdue her.

"SARAH!" I call, reaching across the glass. I see the blurry outline turn towards me and reach for my arm, but as she does so, Ellie lifts a booted foot.

"SARAH, look out!" I yell.

But it's too late; the kick connects with Sarah's chest and sends her reeling backwards, slamming onto a glass partition that holds but crackles and splinters, protesting her weight. She looks up at me.

"NOOOOO!" I scream with outstretched arms, but it's futile. The glass gives way, and she disappears through the frame.

"NOOOOO!"

I half walk, half drag, half feel my way to the other side of the glass roof. As I do, I see that Ellie is folding onto all fours and is expertly crawling across the glass by using the struts to support her weight.

I slide and slip forward towards the part of the roof that has been transformed into a metal cage over a black hole of a mouth filled with teeth made of jagged shards of glass. Below, lying on the parquet floor of the entrance lobby is the axe.

Oh, Jesus. To my joy, I also see that Sarah, legs dangling into the abyss, is still clinging onto the frame. But my relief is short-lived as I watch Ellie crawl towards her.

"Didn't think that one through, did you?" she says before plucking a shard of glass the size of a dinner plate and looking across at me. "Now, we're going to have some fun."

"NO!" I can't reach Sarah from here. I would have to climb onto the frame with no idea whether or not it'll hold all three of us. But worse, something's happened to my vision. It feels like someone has turned out the lights, but a glance upward tells me that the moon is still shining brightly. The problem is with me. I'm closing down no matter how much I try to resist it.

I try to shake away the fuzziness, but it doesn't work.

"You alright, there, Marc?" Ellie teases. "Not looking too good. Look like you're going to pass out any second. I best hurry up," she adds, tongue hanging with deep concentration as she sets about using the glass on Sarah's fingers.

"Ell... liie. P... l...lease not... this...'t do this," I beg, holding out my good arm and wincing at the grinding sensation and pain emanating from the other as I slip and slide in an attempt to stay upright. "You... not... have... don't to this.... PLEASE, Ellie... please. I'm beg...s you..." I say, but I think it's more of a slur.

"What was that? Sorry, Marc. Can't quite hear what you're trying to say," my wife mocks.

"ELLLLIE!" I wail. Tears of frustration fill my eyes as I attempt to climb up and onto the metal frame.

Sarah's scream echoes up from the gaping hole as my wife prods at her fingers with the shard of glass.

"NOOOO!" I pull on the metal frame in an attempt to climb up, but it creaks and moves under the strain. "Nooo...... Sarah..."

But my numbed fingers lose their grip, and suddenly, I realise that I'm no longer holding on to anything for support and promptly fall backwards into the snow.

I wail at the sickening agony of pain that shoots through my whole nervous system, burning out the lights, and I turn my head to the side to wretch. The spasm is strong but ejects nothing, for there is nothing left.

I can't see us getting out of this, so if this is a dream, now would be the time to wake up, Marco.

Wake up!

But I don't. The freeze of the snow continues to seep into my trousers and my jacket. My heart continues to thud irregularly in my chest, and I'm ready to let go. No more struggling.

If Ellie, the woman I loved for so many years, the person with whom I raised a wonderful, beautiful boy, has turned on me like this, then I must have wronged her so severely that I deserve what awaits.

Sarah. I weep. Sarah, I'm so sorry. I'm so sorry I can't do more.

And here I find myself once more. Faced with the inevitable. Resistance is futile. Perhaps I should never have survived Dolce Vita and my existence beyond that night was some cosmic anomaly that death is now seeking to correct.

But then I hear Sarah's scream and Ellie's maniacal laugh. She used to laugh like this when playing with Toby or when I used to tickle her. A shrill series of laughs, each following the other.

"Ellie... p...p...lease......p...p... pregnant" is all I can tremble because I realise I am shivering. I've no idea if it's because I'm in shock or if it's the freeze.

"Pregnant?" I hear my wife say. Then there's a pause. I look up, hopefully, but all I can see from this angle are stars blurring in and out of focus like gems specially lit by a giant moon in a beautiful wintry sky. *Oh, god, please.*

I think I have got through to her, but then I hear her sneer, "So was I!" It is followed by another agonised scream from Sarah that may as well be that shard slicing at my heart.

I try to move, but I can't. My limbs no longer respond to the instructions from my brain. Or maybe it's my brain not even sending the signals. I can't tell anymore.

"Sa...rah...." I gasp. "Sa...rah...."

Get... up! GET UP! GET UP!

Oh, I think it's working. Is it? I try to sit up, but the action proves awkward with my left hand, but I persist. Head throbbing. Pain burning. I manage to lift myself almost to a sitting position, but I suddenly feel the support knocked out from under me and fall back into the snow.

I can see the sky again, twinkling diamonds winking at me. You don't see this in the city.

D...addy!

I only started to appreciate the view from our planet when I first arrived at Dolce Vita.

D…addy!

Toby? I thought I was dreaming. I *am* dreaming, aren't I? Toby? Can you hear me, daddy?

Toby? Is that you? But I've barely asked the question when I realise that I already know the answer. I know because of that peculiar warmth spreading through my veins just like it did that night in the water, transforming the freeze of the Atlantic into a comforting shroud of warmth.

Toby? I gaze at the stars, expecting my son's face to miraculously appear among them like some mystical constellation, but then I hear a crunching sound to my right, behind one of the snow-covered arches.

Gingerly, I turn my head in that direction, but there's nothing there, just snow dust drifting on the wind.

"T…t…toby?"

Is this real? Am I imagining this? Toby. Have you come for me? I don't know if I asked that aloud or not.

Daddy. You need to get up.

I think I have tears in my eyes. I'm so numb right now I can't even tell. I squeeze my eyes shut and reopen them.

I can't, buddy. There's nothing left. I have nothing left. I think this is it, I think I'm on my way to you.

No daddy. I won't be alone this time.

A l o n e.

Alone. I start chuckling to myself. Again, I don't even know if it's in my head or not. *Alone.* I didn't write that stuff on the wall, did I? It was you trying to warn me. Mummy wasn't with you. She was still alive.

Daddy. There's no time. You need to get up. You need to listen.

I can't, buddy. Not this time.

You need to get up so you can start again.

I don't understand. What do you mean? Toby I –

But my thoughts or my words or whatever the hell these things are, they're cut short because, in that same spot where I could see nothing, I can now see what looks like the outline of my boy. "Toby? Is that you, buddy?" I smile. I think I'm smiling and crying. My beautiful boy. Sandy blonde hair. Smile now as bright as the moon, and it's radiating me.

I love you, buddy.

I know. Daddy. I love you too. But I've got to go now. You need to let me go so that you can start anew.

What? I don't. I still don't understand–

But this thought is also cut short when I see my boy point past me towards what remains of the skylight. I glance that way and then back again.

When I do, I have to blink several times to make sure I'm not imagining it. Am I? I don't think I am.

Where Toby was once standing is now… Buddy, sitting on his hind legs, tail fanned out in the snow, fur ruffled in the wind.

"B…buddy…my boy…"

I need to go now, daddy. You need to let me go so you can start anew.

What…wait…Buddy…

I love you, daddy.

"Oh, no…. NO! NO! BUDDY, NO!"

But the words have barely left my lips, and the golden wonder is already bounding through the snow, *scrunch by scrunch by scrunch* until he's leaping over me.

"NOOOOO! BUDDY! NOOO!"

I can do nothing but watch as the giant slash of gold sails over me in a cloud of white powder. I hear a bark, and then the sound of those sixty-something pounds slamming into my wife, then a long-drawn-out scream fills the night, becomes echoey, and then is suddenly cut short by a loud thump and tinkling of glass.

Then there's nothing but the whistling gale once more.

EPILOGUE

CHRISTMAS EVE.

I don't know how we survived that night.

Sarah insists that she survived because of me, that I somehow managed to get to my feet, drag my freezing arse over to that gaping hole in the roof, extend my one good arm and help her climb back to safety.

I have my doubts. You were there. You saw the condition I was in. The paramedics agreed I was concussed and lucky I didn't end up in a coma. My money is on the fact that she's just saying that to make me feel better. But then, I may be wrong.

Speaking of money. Try not to fall off your chair, but the lads returned to Frost Lake Manor and got the job done despite recent events. This final leg took the best part of two months, but it finally got us over the finishing line. Contracts were exchanged at 13:58 yesterday. The transfer of funds took place shortly after. The sale of Frost Lake Manor to Carson Holdings is complete.

How about that for an early Christmas present, eh? I still can't believe it. Me being me, I was expecting some last-minute disaster, but no, it's done.

Irvin and the crew have already been compensated. I wanted them to have a very special Christmas this year, so I paid them their final fee plus a very generous bonus for the *pain and suffering* of putting up with me.

In the meantime, Irvin and I have agreed to one more project before we put our partnership on hold. I think the man needs a break from me, and also, I don't really know where I want to go with Battista Properties now. The business has forged a decent reputation in the industry, so I don't think it would be too difficult to sell it as a going concern.

We'll see.

David thinks I won't sell and that it'll only be a matter of time before I find something else to obsess over. He says I'm addicted to the stress and drama of it all. I was tempted to swear at him, but instead, I just smiled. *Well, you know I always value your opinion* was my response to that.

Yes. It's good to have my friend back. Although technically, he isn't back. At least, not in London anyway. Nope. Mr and Mr have moved out of David's redbrick luxury pad in Camden, London, and into some swish barn conversation in the middle of nowhere. It features a set of outbuildings that he's asked Irvin to convert for him as part of his new business venture.

We don't talk much about the wedding day. Or, more specifically, we don't talk about the fire. The boys simply omit it from any reference to that day as if it never happened. And I'm fine with that.

The official investigation into the fire at Holt concluded that it was the result of *Arson* and that the point of origin was the utility room. Who exactly started the fire remains a mystery since someone had disabled the security and fire systems before starting the fire.

There's no doubt in my mind that it was my ex-wife, Ellie. As a psychoanalyst, I've concluded that her actions were a by-product of her own form of psychosis brought on by the grief of losing our son.

And who can blame her? I certainly can't. And I don't. Not even for what she tried to do that night. I know that sounds weird when you consider what she tried to do to us. But ultimately, she was sick. She was very ill, and the only thing I believe she was truly guilty of was not seeking the support when it would have helped her the most.

Buddy, who is lying at my feet, emits a long groan.

"Yes, alright, I heard what I said. I know I was just as bad. I don't need you to remind me," I say, reaching down and stroking his fur.

When we eventually made it down from that rooftop, and I saw my boy slumped over Ellie's dead body, I really thought it was curtains for the big guy. I've no idea how he came out of that with just two broken legs. Sarah believes that Ellie must have somehow broken his fall. Me, I don't know. After everything I've seen, I believe anything is possible.

It's cute, though. Not the pain bit. That's seriously shitty, and no doubt it's been for him too. No, I'm talking about the way we're both convalescing together. They believe that there's a good chance he may be left with a permanent limp. No more bounding about for the big guy, but I think that's a small price to pay considering the alternative, which, in hindsight, I can't even bring myself to think about without getting misty-eyed.

I don't honestly know what happened that night since most of it remains a blurry haze, but what I do remember is that Buddy saved us. I doubt very much that Sarah and I would be alive today but for the actions of this beautiful animal.

Something happened that night. Something that strays beyond the realms of the rational and the comfortable and veers more towards the fantastical. You know that kind of stuff that you tend to shift awkwardly in your seat when you hear about it.

Toby, my dead son, spoke to me. He told me that I needed to make a choice. I did. Not necessarily a conscious one, but in my mind. We survived. It's only now, in hindsight, that I truly understand what that choice entailed.

Sarah miscarried our child just days later. The doctors say that it was to be expected given the trauma that she had been subjected to, but she's young, and they could see no reason why she wouldn't be able to try for another baby in the near future. The thing is, I don't think Sarah necessarily wants to try again, at least not with me.

After what happened, she went to stay with her mother. A few days became weeks, and weeks became a month. We're now officially on *a break*. As a therapist, I know that most so-called *breaks* are simply the prelude to separation. And on a rare visit to Porthcove, I told Sarah so.

She agreed.

You don't blame her, do you? I certainly don't.

Re-evaluation after a traumatic event is only natural. Ethan's words, not mine, but most therapists, including me, would agree.

So, it's just me and the golden wonder now.

And given that David's pad was empty, he's agreed to let us stay here, convalesce, and contemplate the future that right now is looking... well, um, different.

I finally made a call to that publisher. Via that pushy agent, of course. Do you remember him? *The Cockney Geezer.* Given everything that came before, after, and no doubt is yet to come, he managed to get me a decent advance on a three-book deal as well as a good royalty share, subject to my meeting the various deadlines. Now, I just need to get on with it.

Can you believe this? Me, Marco Battista, a bloody writer. I can't even put this down to one of those bad dreams because, well, they've calmed down again. I can't imagine why. Oh, and I'm back on the meds—for now. Ethan and I have agreed to review this regularly.

Of course, with my arm in a cast, I haven't quite experienced what it's like to feel the so-called *keys beneath my fingers,* but thanks to the powers of dictation, I've been able to make a start. I've agreed to print out some of the pages and let the boys have a read. You know, for some initial feedback. Maybe you'd like to take a look too. After all, you were there with me.

Oh, the carol singers are outside.

I go over to the window and push it open. The cold, carbon monoxide-infused air rushes in. No. It isn't the forest, but it'll do for now. Besides, London is beautiful this time of year. The avenues and walkways around here have been festively decorated and lit by an array of multicoloured lights. Revellers and last-minute shoppers bustle back and forth. A barge decked out like the *Coca-Cola* truck is meandering down the canal. Its deck is jumping with partygoers wrapped against the freeze. And now, right outside my window, the carol singers are performing an acapella of *Carol of the Bells.*

It reminds me of Sarah. I miss her. But I understand and respect that she no longer wishes to be around the calamity that is me. And I love her enough to not want that for her either, as cowardly as that may sound. *It's not you, it's me* springs to mind, but I think it applies in this case.

Speaking of calamities. Did you know that in provincial Italy, particularly in the remote and smaller villages, there's still a strong belief in the practice of *cursing* someone with just a *look* of envy? It's called *Il Malocchio* or *Evil Eye,* and it can be used to bring misfortune intentionally or even unintentionally on a hapless would-be victim. I discovered this during my research into folklores around the world.

I've been toying with the idea of taking a trip to Italy. Tuscany. Venice. Rome. You know, find out more about my ancestry, do a little research. I have the means and the perfect job for that now.

The police still haven't found Maja. She seems to have disappeared into thin air. Yes, I know what it looks like, but the facts do speak for themselves.

Maja did, does exist.

You may roll your eyes at this next bit, but there are still some things that cannot be explained. And I am prepared to believe, especially after all of our misfortunes, that Maja somehow – and I don't know how – did curse us. The terrifying part; there is no way of knowing if it has run its course.

I guess only time will tell.

Ultimately, you know everything that I know. What you choose to believe is for you to decide.

But it isn't all doom and gloom. My ex-father-in-law's lawsuit collapsed, given his daughter's miraculous and terrifying resurrection. Amanda told me that she heard a rumour that Stevenson was considering a different kind of civil suit that would see me cited as the individual that drove his daughter to do the things she did, but nothing has come of it yet. As shocking as that may seem.

Amanda. Yes, you may well be wondering what exactly happened in that hotel room that rainy night. The reality is, I still don't remember much about it – something that didn't help things with Sarah – but I'm told on good authority that it wasn't much beyond a drunken kiss. It would appear that the lightweight that is me who hadn't sipped booze in a while coupled with my exhaustion from everything else that had been happening meant that when push came to shove, I…. um fell asleep!

Fell asleep?! When Amanda first told me, I didn't know whether to be pleased or disappointed with myself. Asleep?! Oh, how the mighty have bloody fallen or are getting old.

Ugh.

I'm glad, though, because although I still firmly believe that Amanda is a sexy and attractive woman, we had our time. Besides, I much prefer her as my lawyer.

"Dude. Come on," David says, walking into the room. "You know we'd actually like to get there *for* Christmas, not after it," he adds with a roll of the eyes.

He's come to pick us up so we can spend the Christmas holidays together in their new home. The lads will be joining us at some point, too, for a special celebration.

Woof!

"Don't encourage him, you," I say to Buddy. "Have you finished chatting up the help?" I ask with a wry smile.

"Oi! I'm a happily married man," he says seriously. "But he is cute. Way too young for me, though—*if I* was in any way interested, of course."

"Oh, of course," I say, closing the window.

Tom is a veterinarian student. He works part-time at our vet's here in London and helps me out with Buddy since the poor guy can't get around easily, and I only have one hand. He is way too young for David and straight. He just enjoys teasing him because he's warped that way.

"You good?" David asks, and I know that it's a question that reaches beyond the journey we're about to make but further into the rest of our lives.

"Yeah," I say confidently, "I just need to turn off my machine, and we're ready to go."

"So, you've made a start then?" he asks, looking at the printed sheets of paper on my desk. "*Psychosis.* Is that what you're going to call book 1?"

"Yes. What do you think?"

He nods. "I think it's perfect. So, what's it like going back to where it all started?"

"Weird, but oddly cathartic."

"Are you still thinking of including everything?"

I nod. "Yeah. I'm just going to tell my truth. I'll let people make up their own minds. I think it's important, you know. Also, I've decided that from now on, I'm going to have an open mind. If there is any way I can help others out there, then I'm all for it."

"Bloody ell, mate, I only asked a question. I wasn't expecting a whole lecture," he says with a wink before reaching down and helping Buddy up.

I've no idea what the future has in store for us, but I feel that I've learned enough now to understand that there's no point in surviving if you aren't going to live.

PSYCHOSIS

A MEMOIR

BY MARCO BATTISTA

FOREWORD

This is my truth as I know it. Some of these truths I can explain. Others, well, I cannot. At least not in any rational sense.

Ultimately, what you choose to believe is for you to decide. Just know that some of what you're about to read is deeply disturbing.

Marco Battista

CHAPTER ONE

ELLIE

Friday. 12:03 PM.

London in September —hot, busy, and stifling.

I can't tell if my shirt is sticking to my back because of the meteorological conditions or the fact that Ellie has finally agreed to meet me for lunch….

If you enjoyed

CURSED

Please leave an Amazon / Goodreads rating
so that others may enjoy it also.

Generally, only a fraction of satisfied readers will leave
a rating, so yours really will make a difference.

THANK YOU.

FOLLOW TONY

If you can't wait for Tony Marturano's next thriller,
subscribe to the blog, mailing list, or follow on social media for
the latest news, special chapter previews and exclusive giveaways.

VISIT
www.tonymarturano.com

JOIN THE MAILING LIST
visit www.tonymarturano.com,
click on contact and subscriptions.

LIKE THE FACEBOOK PAGE
facebook.com/tonymarturano.author

BROWSE INSTAGRAM
instagram.com/marturanotony

FOLLOW ON TWITTER
twitter.com/tmarturano

or google tony marturano

ACKNOWLEDGEMENTS

As always, I'm so very grateful to everyone at a Different Angle, who has supported me throughout this book's journey, from manuscript to print. Special thanks to the following who have actively contributed to its realisation.

THE CURSED FOCUS/READER'S GROUP
My heartfelt thanks to all members of the Cursed reader's group, for giving so generously of their time and opinions!

(In no particular order)
Francesca Marturano-Pratt – Anna Pratt – Renee Owens –
Lisa Hall – Nicola Ramsbottom (for trying) – Cheryl Green

YOU, THE READER
If you're reading this book, there's a good chance you bought it. I'm obviously very grateful for that. Thank you!
On the other hand, if you borrowed from or were gifted this book by somebody else, even better! It means they thought it was good enough to pass on.

ALSO BY TONY MARTURANO

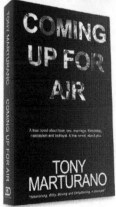

COMING SOON